TRASHLANDS

Also by Alison Stine

ROAD OUT OF WINTER

TRASHLANDS

ALISON STINE

mira

For Andrew Villegas

TRASHLANDS

The world is an old grave.
Women sparkle like cheap/glitter.

—Rebecca Lehmann

It's only a region of trash so, why not trash it?

—Barbara Ellen Smith, *Hillbilly*

1

Early Coralroot
Corallorhiza trifida

Coral was pregnant then. She hid it well in a dress she had found in the road, sun-bleached and mud-dotted, only a little ripped. The dress billowed to her knees, over the tops of her boots. She was named for the wildflower which hadn't been seen since before her birth, and for ocean life, poisoned and gone. It was too dangerous to go to the beach anymore. You never knew when storms might come.

Though they were going—to get a whale.

A boy had come from up north with a rumor: a whale had beached. Far off its course, but everything was off by then: the waterways, the paths to the ocean, its salt. You went where you had to go, where weather and work and family—but mostly weather—took you.

The villagers around Lake Erie were carving the creature up, taking all the good meat and fat. The strainer in its mouth could be used for bows, the bones in its chest for tent poles or greenhouse beams.

It was a lot of fuel for maybe nothing, a rumor spun by an out-of-breath boy. But there would be pickings along the road. And there was still gas, expensive but available. So the group went, led by Mr. Fall. They brought kayaks, lashed to the top of the bus, but in the end, the water was shallow enough they could wade.

They knew where to go because they could smell it. You got used to a lot of smells in the world: rotten food, chemicals, even shit. But death… Death was hard to get used to.

"Masks up," Mr. Fall said.

Some of the men in the group—all men except Coral— had respirators, painter's masks, or medical masks. Coral had a handkerchief of faded blue paisley, knotted around her neck. She pulled it up over her nose. She had dotted it with lavender oil from a vial, carefully tipping out the little she had left. She breathed shallowly through fabric and flowers.

Mr. Fall just had a T-shirt, wound around his face. He could have gotten a better mask, Coral knew, but he was leading the crew. He saved the good things for the others.

She was the only girl on the trip, and probably the youngest person. Maybe fifteen, she thought. Months ago, she had lain in the icehouse with her teacher, a man who would not stay. He was old enough to have an old-fashioned name, Robert, to be called after people who had lived and died as they should. Old enough to know better, Mr. Fall had said, but what was better, anymore?

Everything was temporary. Robert touched her in the straw, the ice blocks sweltering around them. He let himself want her, or pretend to, for a few hours. She tried not to miss him. His hands that shook at her buttons would shake in a fire or in a swell of floodwater. Or maybe violence had killed him.

She remembered it felt cool in the icehouse, a relief from the outside where heat beat down. The last of the chillers sputtered out chemicals. The heat stayed trapped in people's shelters, like ghosts circling the ceiling. Heat haunted. It would never leave.

News would stop for long stretches. The information that reached Scrappalachia would be written hastily on damp paper, across every scrawled inch. It was always old news.

The whale would be picked over by the time they reached it.

Mr. Fall led a practiced team. They would not bother Coral, were trained not to mess with anything except the mission. They parked the bus in an old lot, then descended through weeds to the beach. The stairs had washed away. And the beach, when they reached it, was not covered with dirt or rock as Coral had expected, but with a fine yellow grit so bright it hurt to look at, a blankness stretching on.

"Take off your boots," Mr. Fall said.

Coral looked at him, but the others were listening, knotting plastic laces around their necks, stuffing socks into pockets.

"Go on, Coral. It's all right." Mr. Fall's voice was gentle, muffled by the shirt.

Coral had her job to do. Only Mr. Fall and the midwife knew for sure she was pregnant, though others were talking. She knew how to move so that no one could see.

But maybe, she thought as she leaned on a fence post and popped off her boot, she *wanted* people to see. To tell her what to do, how to handle it. Help her. He had to have died, Robert—and that was the reason he didn't come back for her. Or maybe he didn't know about the baby?

People had thought there would be no more time, but there was. Just different time. Time moving slower. Time after disaster, when they still had to live.

She set her foot down on the yellow surface. It was warm. She shot a look at Mr. Fall.

The surface felt smooth, shifting beneath her toes. Coral slid her foot across, light and slightly painful. It was the first time she had felt sand.

The sand on the beach made only a thin layer. People had started to take it. Already, people knew sand, like every-thing, could be valuable, could be sold.

Coral took off her other boot. She didn't have laces, to tie around her neck. She carried the boots under her arm. Sand clung to her, pebbles jabbing at her feet. Much of the trash on the beach had been picked through. What was left was diapers and food wrappers and cigarettes smoked down to filters.

"Watch yourselves," Mr. Fall said.

Down the beach they followed the smell. It led them on, the sweet rot scent. They came around a rock outcropping, and there was the whale, massive as a ship run aground: red, purple, and white. The colors seemed not real. Birds were on it, the black birds of death. The enemies of scavengers, their competition. Two of the men ran forward, waving their arms and whooping to scare off the birds.

"All right, everybody," Mr. Fall said to the others. "You know what to look for."

Except they didn't. Not really. Animals weren't their spe-cialty.

Plastic was.

People had taken axes to the carcass, to carve off meat. More desperate people had taken spoons, whatever they could use to get at something to take home for candle wax or heating fuel, or to barter or beg for something else, some-thing better.

"You ever seen a whale?" one of the men, New Orleans, asked Coral.

She shook her head. "No."

"This isn't a whale," Mr. Fall said. "Not anymore. Keep your masks on."

They approached it. The carcass sank into the sand. Coral tried not to breathe deeply. Flesh draped from the bones of the whale. The bones were arched, soaring like buttresses, things that made up cathedrals—things she had read about in the book.

Bracing his arm over his mouth, Mr. Fall began to pry at the ribs. They were big and strong. They made a cracking sound, like a splitting tree.

New Orleans gagged and fell back.

Other men were dropping. Coral heard someone vomit-ing into the sand. The smell was so strong it filled her head and chest like a sound, a high ringing. She moved closer to give her feet something to do. She stood in front of the whale and looked into its gaping mouth.

There was something in the whale.

Something deep in its throat.

In one pocket she carried a knife always, and in the other she had a light: a precious flashlight that cast a weak beam.

She switched it on and swept it over the whale's tongue, picked black by the birds.

She saw a mass, opaque and shimmering, wide enough it blocked the whale's throat. The whale had probably died of it, this blockage. The mass looked lumpy, twined with seaweed and muck, but in the mess, she could make out a water bottle.

It was plastic. Plastic in the animal's mouth. It sparked in the beam of her flashlight.

Coral stepped into the whale.

2

Mr. Fall
Autumnus

They were pluckers. Their work was seasonal. They followed the plastic tide. After the floods destroyed the coasts, rewrote the maps with more blue, something was in the water that lapped at Ohio and Georgia and Pennsylvania.

Plastic.

People learned quickly that it was useful. It had to be.

China had stopped accepting electronics and batteries to recycle. Too expensive to process, too much of a waste of electricity and precious clean water. Acid seeped into the earth, and people held on to their computers and phones long past their breaking, knowing there would be no others. The people out in the country became a people of hoarders. They became junk lords. The center of the United States, which many people had not bothered with before, became the great vast orchards of scrap.

Scrappalachia.

The factories had closed to try to stem pollution, all the countries—even the States eventually—moving to ban new polymers. There would be no new water bottles, no take-out containers, no packaging or stereos or ball pits or flip-flops or dashboards or sunglasses or tubs.

But plastic lasted. It could be shredded, melted, pressed into bricks. The bricks could rebuild the police stations, the government offices that had been torn down in riots or wiped out in waves. As for everyone else? Their lives were almost entirely junk. Finding and trading, making do, discovering new uses, haggling prices.

Mr. Fall was old enough to remember the water.

Mostly he remembered the news. The television blared in his household, telling his family…something. *What*, Mr. Fall didn't remember exactly. Something about a warning, how they needed to get out. *Evacuate.* They didn't have enough time, or they hadn't listened. Red bars scrolled across the bottom of the TV; a beeping sound emitted from it. Then the water poured in from under the windows.

Mr. Fall remembered the rain: hammering on rooftops, streaming past the overhang. The pounding of their feet to the attic where his family ran, hiding from the water, climbing up and gathering to await rescue, which never came.

Water followed them. The TV was knocked off the counter. When Mr. Fall looked back, it sparked, went to black. His father yanked him upstairs, water trailing like a puppy. Mr. Fall ran as fast as if he was escaping a beating. Faster. So fast, he fell to his knees and crawled.

Water was coming.

He had never liked the attic, as he had never liked the basement. Avoided both. Both smelled funny, of monsters and darkness, spiderwebs and shadows. The basement shelves crowded with food they didn't eat, murky jars of things that went bad. After the floods, they would find some of these jars bobbing on the surface, dusty glass finally washed clean. His family would grab them. Eat every one.

As for the attic, junk filled it, broken items that had never had a use, or that seemed to have outlived their usefulness. His life, his life of junk, was only just beginning.

Uncle hung a white sheet out of the attic window with their names spray-painted in black and *SOS*. Mr. Fall didn't know what those letters meant. Nobody was answering his questions. He knew it was something to do with ships, the navy—which would be gone soon, along with airplanes except for government and medical use, the internet, commercial trucking.

Whatever *SOS* meant, it didn't work.

They waited in the attic for a long time. Uncle had also spray-painted the family's ages, as if that would help. He was 17. Mr. Fall was 5. His brother, 12. He grew hungry, but there was nothing to eat. He grew too tired to be afraid and fell asleep, curled against a big green jacket, which smelled of mice and bore their teeth marks.

When he woke up, the world was water.

3

Coral

Coral waded in the water, waist-deep. Her boots only reached her thighs, and when she came home, Trillium would know by her damp clothes how deeply she had gone in.

Her pack felt full already, but something bobbed in the river before her. Everything was hot: her body, the river, the air. The setting of the sun would offer little relief, the sky flushed orange and pink. It was brilliant, as was every sunset. Mr. Fall said there used to be a color called *Dayglo* that would burn so brightly it hurt your eyes. Coral didn't understand how a color could just disappear. But whole cities could disappear. Coasts could disappear. Trees and flowers and animals.

Children could disappear.

She grabbed the plastic in the river. It was thicker than the flimsy water bottles. This object was rectangular, open at one end. It had a hole in its side, punched or broken through. But a hole could be mended. The whole thing could be cut up into soles for shoes, or it could be ground to pave a path or fill a mattress. Really, though, she knew what would happen to the plastic. It would be pulverized, melted, and pressed into bricks.

She might know the small hands that pressed it.

Her family had camped in the junkyard for a long time. Maybe too long. But as long as plastic washed up in the river, they could stay, in the southeastern part of what had been Ohio. Trillium felt uneasy about staying in one spot for too long—his business thrived on the novelty of a new place, new people, new skin—though Mr. Fall didn't mind it. But Coral needed to stay. The bus tires could rot in the dirt, but that was the only danger in staying, she thought.

She needed to be rooted. Her son had to know where to find her.

She climbed out of the river, and stood on the bank down the hill from the junkyard. The river had a smell. Different, depending on the day. The white in the water was not surf, not cresting foam—but plastic. People waded in the river below. New Orleans, the rest of the crew. They trudged, heads down as their arms swept the water. Most carried nets woven from plastic bags. Packs strapped to their shoulders bulged with the things they had pulled from the river. Plastic was light, but when the backpacks grew heavy, the pluckers were supposed to return home, dump their finds, and return to the river. Repeat until dusk. Every day.

The bus where Coral lived was parked down an access road that led to an old quarry. A small hill separated the bus from the rest of the junkyard, enough to have some space and privacy, but not too far that customers couldn't find it.

The bus had been a school bus. Coral tried to imagine

a time when buses would have been so plentiful that children rode them every day, gas flowing freely. The bus had belonged to Mr. Fall's school, back when he had been a real teacher. No, someone higher than a teacher. What was the word? Someone who, when the wildfires came, took a bus that didn't even belong to him, rounded up all the children he could and drove them out through the smoke. It took all the gas they had. He had never driven a bus before.

It had always been black, but many years ago Mr. Fall had painted a rainbow stripe around the bus to help teach color names. She knew he had scavenged and saved for the paint. Trillium hated the stripe, but it was useful. The rainbow bus, people could say. When it was parked, Trillium hung his sign. *Tattoos.*

Trillium had his shop in the back. They lived up front, sleeping on a bed that folded out from the wall like a jointed, wooden toy Mr. Fall had pulled from the water for Coral when she was a child. He had made it move, pulling a lever on its back to kick out the legs—and then the whole thing had rotted, collapsing into sticks as she reached for it.

As she approached the bus, water squelched in her boots. She dropped her pack into the dirt. She had been carrying the big plastic piece with the hole in its side. This she set down more gently, sliding it under the bus. Sometimes Mr. Fall slept there, if it hadn't rained, and if he wanted to give her and Trillium space, but he had placed his bedroll on the far end, under the driver's seat. She took off her wet boots and wrung the hem of her clothes.

She heard a laugh from inside. Familiar.

Foxglove.

The accordion doors were open. Coral went up the steps

into the bus. At the back, a girl with long auburn hair lay on
her stomach on a table. She was naked from the waist up. Her
hair streamed over the edge of the table like rainfall, hiding
her face.

"What has he done to you this time?" Coral asked.

The girl lifted her head.

Trillium leaned over her back, the tattooing needle still
in his hand, though he was done. Coral could see a patch
of Foxglove's skin glistened. Trillium wiped the patch carefully with a rag. "You're soaked," he said to Coral. "You
went deep."

"There was something good to get."

"Coral," Foxglove said. "I wish someone would tattoo
me with a nice name like that." She sang it out. "Coral."

"Let me see that tattoo." Coral peered over the girl, her
skin smooth except for the tattoos, like the barcodes Coral
had seen on sturdier plastic. The ink was mostly black, and all
of the girl's dozens of tattoos were names: *Alexandria, Osaka.*

Hague. That was the new one.

"What's a *Hague*?" Coral asked.

"A very rich man," Foxglove said.

"It's a city," Trillium said. "Or, it was a city."

"It's a well-fed, smelly, rich man."

"How can anyone be well-fed?" Coral said.

"Trust me. This man can." Foxglove flipped her hair
back and slid up on the table, exposing the slow curve of
her stomach. The tattoo there read *Charleston,* sloped to follow her hip.

Coral hadn't seen all of Foxglove's tattoos, though she
could have. Anyone could have, for a price. Foxglove danced
at the club at the edge of the junkyard. Its sign glowed pink,

day and night, pulsing with a light you couldn't buy or make anymore, a color that always burned. Mr. Fall said the glow was called neon.

The club was called Trashlands.

So was the junkyard surrounding the club where they lived. She was sure Rattlesnake Master, the man who had started the club, fixing up an old theater, and made the path leading straight there, liked it that way: he had named all he could see.

Coral had met Foxglove years ago when the dancer had wandered up to the bus with money in her hand. Foxglove had worn shoes made from small wooden boxes, lashed to her feet with ribbons that had once been pink. Her toenails, exposed in the shoes, were red. At first, Coral had thought her feet were bleeding. The box soles lifted her taller than the man who stood behind her, kicking at a bit of plastic on the ground. The scruff of a beard made his face look dirty.

Foxglove wobbled on the shoes. She had drawn her eyebrows on shakily. Her lips were dark lines. She had a mark by her eye. Coral thought it was a birthmark or a scar. Only later, the first time Foxglove lay on Trillium's table, did Coral see it was a tattoo. *Baby.* She could barely read the name.

Foxglove didn't like to talk about that one.

Coral's hair was red too, but not like Foxglove's. Coral's hair came out of her head like she imagined electricity had come out of walls: frizzed, streaked with white like lightning. Foxglove's hair shone with the kind of glow that came from chemicals, and from not spending time outside or in the water. She was no scavenger.

Anyone else would have been laughed at, wearing the

clothes Foxglove wore: a tube on top, shorts on the bottom. She would get scratched by branches in those clothes. Her bare legs would be bit. She might get an infection if she brushed a bit of metal in the yard. Her skin should have been burned and spotted, like Coral's was. But dancing kept Foxglove out of the sun. Generators fed chilled air into Trashlands, where it was always dark, always cool, always night.

Foxglove had waved her money. It was the color of shallow water.

"We don't accept paper money," Trillium said. It was hard to trade it, hard to know it was real. "Plastic only."

"Oh." Foxglove sounded disappointed, like a child.

"We could take your shoes?" Coral said.

"Don't be ridiculous," Trillium said. "Where would you wear them? She can't even walk."

"She's not supposed to walk," the man said.

Foxglove said nothing.

Coral tried to imagine a life where she had chemicals in her hair, where she kept out of the sun, where she stood as tall as Trillium, bending over him as he lay on their mattress stuffed with plastic ground fine as sand. Coral still remembered sand. She still remembered Robert's face in the icehouse, the hush of his breath, as if it hurt to even look at her. Trillium used to look at her like that; he used to speak to her softly. Could high box shoes help him do that again? Would Coral look different, sexy? Would Trillium see her differently?

Foxglove turned to the man behind her. "What else you got, Polar?"

Polar, whose full name was Polar Bear, had a lawn chair—and that, they took. In exchange, Trillium gave Foxglove a tattoo.

★ ★ ★

Polar Bear had watched when Trillium worked on the dancer. Some of the men did. That was part of it, not only owning Foxglove, possessing at least a part of her body, the part that bore their name—but also watching her suffer through pain, watching her bleed for them. They liked it when she cried out. She didn't need to—she told Coral later she could take great physical pain, had grown a kind of armor against it—but she did it for the men. Whimpers. The tiniest of tears. She was onstage even when she wasn't.

The man called Hague hadn't watched. He wasn't even in the bus.

"He said he's squeamish," Foxglove said, turning her head to see the new tattoo in the mirror Trillium produced.

"Squeamish and well-fed?" Coral said. "Must be nice."

"He isn't. Nice."

"Where does Rattlesnake Master keep finding these men?" Trillium muttered. He stood behind Foxglove, holding the mirror.

"He advertises. The cool air is a big draw. Plus, he has those little shows sometimes, you know." Foxglove twisted to find the right angle. Coral wondered for a moment if this was how she moved onstage, if this was what the men paid for. Coral had never seen a show or been in the front part of Trashlands. It remained a mystery to her, behind a velvet curtain. Foxglove reached for her shirt. "The tattoo looks great. He'll love it."

"Anytime." Trillium put the mirror down, stripped off his patched gloves into a bucket, and washed his hands with the jug in the sink.

Coral watched the water closely. They were getting low.

Foxglove pulled her shirt back on. She had been at Trashlands since she was a child, but all of life was work, really.
Children were just the ones who did the small work, the
nimble-fingered labor.

Coral tried not to think of him. Her son was older now.
He had never been in the kind of danger Foxglove had been
in. And even she wasn't in danger anymore. Not as much,
anyway, Coral hoped. Foxglove could take care of herself,
keep her tips. She had a trailer in the junkyard, and years ago,
Rattlesnake Master had hired a bodyguard to watch over her.

Foxglove was younger than Coral. Not a single line on her.
Not a scar she had not been paid for. Sometimes Coral worried about Trillium alone in the bus with the girl, her body
unrolling like a beach. But he had promised. He had sworn
an oath to Coral, long ago. They were as good as married.

Foxglove reached into her blue Walmart bag, and pulled
out a naked plastic doll. She handed it to Trillium, feet first.
Its hair stuck up like dead grass. "Is that enough? I wish it
were more."

Trillium took it. The plastic would be melted. Children
didn't play with plastic toys, not whole ones. "It's fine."

Foxglove turned to Coral, and her eyes in their outlines
of ash looked so kind, Coral reminded herself she did not
have to worry about the dancer being alone with Trillium.
Foxglove wouldn't hurt her like that, either. "How close
are you to getting your son back?" Foxglove asked. "How
much more do you need?"

"I wish I knew," Coral said.

Ink for tattoos was expensive and difficult to find or make,
which factored into the price. Coral had observed Trillium

use many things over the years: ash, pulverized lead, iron oxide. Sometimes he used car paint. Once, Coral watched him carefully crack open a dozen pens she had found sealed in their container in the river.

Coral had been fascinated by the package. What a waste. Why did pens need to be encased? They weren't medical supplies. She had brought them straight to Trillium. He pulled them from the package, the sodden cardboard falling apart in his hands.

"You could make art with these pens," Trillium had said to Coral. "If you wanted to. Draw."

She thought about that. She looked at the pens. The ink inside might be dry but it didn't look it, so dark blue it was almost black.

"You take them," she said. "I don't need anything."

He was patient. Unscrewing the pens, laying the parts out, tipping the ink into a bowl. The ink had not dried up. What he could not get out by pouring, he extracted using a syringe. It was like watching string unspool, a spider's web draped in oil.

They ate well, after a tattoo. Trillium came back from the market with jars of cooking oil, bread made from acorns, and cornmeal. "There's something else." He pulled it gently from his bag, and unwrapped it from its casing of plastic bags, grubby and gummed with a feather.

"An egg?" Coral took it from his hands. It felt heavy, or she imagined it was. She held it up to the light, as if she could see inside. "Who has a chicken?"

"Someone passing through, going to Trashlands."

"We should convince them to stay." No one could keep

chickens in the junkyard. They were too loud, and Rattle-snake Master would find out. Rattlesnake Master would want some, take some. Or take everything. Coral gave Trillium the egg back. "How will you cook it?"

Some things she had learned. Some, she had not. How to cook an egg, for instance. Trillium, older than her, had learned more. In the tent city where he lived as a child, he remembered seeing something Coral could barely believe had existed: plastic eating utensils, meant for one use. Coral would find plastic bits in the water sometimes and wonder: Had this been a fork, thrown away after a single meal? No forks survived the river whole.

Some things she thought Trillium only pretended to re-member, like running water, or the lost season from which Mr. Fall had taken his name, when trees would explode into color. Trillium said it would last for a few weeks, the fall-ing bright leaves. People would brush leaves into piles to be thrown away, not even used for mattresses or compost. Kids would jump into the piles for fun.

Coral would ask him to tell her about those old times, knowing it would lead him to touch her. Something about being back there, picking leaf crumbs from his hair, breath-ing in the sweet dark—happier times. There were radios then. Stores that sold food. He would tell her these stories, then start to kiss her. Only a few kisses, openmouthed. He didn't linger on her body anymore; they had been together for so long. He touched her through her clothes, a hard, pressing touch, as if to make sure she was still there. Then their clothes came off—carefully. Clothes took time to make.

If Foxglove's body looked like a smooth beach to Coral, Coral's body was the waves. She went in and out. Her legs were sturdy, her arms full and strong. Trillium said Coral was all fire when he first fell in love with her. He said she was like those trees, the flaming trees from his youth.

"Were those trees even real?" Coral whispered.

"Real as you." From behind her, he pulled her hair.

It was a time of impulse, after the levees had broken for the last time. After the sea walls would not be rebuilt. The roads would not be repaired. Maps had been redrawn with the oceans farther inland. Desperate things happened: people married, left lovers, spent their savings, said things they'd regret and did things they couldn't come back from. They had thought there would be no looking back, that they couldn't go home. There were no homes. They had thought everything good was behind them.

But babies were still born.

They were practiced, Trillium and Coral. Careful. They could not afford the sadness of children. Coral worried, as she always did, about Mr. Fall overhearing them. But he knew she was grown up. This was part of life. Besides, he was hardly ever home anymore.

Coral used the last bit of the water in the jug to wash up while Trillium, wearing only the faded shorts he had stitched himself, cooked the egg in a tiny bit of oil.

In the morning, Coral returned to the big piece of plastic under the bus. The plastic from her backpack Trillium had already traded at the market. It was better if men went to trade and sell. They were treated better, given higher prices. But she hadn't told him about the big piece.

"That looks like a trash can," Mr. Fall said.

She had thought she was alone. But there was Mr. Fall,

stretching. He was really too old to be sleeping on the ground. He should be inside, safe with them at night. "What's a trash can?" Coral asked.

Mr. Fall looked down at the plastic. "When people used to just throw stuff away, they needed a place to put it before it left their homes. They needed, well, cans for trash."

"People would keep trash in their houses?"

"I suppose you could say that."

Coral studied it.

"It's sturdy plastic. Only a small hole. Easily patched. That'll fetch a decent price at market. Unless..." Mr. Fall paused. "You want to do something else with it?"

She had only an inkling. More image than idea. "We shouldn't waste it," Coral said. "We could use the money. I could use the money."

"You can always make more money, Coral."

The sun soared in the sky, getting higher and hotter. Trillium wasn't up yet. Nobody wanted tattoos in the morning. She said goodbye to Mr. Fall, trash can in her arms, and hiked up the hill to the junkyard.

Most of the good stuff in the yard had been scavenged long ago. All that was left were trifles: a charm hanging from a mirror, a pacifier in a back seat. The cars, covering acres, were shells that kept out the rain. People lived in the junk, in RVs with rotting roofs, trucks with spring-torn mattresses. The junkyard was home to a large camp, mostly pluckers who came back every year. Laundry flapped in the wind. Children played in the dirt, their bare feet flashing.

The children reminded Coral of Shanghai. He would always be in her mind about seven, his hair crisped by the sun, his skin bronzed, kicking a ball made from stitched-together carpet.

Her son was not that age anymore, she reminded herself. He was different now.

They said the factories changed you. Her son would be stronger when she got him out. He would have a skill. He would remember her. And he would not be angry at her, not blame her. No. He would understand what had happened, that it was not her fault. It was no one's fault. People took children.

The playing children disappeared, shrieking down a hill patterned with oil pans. Outside the trailer nearest the woods, Foxglove stood smoking. Behind her was a large man.

"Morning," Foxglove said. She saw the plastic. "Is that a present for me?"

"It's a trash can," Coral said.

"A what?"

"Did you know that people used to keep trash in their homes?"

"I knew that," the man said. "Trash cans."

"No one asked you, Tahiti," Foxglove said.

She had plastic flowers stuck in front of her trailer in a bed made from a bald tire. She had used ground-up plastic for the dirt. Trillium swore he had seen her watering the flowers once. High as a kite, he had said. That was still around. People couldn't figure out a way to get power back into the poles, or to get all the screens turned on. But they could figure out how to get high.

"You're not working?" Coral said to Foxglove.

She took a hit off her cigarette. "Nobody wants nudity in the morning."

"Nobody wants a tattoo, either."

"Is that trash thing for scrap?"

"I don't think so. I think I'm going to make something with it."

"You and your art." Foxglove had finished the cigarette, smoked it down to the tip. She put it out by stamping the end on her tire planter, then Tahiti stepped forward and took the butt from her, the tiny end in his big, careful hands.

It would be unrolled and saved, the last bit of tobacco or pulverized plastic or whatever it was, tipped back into a pot, stirred with sawdust and spices, wrapped in paper and sold again. Foxglove might even buy it back herself.

Coral shifted, the trash can awkward in her arms. "I think I'm going to put it in the woods. Up the rise, where there's that old white tree."

"Birch," Tahiti said. "Mr. Fall said it's called a birch."

Foxglove didn't turn back to look at Tahiti when he spoke. She was used to men around her, buzzing like hornets all day. "Be careful," she said to Coral. "There were new men in the club last night. They were *not* happy when their plastic ran out. They might still be around."

"Trillium said there were new people at the market."

"I don't like strangers," Foxglove said, though her body was marked with them.

Violence happened in the woods. Men came from there. Sometimes they camped, living or what passed for living among the scrawny trees. Usually only men traveled alone. Women tended to find a place and stick to it, or to get stuck there by children, family. There was protection in a group, in a family unit, even a flawed one.

Coral had been born into plucking, born in Scrappalachia (Mr. Fall said it had been called *Appalachia* without the "scrap" once). The old states that made up the region stretched from what was now the border of The Els—short for The Elites, the coastal cities that still had semiregular power and newspapers—all the way down to the edge of The Deep, or Deep South. In the middle of the country were The Flyovers, overgrown farmland and old manufacturing plants whose empty shells rose out of fields.

Scrappalachia had the trash. Mountains of it.

After the floods, some regions were lost. Some were given up on. No one worked to restore power to Scrappalachia, for example, though Mr. Fall said there were hundreds of people who worked on electricity in The Els, doing what they could to keep the lights on for the cities.

Why them? Coral had asked him. *Why not us?*

We were poor, he had said. *We didn't have voices that anyone important would listen to. People didn't understand what it was like to live here.*

Who is important? Coral had asked him. *And who is not?*

He didn't have an answer to that.

Appalachia already had scrap, junkyards and compounds. But there was room in the woods and mountains, in the rivers, for more. Appalachia had miners, people used to digging out a living. That kind of life doesn't wash off, Mr. Fall said. Appalachia had scrappers, people who knew how to reuse. They had scavengers, used to foraging, hobbling meals together, to stretching and skimping and hoping for the best.

It's in your blood, Mr. Fall had said to Coral.

And they were lucky, in a way. A consistent stream of plastic washed up. There was so much plastic in the world, Mr. Fall said, it would never run out. Some, like the white brittle Styrofoam, would never leave this planet at all. Never decompose back to ground, or back to what it had been before—chemicals, mist in the air. Was that good or bad?

Another question for which he didn't have an answer.

Walking through the woods with her trash can, Coral was wary of men. Lost ones, drunk ones. Men looked for trouble, Coral had realized. Women mostly just found it.

But the woods felt empty to her, ringing with a kind of hollowness. Plastic bags and bottle caps dotted the pine needles. On another morning, she might have collected them; caps could be used for buttons. But today she had something to do.

Deer had scratched up the bottom half of many trees in the woods, trying to eat what they could. She had never known trees to look otherwise. The white tree Tahiti had called *birch* had the worst scars of all. Deep lines bore into its bark, peeling off in curls.

A seam of dirty water pushed up through the ground. It was dead pine needle–colored. Its red came from acid, which came from the mines. There was nothing in them anymore. The coal had been gouged out, the minerals dried to dust. Nothing was left except acid. It slid down the mines and slipped into the water.

Coral stopped at the red stream. Mr. Fall would tell her not to touch it. But Mr. Fall said that about everything. The whole world couldn't be off-limits. They lived in the world; they had to. She reached into the water and dug into the stream bottom, scooping mud into her hands. She squeezed out the moisture, then slapped the mud on the trash can, which she had propped on the bank.

She didn't have a shape in mind, not exactly. She let the mud speak.

The mud decided it wanted to be a column with a circle at the top. She used supple bits of plastic to support the circle, a frame she patted mud around. The mud was old car–colored. It would dry to the color of the birch's trunk, beneath its torn bark.

Soon, the piece was finished, as much as it could be, with the time she had. The deer might knock it down, what was left of them. A tree might fall, smashing it. Would anyone see it? Likely, one of the men who wandered out from Trashlands would slap it to bits, sell the trash can for scrap.

But maybe it would last until then.

Coral washed her hands in the stream. She looked at the mud and junk sculpture one more time. Whatever it meant, whatever else she did today, she had done that. She had made something from trash, from a castaway, gone life. She had given it new life. She turned and went to work.

When she came out of the woods, there was a stranger in the junkyard.

4

False Foxglove
Aureolaria

After Coral left, Foxglove went around the back of her trailer
to shower. She had had her morning cigarette, talked to
someone—Coral—before she was ready, before the clove
or tar or whatever the fuck they put in those things flooded
her blood; they tasted different every time. Now she just
needed to relax.

Once, a girl called Artemisia had sold Foxglove a cigarette
full of artemisia. How fucking wonderful to smoke yourself, Foxglove had thought. She had never seen a picture of
False Foxglove. Mr. Fall had not been able to find one. He
thought it was yellow, but there was also a purple one. She
couldn't have known which plant she had been named for,
which had disappeared from her family's village, wherever
that was. So she had dyed her hair red. She thought that was
a nice compromise. She had dropped the *False* from her name

years ago. Rattlesnake Master had said men might think her tits were fake, with a name like that.

She had accepted the artemisia cigarette, paid too much for it—a whole bottle of the fruit piss Tahiti was making on the side—because it felt like a privilege, a rare thing that would not come again, like her two cherished hair bands, the rubber so worn she could no longer wear them, only look at them sometimes; like the hard stick of pink called *bubble gum*.

Rattlesnake Master had given bubble gum to her when she first came to Trashlands. Foil had still wrapped it, silver paper that glinted in her hand. It would have been good material to keep, to trade maybe, but she tossed it as soon as she could. And once Rattlesnake Master's head was turned, she had spit the bubble gum into the weeds. She never tasted bubble gum again. But she had never wanted to.

What did the artemisia cigarette taste like? She couldn't even remember, for all it had cost. But she remembered bubble gum. It tasted like the bile that rose in her throat when she watched her mama walk away, leaving her at Trashlands.

Behind the neon sign on the club's roof, solar panels tilted to the sky. Plenty of sun juiced the panels, ran the chillers that pumped icy gusts and cooled off drinks the dancers sold to men. Rattlesnake Master also had a generator. Trashlands sold beer made in bubbling vats in the back, and an alcohol that came from leaving fruit in the sun. They called it rot wine or fruit piss.

Every now and then at Trashlands, they also had sugar drinks, the kind Mr. Fall remembered, with names like Pepsi and the Doctor. Those drinks sold for more money than a dance, more than a tattoo, more than Foxglove could imagine. Only once had she been there when someone ordered a sugar drink. It was a big production: the can taken from the back office where Rattlesnake Master kept it in a safe. It was dusted off, placed in the middle of a clean white napkin on a tray.

Foxglove was tasked with delivering the drink. She wore only a ribbon around her waist, a ribbon that had been in another dancer's hair. Her legs were shaky from dancing all night, but she had to walk straight and hold the tray high, smiling.

The man who ordered the drink was a paper money man. Some of the cities still used that currency, but it was so rare that Trillium wouldn't accept it. Paper was fragile, not like plastic. It could be faked. The man sat, surrounded by other men who laughed at everything. A girl had already left their table in tears.

Foxglove made it to the table, setting the drink down amid the empty fruit piss jars and the smoked-to-nothing cigarettes. During slow hours, dancers would go around and collect all the cigarette butts. Rattlesnake Master would sell them, as he sold everything. She straightened up, using the tray as a shield for her body.

She should have left right then. Paper money men never tip.

But she wanted to see. She wanted to witness the drink being opened. She had heard there was a sound. She had heard you could see something come out of the top, like sparks. It all sounded like magic. There wasn't much magic in the world.

So she lingered. And the paper money man did a funny thing. He reached for the drink, but he didn't open it at first. He held the drink in his ham-colored hand, his hand that had been all over the women, grabbing and coarse. And then he shook the can.

The other men began to laugh. It was nervous laughter. They had been doing it all night, but this time it sounded worse. This was the high laughter of animals in fear. The man shook and shook the sugar drink. Then he pressed his fat thumb on the tab.

There was a sound. A high hiss. Foxglove flinched, already backing away, but the spray hit her. Liquid shot out of the can. It arched up, the man directing the can at her. The drink splattered over her breasts, her hair. It dripped down the tray. It soaked her ribbon.

The men reared back to avoid being sprayed. They were doubling over themselves, laughing so hard. The man shook the can again and again, aiming it like a weapon. The drink felt cold and sticky.

Then the man stood up. He was shorter than Foxglove in her shoes—the men usually were, but for some reason, this seemed to make the men feel more powerful, not less. He wasn't hobbled by heels. He could outrun her. He wasn't weak from working all night and not eating enough. He reached over her head and dumped the last of the can over her, shaking to make sure he got out every sweet drop.

He didn't taste the drink at all.

He had paid so much for it, and none of them at the table tasted even a bit.

The men laughed at Foxglove for a while, standing in front of their table, shivering and wet. She noticed for the first time how the club smelled like rot. Did it smell that way all the time? She heard the skip in the song of Trashlands, louder than ever before. They only had the one song: the

pounding bass from a band that had died years before anyone in the club had been born, and at one part the sound
hiccupped until the DJ pressed the button again. Everyone
knew there was no new music anymore, not that Rattlesnake Master would pay for.

The paper money man took her tray away so the men
could look at all of her. He forced her to give a little turn.
She stayed there for what felt like forever, being their joke.

Then the men's attention turned to something else. The
music shifted, grew louder. Maybe that was on purpose.
Maybe the DJ had seen what was happening at the table and
had cranked it up, hurrying a new dancer onstage. Whatever it was, the men moved on.

Foxglove only hesitated a moment—no tip had come, no
tip was coming—and then she fled. Later, another dancer
collected the can—Foxglove refused to go back there—and
Rattlesnake Master sold it for scrap. Someone likely turned
the can into a surgical tool. The metal was sharp and thin,
suited for scooping out hurt or burned flesh.

But as for Foxglove, she disappeared into the darkness of
backstage. Behind the curtain, where no one could see her,
she licked the sugar drink from her skin.

The most expensive drink in Trashlands, maybe in all of
Scrappalachia, priceless really, never to be made or remembered again. She drank the sweet film from her body.

How did it taste? Coral had asked her.

Like the future we lost, Foxglove said.

The plastic bag that was her shower hung on the far side
of the trailer, facing the woods. The other sides of her trailer
looked toward the junkyard, cluttered with shadows. No

good came from the woods, but what came out of the junkyard for her was worse.

You could hear someone coming from the woods. They
rustled leaves, snapped branches. But sounds came from the
junkyard all the time. Sounds of the scrap shifting, children
playing, men weaving to and from the club. It was difficult
to discern which sounds meant danger and which meant
ordinary, stupid life.

So Foxglove had strung bells on the junk closest to her
trailer. Friends, like Coral and Trillium and Summer, knew
to duck. But a stranger might blunder into the bells, setting
off the alarms tied to the fenders and shipping containers.

In that case there was Tahiti. A man as broad as a door—
and too tall to fit into Foxglove's door without stooping.
Sometimes she would turn in her bed and see, through the
tapestry over her window, his shape patrolling the night. Tahiti said he was a light sleeper, and anyway, he didn't need
much sleep. He had learned to live without it. And it was a
better situation here at Trashlands than what he had done
before, which was wrestling, he said. Sometimes alligators.

Foxglove didn't know what *wrastling* was. She had looked
up a picture of alligators in Mr. Fall's book and they looked
like darkness with teeth. She wondered if these creatures
were the source of the scars up and down Tahiti's arms, the
missing bits on the side of his face. His cheek dimpled in
there, like tin. A thin scar ran around his neck, but she knew
the story of that one.

The plastic shower bag was heavy. A hole had been poked
in the bottom, edges melted to cauterize them. A cork stop-
pered the hole.

Coral and Trillium had clean and dirty days. Most of their days were dirty; Rattlesnake Master charged a lot for water. But Foxglove liked to wash more. She needed to. Once, a man had complained. And you couldn't use creek water from the woods. There wasn't much of it anyway, and anyway it was red. That wasn't a color for water.

Water had to be passed through sieves to get out all the plastic, and even that didn't work. Almost every time she washed, Foxglove felt something sharp. She barely noticed it anymore. It was a small pain from the past.

She thought of plastic as time traveling. She knew that most people viewed it as money. But to Foxglove, plastic told a story. If only it could talk. What would it tell her? What had the world been like? What had the plastic in her water been—a toy or a shoe? Mr. Fall said that most plastic had been packaging. What a world that must have been, to have had to protect everything.

She knew that Coral sometimes imagined the shit she pulled from the river would end up in her son's hands. But for Foxglove, the imagining was about what had already happened, what the people who had lived before her had done.

Those fuckers.

When Foxglove came out of the trailer in her tire-tread sandals and robe, Tahiti stood up from the stump where he had been sitting. Foxglove stood under the shower bag, and Tahiti picked up the vinyl curtain, his face giving away nothing.

Most men paid to look at her. Tahiti was paid not to look.

She took off the robe and slung it onto his shoulder. He spread out the vinyl. His arm span was so wide he blocked her from view, like the red curtain. It was hard not to think of that. Not to feel she was always onstage, performing all the time.

She turned her naked back to him and pulled the cork from the bag. The water was warm from the sun, but not warm enough. Never warm enough. She tried not to shiver. Water splashed down her shoulders and she lifted her arms. She tried to forget that a man was always with her.

5

Coral

Trashlands drew men. Coral could see its sign wherever she went—in the woods, by the river. All the cars in the yard, and many of the trees, were bathed in its light. She didn't understand how the club could spare the power, even with solar panels, but Foxglove said Rattlesnake Master had buried canisters of diesel. He had a secret supplier. Between the fuel and the solar, they could burn light for years.

After Foxglove's trailer at the border of the woods, the junk started fast. The old trucks and cars where people lived looked indistinguishable from trash. Rust blended with the scrubby brush, the dirt ground, the dry and skinny trees. They were past the green time. The trees had mostly shed their brittle leaves in the wind, all at once like a shrug.

The path through the junkyard was not obvious, and that was on purpose. One path led straight to Trashlands, lighted with solar lamps made from tin cans. But getting anywhere else, any other way through the junkyard, had been made difficult on purpose. Difficult for the men to find the dancers, like Foxglove, who lived in the yard. Difficult for the men to find the children.

It was a man who picked his way through the junkyard now, the stranger. He walked on a large metal sheet that had been welded onto piles of scrap, making a teetering roof.

And he was lost. Coral could tell from the way he scanned the sky. He didn't belong here. Any person who knew what they were doing, the way through the junk, would look straight ahead, eyes focused on the direction they were heading. Any person who knew what was good for them would glance at the ground too, alert for the many obstacles. That metal roof, for instance, would drop off at any moment.

This man looked up. What was he looking for? The light hit his face in a strange way, as if bouncing off a surface. Dark hair flopped over his features. Probably he was drunk, wandering back from the club. She would ignore him, and he would go away.

She ducked under a plow blade. Mr. Fall said that so much snow used to fall from the sky, people had to push it away from the roads with plows. It piled up in great mounds, flecked with soot. People didn't even need to melt the snow for water or cooking.

Trashlands, like many places, still had snow and it could get bad: thick, deadly storms that would incapacitate, though not enough infrastructure remained to do something as organized as remove the snow, not from the roads, which belonged to everyone and no one.

Coral had to crawl under a squashed car. A cat darted away. She could hear rats scrambling around. Children would

catch the rats and sell them to Rattlesnake Master, who had
hired a cook to fry them up.

But Coral could still hear the man above her. She passed a
semi cab, climbed up a ladder propped against a van—there
was a circle in the windshield where someone's head had gone
through—and then she was at the rim of the junkyard. She
could see the man. There was no way she could hide. She remembered the new men Foxglove said had been thrown out
of the club, remembered Trillium's strangers at the market.

The man looked over and saw her. He wore city clothes,
clothes that didn't belong in the junkyard, that wouldn't stay
clean or would be stolen from him while he slept: neat pants
and a shirt with real buttons. But the strangest thing about
him was on his face. Eyeglasses.

"I could hug you," he said.

"I've got a knife," Coral said.

In truth, the knife was home on the bus. She had a ten-
dency to forget things when she made her pieces, to think
only about the plastic, and what she could create with it.
But the man didn't need to know that. All men needed to
think you carried a knife at all times.

"I just mean," the man said, "I don't know what I'm doing
here. I'm grateful to see somebody else. Another living soul.
Do you know the way around the junkyard?"

"The path to Trashlands is behind you. I don't know how
you missed it."

"I'm looking for something. But not Trashlands. Whatever that is."

Coral peered closer at him. "The best strip club in Scrappalachia. Don't you read the ads in the papers? Isn't that why
you came?"

At this, the man laughed. "I am the paper."

★ ★ ★

The stranger's name was Miami. Coral helped him find the way down from the roof through a boxcar, resting on its side. It always reminded Coral of the whale, every time she passed it. The boxcar was red, the color of a scab. No one lived in the boxcar, because it leaked. Sometimes desperate men would camp there for a night or two, before it rained on them.

But today, they were lucky. The boxcar was empty. Coral opened the hatch in the bottom, and directed the man through. They crawled until they reached one of the hidden paths, a path that didn't go to Trashlands. It would get the man safely to Summer's truck, or to Ramalina's place, and then back onto the road—or to the woods, if he wanted to go that way. Coral wouldn't recommend it.

"This place is amazing," the man said, straightening. "I'd heard that. But to see it with my own eyes—I've written about you even, referenced it, as much as I could without visiting. Which isn't very much, I guess. I'm a reporter."

The word sounded familiar, but she couldn't remember it. She waited for him to explain. Mr. Fall always explained. When Miami didn't say more, Coral said: "Define that, please."

"Define?"

"Define that word for me."

Still he was puzzled. "What word?"

"*Reporter.*"

He looked at her. Sweat had made circles on his nice shirt, made his forehead and cheeks shine. His glasses were small squares, flecked with dust. Neither of the lenses seemed to be broken. "You've never heard of a reporter before?"

"It's a job?"

"Yes. You research and write about people, about things that happen, to inform others."

"So you're a gossip?"

"No." Higher circles of red appeared on his face.

"The jobs we have here are dancer and bodyguard. Teacher, tattoo artist, healer. But most of us are pluckers. That's me. That's what I do."

"You pluck plastic from the water?"

"That's right."

"And sell it by the pound?"

"It's a living," Coral said. "Almost."

It was something Mr. Fall would say.

Clear plastic was worth more than cloudy. Plastic that hadn't been recycled before was worth the most of all, but that was hard to find. And the price kept dropping.

Miami started walking again, even though he didn't know where he was going. "I thought pluckers were migrants, moving from place to place?"

"I know what migrant means. And we do. We move where the plastic is. But there's a lot of plastic here in the river." Once she had found a radiator, and a few times, something called a toaster oven, a black box with coils inside. Mr. Fall said the coils would heat up and glow, just like the Trashlands sign, to heat food. Trillium said that sounded like a waste of heat and plastic. "We always used to come here, every year, but we've ended up staying for a long time. The plastic hasn't stopped."

"Will you leave when it does?"

She didn't want to tell him that it wasn't the plastic that bound her to Trashlands. "Why are you here?" she asked instead.

They had reached the end of the path. A food truck sat

there. The order window was boarded up, and the awning had mostly rotted. But steps led up to the door, cement steps, which meant the truck had been parked awhile.

The screen door opened and a woman, perhaps in her forties, with long black hair, leaned out. "Hey, Coral," Summer said. "Who's this?"

Summer had a kettle boiling over a fire outside, near a barrel and a lawn chair with a busted seat. She ushered Coral and Miami inside the truck and instructed them to sit. The truck was only one room: a kitchen with silver countertops, which Summer used for a workshop, and a bed with a flowered bedspread, which took up the whole back. Summer fussed around the kitchen, taking a tin from a shelf, tossing a pinch of dried leaves into a jar. Coral settled onto the bed. Miami looked around, not wanting to choose the bed beside her.

The kettle sang. It was a discordant song, deranged from the mangled whistle in its throat. Coral had found the kettle in the river and bargained for a year's worth of haircuts from Summer. Coral liked to hear the kettle. She imagined it was a train—or maybe the whistle at a factory, signaling to the workers it was lunchtime. It was the time at the end of the day when they could go.

Better to think of a train, a train taking a lady far away.

Miami chose a plastic tub, and turned it over to sit on. Summer went outside with her jar. Through the screen door, Coral watched her take the kettle off the fire, a stocking cap wrapped around the hot handle. She had long, curved nails, painted orange today; Foxglove had once told Coral they were plastic. Summer poured the steaming water into the

jar, then balanced a plate on top to keep in the heat. She left
the jar and came back inside.

"There," she said. "That'll steep for a few minutes." She
sat up on the counter. "Now tell me about you."

Miami said, "You don't get many strangers here?"

"No, we don't."

"None that don't go directly to Trashlands." Coral said.
"Miami is a reporter."

Summer raised an eyebrow, as full and brown as Foxglove's was thin and red. "What is that?"

"I want to experience everything I can," Miami said. "See
it all. Observe. Because—"

"You're a man?" Summer laughed. "You think you own
everything?"

Miami didn't seem rattled. "Because it's my job to write
about things. I tell stories. In a newspaper in The Els."

"Oh, The Els." Summer leaned back against the cabinets.
They held chemicals and potions, for curling and coloring
hair. Coral would bring bottles she found with any solvent
still inside straight to Summer, who added clay and crushed
berries, her formulas as mysterious as Trillium's ink. The
cabinets also held wires, screws and bolts that weren't rusted,
fabric and glue for Summer to make shoes and costumes.
"That sounds fancy," Summer said.

"Not really."

"Fancier than this."

"It's just different."

"What are the cities like?" Coral asked.

Miami turned to her. "Hard to sleep at night. They're
loud, crowded. My apartment—the building gets broken
into sometimes."

"Looted?"

"Yes. There are bars on the windows, but no glass. It's too hot."

"You don't have chillers?" Summer asked.

"Not where I live. And not where I work. We're not important enough. The government, maybe. What's left of the police. But not us. There are buses that run, but they're crowded and late. They break down. They're all so old. People get run down sometimes in the street. And sometimes people just...walk in front."

Coral fell silent for a moment. "Why are you here?" she asked him again.

"How is the food there?" Summer said at the same time.

Miami answered Coral first. "Two things. I'm looking for something in a junkyard."

"And?"

"I told my boss I would write a story if he let me come here. A firsthand account of life in Scrappalachia."

"That's no story," Summer said.

"What are you looking for?" Coral asked.

He did not want to answer, she knew. She was not like Foxglove, who could have any man she wanted just with a look. Or Summer, crossing her long legs and shifting so her hips wiggled on the counter. But Coral still knew when a man was avoiding something.

"The food is a little scarce," Miami said to Summer. "Depending on the day. There are long lines. You can get noodles pretty regularly. But meat can be difficult, and vegetables spoil before they reach us. I bet you eat better here."

"I had groundhog yesterday," Summer said.

"Well, I'd try that."

"For your story."

"Yes. For my story."

"We can't grow vegetables," Coral said. "Not without paying for them."

Summer had a garden once. Rattlesnake Master had sent men to burn it in the night. Coral still remembered the spicy smell of tomato vines, the whorls of lettuce. She'd never gotten to try anything from Summer's garden.

Summer hopped off the countertop. "Tea's ready. I'll be right back."

Coral waited until the door smacked shut. "Is that one of the things you do for your job? Ask questions?"

When Miami removed his hand from his knee, Coral saw a sweat stain on the nice fabric. His glasses had slid down his nose and he pushed them back up. "Yes," he said.

"You're answering more than you're asking." She leaned back on the bed. On the ceiling above, Summer had hung up scraps of black fabric with radiant stars. Some of the stars still glowed. Fabric was expensive, but we all had our things, Coral thought. We all had our ways to get through. "What are you looking for in the junkyard?" she asked the ceiling. "A car?"

"Much smaller than that. Why can't you grow vegetables?"

"We're supposed to buy our food at Trashlands."

Summer came back. She poured the tea into cups and passed them around. Miami took a cup with a broken handle. Coral took the one that read *Season of the Bitch*.

"I'm looking for something from my sister," Miami said. "Something that was lost in an accident. Involving a car crash."

"Oh, almost everything valuable's been taken out of the junkyard by now," Summer said. "People picked over the good stuff long ago. Even the plastic that washes up from the river is mostly ground up these days. Isn't that right, Coral?"

That wasn't true. Coral had found the trash can just yesterday, but she wondered if Summer was trying to get rid of the man. Or more likely, trying not to get his hopes up.

"Most of the junker cars have been here a long time," Summer said. "None of them run. We all just settled in around them."

Miami placed his tea on the tub beside him, and pulled something out from his shirt pocket. A slim book with a blue cover, smaller than his hand. A notebook. He took a pencil from the pocket, stubby, sharpened almost to the end but still, a pencil. He flipped the book to a clean blank page. "When did you come to Trashlands?" he asked Summer.

"Oh, I haven't seen one of those in years!" Summer said, more interested in the pencil than the question. "Can I hold it?"

Miami gave the pencil to her. Coral stared at the notebook. How many pages were blank? How many had been torn out to use as insulation or to start a fire? Did he really use paper just to write?

Summer leaned over the mirror she had propped on the counter. It had a broken frame, gold and plastic, meant to look like a crown. Squinting at her reflection, she took the pencil and went over her eyebrows. "Faint, but I like it. So easy to use." She smacked her lips in the mirror, smoothed one hank of hair over her eye, then handed the pencil back to Miami.

"What do you normally use?" he asked her.

"Clay, arrowroot, charcoal. Whatever."

He was making notes, now that he had his pencil back, writing in the way they all did: tiny, cramped, conserving room. Once he had filled the center of the page, he would turn the book and write sideways, around all four squares, then in short lines angled on each of the corners. That was the way you used paper: you used it up.

Coral caught herself eyeing the notebook's flexible plastic spine. A coil like that could be used as a splint for a broken finger, or a hair tie. Or—she couldn't stop herself thinking it—a sculpture.

That was the problem: You couldn't stop remaking. You couldn't stop breaking down everything you saw in the world into parts. How much could it be worth? What else could it be? She tried to imagine a world where objects had only one use, where a bottle of plastic held water only once, quenched one person's thirst. She couldn't do it. How could you look at something and not see what else it might make?

Miami's lips turned down when he was writing. Trillium's mouth did the same thing. Lines radiated from Trillium's mouth, from all the years of frowning, concentrating on a tattoo. Then she noticed the ink on Miami's finger. A band she had mistaken for dirt or shadows. It was neither. It was a ring tattoo, a faded circlet of ink.

That meant he was taken, branded by someone on the finger that, in the past, might have held jewelry. Jewelry was difficult to find and afford. But ink was forever.

Miami was married.

Self-consciously, Coral felt for her own finger, squeezing it with the fingers of her other hand. She had no tattoo there. Trillium didn't either. He didn't want to waste the ink, spend the money on himself or her. And what did it matter? they told themselves. It was an old tradition, outdated. They could be committed to each other without rings.

"Let me cut your hair," Summer was saying. "Just a quick trim, to get it out of your eyes? It'll be a nice change, for both of us. All these dancers in here wanting straight hair and curls and to cover their gray." She pointed her cup at Coral. "I've been trying to get this one in here for that."

Coral felt heat in her face. "It doesn't matter."

Miami looked at her. "I like your hair."

"I'm not onstage so who cares what I look like." The tea was minty and sweet. She drained it, her tongue finding the sodden leaves at the bottom.

Summer picked the nettle leaves herself and dried them. Nettles would leave welts on your skin if you collected them the wrong way.

"Are you staying, then?" Summer asked Miami.

"Staying?"

"Staying here for a while? For your story?"

Miami closed the notebook and put away his pencil. "I guess I am."

"Do you have a place to sleep?" Coral said.

"No room here," Summer said. "You have any money? You could stay at Trashlands?"

Miami looked at Coral.

"They take old paper money," she explained. "Most places around here will only accept plastic. But…" She paused. "It's pretty loud there, and—"

"Sounds like my apartment."

"It's fine," Summer said. "They've got rooms above the club for boarders. Locks on all the doors. You have any stuff? I can show you."

Coral stood. "I'll take him."

★ ★ ★

Not all of the pink light across the junk-scape came from
Trashlands. Some of it leaked from the sky.

"It's from The Els," Coral explained to Miami. "Your
pollution comes all this way." They started walking below
the sugary, orange-pink clouds. "Strange to think how bad
things can make good things. Pretty things."

"Do you see a lot of stars out here in the country?" he
asked.

"I don't really know. We fall asleep pretty early." They
were always so tired, Coral and Trillium. Exhausted enough
to overlook the rumbling of their stomachs, to tune out
other wants.

Miami carried only a thin bag, so slack she hadn't even
noticed it, hanging off his shoulder like a broken arm. It
couldn't hold much, only an extra shirt or two. The bag
was made from leather, patched in several places. Who had
patched it for him? The person whose tattoo he wore?

The club Trashlands was three stories tall, the highest
structure in the junkyard, soaring over the cars. That was
by design, Rattlesnake Master's plan, so you could see the
sign from anywhere. So it could lead you, a hungry man,
to water—that was what he had said.

Thirsty man to water, Coral had thought.

But you did not correct Rattlesnake Master.

When her group first came to Trashlands, they came lured
by the promise of a job—Mr. Fall's job. An ad had been published in a newspaper that made its way to the warm weather
camp where they had been staying, near an old casino.

Seeking a teacher for the many children of Trashlands.

It was a pricey thing, to place an ad—and a dangerous

one. The dancer who had scrimped and saved for it, looking to help her children and more, the dancer who could
read, was gone by the time Mr. Fall and the others arrived.
But children were there, peeking out from behind the trailer
windows and the busted fire engine. Their mothers could
pay a bit. And the river was there.

Coral remembered the plastic bobbing in the river her
very first glimpse of it, like white ducks lining up for her.
There was a sheltered place to park the bus. Shanghai would
have friends. The camp back at the casino had only a few
children.

Coral did not know why yet. No one had told her.

Their first night at Trashlands, as they gathered kindling
for a cookfire, Rattlesnake Master came out to greet them,
and to explain the rules of his junkyard, the price they would
pay for living there. Water cost and was limited. There was a
cost to till the dusty land, and if they wanted to grow crops
they would have to turn the harvest over to him so he could
select what he wanted. There was a curfew for women.

"And when will you start working?" Rattlesnake Master
had asked, turning to Coral. He had conducted the entire
conversation about rules and rent with the men, speaking to
Mr. Fall and Trillium only, as if Coral didn't exist.

But now he looked at her like she was the only thing in
the world. She filled his eyes and face with a kind of hunger, deep want mingled with contempt and an expectation
that seemed inevitable. Of course he would have her.

She had difficulty reading his expression at first, and then
it came to her. Smug. His lips turned up in a thin, nagging
smirk, as if he was resisting laughing at her.

Coral tried not to glance at her backpack, full of the plastic she had already gathered that evening. Would this man try to take that from her too? "I'm already working."

"Women do one job here," he said. "You'll see."

It was not that Rattlesnake Master reminded her of Robert so much as he reminded Mr. Fall of him, as did many men. Those who stood too close to Coral in the river, who looked at her a little too long. What was different about this man, with his smirk and his way of licking his lips, was that Trillium too felt it. He and Mr. Fall promised they could keep Coral away from Trashlands, keep her safe from that man.

Inside the club, a spotlight lit a stage and pole. So Coral had been told. She had never actually been in the front way, below the neon sign. Only through the back. An office was back there, a dressing room, a kitchen where children sold rats at the door. Coral had been to the office exactly once. After that meeting by the fire, she had gone with Trillium to the club to collect some plastic. Trashlands had a scale, and they went to settle Foxglove's first few debts.

Until Coral and Trillium were ushered into the office and left to wait, they thought they were meeting a lower associate, not Rattlesnake Master himself. Coral would never have come. Trillium would not have let her.

A velvet curtain, dyed a dull red, separated the backstage from the rest of the club. While Coral had waited, the men doing all the talking, she watched the dancers going in and out. When the curtain parted, it was like an alien creature walked in from the shadows, all skin and sparkles. Each time the curtain gaped, she caught a glimpse of the main club floor, heard a shout or two. The music grew louder for an instant. Then the curtain closed up. The music continued, but dull and distant, like a headache.

Rattlesnake Master had looked down at her, sitting on a couch in the corner. *Real red?* he had said. *I've been wondering.* But he wasn't speaking to her, only about her.

Trillium hadn't responded. He indicated the plastic, spread out on the desk. He accepted a price, which was lower than they had hoped. Coral knew it was to redirect the man called Rattlesnake Master.

Named for a root. From the parsley family.

The music pounded as she led Miami around the back of Trashlands, where the door was splintered wood. Everything was shabbier back here. No sign, only a busted porch where dancers would sit or smoke. A staircase led up the side of the building to the top floor, an exterior hallway of doors. These were the rooms rented to boarders, mostly men who were too drunk to find their way home—but not too drunk to find their wallet, or have it found for them—or men who didn't want the night to end, to be left alone in it.

Miami stared up at the big, crooked building. "Are you sure there's no hotel?"

Hobbled together with boards and metal siding, it looked like a giant shed from the back, Coral knew. It tilted slightly to the left, but the ground underneath was solid. Trashlands, like any building that had survived, had been built on a hill.

Higher ground, for when the floods came.

"It'll be fine," Coral said. "There's a lock on the door, and nobody bothers a man alone." And when he looked at her in a way that seemed to indicate it was different where he came from, she said: "Here a man is usually safe."

A man blocked the back door. A big man. Tahiti stepped

closer—he was nearsighted—then broke into a grin when he saw who it was. "Coral! Come to see your girl, Foxy?"

"Not tonight." Coral had never visited Foxglove any night inside the club, but Tahiti always asked. "I've got business for you. A man who wants a room."

"Does he have money?"

"Paper money."

"Excellent. Boss will like that." Tahiti stepped to the side, indicating the stairs.

"Are those safe?" Miami asked.

"Perfectly. I helped fix them up myself. Material called *Ikea*. Very structurally sound. Unless—" he tilted his head, exposing the scar on his neck "—would the gentleman like to visit the club first, before you get settled? Foxglove is dancing tonight. She's got a space for your name."

"He's not here for the club, Tahiti," Coral said. "He's here to write a story. He works for a newspaper in the city."

"A newspaper? That's something! You've seen our ads? I wrote some of them myself. Are you here to write a review? That would sell your papers."

"No, I—" Miami began, but Coral touched his arm. She was surprised to feel warmth.

"I'm sure Miami's tired," she said. "Could he just see a room?"

"Of course," Tahiti said. "We can talk later."

"I'll leave you here, then," Coral said to Miami. When she turned to face him, she realized they were almost the same height. To be looking eye to eye with a man was new. She had to crane her neck to look into Trillium's eyes. She could not, she realized, remember the last time he had looked her in the eye.

"Can I hire you?" Miami said. "To be my guide through the junkyard?"

The request threw her off for a moment. "I have work."

"Please."

"I have a lot to do."

"You know this place better than anyone. Please," Miami said again.

It was not a word she was used to hearing. It was not a word it was easy to say no to.

"All right," Coral said. "I'll do what I can to help. But you can't distract me. I still have my work."

"Of course. I'll meet you whenever you have time tomorrow. Maybe in the morning? I'll be in room..." He looked to Tahiti for guidance.

"Two," Tahiti said, making a decision.

"Perfect. My favorite number."

By the time she began the long walk home, it was twilight. At night, the familiar structures of the junkyard took on other mysteries. The only lit path was the path to Trashlands. All the other, hidden ways depended on mercy and kerosene, juiced solar lamps or precious batteries. Most people didn't have light to spare. They certainly didn't have gas for a generator, which was a luxury only for rich men in cities.

And for Rattlesnake Master.

Coral knew the way. Long ago, she had memorized the paths. But she was not supposed to be out after dark. There was Rattlesnake Master's curfew. If you broke one of the laws of his junkyard, you had to pay. He demanded plastic. *Or you can work it off,* he had told them—told her—that first day, in his joking manner, which was not a joke, with his smile, which was not friendly.

It had been a long time since Coral had strayed from the bus after sunset. She had forgotten how the small animals moved, how the rats and raccoons, which were kings of everything, could scurry, shifting the metal of the junkyard. She was ducking around a truck when she heard the creaking. For a moment, she was jarred out of place, thinking again of the whale.

There had been screeching from the birds on the beach that day. A single boat, tied to a dock, hung on by shreds. The boat squealed as it rocked. Something clanged against a pole—a mast, she thought it was called. The dock tilted into the water like a pile of old piano keys. The boat, she remembered, had a hole in its side, like so much of the plastic she pulled from the water.

In the junkyard, the pile next to her groaned. It was tilting, jarred loose with a sound like screaming. That day with the whale, Shanghai had kicked inside her for the first time. Mr. Fall had joked that it must have been the smell of the beach that had set him off.

A yard cat dashed out of sight, yowling. A hubcap rolled out from the dirt, spinning like a coin, and the column it had been underneath buckled. She turned too late as the junk fell: a broken pallet, metal barrels, strange arms of cranes collapsing, kicking up a spray. How had they ever thought that would hold? Coral was clipped by the falling metal. She landed in the dirt, surrounded by broken bits. Now they were more broken.

"What the fuck was that?" said a man's voice.

Nobody came to see what the fuck it was.

She should have scrambled up immediately. Somebody might be coming. The wrong person might have heard and sent out muscle from Trashlands. The men were not all kind like Tahiti. She was out late, breaking the rules. But she couldn't get up, couldn't move fast at all.

There was pain. Pain in her jaw, pain in her leg. Miami was closer than home. Miami was in Room 2 of Trashlands. She could hear the music start up at her back, the whirl and scratch that meant the one song was beginning again.

But she couldn't go there, that was reckless. To seek help from a man she'd just met?

She pressed her hand against her jaw, which pulsed. Her face had smacked the earth. It would feel better in a bit, with a compress of comfy, maybe. Another moment, and still no men rounded the corner with torches and clubs, to survey the fallen column, to drag her to Rattlesnake Master. Coral was not sure what the penalty was for breaking curfew. The punishments kept changing. They were different for women. Lately, women were pushed onstage, stripped, and shown to the crowd.

Coral couldn't do that. She *couldn't*. Two men had seen her body, only two, and the first had hurt her. It had been wrong. *She* had been wrong. She pulled her shirt tighter to her chest. She tried to listen for the sound of boots on dirt.

Trillium would have questions. Where had she been? Why was she out so late? She wouldn't know how to answer them. Another moment, until she felt she was safe, then she bent under the truck and limped back.

6

Trillium
Trillium grandiflorum

This was an art that worked. That you could be paid for, and live on, and keep doing. To mix the colors, so visceral, so changeable. To improve the consistency of the ink, its staying power, its vibrancy. To make its poison not poison.

In this life, you were constantly innovating. Even the simplest tasks required imagination. Where would they live? How would they cook? How would they wash? How would they make love in the bus with Mr. Fall, Coral's adoptive father, everywhere? They would figure it out.

They figured it out.

Tattooing was an art he fell into. He had always wanted to draw, was always scratching figures. Impractical, waste of time, his daddy said when Trillium had found a piece of relatively clean paper and used it to draw. *It won't keep us alive*, his daddy said. Paper is for fuel. Paper is for messages.

Nothing is for art, his daddy said. *Nothing*.

When his paper was taken away, Trillium drew pictures in his head. He thought of a bird on top of a crooked pole. Once the pole had carried wires, his daddy said, which spread power and light and pictures from house to house. Pictures, he had said pictures—but then he quickly tried to cover it up by saying *words*. The lines had spread words.

What happened to the lines? Trillium had asked.

The same thing that had happened to air travel and the internet: not paying enough attention, then they were taken away. *Pay fucking attention*, his daddy said. He slapped the side of Trillium's head by his ear.

That ear rang for a long time. One day it stopped or he just didn't notice it anymore. Another day his daddy would hit him again, and the ringing would begin anew. Could he hear it now? Could he hear it still? Sometimes he felt the ringing was in him, in his bones, a vibration as resonant as the tuning fork Coral had scavenged once. She had a gift for finding objects that reminded him of old times. Or maybe he was just always thinking of back then.

Trillium and Coral were makers. This was mostly what bonded them. They belonged in this society of scrap, they could lose themselves in it. They spent hours finding materials, selling them, then refining that which they did not sell into something else.

Trillium dipped a needle. This was art that was alive. You could feel it under your fingers. The needle vibrated, hollow, bloodied with ink. Once it had belonged to a bird, the thin feather that became an instrument. Once Trillium had drawn in the dirt with a stick, on his own hand with the fingers of his other hand, tracing, trying to remember what he wanted to create.

Now he drew on the arm of a man.

The man had asked for a swan with his woman's name tattooed beneath. He had come from Trashlands, Trillium could tell by his sour smell. Half of Trillium's customers were dragged from the club by Foxglove, flashing her mile-long legs. But half were rueful, like this man. He had been drunk but he was sobering up quickly. His eyes looked like he hadn't slept in days, crimson as the ink Trillium made from red cabbage. The man's clothes were rumpled. He had spent the night—maybe more than one night—in a chair, maybe hopped up on something one of the girls had sold him.

The man's hands shook. He was sweating heavier than he should have been on an early evening in the rainbow bus. It was warm but cooler nights were coming. The bus had been parked in the shade.

"Almost done," Trillium said. Ink came from the needle in careful dabs. Redness came from the man.

Coral joked that Trillium could coax blood from anyone, give him time. Maybe that was his daddy's influence. His daddy could raise a knot, bloom a bruise from nothing, a slight that only he could hear or see, some kind of indecipherable shift in the atmosphere. The temperature one degree warmer, the air one droplet wetter could set him off. Crickets or the absence of crickets. The absence of food. The absence of liquor—there was never enough liquor in the world for his old man.

"Georgia Aster," Trillium repeated the name he was tattooing on the stranger's skin. He wiped any blood away with a rag, and pressed the needle down at an angle, pricking the image out, dot by dot. It was the slowest kind of drawing, and it was an image that would live as long as the man did.

Who knew how long that would be.

"What a pretty name."

"She's my sweetie," the man said, huffing through his teeth. Sweat rolled down his face. "She swore she'd never leave me, but…"

"Good to show her this."

He didn't like it when they talked.

"I made a mistake," the man said.

Fuck. Here we go.

"It was only the one time. I mean, it was only one night. Maybe a couple of times. Maybe five or six."

"Sure, five or six."

"Eight or nine."

Fuck this guy. Trillium bent closer to the swan named Georgia Aster. He doubted the man had seen the flower or a swan—Trillium only knew what the bird looked like because of Mr. Fall's book—but the man had insisted: a swan with a long, graceful neck. *That's what she has*, he had said. *My love.*

But now that the tattoo was almost done, the man was hedging. "One of them has it," he said. "A long neck."

Trillium paused with the needle posed above the man's skin. "One of them?"

"One of the girls. Long neck. I remember that."

"It's fine. Lots of people have long necks. She'll know in her heart this is for her." Trillium finished the beak of the swan, tapered and delicate as its noodle neck, the neck that could have belonged to any girl. He preferred tattooing people like Foxglove, who just lay there, head down, eyes closed. Trillium didn't have to hear Foxglove's sad story.

He already knew it.

He heard the screech of the bus doors. The glass panels had been replaced with cardboard, but the vinyl material between them still folded and unfolded, mercifully. If you were inside the bus, you used the lever at the driver's seat to unfold the doors. From the outside, you opened by pushing hard. This person wasn't pushing hard enough. They were probably drunk.

Trillium looked away from the man. "Push harder," he called.

The doors wheezed, but did not open all the way.

Trillium put down the needle. The man on the table shifted. "Don't get up." He raised his voice to the drunk, "Push—"

And then the person did, tumbling inside and tripping up the bus steps. Trillium saw matted red hair. It wasn't a drunk. It was Coral. He hurried to her. "What's wrong?" He noticed the tiny windows of the bus reflected darkness. He hadn't realized night had fallen. "You're home so late. Too late. Are you all right?"

"Women shouldn't be out late," swan man called from the table. "My Georgia Aster was always home right on time, making me supper."

"Shut up," Trillium said. The man could keep his plastic, a pod coffee maker—those were as common as sunburns. Coral looked strange. "You're hurt."

Her eyes that rose to meet his were teary. "I fell and bumped my jaw."

"Let me see." He tried to touch her face but she wouldn't let him. "Where were you?"

"Working. We can wrap it. It's fine."

"I think you should see Ramalina."

Her eyes flashed. She lifted her chin, and he remembered falling in love with her. He always did. She stood out among the other pluckers like a flaming tree. The shortest among them, and yet the one who seemed, by her very presence, to search him out. To call to him, like an emergency. He'd heard the story of her before he met her. And once he saw her...

"No," Coral said.

"We can afford it."

"No, we can't."

"Yes, we can." He called to the back of the bus. "Leave your plastic on the counter, please."

"Am I done?" the man said.

"Yeah, you're done."

He wobbled off the table. Trillium heard him hitch up his pants. "She's got a long neck," the man said. He was staggering up the bus aisle, pointing at Coral.

"Not really," Coral said.

When the man reached them, Trillium saw he had forgotten to go over the last part of the tattoo. The final letters looked fainter than the rest.

That was fine. It was not like the wasted man would remember who had done his tattoo, where he had been for the past few days, why his groin and back ached and his cock burned, or where his plastic had gone. Trillium and Coral both did their work like this: without attribution.

The man's arm could say *Georgia Ass* for all Trillium cared.

"It's my hair people notice," Coral said.

"That's purty too," swan man said. Then his finger dipped. He pointed at Coral's leg. "You're bleeding, honey."

They went to Ramalina's. Trillium was welcome there, as all men were, unless the opening of her yurt was pulled shut. Sometimes Trillium heard moaning in pain at those times, or weeping behind the opening. Coral felt a little afraid of Ramalina, Trillium knew. The healer remembered Shang-

hai as pure and innocent and young. She remembered Coral
as having lost him. Trillium didn't like to think about that,
either. He had offered to carry Coral, all the way across the
junkyard.

She had said no.

The curtains of the yurt were open. Coral looked back
at Trillium once, then went inside. He followed her into
the yurt swirling with warmth and richness, the smell of
medicine. A cot stood in the back, behind carts and count-
ers cluttered with jars of dark liquid. Herbs hung, gathered
into bunches. At the center of the yurt was a fire bordered
by stones.

A woman with long braids sat in a rocking chair, smoking. "What happened?" Ramalina asked, taking the pipe
out of her mouth. It was plastic, small and pink, an old toy.
She had stuffed it with spearmint and mugwort.

"I fell," Coral said.

"Not like you."

"I was distracted." Coral looked at Trillium. What was
she not saying?

Ramalina got up from the chair and drew Coral over. She
had a pot of water boiling over the fire. She opened Coral's
mouth and began to poke around. She had studied from Mr.
Fall's book—which was really a series of books, all with the
same cover. The books looked alike, but there were different sections for almost everyone; Ramalina liked the first
volume, which covered anatomy. She knew the location of
bones inside the body, their names, what they were supposed
to do. Ramalina paused. Coral made a sound like a kitten.

"You broke a molar," Ramalina said.

"Fuck," Trillium said.

"It was probably rotten. Good to get it out. You have enough teeth left. You don't need it. That, though—" she pointed at Coral's leg, where red had soaked through her pants "—that might be a problem."

They helped Coral onto the table next to the fire. Ramalina rolled back the leg of Coral's pants to the calf. She was not going to cut it; they were not going to waste good fabric. Blood could be washed out.

Ramalina dabbed a rag in the boiling water and brushed away grit, revealing a cut as long as a little finger. She washed it but the cloth kept coming away red. Red water ran down Coral's leg. "I might need to sew this up."

Coral made another sound.

"It won't hurt too much. Not like hurt you've already known. You—" she nodded at Trillium "—hold her, give her comfort."

He was not the best at this, not when others were around, when he felt pressure. He felt awkward, too old to give reassurance, even to his own partner. On the table, her hand looked so young next to his. She did not have the spots on her skin yet that he did, the scars, the raised veins that marked him as different than her, a little bit apart. His heart beat hard. He tried to think of the first time he had held her.

Trillium would travel from camp to camp then, setting up shop anywhere. He didn't like to stay anyplace for too long. One night he had followed lights bobbing on the horizon to a meadow. In the middle of the field stood a metal frame, as tall as a factory. The frame had once been covered in a screen, but most of it had rotted, exposing the rusted skeleton beneath. Poles poked out of the meadow every few feet.

A drive-in, Mr. Fall would tell him later. He had names for almost everything.

Those may have been the first words Mr. Fall had said to him, now that Trillium thought about it: *You're in a drive-in theater, son. Once upon a time, cars would come here on Friday and Saturday nights—loads of families, kids. They would pay money to sit in their vehicles, sound coming from machines stuck through their windows or on their car radios.*

And on those screens, Mr. Fall said, *pictures would flicker to life. Stories, music.*

And in those cars, Mr. Fall said, *nobody was paying any attention. They were drinking, eating, kissing. That was much more interesting than what was on the screens, we thought at the time,* he had said.

Long after the movie screen had mostly shredded, tents had been set up in the meadow. A few vehicles parked there. Tarps were spread over the ground, dotted with plastic odds and ends. By the plastic, Trillium knew the people camped in the meadow were pluckers. A big sign with dark, broken bulbs at the edge of the meadow read *STAR-GLOW.* There was a star shape at the top of the sign, with an arrow pointing down into the meadow. When the sign was lit, it must have been visible from the highway.

As good of a place as any.

He set up shop by a concrete building with a caved-in roof. Painted letters on the side of the building had mostly flaked away, reading...*CESSIONS.* A boy, too young to go out with the pluckers, sat on the ground and fiddled with a bike frame. Except for the cry of a baby and a few women talking, the meadow was still. When the others came back, they would be hungry, and if they had found anything of value, they would be excited, ready to spend their money as soon as they thought they had it.

A good time for a tattoo.

Trillium got ready. He laid out his needles, arranged the inks by color. The pigments caught the light and glimmered, which was a good advertisement, but he also had the sign he had painted on a blanket. *Tattoos. Safe Needles.* Below the words, he had drawn a flower—his flower, his name plant, a trillium: three white petals with a yellow center—and a bottle of black ink. He hoped the images would be enough for those who could not read.

Trillium settled on his stool and waited. The only sound was the boy striking the bike with a tool. After a time, Trillium realized the child wasn't fixing it. He was just hitting it for something to do.

At sunset they came: streaming over the hill, the line of them, heads down. Trillium heard them before he saw them. It was a particular noise, the hollow sound of plastic. Milk jugs jostling against water bottles, sunglass arms sliding into food containers. The whispered rustle of a hundred plastic bags.

Then Trillium saw Coral.

He remembered the moment. How could you forget that hair, bright as blood in the sea of dark heads and drab clothes? Her arms were empty and she swung them as she walked, trying to keep her balance with the pack strapped to her back. She headed with the other pluckers down to the meadow, to the tents and cars that awaited them.

Those too old or too young to go out with the crew came out from their shelters and watched. Trillium had been aware of food cooking for the past hour or so, the smells of algae oil and onion, the sweet and slightly arid scent of cricket flour biscuits. Vendors would be busy selling. People would want booze tonight, so certainly one of the tents made it, brewing from fungus or rot.

And who would want a memory, a rowdy night, wildness and art and pain?

Trillium sold those.

It only took a moment. A man nudged his friend. Trillium saw the look light up their faces, the *aw yeah* on their lips as they read his sign or figured out the pictures.

They came over to Trillium. "What do you accept?" the first man asked.

"Plastic is fine," Trillium said.

"Can you do a naked girl on me?" the second man said, exposing his biceps. He slurred the words a bit, so the men must have already been at the wine stands.

"I can. But I don't advise it. Unless you have her permission."

This was not the answer they were hoping for. There were guffaws from the men, some discussion among them. Trillium took this time to look back at the hill of pluckers.

Coral raised her head then. Her mane of red gave way to a round face with freckles, a pattern that repeated up and down her arms. He couldn't see any tattoos. She looked smaller than the others, but she walked confidently among them.

"Who is that girl?" Trillium asked.

"Oh, Coral," the first man said. "She's a strange one. Plucks a lot—but then something always seems to happen to her plastic."

"What do you mean?"

"She don't sell it all," the second, drunker, man said. "She uses it for something. Building something way out in the woods, they say. Freak."

"She's got a reputation, though," the first man said. "She's kind of a legend."

"What is it?" Trillium asked. "What's her legend?"

In the yurt, Ramalina shook a jar. She unscrewed the cap and tipped a dropper, made from a pen, into the brown solution. She dropped the oil into Coral's mouth. Clove oil. Trillium could smell the spice from where he stood. It would numb and soothe her tooth pain.

Next, Ramalina closed the cut on Coral's leg. This was trickier. Coral winced at the dabs of the rag, the sweeps of a blood-colored liquid. Iodine, Trillium thought. Peroxide was too precious, too expensive. Ramalina went for her sewing bag.

"Look away," Trillium said. "That helps with the tattoos. People don't really feel the pain until they see the needle."

"I know that," Coral said.

Ramalina got out thread, scissors, the large silver needle. Mr. Fall said there used to be drugs for knocking people out, for making them feel no pain. Legal, safe drugs for hurt as common as a pulled tooth, a stitch in skin. Ramalina had none of those drugs.

"I have rot wine?" she offered.

"I hate that stuff," Coral said.

"It would take too much, anyway. You'd be sick all night." She threaded the needle.

"Look at me now," Trillium said to Coral. Her face was lovely, even in a mask of pain.

Ramalina tied a knot with her hands that had held so

many children, that had pulled them out of their mothers, that had buried some of them. Trillium didn't understand how you could bring a child into the world, *this* world, why you would want to.

But he also knew you didn't have to want to. There was so much forced onto you, if you were a woman. The world was full of thorns. Coral had taught him that. The world was a long night and you could never sleep, never rest. He remembered when Coral had told him the story of the icehouse, as much as she could, which he knew was not everything. She could never tell everything, not even to him. He reached for Coral's hand. Ramalina cut the thread with her teeth.

7

Shanghai
Shanghai Municipality, China

After the first few weeks he stopped wearing gloves. What was the point? They snagged. They made his skin slippery and wet. He kept having to strip them off, put on his spare pair—but save the first, of course. He would have to wash them, mend the thin material. You were only given two pairs.

And not *given*. You had to work for them. Pay for them. The gloves were added to your debt, as was food, lodging, clothes, anything you bought from the factory store like cigarettes, rubber chewing sticks, foam plugs for sticking in your ears and trying to sleep at night if your bunkmate snored, which they all did. Socks. Tire-soled shoes. Washing powder for your teeth, or face, or hair. Soap. Pens or pencils. Paper. Thin, expensive paper. Though what was the purpose of that?

Some of the others got letters sometimes, from the irregular post or from family members who had discovered where they were, who waited at the gates and pressed folded messages through the bars, after bribing the guards. The others took the letters away to read in places where they thought they were alone, squeezed into a corner, backed against a wall, cupping the pages as if words could keep them warm.

But Shanghai had learned you were never alone in the factory. Even in your bunk, others could hear the rustle of a letter's pages, could hear you weeping.

The smart ones ate the letters, or somehow destroyed them after reading. Otherwise, someone would eventually find them, read them, and know all about the lies.

Love. How much. How soon coming. How bad it felt. How strong the regret. What the price for selling their child had bought the letter-writer: food for a few more months, or shelter, or another child come home—a girl brought to safety, maybe a mother.

Girls were always at risk. Shanghai was too, but he had hit back right away, lashed out with his feet, bit the air, growled. And then they left him alone, those who would do him harm, who waited in the shadows, offering food and promises.

Everything was a lie.

Shanghai got no letters. At first he wondered why. Did she not care? Did she not remember? Did the collectors take the letters from her, or not let her send them? Had something happened to her? Did she not know where he was?

Then he got angry. His mother wanted to forget him. She wanted to wash her hands of him. He knew she would never really be able to, like when it was his turn to wash up and he had only a few seconds of greenish-gray water. That water did nothing. He would never be clean, never rid of the filmy sludge, the muck from the shredded plastic.

So too his mother would never be free of him. The *patina* of him.

He had learned that word from one of the older boys at the factory. The boy had once been a painter, or wanted to be. Shanghai had met the boy when he graduated from sorting plastic. Sorting was the worst job, the most dangerous: putting your hand onto a moving conveyor belt and grabbing bits of plastic. It was the dirtiest, reaching into mud and food waste. It was work meant for the smallest, quickest of fingers. Not every child survived that job, and Shanghai was grateful when one morning the guards relocated him to a new spot, beside some older children. He was not given a reason for the move, but he knew: his hands had simply grown too big. Now he would take the plastic, ground to bits then melted, and extrude it into a brick-shaped mold.

This job had its dangers too. The mold was cumbersome and latched on the sides and top. Screws had to be tightened to press the shape. The plastic sludge was hot, and to cool it, the whole mold had to be plunged into a barrel of water, which hissed and steamed. The steam rushed to Shanghai's face. His hands shook from the heavy mold.

For a long time he had been plucking plastic from the conveyer. He had learned what could be salvaged and what was trash. He had grown used to flinging muck from his fingers, dipping the plastic in another barrel to rinse it, then tossing the plastic into sorted piles. The water in the barrel to rinse the plastic was fetid. Sticks and garbage swam at the top, and he suspected this was the recycled water the children used for washing up. At night, his eyes also swam with images of plastic flashing by him, the blue and green, the clear, the bags strewn about the conveyer like loose skin.

Now he would shape plastic bricks. For how long? No one knew. The painter did not know his own age, and one morning he too was gone, replaced by a boy around Shanghai's height with reddish-brown hair. The color reminded Shanghai of something.

It was walking in the woods with his mother.

In his memory, he followed her hair. Followed that bright cloud over a hill and across a stream, fronds and branches brushing by him. The two of them were searching for something but he couldn't remember what. Food probably, or plastic; those were the only things they looked for. Except, shortly after crossing the stream, his mother stopped, bent down, and put a finger to her lips and a hand on his shoulder. He remembered the press of that hand, its softness and gentle weight. She pointed across the trickle of red water. Something flickered between the trees, in and out, in and out, an animal with light fur. If he squinted it would disappear.

"A deer," his mother said.

The creature looked scrawny, he remembered that. They could count its ribs. Still, he said, "We should shoot it! For dinner."

But his mother shook her head. "Let's just watch it. Let's just let it be."

The creature lowered its head to nibble at something on the ground. Its muzzle was dark and wet, and its eyes, shining but not seeing them.

His mother watched the deer. He watched her hand on his shoulder rise and fall, rise and fall with his breathing.

★ ★ ★

Plastic oozed past him into a hose. He had to fit a nozzle onto the hose, and fill the mold with liquid, squeezing it off at the right time. But the hose was patched in many places, tied with rags, and hot melted plastic escaped from it, searing his hand. He dropped the hose, stuck his hand in his mouth.

The boy next to him stared. Shanghai picked up the hose again.

He hoped he haunted his mother. He hoped she hadn't been able to sleep for seven years. The way he hadn't, turning in the dark, the bunk frame squealing. It was a wonder his bed hadn't collapsed into twigs by now. Nothing wood could stay. Nothing made of metal. Or love.

Only plastic was forever.

Sometimes, not too often, but every now and again, he set aside a chunk of it. Just a little of the plastic slurry pinched off the hose that was an especially bright color, or contained interesting bits. Once, he had found a piece of sludge that was blue-green with glitter stars. You saw glitter a lot, but usually in the bodies of animals. You would spit it out of your food, as you would spit tiny plastic shards. It wasn't rude. Plastic was everywhere. It was like expelling the bones of fish, though Shanghai thought he had never eaten fish.

He knew his mother's story. Was it supposed to mean something? Supposed to make him brave—that his mother, pregnant with him, had walked into a whale? Was it supposed to keep him safe, protected by the myth of a dead monster?

Well, it hadn't worked.

He set the glittery plastic aside. Later, when the boys on either side of him on the line weren't looking, and when the plastic had cooled a bit, Shanghai took the blob out and shaped it. Not with the mold, the sharp frame that had cut or burned him many times already. Not into the brick he had been making out of plastic slurry, as they made bricks every waking moment, hundreds of bricks a day.

He shaped this plastic into something...else. Whatever the plastic wanted to be, whatever it told him to make of it. Maybe what it had been before.

Sometimes Shanghai imagined he could envision it, though of course that was impossible; he was born too late. Almost all of the plastic he saw had already been broken.

By the time plastic reached his hands, it was a stew, a mess of ground-up, pulverized polymer. Children down the line had picked out the metal bits: the razor blades, springs, the human teeth—anything that might make the bricks less useful, less structurally sound. Corruptibles in plastic weakened the bricks, pockmarking them with holes. Children were punished for neglecting to pick out contaminants.

Or anything that could be sold for scrap elsewhere.

Once someone had found a ring, and the rumor was that they had kept it. Later, they had been found out and beaten. So the story went. It was rare for something like a ring to survive the melting process the plastic went through. It had to be very tough metal to not melt down.

Or it had to be teeth.

Sometimes Shanghai made hearts or balls or bracelets with the bits of moldable plastic he swiped. Often he made animals, ones he remembered or had seen pictures of somewhere. He pressed their bodies into the melted material. It took the shapes easily. It wanted, like all plastic, to be something else.

He made the faces of the boys around him (there were very few girls at the factory; Shanghai was not sure why, where they went or were taken). He made his own face, the face he knew most of all, even without seeing it that much anymore.

And he made her. His mother.

She was young. She was beautiful, in a way. All mothers were. Her way was wild, elbows and hands rough from work, an upturned nose, slightly gapped teeth she tried to hide with her hand when she smiled. He didn't remember her smiling much. She was slight, shorter than he was going to be when he grew up, she always said.

He mostly remembered her hair. Burning, an untamed thing. He had liked to twist it around his fingers. It always sprung back into the same coils. He remembered her pushing him gently away when he pulled on her, hung on her. As a child, he couldn't get enough of her—he remembered he could never be close enough.

He hurt her. She asked him to stop, to give her a rest. It was like he knew even then, it would all be taken away.

He made the glittery plastic into a whale. An animal he had seen in a book, long ago. The animal was majestic, with a huge, powerful body. What did that animal do, other than make a good story for his mother? What had it been used for, what was its purpose? Everything had a purpose. Were any whales still around? Shanghai made the creature the best he could. He wished he had more of the blue plastic. His whale looked small, shimmering in the light.

"What's that?" the boy next to him said, ruddy-faced and red-haired with a beard he could barely grow. His name was

Outer Banks. Shanghai had heard a guard say it. The boy
nodded at Shanghai's whale.

"Nothing. It's nothing."

He didn't like how the boy reminded him of his mother.
The hair. How dare he have her hair? How dare he look
anything like her?

Shanghai pushed the animal down, squashing it flat with
his hand. He threw the blue glitter plastic into a tub being
funneled into a hose, adding it to the other sludge until it
became just more melted plastic, nothing special. He didn't
look the boy in the eye.

It would make a lovely brick. He wondered if anyone
would notice, the rich man who would buy the brick for his
house or business, in his safe and distant city; if he would
recognize how different this brick was, how it had almost
been—what was the word? His mother had taught him—art.

8

Coral

After the long night at Ramalina's, Coral forgot she was
supposed to meet Miami. Miami didn't forget, though. The
murmur of male voices woke her. Trillium was gone from
the bed they shared, and heat spilled into the bus from the
open doors.

Trillium leaned out of the bus, his arm blocking the way.
"I'm not set up for tattoos this early," he was saying to someone outside. "You must still be tanked from last night?"

"Not at all," Miami said. Coral pushed under Trillium's
arm, and Miami saw her. "I'm here for Coral."

Trillium looked down at her. His eyes were tired, the
skin underneath them creased like blankets. He had been
up late—they both had been. Coral had needed help walking, climbing into the bus and into bed.

She knew her face was swollen, but she tried to hide it
from Miami. "He hired me," she told Trillium. "As a guide."

"A guide to what?"

But Miami had noticed. "Are you all right? What happened?"

"I fell on the way home. Things move around sometimes in the junkyard."

"On the way home from what exactly?" Trillium said.

"How did you find me?" Coral asked Miami.

"Tahiti led me. I didn't know you got hurt"

"Well, he can lead you right back, then," Trillium said. "Whatever you need a guide for, Coral's out."

"I'm not out," she said. "We need the money. It's fine. Miami and I arranged it already."

"When did you do that?"

Was this trouble? His eyes looked different, both hard and empty at the same time. "Yesterday," Coral said. "He's looking for something in the junkyard. That's why he needs a guide."

Trillium glanced at the man. "What do you want in the junkyard? Plastic?"

"Yes," he said. This was news even to Coral. "It's something my sister lost."

Trillium looked back at Coral. She knew he was taking in her swollen face, the stiches on her leg. She had no plastic to show for yesterday. No finds meant no money.

Faintly, she heard the music from Trashlands, the dull thump that didn't seem to have a melody, a beginning or an end. *The loop*, Foxglove called it; she could do hip circles to it in her sleep. It wasn't a beat so much as a thrum. Not a heart pumping life as much as a heart beating to death, marching, marching, unstoppable.

Coral knew people still made music but it wasn't recorded,

pressed onto a disc that could be replayed. They made what they could, what occurred to them on the instruments they could find or make: strings stretched across the belly of a box, holes in a plastic tube, singing. It was a rare night that Coral heard new music coming from the junkyard or woods. It was risky; travelers could give themselves away like that. But she and Trillium always sat out on the bus steps on those nights and listened for as long as they could.

Today was like every day. Heat would burn the fog that hung over the river, down from the hills. Soon would come the cooking smells, the sickly odor of wine and beer fermenting. The flies the liquor drew, the gnats, the biting bugs. Soon would come the punishing sun. Men would stumble to the rainbow bus because they were bored, because they were lost, because they were drunk or hungover or in love. Because Foxglove led them. Trillium needed to set up his tools, start his day and long evening.

And Coral needed to leave. Get away from the stifling bus. "I'm going," she told Trillium. "You have stuff to do, anyway."

"We haven't even had our coffeetree pods yet."

"We can get something," Miami said, "on the way."

"You're from The Els, aren't you?" Trillium asked. "You'll find it's different here."

Coral had put on boots. She had picked up her empty bag and slung it over her shoulder. She kissed Trillium's cheek. "I'll be careful."

Trillium didn't say anything. She slid past him down the steps.

Her tooth ached but she expected that. The pain would last awhile, Ramalina had said, despite the numbing clove.

What Coral didn't expect was the pain in her leg. A scratchy feeling from the stitches. She fought the urge to tear at them.

Coral looked behind her. To his credit, Trillium waved. Then he went back into the bus without closing the doors. The space under the bus was empty. Mr. Fall had already woken and left. Or maybe, not slept there at all. He spent a lot of time with Summer.

Coral had been walking in step with Miami without paying much attention. Now she stopped. "We should plan this."

He stopped too. "You're right. Sorry."

"I don't even know what it is you're looking for, really. Can you tell me?"

He paused. "A bracelet."

"A bracelet?"

"Plastic. Pink glitter. With a gold charm."

Why did she think he was not telling her the truth, not telling everything? "Well, the gold will be gone. And maybe the plastic too." Sold. Melted down. Pressed into a brick. "Why do you think the bracelet is here?"

"Her accident happened here."

Coral didn't ask why. The world brought people different places for the strangest of reasons and no reason at all: a rumor that there might be food in a place, or power, or good plastic. Mr. Fall had taught her that a battle was once fought over shoes. And not even shoes, but the rumor of shoes. Coral understood moving—how the smallest, most inconsequential thing could make you leave a place, and once gone, you could never get back.

She didn't ask where Miami's sister was. Dead maybe, or far away. It was a strange thing to want, a bracelet. Possessions were temporary, swiftly lost, stolen, or made into other things. Coral had nothing of Shanghai's. She was not sure she would have wanted something. It was better not to be faced with the loss of him daily.

"Let me lay it out for you," she said. "The junkyard is hundreds of what we call acres. About a third of it is occupied, mostly with dancers and pluckers, but they move in and out. Where the plastic goes, we go."

"What's it like, moving around like that?"

"Trillium likes it." New customers, a chance to see new places, though they mostly saw the same places again and again.

At first, they stayed at Trashlands only in the cooler months, camping farther north in warmer times. That camp, the summer place, bordered an old casino. It didn't have the cover of the junkyard, which kept out strangers and kept in friends. Coral had always felt protected by the junk. It had never harmed her. Before yesterday, she had never gotten in its way.

But at the casino, they were in a vast space. The pluckers circled their camp. They built a huge bonfire. It was difficult to sleep. People stayed up tending the fire, talking and drinking.

In this way, Coral had always preferred Trashlands. The people who wandered through the junkyard were almost always going to the club. But at the casino, anyone could come out of the evergreens, drawn by the fire. Desperate people, people who had spent everything they had at the patched velvet tables of the casino.

"You have to go where work is," Coral said to Miami. It was what Trillium would say. "Plastic is work. Plastic is life."

But also... Shanghai knew Trashlands. Shanghai had been

here before, year after year. It was their winter camp. He knew that. What if he was released and couldn't find her? What if he came back to Trashlands and she was not there?

"I'd prefer to stay in one place permanently," Coral said. "Settle down. But except for the garbage patch, plastic moves. So we move. You've traveled for your work? Have you ever seen the garbage patch?"

"No. I'm not rich enough for a boat or a plane. That's the only way you can get out on the ocean."

"But people live there?"

"Yes," Miami said. "There's a school. A restaurant. There's talk of secession."

"Secession?" That was a word Mr. Fall had used, but she couldn't remember what it meant.

"Forming their own government, their own country."

"The country of the garbage patch?"

"It still moves," Miami said. "That's what they say. It moves slowly, spinning in the ocean. If you're not used to it, you can feel it, they say. Like feeling gravity."

"That sounds horrible." Coral tried to imagine walking on floating plastic, building a house on plastic ground. She couldn't believe people didn't pull the garbage up, tear away the very bones of the island, the land they walked upon, to sell it.

"Maybe I'll get there someday. In the meantime, here we are," Miami said. "Scrappalachia is just as exotic to my readers as the garbage patch."

"I find that hard to believe."

"Most people in cities have never traveled far. It's too hard to get back. Too expensive. Your apartment might be looted or taken over by the time you come home."

"Aren't you worried about that?"

"I don't have that much to return to. I just have my work."

Coral understood.

"It's hard to get too far out of the cities. There are robbers on the roads. Worse."

"How did *you* get out?" she asked.

"I'm a man," Miami said. "And I sold a lot of my things, for the trip. I have money to pay my way."

"Don't say that too loudly." Coral started walking again, and he followed. She moved slower with the hurt leg. "It's best if folks think you're just here for Trashlands. That's why strangers come. To look at the girls. Not to search in the junkyard and definitely not to write a story about it."

"What's so special about Trashlands?"

Coral realized she didn't know. It was the only strip club she had ever seen, the only one she had even heard of. And she had only ever been backstage. The club was not why her family had come, not what had drawn them. But it was a special thing, a spark to make the miles of junk and rust different, set the area apart.

Camps would be known for a landmark, the biggest structure still standing, so you could navigate to them, find their safety from far away: the casino; the Star-Glow; the Settlement where the icehouse had been, where Robert had been.

But none of those camps had the kind of halo that encircled Trashlands. It was like the camp had its own sun.

She tried to explain. "It's just magical. The pink light, the DJ. They have these beautiful costumes. Sparkles and gold paint." Tall box shoes. Eyelashes as long as fingers— Foxglove said those were called *falsies*, which was also the name of the jiggly cups of soft plastic she slipped into her top sometimes, depending on the night.

Coral and Miami had followed a path she knew and were at the well. It was circled by tires, a rusted metal grate on top like the lattice on a pie. Water lapped at the opening, but the grate was locked. Rattlesnake Master had the key and you had to pay for it, if you wanted water.

"We don't have a lot of glamour," Coral said, "outside of Trashlands."

A line of mostly women waited by the well. She saw Miami take in the locked grate, the guard who was as big as Tahiti but had none of the kindness of his eyes.

"You said your sister was in an accident?" she asked.

Miami said, "A car accident in Scrappalachia. That's all I know."

A working car—it was probably not working well or for very long. It might have been forced off the road, men setting upon it like feeding animals, trying to take the wheel. And if they couldn't do that, they would tear off what they could, ripping at the mirrors and bumpers.

"We're a big region," Coral said. "Why did you choose Trashlands?"

"This was nearest to where the bus stopped. I walked for a long time after. This was the first place I came to, the first civilization I could see."

"What did the car look like?"

"It was our father's. And his father's before him. An SUV, it was called."

"Your family must have kept it in good shape, to keep it running."

"We hid it. My family had a garage. A house farther

outside of the city, before the floods. We stayed there for a while, but the neighborhood got overrun. Too many people came together, and then they wouldn't leave. So we had to."

Coral had heard of this, whole communities taken over. She had never lived in a house and had no memory of her parents. Her life began, as far as she knew—her mind began—with a circle of sky as she lay on her back on a blanket that smelled of smoke. Her first memory. A sky swirled with clouds.

Mr. Fall had found Coral in the rubble of a Dairy Queen. He had set her on a blanket outside the building. She swore she remembered this, or maybe he had just told the story to her so many times. Maybe she had been born in a factory, Mr. Fall had told her when she was old enough to ask. Maybe her parents were young and couldn't keep her. Maybe, though Coral thought this only later, her mother's pregnancy had not been her mother's choice.

Mr. Fall had found Coral on a mission. They had netted a lot of plastic that day in the burned-out Dairy Queen: tables and chairs, plastic dishes. The door was smashed, the entrance smoldering. But not much had been destroyed inside. No one could tell her why the building had burned, why Coral had been left or survived there behind the counter, which the pluckers ripped apart.

It was a long time before Coral understood what a Dairy Queen was. A store, just a store that sold food. A long time before she understood that she was not royalty, like she had mistakenly thought. Not a princess left in the ashes for her parents to reclaim, left a throne to retake later. She was not magic. She was not special.

Though Mr. Fall said ice cream was special, very special indeed.

Coral led Miami beyond the well, around the walls made of pressed-together cars. She used the wrecks to guide herself. There was the car without a roof, *just married* spray-painted on its side. There was the long, dark vehicle Mr. Fall said had been used to carry the dead.

She paused on top of a hill. Below them, near a bend in the river, was the market. People shook plastic out onto scales. There was haggling, shouts, sometimes pushing or worse, knives drawn. Then a price was decided upon and exchanges made: plastic for food, for clothing or tools.

"It's only men down there," Miami said.

"Yes." She watched him take in the sight of the men, dumping the weighed plastic into giant baskets and bins, then loading them onto boats in the river.

"You don't sort the plastic?"

"Children do," Coral said. "I thought you knew that."

It was terrible work. Dirty, dangerous. Coral couldn't look at the market anymore. When the boats passed her in the river, she turned her face away. Once, she had tried following them, swimming until the water reached her chin, her nose, until she began to swallow it, to sink low in the waves. New Orleans had run back to the school, to get Mr. Fall. The two men shouted for her to stop, wading after her until she listened, let herself be pulled back. They were all soaked to the neck, Mr. Fall's face wet with tears.

On land, in the trees, she lost the river's path. She couldn't find where the boats went. Was it where her son was? Some people said the boats took the plastic to horse-drawn wagons, which carried it to factories. Other people said there were no horses anymore, and the collectors used cars.

Coral knew that part of the story to be true.

She took a metal rod leaning against the nearest pile of junk and began to draw in the dirt. She drew Trashlands, Summer's and Foxglove's places, the rainbow bus down its hill. She drew circles for the well and the market, and marked where she and Miami stood on the rise.

"People don't bring in a lot of new scrap these days, not big like a car," she said. "If they do, it'd be near the entrance. You can't get stuff very far in." She made a line in the dirt and set the rod down. "I can only give you a day of my time."

"One day?"

"If we haven't found your bracelet by dark, it's probably not here. Or you won't ever be able to find it." She straightened, adjusted her empty pack on her shoulders, not looking at him. "And I get paid no matter what. Whether you find what you're looking for or not."

"That's only fair. How much?"

"How much?" She had expected he would argue over her time. All men wanted more for less. That was what Summer and Foxglove had taught her. That was what Coral had experienced herself. She remembered staring at the icehouse door, and still Robert would not move from her.

"What's your price as a guide?" Miami asked.

Coral looked down at her leg. The clove oil burned in her mouth. She thought of the most expensive plastic she could imagine. "PMMA," she said at last. "Acrylic."

"I don't have that with me."

"You can get some at the market, buy it with paper money.

Or give me what it costs, and Trillium can go. You don't have to pay me right away, though."

But he said, "I will. I'll pay you as soon as I'm back to my room."

She looked at him. He squinted in the light, behind his glasses. The sun was blinding, yellow-white. He didn't wear sun protection, though his hair covered his ears. He wasn't wearing plastic boots. What had led him to Trashlands? Was it really just the first place he came to? Most outsiders couldn't handle a day in the junkyard.

"Do you have a hat?" Coral asked him.

9

Mr. Fall

It was easy to wake up. Achiness woke him. Achiness and dew.

The pain radiated in his bones, and the dampness seeped from the ground. The sun might grow hotter, as the ozone protecting the planet thinned to nothingness, like the stringy white of an egg. The earth might grow arid with dust, he knew—history had taught him—could blow the very roots of the plants out of the ground and sweep them away. But under the bus, Mr. Fall still woke up.

He didn't mind the dew. That was Nature. Nature continuing, and that was good to feel. The achiness, however, the pain in his joints—that would end him. He balanced on his elbows and rose slowly. He wondered if Coral would get this pain eventually, if she would know arthritis.

He had protected her for so long. She was grown before she even had so much as a broken bone—and it was a tooth, at that. Maybe that wasn't best, though. Children healed faster than grown-ups. Grown-ups might not heal at all.

He had protected her from bad men, of which there were many. He had done a good job since that teacher hurt her, he told himself. Trillium was good. Mr. Fall had had his suspicions at first. A man older than her. An artist. A quiet man. But Trillium had proven himself, he had been loyal. He had not forced her to have more children. He had supported her in her art in the woods, work she felt she needed to do, though neither Mr. Fall nor, he suspected, Trillium, understood it very well.

He had let her down about Shanghai. But they had all been helpless about that.

Mr. Fall crept out from the bus. Luckily neither Coral nor Trillium were around to see him struggle. They would protest, insist he sleep inside. He reached back under, feeling as he did the pain in his back. He managed to roll up his blankets inside the foam pad he slept on. He tied the roll with a rope of plastic bags.

He put on his boots, found his hat and placed it squarely on his bare head. Only skin up there now, tanned till it peeled. He had freckle-like spots he didn't want to think about. There was nothing to be done about them, anyway. No doctors to see, no insurance to worry about, no bills to come in the mail. No mail at all really, nothing reliable. Nothing to do except see Ramalina, who could soothe with plants, and who would cut when soothing failed, slice out from his body what the herbal medicine couldn't help.

There were still medical drugs in some places, he imagined. He had read about that in the newspapers that made their way to the yard. Everyone traded the papers, and when they were done, Mr. Fall used them for teaching. One day he would organize them by date. Or maybe that was a job for the children, to keep them occupied, help them remember their numbers.

Maybe some of the children would keep up the act of preserving, after Mr. Fall was gone.

It was because of the artifacts that he couldn't sleep in the school tent. Books crowded it, stacks of papers, chairs they had salvaged or made. And the found things that he thought the children should see. It was a library of items that had outlived their usefulness, items that weren't plastic and couldn't be melted down, and those he had kept from Coral's curious fingers. The library included computer parts, a flip phone, a scooter whose motor and tires had been stripped. He let children take apart clocks and coffeepots and circuit sets, and try to put them back or arrange them into something else.

"Everything is useful," Mr. Fall would say. "But everything also has a story. Sometimes an object's purpose," he said as a girl fiddled with the phone, "is just to tell the story."

The flip phone didn't flip anymore. Its hinges had snapped, and now only cords connected the two pieces. The child was careful not to rip the cords. She ran her fingers over them, thinly ribbed. "What's this thing's story?"

"I don't know," Mr. Fall said. He had learned the best way to teach was to ask questions. "What do you think?"

"People loved to talk a long time ago?"

"Maybe."

"Did they use this for more than talking?"

"Yes," Mr. Fall said.

The girl tried again: "People loved to have possessions,

things to occupy themselves? Things to make them feel special, help them belong?"

"I think so," Mr. Fall had said. "I think that was it."

On his way up to the school he saw a man, heading down the hill. The only thing down that way was the bus. The man was dressed nicely, too nicely. He must not have been in the junkyard very long. There was only one place he could have come from: Trashlands. No one emerged from the woods this early in the morning, not unscathed. Mr. Fall saw no wounds on the man, no tatters on his clothes, which were a little dusty, that was all.

And the man wore glasses. With unbroken lenses.

"A little early for a tattoo, isn't it?" Mr. Fall said, friendly.

The man looked surprised.

"Do you know what you want?"

But the man didn't respond. It seemed like he didn't know what Mr. Fall was talking about. How strong was the wine they were serving at Trashlands these days?

Mr. Fall gave up.

Then he heard the man say, "I do know what I want, thank you."

It was pleasant, neutral. Mr. Fall waved over his shoulder and kept on walking.

Summer was up. She usually was, whatever time he came by. He knew she had trouble sleeping. She had dressed already, in a faded flower-print dress and shoes with high clear heels.

Mr. Fall took off his hat and called through the screen door. "Are you working today?"

She kicked her heel. "Would I wear these if I wasn't? Actually, I probably would. Coffee?"

Mr. Fall opened the door. "Yes, please."

"Breakfast?"

"What do you have?"

She rattled something in a metal can. "Black walnuts. I was going to roast them, once I get the fire going. Or raw, if you can't wait."

"I can wait," Mr. Fall said. He hung his hat beside the door and pulled up a turned-over plastic tub to sit on. "I saw a man headed down to the bus this morning. Man I'd never seen before. Nicely dressed. Young."

Summer looked up from the can, where she was picking out walnut hulls. "Glasses?"

"Yes," he said. "You know him?"

"I bet he's that reporter, hanging around Coral."

"Coral knows him? A reporter from a newspaper?"

"All the way from The Els. He's here to write a story. And to look for…something or other. Coral's helping him. I'm pretty sure he's sweet on her, though. Who wouldn't be?"

Mr. Fall said, "Does Trillium know about him?"

"No."

"Well, he will. The man was headed that way. A reporter, you said?"

"From a paper in the city."

"What would he be writing about?"

Summer said, "Human interest story?"

He was surprised she knew that phrase. But it was probably from one of the old newspapers. Mr. Fall realized the man might have papers with him, more recent editions. He might be able to speak to the children about being a reporter, about life in the city. He tried to temper his excitement. "Why was he interested in Coral?"

"Are you kidding me? Your baby is grown up and beautiful." Mr. Fall must have looked horrified because Summer said, "He said he was hiring her. As a guide. He lost something here and he thinks our girl can help him find it."

"Here in the junkyard? Good luck."

"I've gotta get that fire going if we're gonna have breakfast."

She moved to go past Mr. Fall but he touched her leg. "Let me take a look at those shoes. What are the heels made of?"

"Broken wine glasses."

"How did you manage that?"

She kicked her heels again. "I took off the stems and attached them to old soles."

"You're a genius," Mr. Fall said.

"I just don't want to waste money for shoes." She kissed him. She tasted of the bitter Kentucky coffeetree pods they boiled and drank.

"I wish you wouldn't go in today."

"I've got to eat," Summer said. "And so do you." She took the can, rattling with walnuts, out the door.

Mr. Fall made enough to keep the bus repaired, enough to contribute some to their food stores. Parents gave what they could to Mr. Fall, when they could. Some gave nothing at all and that was fine too. Better the children learned to read, learned history. So many of them slipped through the cracks. So many were lost in the woods, locked in apartments, especially the girls.

Summer felt lucky, she said. She had a roof over her head,

a roof with wheels that could, in theory, roll again. She tried
to keep the tires patched and had stored a small canister of
fuel for the future. She hid the canister under her bed. She
didn't like dancing so much but she was paid, and she made
more money selling food and doing hair and costumes. She
was saving, he knew. She would be ready if she had to move
again quickly.

If *they* did.

Approaching the school tent, Mr. Fall waved to the
woman who lived next door. She was hanging clothes to
dry on a satellite dish. He pushed open the tent flap. Already a boy waited inside, Golden Toad. He often arrived
early. His mother worked at Trashlands, and he didn't like
to stay in their car alone without her.

Mr. Fall didn't blame him. He nodded at the boy, sitting
on his knees in the center of the circle, in front of a pile of
ashes. "Have you eaten today, Toad?"

The boy shook his head.

"Get some kindling from the box and we'll get a fire
going. I've got some walnuts for you." Mr. Fall pinned the
tent flap back with a rusted clip. He waved to the two girls
coming through the yard, sisters. He hoped he had enough
walnuts for all of them. Behind him, he heard Golden Toad
scrounging around for kindling.

It was important that the boy learn not only reading and
history, but how to forage and cook and build a fire too—
that all the children learn. It was important that they had
somewhere to go while their mothers worked, that their
mothers *could* work. He had seen what had happened when
families didn't have enough to eat.

He wouldn't lose another child to the collectors again.

10

Coral

Coral felt less safe around people than she did around trash. She and Trillium hadn't made love much the nights they spent at the casino camp. It felt like they were never alone there.

The pluckers had set up their camp on the outskirts of a parking lot, against a line of trees. Evergreens, Mr. Fall told her. The trees lived up to their name, sticking around and staying verdant. On the other side of the camp stretched rocky dunes. Dirt would blow in the wind, stinging her eyes, getting into her hair and mouth, and hissing in the campfire. At night the wind peppered the bus with a sound like rocks in a can.

The collectors had come to the casino camp at night. They had come in a caravan of cars with fire to see their way, and guns to get their way. Coral knew the guns were loaded because the men proved it. They wasted ammunition, shot bursts into the sky that, from a distance, sounded like thunder.

"Is there a storm?" Shanghai asked in his sleep.

They slept three in the bed then, Shanghai nearest the window, Trillium by the aisle. Mr. Fall slept on the floor. It was cramped in the bus and cramped in the bed. Coral knew Trillium wasn't thrilled with the arrangement, but what could he say? What else could they do?

They were married now, Coral and Trillium, as married as they could be without rings or ink. Sometimes at night Trillium would touch Coral's hair above the child's head. Or they would exchange long looks. But the moments they had alone together were stolen, in the woods or in an abandoned car, and only moments. Coral associated the smell of mice with making love. Mouse droppings and leaf rot and mold. It was better than associating love with ice, as she had before. And touch with pain.

Shanghai was about seven, a blond head between them, hair as white as a slice of moon. He asked again, "Is there a storm?"

"No, honey," Coral said.

Then she heard the screaming.

She sat up. Shanghai rolled over, bumping into Trillium, who was waking too. It wasn't dogs she heard. And not a single scream either, which could mean anything: grief, labor. Coral heard the yelling of multiple people, and the rumble of cars moving through the camp. Running cars?

"What's happening?" Trillium said.

"I don't know."

Shanghai sat up and swiped at the condensation on the window.

Trillium was already pulling on boots. "Mr. Fall." He
shook the older man to wake him.

"What do you see?" Coral asked Shanghai.

The child squinted at the window. It was so dark, the dead
of night. "Nothing."

Coral leaned forward to the window. Debris hit the pane,
sticks or gravel, with a force that made them both jump back.

"Get your shoes on," Trillium told them. "But stay inside."

"What's out there?" Coral said.

"I don't know. Stay here." Trillium opened the doors to
a rush of cold air and darkness.

The air had a smell. Smoke but not campfire smoke. Gun-
powder. And gasoline. Coral was surprised she remembered
it. It had been years since she had smelled it that strongly.
Trillium and Mr. Fall pulled handkerchiefs over their noses
and mouths. Coral knew they had knives strapped to their
legs—they all did.

Nobody had guns.

But somehow, somebody out there did. She heard again
the sharp retort.

"Trillium," she said.

"Shut the bus after us. Stay here."

She did as he asked, yanking the heavy accordion doors
shut. "Get your shoes on," she told Shanghai.

"Why?"

"I don't know. In case we have to run."

"Why would we run?" he said. "We have the bus."

"I don't know. Just get your shoes on. Give me a break."
She said that to him a lot. *Give me a break. Don't fight. Stop
arguing with me.*

Coral had put on her boots. She had checked her knife,

saw that a bag was in reach and packed with a water bottle, some dried fruit, sweaters. Shanghai still hadn't put on his shoes.

"Shanghai," she pleaded with him.

"I don't know where they are."

"Where did you leave them?"

Something exploded outside, a boom followed by a rainfall. Small bits of plastic smattered against the windows. Coral yanked up the blankets and looked under the bed. She saw his shoes, as she knew she would, a pair she had scavenged that still fit. She pulled them out by the laces and threw them down the aisle. "On, now!"

Was that really the last thing she had said to him?

She didn't tell him that she loved him. She didn't tell him to be careful or be safe, or that she would come for him. She didn't know what was happening, until it happened: Shanghai saw someone out the window, someone he knew from the camp, one of its few children. A little girl.

"They have Tybee!" he said.

It was enough of a shock to propel him against the door lever, to give him the strength to wrench it open and fall outside.

"No!" Coral ran down the steps after him.

Outside, the world was dark and full of smoke. Mr. Fall and Trillium stood in front of the bus. They both had their knives out. But the men in the cars barreling through the casino camp had guns. They shot them out of windows, into the air.

Mr. Fall turned and saw her. Coral should have told him to catch Shanghai. She should have warned him and Trillium, but the child was already slipping through them, escaping like a cat into the space between his family and the cars.

"No!" Coral said again.

Trillium swiped at the air, grasping and failing to grab Shanghai. One of the men leaned out the front passenger side of a car, the space where a door should have been—it had been wrenched off its hinges—and snatched the child.

Her child.

Shanghai, who struggled. Shanghai, who fought everyone about everything—including sleeping, eating, wearing warm clothes. Shanghai went into the car. He went with the man. He folded up like a knife. His limbs, his small bare feet without shoes, his lightning-white hair, his father's eyes wide above his kidnapper's arm. It happened so fast. He said nothing.

Not even her name.

Coral screamed. Trillium and Mr. Fall ran after the car. Trillium reached for the door frame, but the man holding Shanghai kicked at him. The man's boots were heavy, barbed with spikes. Only later, Trillium would notice how badly his hand had been cut. His tattooing hand. He would not be able to work for days.

Later, only later, Coral would think how strange it was that certain details were burned into her memory—and others she couldn't recall at all, like the faces of the men who took her child. If they were wearing masks. The kind of car they drove or what they said, if they said anything.

What she did remember: Shanghai's feet, bare as flowers. How his hair had looked, sticking up and mussed from sleeping. The rise of his eyebrows and the shrinking of his pupils into the tiniest dark dots. He was terrified. He was all she could see.

She ran after the car. It was the last in a long line. The rainbow bus had been close to being spared, so close. If only they hadn't left the bus. If only Shanghai hadn't seen his friend. Maybe the car would have missed them.

The caravan had torn through the camp. Coral did not know yet the human toll that the collectors had taken. She did not even know that the men in cars were called *collectors*. She did not know that every family had lost someone. That was the price for staying in the camp in the shadow of the casino and the sheltering evergreens.

One child.

Mr. Fall stumbled, racing after the car too, but Coral passed him. She couldn't worry about him yet. She couldn't stop. The car did not have taillights; she couldn't even follow its red glow. She ran after its dust, its gasoline trace. Shadows restitched themselves after the car as if it had never torn through them. The shadows would go on. Night would go on. Not her.

She couldn't remember how long she ran. Long after she had lost sight of the caravan, long after she had seen any other people. Her son was coming back. The cars would turn around.

Finally, she fell or tripped. She found herself in the dust, on the ground far from home. A stranger was helping her up, an old woman.

"There, there, child," the old woman said.

But there was no child.

"They took him, they took him," Coral said.

"Who did you lose, child?"

She shook her head. She couldn't say it. If she said *my son*, if she said his name, it would be real. It would be some kind of spell. She bit her lip hard enough to bleed. Her eyes swam so she could barely see the stranger, patting her arm. The woman's hands felt soft. Coral would remember that.

"They take them, child. One from each family. That's the blood price for staying here," the old woman said. "But you never know when they're coming. So you keep thinking you can leave in time. You can beat them. But you can't, love. You just can't."

"Why did they take him?" Coral sobbed. "What are they doing with children?"

"It ain't bad, child. It ain't for…" Here the stranger paused, uncertain how to say it. She patted Coral's arm again.

Coral gasped, the sob lodged in her throat. She would choke, she would die. She could not stand this.

"I know where they go," the old woman said. "It's the brick factories. Far away."

"Brick factories?"

"They have them sorting plastic. Their little hands, see? That's why they want children. It's their little hands they need."

Coral knew cities were rebuilding with plastic. Dredging for concrete sand ruined the oceans, and dynamiting for stone destroyed mountains. But plastic, melted, made bricks. Cities were building plastic houses, plastic schools, Mr. Fall had read. She knew the plastic she sold went somewhere, but to factories? To children?

"They're kind, the collectors," the old woman said. "They feed the little ones, better than we could. They take good care of them. They won't harm your child. They need him."

"Why didn't they take me? Take me instead?"

"Our hands are too big. We're too slow at sorting. We're no good to them. Believe me, I tried. I begged them. I walked all the way to one of their factories and begged at the gate."

Some of the tears cleared from Coral's eyes. "What did they say?"

"They told me the price."

"The price?"

"For getting your child back."

Coral sniffed. "Did you pay it? How much do they want?" She could see the old woman better now. Her hair was snow white.

"It was too much, love. I couldn't. They have guards with guns. I have to wait."

"Wait for what?"

"Until he's worked it off. At the factory."

"Where is the factory?"

"There are many, child."

"Are they close?" Coral asked.

But the woman didn't answer. "It was no use. I have to wait until he's worked enough and then they'll let my grand-son go."

Coral broke away from the old woman. She didn't thank her or ask her name, if they could walk back together. She began to move alone, stumbling as if drunk, back to the casino camp. Soon she saw someone running up the road toward her.

It was Trillium. "Did you catch him?"

"No." Coral was broken by her sobs again, blinded by them. In a fog, she let herself be led home.

She was not even sure how they made it. She had traveled much farther down the road than she thought, farther than she had ever been. Everything looked strange to her: the broken and curving road, the dusty trees.

Trillium supported her. His cut hand bled into her hair. Mr. Fall had sprained an ankle running for the car, but wouldn't say anything about it, and Coral wouldn't notice his limp.

There was a lot she wouldn't notice.

She would think about the woman with the snow-white hair, the way she had been so resigned. Collectors come into the camp. They take our children to work for them. They say it is their right, their price. The woman had tried to reassure her: the work wasn't that bad. It could have been worse. The collectors were kind, she had said.

What *kind* people steal children?

There was a word for how the old woman had behaved, how she had been conditioned to think. Mr. Fall had taught it to her. She had read about it in his book. But she wouldn't recall the phrase or what it meant—sympathetic to the one who hurts you—until years later, after Coral and Trillium and Mr. Fall had left the casino camp by the evergreens, never to return, never again to leave the seasonal camp of Trashlands, which Shanghai was familiar with: the place that had needed a teacher—and where Coral thought the boy might return to look for them.

There, they would meet a young dancer named Foxglove, and Trillium would tattoo a word on her body. Coral would remember it then. *Stockholm.*

11

Miami
Miami-Dade County, Florida

He could not say what it was about Coral. The surety with which she walked through the world, this world of trash and men. He didn't know what that was like, except for what his sister had said, and how his sister had suffered. The comments, some of which she related to him. The attempts to grab her, to touch her, to pull her into an alley—or once, out of a bus. He was certain his sister hadn't told him everything.

Mangrove never told him everything.

She didn't know the man who had tried to take her. She couldn't conjure his face or much about him. Only his hands, which had felt rough, she said, groping for her on the hectic and crowded bus. She had shuddered to remember, telling Miami about it. The man's skin was so dry, it was like his fingerprints had worn away.

What difference did it make, anyway? No one would catch the man. No one would look for him. There were barely any police, and they really only worked for the wealthy. Girls were taken every night. Girls were hurt and killed. Girls much younger than Mangrove. She knew it could have been worse. She wasn't going to look for sympathy or retribution. She just wanted to forget.

Miami couldn't forget. Not any of it.

He couldn't let go. He couldn't move on, not without knowing and not without punishing the last men who had hurt her, the men who had ended her life. How would he know them? And what would he do to them? Walking through the junkyard with Coral, he could feel the handle of a knife, pressing into his back.

Or maybe he only imagined he could feel it. The knife, like the old car, had been his father's and grandfather's before him. Miami had kept it sharpened. Ready, he had thought, for men breaking into the apartment, or jumping him as he walked to work. He was always ready.

But the men were here, not in the city. The ones who had killed his sister were in this region. The threat had not been for him all along, but for her.

And he was not ready.

Coral he had not counted on. The way she navigated the junkyard, the map of it deep in her brain. The way she de-manded definitions to words she didn't know. He had not expected that from a person in Scrappalachia, the dump of the world. He was embarrassed to think how seldom he had thought of this place and how low his opinion of it had been. Yes, the bricks that made up his office and the medical clinic, and the new school they were building in his neighborhood had to come from somewhere, were made out of plastic that had been harvested somehow, but he never thought much beyond that.

He couldn't have imagined Coral. A small person with wild hair, who confidently threaded her way around, including up to a strip club, walking right up to a giant of a man who smiled only for her.

The giant—Tahiti—had knocked on his door last night, and when Miami answered, tentatively, the flimsy chain still on the flimsier door, the man had held up a bottle. "Drink?" Tahiti had offered. "I'm on my break."

Miami unfastened the chain. He sat on the one rickety chair in the room, and Tahiti sat on the bed, because he was worried he would break the chair.

"If you want to tattoo Foxy with your name, you can," Tahiti said. "It's expensive, but then she'll always wear you."

"Are you looking for work for her?" Miami asked.

"It's part of my job." Tahiti drank from a tumbler that looked like a child's cup in his hand. "It's more than my job, though."

"How long have you been in love with her?"

It was maybe too far, even for Miami, but Tahiti considered the question. Miami could see the thoughts cross the man's face: all the words he could have said. He didn't deny it, but he chose not to answer it.

"You ask a lot of questions." Tahiti passed the tumbler to him.

"Well, that's my job. Does she know you're in love with her? Does she wear your name?"

"No. And no, of course not. I can't afford it, and that doesn't seem right to me, to tattoo her like that. She looks down on those men."

"As well she should," Miami said. "Who pays for something like that?"

Tahiti looked at him. "Lots of men do. Why are you at Trashlands?"

"To write a story."

"Why are you really here?"

It must have been the alcohol. Harsh and strong with a scent like corn. "My sister died here," Miami said. "She was killed by some men."

"Recently?"

"Yes." He passed the tumbler.

"They'll be long gone," Tahiti said.

"Have you heard of a crime here lately? A big car crash? An explosion? A woman dying?"

"Those kinds of things happen all the time. People don't talk about them. And they sure don't stay around after they do them. But a running car—" He took a swig of the alcohol. "That would be something." He returned the tumbler to Miami. They only had the one glass. "What was your sister like?"

Miami looked down into the drink. "Fearless."

"Well, she'd have to be, to come here from the city. She was like you, then."

"No. I was the shy one, the writer. She was the brave one. Doing things people told her she couldn't do."

"Sounds like Coral," Tahiti said.

Mangrove would have loved Coral. Her careful eye, her quiet steadiness, her will. Miami knew Coral was a good friend to her friends, like the woman he had met, Summer, and the man she seemed to be partnered with, Trillium. Coral was kind. He knew she was loyal.

Maybe, he thought as he stared into his drink, that was why he was starting to want her, desperately, not to be.

They searched the junkyard, mostly without speaking. Coral watched the ground and Miami watched Coral. She opened the doors that could still be opened, after first knocking to make sure the cars were not occupied. The most pitiful-looking structure, little more than a pile of scrap, could shelter someone. A tiny door would creak ajar, seemingly from nowhere, and a face would peek out. They always looked happy to see Coral. They let her search near their dwelling. They always asked if she and the stranger with her had eaten, if they could fix them something.

"You're loved here," Miami said.

Now she turned her smile on him, but it was hard to read. "I have a reputation," she said. "It's because of the whale. And because I was pregnant at the time."

He felt stunned to hear the word, then ashamed to have been taken by surprise, to have just assumed...

Pregnant.

When? Had she given birth to the child? Had they lived? Why had she not spoken of this? He had seen no children around the bus. And what was that about a whale?

Some children were spilling out of a tent on top of a hill, next to a satellite dish strewn with clothes. Satellites pointed at trash now, in the sky, which was silent.

All of the children seemed to know Coral. Was her child among them? "Listen up," she told them. "This man is looking for something. It's plastic and pink. Small." She made a circle with her fingers. "We'll pay for it. Two cans. Look on your school breaks, if you like, or tonight before dark."

The children yelped and set off in different directions.

"Be careful!" Coral called after them. "Small eyes, small hands—they can get into smaller spaces," she explained to Miami. "They're closer to the ground. They notice things we miss."

"You said we'll pay them two cans. Of what?"

"Something edible. That's all that matters."

Miami thought the skinny children probably needed to eat more than two cans. They disappeared into the thicket of scrap. He wanted to ask Coral about her own child, but a man came out of the tent before he could find the words. It was a man Miami had seen earlier, when he had gone to the bus to find Coral. Tall and bald, the man could have been anywhere from fifty to seventy years old.

"What did you do to my students?" the man asked Coral.

"I sent them off on a mission. This is Miami."

"Ah, the reporter." The tall man held out his hand.

An old-fashioned greeting. He was maybe leaning toward sixty, then. Miami took the man's hand, leathery and soft, and moved it up and down, as his grandparents had taught him. He felt funny doing it.

"This is Mr. Fall," Coral said.

"You're the one distracting Coral," Mr. Fall said.

Miami tried to laugh. "I just hired her, as a guide to the junkyard. I had no idea she was so busy."

Mr. Fall still pumped his hand up and down. It was feeling stranger and stranger. "She is busy. And irreplaceable."

"I'm working," Coral said. "We should get back to it before it gets too hot. We break in the middle of the day, when the sun is the hottest," she explained to Miami. And then to Mr. Fall, "He's from The Els."

"I heard. A real reporter. You don't break midday?"

"In the cities, we try to stay inside as much as possible."

Mr. Fall had finally dropped his hand. "Interesting. What do you do for cooling? Do you have chillers?"

"Some. But only the important places, like government offices. My paper doesn't have a chiller. We're not that important. We keep curtains on the windows to block the sun during the day, soak the curtains in cold water. Sometimes, when it's real hot, we soak our clothes even."

"Interesting," he said again. "We do that here too. Do you have power?"

"Off and on. A lot of brownouts."

"You know, I have a large collection of newspapers here at the school. I've saved them for years and tried to preserve them. Would you like to look at them sometime? Would you consider speaking to my class, about life as a reporter?"

"I'm not sure how long Miami's going to be around," Coral said.

But Miami said, "I'd be happy to." He tried not to feel disappointed that Coral thought he would be leaving.

"It would be good for the children to hear about other jobs," Mr. Fall said. "Other lives they might have available to them."

Would they have those lives available to them? Miami thought after they had walked away from the tent, the children scurrying back like insects. Those children would probably just do what their parents had done. How could they learn anything else? Plucking plastic was the job of Scrappalachia.

"Mr. Fall is our teacher," Coral said.

"I figured. Is it usual for pluckers to have a teacher?"

"I don't know. These are the only people I've ever lived with. Mr. Fall raised me." She glanced at Miami. "He found me as a baby, after I was abandoned. Or maybe my people had died. There was a fire."

"I'm sorry to hear that."

"It's all right. I don't remember anything."

This was the moment that Miami could have told her about Mangrove. About how they were born less than a year apart, Mangrove first. About how, his whole life whenever he felt something that didn't make sense, that came upon him quickly and inexplicably, a feeling like a wave or rush, he knew it must be her, something to do with *her*. And he needed to call, to reach her, to see if she was all right.

The day she died, he felt panic from the moment he woke. In the fragment of glass that passed as a mirror, his own eyes had looked empty to him. He knew something was gone from them, but what? The light. Her light. His older sister, his last surviving family member, had died.

The moment passed.

This was the time he could have asked about Coral's child too, but she fell silent. So he did too. She had said they would rest when the sun bore down the hottest, but he knew already that something was wrong.

Coral was pointing out a weather vane, made from shingles, on a pole at the outer rim of the junkyard. "I made that."

He saw the shingles had been cut into arrows. There was a plastic moon on top. "Why?" he asked. An automatic question.

"I don't know. I just make things sometimes."

The weather vane wasn't useful. He doubted it could tell

the direction of the wind—he thought that was what weather vanes did. But the weather was so wild, the wind always hot or dry or wet, and coming from everywhere and nowhere at once. The plastic weather vane seemed feeble in comparison to the wind they faced. The wind might snap it. That plastic could have been sold and melted.

Miami noticed Coral was breathing differently. "What's the matter? Do you need to stop?"

Sweat ran down her face. "My head feels strange. Hot."

"We should stop." He wanted to reach for her arms, to steady her, to feel for the fever on her skin. But he just looked at her without touching her. There were stitches on her leg, angry and black, and her face was swollen along her jaw. Red lines, which meant infection.

12

Trillium

"You don't understand," Ramalina said. "We don't have any antibiotics."

The man from the city, Miami, was not getting it, though she had repeated herself several times. "How can you not have any in this whole place?"

Trillium exchanged a look with Mr. Fall. No one had asked the reporter to be here, and yet here he was, standing outside the bus. Inside, Coral was supposed to be napping, but Trillium knew she likely sat up, wide awake, listening to herself being talked about.

Ramalina chucked a washrag into a bucket by the doors; Trillium would have to boil the rag later. She had used it to wash Coral's cut again. "Antibiotics got real expensive. When Golden Toad was sick, I used the last of them. I haven't been able to replace the drugs since."

The boy had been bitten by a hornet. People were bitten

all the time. Mosquitos bred in the loops of tires, though every few days men went around and dumped out the standing water. Sometimes people came down with fevers after being bit. But this time, this boy had swelled, his hand ballooning up like a rubber glove with no rips in it. Ramalina said the bite had gotten infected, though his mother had washed and bandaged it.

Trillium knew the mother felt awful. She worked late at Trashlands. She worked a lot. Toad spent as much time in the school as he could. He was lonely, Trillium thought. In a way, Toad reminded Trillium of himself as a child, looking for a place to belong. If circumstances were different, maybe he and Coral could have helped the mother out, cared for the child. Perhaps if Trillium was not so old...

But Coral had her art. They both had their work. She had already lost one child. What if times got hard again, and they had to give up another one?

Ramalina had given the last of the antibiotics to the boy for free. Now there were none for Coral. The wound in her mouth, where the tooth had been, festered, speeding to her heart, trying to seep into the bone.

"The infection will spread," Ramalina said, "if left untreated."

"I don't understand how the infection happened," Trillium said.

"Sometimes they just happen."

"I don't understand how you don't have a med center here," Miami said.

Ramalina ignored him. "There are still antibiotics for sale at the Strip. But it's a trek to get there, and it's not the safest place."

"How expensive?" Trillium said.

Ramalina just shook her head.

That meant *a lot.* "How bad could the infection spread? If we don't get the medicine? Could she die?"

"Without antibiotics, it's possible."

"We'll pay, then. Whatever it takes."

Mr. Fall looked at Trillium again. He knew what that meant. Their savings—gone. Coral was dependent on luck, on the whims of the river. What if, in the days to come, it gave up nothing?

"It's not just a question of paying," Ramalina said. "It's a question of going to get the medicine. A day's walk. At least, when I last did it. Maybe you could make it there and back in less time. You're stronger than me. Faster. But it's a dangerous place."

Trillium had heard of the Strip, another market. But they had had no reason to go there. To make an unnecessary journey was to take an unnecessary risk. Everything they needed was at the marketplace in the junkyard—and the Strip was inside a building. That increased the risk: of an illness spreading, of a stranger jumping them, of something bad happening where no one might see.

"We could take the bus?" Mr. Fall said.

"No bus. You don't want to attract attention. You don't want the wrong people to know you have fuel."

"Who are the wrong people?" the reporter asked.

Nobody answered him.

"I'll tell you where to go," Ramalina said. "I'll tell you what to look for. It's in the old post office."

"If we go without you," Trillium asked, "would the people sell to us? Would they trust us?"

This was a complication in the plan. Trillium saw worry cross Ramalina's face, creased from the late nights waiting for babies. She paused. "Summer's been to the Strip a few times. They would know her there. They would sell to Summer."

"No," Mr. Fall said. "You just said it's dangerous."

"Why can't you go?" Miami asked the healer.

"I'm needed here. Some babies are coming any day."

Another problem was Coral. Coral who was stubborn. Coral who was strong, despite her infection. Coral who demanded she come along too.

She had eavesdropped on the whole conversation in front of the bus, as Trillium had known she would. She had formulated the plan, ambushed him with it as soon as he cracked open the doors. "It makes sense," she insisted. "I can take the medicine right away."

"And what if you get too weak on the way there?" Trillium said. "What if you never make it to the medicine?"

"Then leave me somewhere to rest. I know how to hide. I'll be fine. It won't happen, anyway. I won't get too weak. I know myself."

"This is ridiculous."

"It's my money," Coral said. There was the fierceness Trillium knew. There was no arguing with that fierceness, no way to win against it, against her.

She stood on the steps, blocking his way.

She should not have been standing. She should not have been out of bed. But she said, "It's my plastic. It's my injury, my problem. I deserve to go. And it's my money for Shanghai." Her voice cracked on the last bit, the only waver.

Miami stood below the open bus doors. He didn't understand. How could he? Trillium wasn't going to fill him in. But he was coming. This stranger who had butted into their lives was coming too.

They packed water bottles, fruit, and nuts. They packed plastic for bartering—and this was the hardest part. Not knowing what the men who sold the medicine would want, not knowing how much it would be. The price always changed based on who was asking, the color of their skin, how dirty it was, how ragged their clothes, how red and urgent their infection. If Trillium went alone, a man, the price might be expensive. But for Coral alone, it would be untenable.

Ramalina traded medicine for medicine. Helpful plants didn't grow around the Strip, she said, or the people there didn't know how to cultivate them like she did. She hoarded water for her plants. She sacrificed for them, checking in on them deep in the woods, and when she harvested she always left some behind to keep growing.

Trillium carried the bartering plastic, because it was the heaviest load they had, and because he felt Coral shouldn't be burdened with it, shouldn't be reminded of what she was giving up with every step. Coral had the lightest bag, with sweaters and a tarp in case of rain.

Mr. Fall and the boy Golden Toad saw them off, standing in front of the rainbow bus. Trillium thought the child had just come around looking for breakfast, which Mr. Fall would certainly give him. Trillium had put away his sign. He had packed a few needles and ink in case he ran into business on the road, or in case the men who sold meds wouldn't take their plastic.

He filled a gallon jug with water, capped it with duct tape, and handed the full jug to Miami. "Be useful," Trillium told him.

Miami looked at the jug. "It won't fit in my pack."

"Tie it to your belt, then. Make sure the rope is sturdy. And if we meet anyone on the road, hide the water away. We're not sharing."

Miami did as he was told. Coral was hugging Mr. Fall.

"Keep my girls safe," Mr. Fall said to Trillium.

Summer rolled her eyes, brushing her hair out of her face and tying it up with a knotted rope of straws. She had changed from her usual heels into sturdy boots.

Coral told the small boy, "Listen to your teacher. We'll see you no later than tomorrow." She started down the path away from the bus. She did not look back.

"Rest if you need to," Mr. Fall called after her. "Stop if you want."

Trillium was not quite ready, but he had to follow Coral. Miami hurried to keep up too, the water jug sloshing. "Don't spill that," Trillium said to him.

"Isn't water precious in The Els?" Summer asked.

"Well, it's different," Miami said.

"How?"

"Water comes from pipes."

"Pipes in your house?"

"Yes, but only sometimes. Some days. And it isn't safe."

"Trust me," Summer said. "Nothing is safe. What can we do? We drink it anyway."

The two women walked ahead. Trillium finally slowed his pace so the reporter could walk with him, the water jug at his side like a cannonball. It was rude to make the man carry it—they had enough water without, and it made him walk lopsided—but he shouldn't have even been on this trip, Trillium thought. A near stranger, an outsider.

"What are you writing about?" Trillium asked him. "For your story?"

Why are you even here?

"I'm not sure yet," the man said. "But people in cities, they don't really understand what it's like to live anywhere else."

"So you want to tell them."

"That's the idea."

"You think in a couple days you'll be able to know what it's like here? You'll be able to say?"

Miami looked surprised. "I don't know."

"You should spend time with some other people. Coral and I and Mr. Fall, we don't have it so bad. But Golden Toad, that boy back there, and some of the women…" Trillium trailed off. "Life is harder for the women."

"I think that's true everywhere."

"But here, you see it. We don't have apartments to hide in."

"You have piles of scrap to hide in."

Trillium thought of the crying he heard at night, coming from some of those piles. The dead cars that were occupied one night and empty the next. He thought of what would be left behind: baby bottles, blood-stained blankets. Sometimes people were left behind. One morning there would be a new little face peering up at Mr. Fall in the circle the children made in the school tent; one night a new dancer onstage, her skin stained by the neon but the bruise still visible on her face.

Miami asked, "Have you ever been to where we're going?"

"The Strip? No. No reason to."

Coral looked back over her shoulder. "Trillium's not fond of people."

"I like doing my work," he said. "We both do."

"He's not fond of crowds."

"Crowds are dangerous," Trillium said.

Privately, Ramalina had told him that the men who sold the medicine were unpredictable. When the men saw the group from Trashlands had women among them, they might demand other exchanges. Summer had dealt with these men before. But Coral...

Trillium tightened his hold on his pack as Coral smiled at him, the hot wind flicking one of her curls in her face. She swept it away, like a leaf, and turned back around.

"You're not excited to go to a new place?" Miami asked.

"You ask a lot of questions," Trillium said.

13

Foxglove

Men came to her when they were young. They came when they were old. They came to her in the middle—and those men were the worst. Running from their lives, from their wives, spending money that they didn't have, plastic they should have taken to their families. They all had children of course, babies they blubbered on about while in her arms. How beautiful the children were, how perfect. How they bore the men's names.

You should go back to them, she said. But only after they had paid her. *You don't have to leave her,* she said. But only after they had tattooed their name or name sign on her arm or ankle, the finely furred skin of her back. *She'll never know,* Foxglove whispered when she sent them off. *Just don't bring it up. And* don't *let me catch you here again.*

"You're driving away repeat business," Tahiti had said to

her once as she shooed a man out of her trailer and down the path, waving until she couldn't see him.

"I don't really get repeat business," Foxglove had said.

She knew what she was. She was pretty, maybe beautiful, but not special. She did not do things that wives didn't, or wouldn't, do. She felt—she knew—that she was not good at sex, or really even at dancing. She just jutted her hips, spun slowly, paced, shook her hair. She didn't like it, dancing or sex.

Art is something you choose, or that chooses you. And she hadn't chosen this, any of this. It just made her tired. She was always so tired. Her bones, her skin ached from the strangers spreading over her like infection. That last tattoo had hurt.

"Just say no," Tahiti said. "No thank you, next time."

"No means no money. Money is freedom."

"Is it, though?"

"For me, it is."

"What would you do if you weren't at Trashlands?"

She looked at him from the doorway of her trailer. No matter how long they had talked, and they kept talking for longer and longer each night, this was where their conversations ended every time: at the door. While she slept, he waited outside. He had never come in her home.

She had never asked him to.

"I have no idea," Foxglove said.

She closed the door. She kicked off her clogs. Her fancy shoes, the ones Summer made from wine stems and table lamps, she kept stashed by the back door of the club. She tried not to walk through the yard in them. Despite the mud and dust all around them, Rattlesnake Master forbid getting dirt on the stage. It was one of his rules. *Shoes off inside, la-dies. I don't track shit in your house.*

He didn't like it when you broke his rules.

She peeled off the small clothes she wore, faded things that shone like candy under the lights. She wadded them into a ball and threw them into a corner. She was hungry but too tired to fix anything, to waste the candle under her tiny pot to heat up broth, or even to mix greens with nuts from Summer. She heard Tahiti sit down on the stump outside.

The light from Trashlands spilled into her sink. Pink stripes, like one of her stage outfits. A pipe had long ago been salvaged from the sink. *Faucet*, it was called. Nothing came out of it, no water. She wished they would have left it, though.

She tried to imagine a family in her trailer. It was small. There was only the one bed. Maybe they would have used the trailer for traveling, sleeping on the road. People used to journey for fun, she knew. For *freedom*. Would they have parked in the woods? Wouldn't they have been afraid? Did the family have children? Did they hold each other at night, on the floor beneath their parents' bed, believing their close-ness would save them?

They were wrong. Nothing would save them.

Foxglove slid the blinds shut. Amazing that she still had those. *Be grateful for small things*, she reminded herself. Half-shredded blinds and a tapestry. She went to her bed and reached below the mattress. It was stained, though she tried not to look at those stains or connect them with any stories. (The mattress was from a family, a family's regular life, their good life; only good things had happened on her bed, her bed where only *she* slept.)

She pulled out a slim, palm-sized object. It was gray and convex, made from two shells. Mr. Fall said they were from a creature edible and no longer around. Once, the shells had been attached to each other with springy skin or muscle, but that had decayed. Coral had found them in the water. She had made the shells join again with a spring of plastic coiled through the two halves. She had attached a plastic fastener where the shells met in the front, like a sealed little mouth.

When Foxglove opened the fastener, the shells sprung open in her hands. And here was the marvel, here was Coral's magic: a tiny plastic doll sprung up too. The doll was pinky finger–sized. Her pink legs hung straight down, her arms raised above her head in an O. She had high pink shoes. Yellow plastic hair in a knot on her head had mostly flaked away. So had her clothes. Her face was gone.

But she danced. When Foxglove opened the shells, the tiny dancer turned. She turned forever. There was a motor Coral and Summer and Tahiti had all conspired to fix for Foxglove's birthday, the day she had picked as her own and celebrated. It was a beautiful, strange present, and it meant a lot. It was the only toy she had ever had.

The dancer turned silently, and Summer had fretted about that. *There's supposed to be music*, she had said. But Foxglove didn't need music. Foxglove heard music all the time.

She watched the dancer turn in her hands. She felt sorry for her. Poor bitch, she could never stop. She had lost all her clothes. She had lost her face. Mr. Fall said dancers like this used to be inside children's jewelry boxes. What lucky children.

She snapped the shells shut, squeezing the dancer, contorting her. Foxglove was not sure what hurt the dancer more:

dancing, or being forced to stop. She stuffed the shells back under her bed.

But the music played on, the call to Trashlands. Foxglove could not really remember a time when it had not been in her head. Coral said there was soft plastic you could scrunch in your ears to dull sound. She said there were cuffs you could place over your head to do the same thing. She had not been able to scavenge either of these for Foxglove, though she was looking.

Foxglove lay down on her bed. She had one pillow, thin as a dress. She rested her head on its edge, and folded the other end around herself. She pressed her arm against her ear to keep the pillow there. It muffled the music a bit.

She imagined she was under water. She pretended she was Coral, ducking under the waves to retrieve plastic. Swimming, to save them all.

She slept naked every night because she could. Because Tahiti, the man Rattlesnake Master had hired years and years ago to keep Foxglove from running away, to keep the child he had bought from leaving the trailer he would make her pay for, was just outside. She imagined she could hear him breathe. She pretended he dove deep for her.

14

Coral

Off the road that led away from Trashlands, they cut diago-
nally through a field. Old transmission towers soared out of
the grass. All the power had left them. The lines, long broken, were bisected by branches and vines.

Coral tried not to stare. She had never been this way. It
was hard, as they walked, not to stop and wonder, not to
look for factories in the trees. She resisted badgering Summer with questions: How many people were at the Strip?
What did they make? What did they sell? Most of all she
wondered: Was a factory close by? Were there children?

It was hard, very hard indeed, not to pause every few feet.
She had seen nothing big enough to ask the others to stop
for. Just plastic bags and the milky bark of food containers,
ripped apart by wind.

Most of the plastic in the bushes looked shredded beyond recycling—plastic could really only be remade once.

She brushed her hand down her legs to discourage ticks and pushed through the tall weeds with a stick she had picked up, hurrying after Summer.

Coral sometimes went far on her art expeditions, farther than even Trillium knew. She went looking, not just for plastic to sculpt into pieces and for quiet places to leave them, but for buildings. A structure in the distance that might hide people. A path that seemed worn with tire tracks.

She hadn't gotten too close to anyplace she had found. The buildings looked old, abandoned. Still, she would watch long enough to make sure their smokestacks were cold; their walls, choked with weeds, unguarded. That there was no movement behind their broken windows. She waited until she heard no children's voices.

She didn't know where Shanghai had gone.

She leaned heavily on the stick, hoping the others didn't notice her pace had slowed. She wished Mr. Fall had come.

Trillium, in his midforties, they thought, was not as old as Mr. Fall. They marked their ages by what they could remember. Trillium could remember running water, but not the internet or heat coming from the walls. Mr. Fall swore these things were real, they had happened. He also swore electricity did not always come from the sun or generators. *Where did it come from, then?* Coral had demanded.

Mr. Fall could have told her more about those transmission towers, maybe. Trillium, worry etched in his face, said nothing about them. Did he not know or did he not want to talk?

Trillium could not remember where he had lived before the tent city. He remembered where he went after, though Coral knew he sometimes wished he could erase that too, blot out his time in the woods. He ran with others. He ran alone. He slept sometimes at the edge of camps that would not let him come closer, pacing in the smoke of their fires, never near enough to be warmed by their heat. He learned to eat moss, to chew the bark that was not bitter.

Everyone had gaps in their memories, of course. Parts of your life were blank for a reason. Better to sleep the blankness of forgetting than to live with nightmares.

In many ways he was still that feral boy in the woods. He could go for a long while without speaking. Much of their time together was spent this way, in companionable stillness. Which was fine with Coral. They could do their work. Coral was used to fitting plastic together to the sounds of Trillium whittling sticks, or the rat-a-tat of him stirring ink. She knew him. She didn't need to speak to him.

As they walked, she could imagine the conversations she and Trillium might have had, about the hills they passed, higher than the junkyard. After the field, the group followed an old road. Maybe there had once been a yellow line running down the middle, but now the road was cracked and broken, no color except gray.

"How long has it been for you," Coral asked Summer, "since you went to the Strip?"

"A while. But things don't change that much anymore, do they?"

That was true. The first changes had been the biggest, Mr. Fall had said. No regular power or water, or trucks to take away trash. No new plastic things. No factories, except the brick ones. The trick, Coral felt, was not to expect anything. Part of her didn't even believe she would get antibiotics.

"The Strip has some nice shopping," Summer was saying.

"What kind of shopping?"

"Oh, it depends. But last I was there, they had fabric."

Maybe months ago, a sheet had washed up in the river. Stretched and ripped into trailing segments, Coral had thought at first it was a body. The sheet was stained. But someone had taken it. Someone always took everything.

They reached the Strip by late afternoon. Down the next hill, Coral could see it: a line of low buildings joined together like bumps on a spine. Before the Strip, in what used to be a parking lot, a camp had sprouted up. Tents and tarps, fire in barrels. People milled about the camp: waiting to trade, wanting to be let inside, or just living off the offal.

But something happened. Coral's view of the Strip tilted, then her vision righted itself, as if she had been turned upside down. She felt chilled. "I can't do it." She sat down on a metal stump. It was—she knew the word—a *hydrant*. A fire hydrant. But the name was confusing. Fire hadn't spewed from it, water had. "I can't go farther."

"What's the matter?" Trillium said. "We made it."

Summer knelt. She brushed the hair from Coral's face, putting a cool hand on her forehead. "She's burning up."

"We're getting the medicine. Right now."

Coral felt dizzy. Hair stuck to the back of her neck. Her legs trembled even though she wasn't standing.

"We're here," Trillium said.

Coral turned her head to him. His eyes looked sympathetic but confused, frustrated, his brows slipping down. He didn't know her. He didn't *know*. Why couldn't he see her? They had such history. They had so many times settled words, hot words, tears, with their bodies meshing together.

They often made love forcefully. She sometimes felt he was determined to burst through his body, his bones and skin, to liquefy with *her* body, to make a new thing.

"I can't," Coral said.

The lines on his forehead deepened. "I can't let Summer go in there alone."

Miami spoke up. "I'll stay with Coral."

Coral had almost forgotten the reporter. But there he was. He smiled. Coral saw he had a scar on his cheek, by his ear. He must have kept his hair longer to hide it. She felt a pang of kindness.

"Don't you want to see the Strip?" Trillium asked. "What if they have art in there?"

"They won't," Coral said.

Summer got off her knees. "No, they won't. Anything you want us to bring you from inside, though? A sweet treat? Fabric?"

"Just the medicine."

Trillium wanted to kiss her. Coral could see it in his eyes, a kind of dividing: She pulled him, the obligation of the Strip pulled him. She knew he didn't want to go inside, but he would. He wanted to kiss her, but he wouldn't. Not with everyone around. "Are you all right staying here? With him?"

"I'm fine."

Another long look, then Trillium turned away. He started down the hill.

"You don't want to go in there yourself?" Summer was asking Miami. "For your story?"

"I've seen old shopping malls like the Strip before." He nodded at Coral. "We'll do an interview or something, if she's up for it."

"Don't push her. And don't say anything I wouldn't say," Summer said to Coral. Then she too was going. The wind flapped the hair across her back like a flag.

Coral watched them skirt the encampment. They didn't want trouble. Trillium's tall figure moved amid the tents and fires, Summer close behind. Then the smoke twisted and she couldn't see them anymore.

"How are you doing?" Miami asked.

"The same."

"Does it hurt a lot?"

"It's more the fever bugging me. My head hurts."

"Anything I can do?" he said.

"If there were willows nearby, I could chew the bark."

But they weren't near water. And there weren't many willow trees anymore.

"That works?"

"A lot of things work," Coral said. "You'd be surprised. What did you want to ask me?"

Miami took a seat on the ground in front of Coral. He crossed his legs. She noticed the inch or so of skin between his pants and his shoes. It must have been the fever, and that was why she focused on that part of his skin she could see.

"How long have you lived in this region?" Miami asked.

"My whole life."

"Did you ever want to go anywhere else? To travel?"

"What for?"

That answer seemed to fluster him. "For a lot of things. To meet people. To see the world."

"I know the world," Coral said. "It's plastic."

Miami shifted. The ground was uncomfortable. He looked unused to sitting on it, or maybe it was Coral, just assuming things, sizing him up. He tried another question. "What was it that Trillium said about art? Seeing art in the Strip?"

"Oh," Coral said. "It's just something I like."

"Have you ever seen any? Real art?"

"What do you mean *real*?"

"By professional artists?"

"You can't make a life, doing art."

"I guess that's true. Not anymore."

"Unless you're Trillium." She felt heat at the base of her throat. It wasn't just the fever, but her impulse to defend Trillium, to stick up for him. "His tattoos are art."

"And Foxglove and Summer, do they think of dancing as art?"

"No," she said. "I really don't think so." Summer made things, costumes and shoes, food and furniture, and she made her truck look nice with curtains beaded with plastic bottle caps that rattled when you walked through, the starry fabric. That felt like art. But Coral said, "I don't think they'd consider dancing art. Just what they have to do. Nobody treats it that way, anyway. Not the men who come. Definitely not Rattlesnake Master. Do you consider your stories art, for the newspaper?"

"I try to do a good job."

"That's not the same as art. Sometimes art is a very bad job."

Miami looked down at the dust on his shoes. There was a small hole on the heel of one of them. Didn't he know that? Couldn't he feel the rocks getting in?

At the Strip, someone new walked into the building but no one came out. The camp rustled with the usual work. A woman beat a blanket on a clothesline strung from a tent to a chain-link fence. Nuts roasted somewhere, filling the air with a buttery scent. Coral heard a child crying.

"Is anyone waiting for you at home?" she asked. "Your sister, or—"

"My sister didn't make it," Miami said.

"What happened?"

"I don't know. I don't know who did it."

"Someone did it?"

"It wasn't just an accident. Someone killed her. I know. We were close, and she got in trouble a lot."

"That's why you want the bracelet," Coral said. "You don't have anything else from her."

"No. After having so much, I have nothing."

"And you want evidence."

"Yes," he admitted.

Not for justice, certainly. There was no justice. There was barely a police force: only the men who had appointed themselves law, who went around doling out punishments and taking what they wanted until they were dethroned by others. Until the others had been taken down too.

Rattlesnake Master was what passed for law in the junkyard. You just tried not to make him mad, or attract his attention. Sometimes Coral hated her hair, how it had drawn him like a light. She avoided the club. It was like skirting a deep part of the river. But someday, even with all your precautions, even if you were a strong swimmer, the current might drag you down.

Did Miami need to see the place his sister had died? Did he want to find the people who he thought had done it? It was intentional, he said. Or did he just believe it was, the way Coral searched for a reason for the loss of her son. It couldn't have just happened. It had to have been her fault.

Coral wanted to tell the reporter about how after Shanghai was born, she felt hollowed out, as if her baby continued to consume her. He took everything, desperate and hungry: a mouse emptying a melon in a field. She wanted to tell Miami that it was then she felt the most pain about Robert leaving, about what they had done. It was like being pregnant had filled up something inside her, an absence she didn't even know was there. But once her son was born, clutching at her shirt, screaming in her arms, she felt it all over again: everything she had lost, everything that had happened.

Miami took off his glasses to clean them on his shirt.

She told him, "I have a child."

He answered right away. "I wondered. You said you had been pregnant. Kids are cool."

She laughed. She couldn't help it. It was such an old-fashioned word. Mr. Fall said it sometimes. It was funny, strange, that she had felt nervous to tell Miami about Shanghai. Who cared what he thought? Trillium was the only one who mattered.

"How old is your child?" Miami asked.

"He's about fourteen."

She saw the surprise pass over his face. "How old are you?"

"Younger than Trillium, older than Foxglove. Some of my hair is gray," Coral said. She stretched a strand over her shoulder, trying to show him. "That's what the red does, I guess. It fades." She wondered if Shanghai's hair was still golden. The midwife said that children's light hair always darkened. Life darkened it.

"Where is your son?" Miami asked more gently.

He had noticed. But not mentioned it, not pressured her.

"Not at Trashlands. He was taken when he was little, by collectors. They make him work in a factory, sorting plastic. I'm trying to get him back."

If Miami was shocked, he didn't show it. Maybe that was his reporter training. His voice rolled over her, quiet and calm. "Do you know where he is?"

Coral shook her head. The uncertainties were piling up. She worked so hard not to talk about it, not to think about it. Now here they were again: all the questions, everything she tried to avoid.

"Nobody comes home, Trillium says. He thinks the children just return when the factories are through with them. When they're no longer small, and their hands are too big. That's why we have to stay at Trashlands. Shanghai knows it. We lived here together. He'll remember it, I know he will. I can't go back to the casino camp where he was taken. I just can't. People disappear," Coral said. "It's unusual to try and get them back. Most people give up trying. That's what Mr. Fall said."

Everyone had lost someone. It didn't make her special, it just made her alive.

She remembered the other mothers at the casino camp. At first, they had cried together, but then, after a time, the other mothers stopped crying. They moved on with their work. There was so much to do: foraging and cooking and finding ways to stay cool. They woke up and worked. Coral couldn't bear to.

For a long time, she couldn't get back in the water and touch plastic. It made her sick, to know where it went, who handled it. Some of the other mothers who had lost children became pregnant again. They celebrated together, talked of the future around the fire at night. Coral wouldn't let Trillium touch her. Soon they left the casino camp and the other mothers behind.

"Shanghai?" Miami's eyes had a sparkle in them. "That's your son's name?"

"I read it in a book." She didn't want to talk about him anymore. "I think I'm a little older than you, Miami. What's the first thing you remember?"

"The radio."

"What did you hear?"

"Updates. Usually the same message again and again. A test of the Emergency Broadcasting System."

Coral nodded. "I love that band."

"What do you remember from when you were a kid?"

"Not much. Plastic. It's a game, when you're a child. It's fun, finding it in water, all the shapes and colors. Only some plastic floats, you know. Other plastic you have to dig for, swim for. But before you know it, that's it, that's all you get."

"Did you ever want more?" Miami asked.

"Yes," Coral said.

15

Trillium

Damn the wound. Damn the infection. Damn the man he had to leave her with. The younger man, the stranger. Trillium didn't like his eyes. He didn't like his questions.

He didn't like how the people had stayed in their tents when he and Summer approached the camp before the Strip. People should have come out to look at them, to wonder about the strangers. Either they were completely used to new people going in and out—or the people in the tents were too drugged, drunk, or starved out of their minds to bother. Either way, it wasn't a good sign. A blanket flapped in the wind. He thought he heard a baby.

But then, he often thought he heard a child.

Guards had been posted at the front doors of the building. Trillium had expected that. He and Summer had nothing to hide and plenty to trade. They had almost reached the doors when a man approached from the encampment. The man looked thin, dirty. He held his hands out.

"We don't have anything to spare," Summer said right away. The man had watery eyes. Trillium remembered his kind of thinness. "I'm sorry, baby. We just can't today."

"Maybe when we come out?" Trillium said.

The man turned away. "Nobody has anything left when they come out."

Trillium and Summer approached the guards, young men with guns, handkerchiefs over their faces. "What's your business?" one of the men asked.

Summer spoke first. "Trade."

The man lowered his handkerchief. "Summer? That you?"

"In the flesh." She smiled at him.

Trillium glanced at the other guard. Silent, holding his rusted gun.

"What are you doing here?" the first guard said to Summer.

"I just can't stay away."

The guard grinned, then remembered himself. He cleared his throat, tightened his grip on his ridiculous pistol. "Do you have plastic?"

"You know we do."

"I'm sorry, I gotta see it. It's the rules."

"Nobody comes in without plastic," the second guard said.

"We understand," Summer said. "You're just doing your job."

Trillium took the bag off his shoulder. He opened it, exposing but not taking out their plastic to trade.

The first man nodded. "You can come in."

The second man opened the glass doors. Cracks webbed

the frames. After Trillium and Summer were through, the guards closed and locked the doors behind them. Trillium didn't like the sound of those bolts sliding closed, but he and Summer stepped forward into a dim hall. The ceilings looked high and only partially rotted. Their footsteps echoed on the tile.

"Do you like doing that?" Trillium asked. "Or do you feel like you have to?"

Summer walked ahead of him. "What do you mean?"

"Talking to men?"

"You know, I don't even know anymore."

It had been a long time since Trillium had been inside a building this big, and it made him nervous. Where were the exits? Despite the soaring ceiling, he felt the walls constricting, squeezing him like a chute.

They walked to the end of the hall, where light shone. The light came from skylights, Trillium saw when they rounded the corner. The ceiling was studded with them—luckily, because the building had no other illumination. Leaves and branches had drifted over the once-clear plastic so the light made a scattered pattern on the floor. Trillium faced a long hallway, with doorways to different shops.

"Where are we going?" he asked.

Many of the shops had rolling metal gates down over their entrances. The gates had been wrenched or broken through, repaired with wire and plastic, or not repaired at all. People must have been living in some of the stores. Trillium could hear voices. He smelled food and trash.

"I think I remember the apothecary is down there," Summer said, "where the post office used to be."

They passed a shop selling fabric. People with drapes in

their arms raised their faces to Trillium as he went by, showing their wares, the fabric shiny with plastic. He and Summer passed a shop with the gate a few inches from the ground. Children's small and dirty feet stuck out from underneath. When they heard the two coming, the children swept their feet back inside, hiding.

But the gate must have been stuck. They couldn't pull it all the way down, couldn't budge it any farther. Someone could slide under that gate, sneak inside. It was dark in the shop. Trillium couldn't see the children's faces, see if they lived with anyone to feed them or protect them.

They passed a stand in the center of the hall. A man stepped forward. "Books?" he said.

"Really?" Summer slowed.

The man grinned. He indicated his stand with a flourish. The sleeves on his shirt were torn like an animal had nibbled on them. He pointed at a pole with what looked like shingles hung upon it. Trillium realized it was paper, faded and waterlogged and patched.

Books.

"I've got a phone book," the man said. "Mansfield city, 2020. Lawn mower manual. A book by one Mr. Gatsby. Supposed to be great."

"Heard of him," Summer said. "Any Encyclopedia Britannica books? It's a big book with illustrations. There's supposed to be a lot of them. Sequels, or something."

The man was looking around his stand. "I've got safety instruction books. From aeroplanes. They were laminated so they survived." He opened one. A smell of mouse droppings and mold released from its folds.

Trillium saw a drawing of a woman and a child in bright

yellow vests. The pictures had partially flaked away into nothingness. Trillium remembered what the vests were. Life vests.

But Summer was already walking away. She waved at the man. "We'll stop on our way back, maybe. We have something important to do first."

What's your favorite book? Trillium wanted to ask Summer. But of course it was likely she didn't have one. He didn't, except for Mr. Fall's. Those were the only books he had seen consistently. Mr. Fall took great care to make sure they survived.

"It's right up here," Summer said.

Trillium heard the faint sound of water. More light fell from larger, less obstructed skylights. The hallway widened, and he saw people gathered in a kind of atrium, grouped around a fountain. Water trickled from a post in the middle. The stream was thin and Trillium wasn't sure how clean it was, but children splashed in the basin. People leaned over the rim, washing clothes.

"Here we are," Summer said.

They ducked below a half-open gate. Kerosene lit the store inside. Such a waste, to use lamps in the day, but the skylights didn't reach back here. A counter took up most of the store. Shelves had been set up behind it, about half of them holding pill containers. One shelf held a rubber-tipped cane. Trillium saw a row of baby bottles, the plastic brown and ancient. A basket of syringes.

A man stood behind the counter, and another one guarded the shelves. The man in the back held a gun, of course. A rifle. Both men looked young.

"What can I do for you?" the man behind the counter said.

"Antibiotics," Trillium said.

"Ooh, high rollers."

"Let me talk." Summer turned to the man. "You remember me?"

"I do," the man with the gun said.

The man at the counter glared at him then turned back to Summer. "We are familiar with your presence at our establishment."

"Then you know I'm good for it. We can pay."

"Antibiotics are expensive."

"We can pay," Summer repeated.

The man pinched the bridge of his nose. "All right," he said. "Do you have a preference? Any allergies?"

Summer looked at Trillium.

"Not that we know of," he said. "She's never had an antibiotic before."

The man scanned the shelves behind him. "Looks like we have amoxicillin, doxycycline, azithromycin. And a zee-pack, all in stock. All at different price points, of course." He rattled off the drugs, pronouncing the strange words easily. He had said them many times.

This was not something Trillium had expected: a choice. He had thought they would have only one drug. How could he choose for her?

But Summer knew. "How much for the zee-pack? It's the fastest," she explained when the man from the counter went back into the shelves. The man with the gun kept it trailed on Trillium and Summer. "It'll start working right away. Mr. Fall had a bad illness, and the zee-pack worked for him."

"I never knew he was sick like that. When? He never said anything."

"He wouldn't."

The man returned with a small square package. It was paper, dirty on one end.

"When was this made?" Trillium asked.

"A few years ago. You know how it is in the cities. They have stuff we don't. If they can pay enough for it, they can get it."

"How do we know it's still good?"

"You don't. But you got a sick person, sick enough to come all the way out here and try to buy these pills—what other choice do you have?" He pulled off the dirty cardboard sleeve. He slid out a card with five big pills, white, under plastic.

At least the pills had been protected over the years. At least, Trillium hoped they had been protected. How long did antibiotics keep? How long did anything? They stretched it. They chanced it all: the dented cans, the chips that tasted like dust. In the tent city, he barely bothered flicking the mold off bread before wolfing it down. Plucking flies from the soup in stainless steel bowls. You couldn't be picky and live.

Trillium nodded at the pills. "We'll take them."

"All right," the man said. "Open your packs."

Trillium and Summer put their bags on the counter. He took out the white grill, sturdy plastic, which Mr. Fall said had been used on an air chiller and could be used again. And their prize, what he had bought with the money from that damn reporter: PMMA, a sheet of plexiglass, as long as his forearm. It had jagged edges, of course, but the center was clear. No cracks.

It might take a long time to save this kind of intact, high-quality plastic. A long time—and luck. Who knew when

Coral would find something this good, when she would be first to reach it in the river? In the dimness of the shop, kerosene flickering, Trillium unwrapped the rags around the plexiglass. It was like unveiling a jewel.

"Yes?" the man at the counter said.

Trillium thought he wanted him to explain, to tell the uses of the plastic. The man might not have seen it before. He might not know. Trillium found his throat felt tight. So much rode on these words. He touched the grill. "This was to cool the air. This—"

"No," the man interrupted him. "What else?"

Trillium wasn't expecting that. He touched the plexiglass. "This is—"

"Not enough."

"Are you joking?"

The man didn't change his expression.

"This is plexiglass. You could light your shop with this. You could make a windshield with this. This will never wash up in the river." Trillium's face burned as he said it. It was true, he realized. They would never again get something like it.

"It's okay." Summer put a hand on his arm. "I got this." She took out a folded object from her bag. It was smaller than her hand, black plastic.

"Shit," the man said. He leaned forward. "Can I touch them?"

"Yes."

He reached for the object. He unfolded it delicately, and Trillium saw.

Glasses.

Summer had brought a pair of eyeglasses.

The man held up the glasses and looked through the lenses. They were dirty but not cracked. Somehow, Summer had found, hung on to, and brought them safely on their journey.

"Can I?"

Summer nodded.

Licking his lips, completely taken in by the object before him, the man slipped the glasses over his ears. His fingers trembled a little on the frames. He pushed them onto his nose. Blinking through the smudged circles, he looked younger suddenly. Trillium wondered how old he really was. Fourteen? Thirteen? Shanghai's age. The glasses were small circles, but on the man—the boy—they looked big.

"Do they work?" Summer asked.

"Yes," the boy said. He looked down at the counter. He looked at the grill. He spun to the shelves behind him, and scanned them. Looking, looking. "They're not perfect, but…"

"Better?" Summer said.

"Yes." The boy turned back. He was grinning behind the dirty glasses. "Much better."

Trillium thought of Shanghai. He didn't think of the child often. He tried not to. But the child had looked like that, hadn't he? Like this boy? He had that same loopy grin, dizzy with hope. What was this boy behind the counter, this boy with an armed henchman, hoping for?

To see.

"You remembered," the boy said to Summer.

She cinched shut her bag. "So are we done here?"

The boy took off the glasses and started to polish them on his shirt. "One minute. I need to talk to your man here."

She gave the boy a pointed glance. "It'll be enough. It'll be plenty. Look," she said to Trillium. "I've got something to take care of in the hall. Are you good? If you need anything, just shout for me." She slung the bag over her shoulder and ducked under the gate.

In the end, the boy took the eyeglasses and the plexiglass in payment. It was both less than Trillium had expected and more. Summer had brought the true prize, the thing the boy really wanted. Trillium felt the boy didn't need or even want the plexiglass, but that he took it out of principle. It couldn't be just Summer who sacrificed. Trillium had to pay too.

Afterward, Trillium found Summer by the fountain. "Everything all right?" she asked.

He tapped the pack of pills in his pocket. He didn't want them out of his reach.

"Do you have anything left over?"

"The grill," Trillium said.

"You should get something for Coral at the fabric store. Just a little present. It's nice to have a treat when you don't feel well, you know?"

They needed that plastic. And Coral would feel better, Coral would feel best, when they had savings again. But Coral had mentioned fabrics; she would like that. When Trillium came out of the fabric store, Summer was talking to someone at the fountain. A girl. She had stringy hair and full cheeks, like they were stuffed with cotton.

"This is Joshua Tree," Summer said. "She's coming with us."

"What?" Trillium said.

"She's coming along."

Joshua Tree tried to smile. Her eyes flitted uncertainly from Summer to Trillium.

"She's staying with you?"

"Maybe," Summer said. "For a time."

"You know her?"

"No," Joshua Tree said. And her voice was full of so much eagerness and hope that Trillium had the urge both to slap her and to ferry her to safety. "We just met. Isn't that the greatest?"

"The greatest," Trillium said. "Can I talk to you for a moment?" he said to Summer.

"Sure thing." She waved at the girl and walked a few paces away.

"What's going on?" Trillium asked.

"She needs a place to stay. She needs a job. I have jobs."

"Since when?"

"Rattlesnake Master has jobs."

"Is this a recruiting trip? Is this why you came along?"

"No. And yes. I wanted to see the Strip again. I wanted to get out of that damn junkyard for a change. And I knew you didn't have enough for that medicine. I knew what the boy who runs the apothecary needed. And..." She paused. "I owe Rattlesnake Master. Anybody I bring in—"

"You get a cut?"

Summer looked at him directly. "No. They get a job. A place to live. Regular food. That girl's not being fed here. And she's doing things you don't want to know about. She's not safe."

"That's none of our business."

Summer dropped her chin and intensified her look. Her eyes were lined with a darkness that sparkled. The makeup she and Foxglove used—Trillium was going to have to ask them more about it. Maybe he could use those colors for his tattoos.

"Fine," he said. "Bring her along."

Summer turned to the girl by the fountain and nodded. Her face split into a grin, like a pumpkin in the weeds.

It was going to be a long trip back.

16

Miami

They walked until nightfall. They walked slowly, with Coral struggling to keep up, leaning on Trillium's or Summer's shoulders. Miami did not offer his own shoulder. He felt it wasn't right. But also it wasn't right walking behind her, watching her limp. When they stopped, it was a relief. Miami couldn't stand to see her in such pain, pretending she was not.

All women pretend. He heard Mangrove's voice in his head.

Had she really said that? Was he remembering correctly? He was starting to forget the sound of her voice. It was high, he thought. In contrast to her deliberate, often forceful actions and confident way, her voice was soft and light. He thought.

They stopped at the foot of a big hill. Miami could see a building at the top, and the remains of another structure at the bottom. That building had three crumbling walls, which were enough for the others, apparently. Trillium checked the woods around them for danger, and Summer and her new friend foraged for dinner. No one was saying much about the girl. She had attached herself to them like a pricker from the grass. Miami didn't feel he could ask any questions about her, and Coral was in no position to. He was left to get Coral settled inside the ruins of the building.

It was large, two stories, though most of the upper floor and roof were gone, rotted or burned out. Junk, broken chairs, and long pieces of timber filled the ground floor.

Miami found Coral standing in front of a gaping black hole in the wall. "There you are."

She turned. "Do you know what this is?"

He studied the wall. "A fireplace? A big one?"

"Do you think it will work?"

"Well, the chimney's probably blocked."

"And smoke would attract attention. Never mind."

He reached out to touch her shoulder. It was the second time they had touched. The first was when she had grabbed his arm at Trashlands. He had felt warmth pierce through him then, like a knife. He felt it now, even just brushing her. She looked at his hand and he dropped it right away. "You should sit down," he said. "Relax."

"I've already had one pill."

"Well, they take a while to work."

"I wish I could take them all at once and be done with it."

"I don't think that's how to do it."

"I know." She settled down beside the fireplace. "I read the directions on the package."

"Do you need anything? Something to eat? A blanket?"

She smiled up at him. "Do you have those things?"

"No. But I could find them. I do have water." He unscrewed the cap and she took the jug from him.

"I'm sorry we haven't been able to find your sister's bracelet."

"That's all right," Miami said. "I don't really want it."

"I know," Coral said. "You want revenge."

Before the journey to the Strip, he had moved the knife from his waistband to his bag, where it waited along with a spare set of clothes, bus tickets home, his notebook, and three pencils. He would move the knife again, to his pocket. His father had not taught Miami how to use the knife. But how hard was it? You stepped forward. You slashed at the pain. Your pain manifested in the form of a man. You tried to stab him out of the world.

"You're not going to find it," Coral said. "You won't find the men who killed her. You know you won't. Men come through Trashlands all the time. Out of the trees. And if you did somehow find the people who hurt her, it wouldn't make you feel better. It wouldn't bring her back."

"I know," Miami said.

Coral traced the top of the water jug. "I go out looking for the factory sometimes."

"The factory?"

"Where my son is. I haven't found it."

"Would you know it if you did?"

"I think I would."

Miami understood. He had thought he would feel that way too. That he would sense the spot where Mangrove had died, as they had sensed so much about each other. The ground would be scorched, the trees red with blood, with her fury. He didn't realize how vast the region was, and how forgettable his own tragedy.

Trillium dumped a pile of firewood at their feet. "The woods are clear," he said.

Coral pointed through the window. "What's that on the hill?"

"The building?"

"No. A railing high above the ground, with a funny little thing on it."

Miami rose and went to the window, jagged with broken glass. "It's a chairlift."

"A what?"

"For skiing." He picked up one of the long timbers strewn about the floor and examined it. "These are skis. We should see if we can find some unbroken pairs. Have you ever skied, either of you? They'd be useful to get around in snow."

Trillium just looked at him. "I'd hang on to your eyeglasses if I were you. Those fetch a high price here."

They made a fire on a cleared patch of floor—avoiding the big fireplace—and ate small orange fruits called ground cherries. The fruits tasted sour, chewy, and delicious. Only a handful each. Miami wished he had a dozen more, wished he could have had a pie of them. Everyone found a place to sleep amid the debris, Coral in the middle.

Miami couldn't sleep. He thought of his first night at Trashlands.

Not long after Tahiti had left his room, Miami was nursing a headache from the strong drink when he heard another soft knock on the door. Tahiti, he had thought, back for another round.

"Come on, it's late," Miami said as he pulled open the door.

It wasn't Tahiti. It was the dancer with tattoos up and down her body. The girl Tahiti loved. She was alone. She leaned through the doorway into Miami's room. "Would you like company tonight?" she asked. "What's wrong with your head?"

He lowered the wet rag he had been pressing to his forehead. There was no ice, of course, and the washrag was filthy. "I have a headache. It's fine."

"You know what cures a headache?" Foxglove said.

"It doesn't actually—and I'm all right. I'm good." He kept his hand on the knob, the door open to the night. Neon spilled from the rooftop sign over the edge of the walkway like sparks from a fire.

The dancer's eyes looked intense but also unseeing. She was not drunk, not even a little. Just tired. And bored. Bored of this? Bored of him? Bored of pretending.

She teetered into his room, but it looked practiced, purposeful. Her only wobble came from those damn shoes. What were they made of? She walked into the room marveling as if she had never seen it before, though surely she must have, many times, or a neighboring one that looked exactly like it. She clocked the narrow unmade bed, the basin of water, his bag.

She looked at him over her shoulder. "We don't even have to do anything. You can pay me to wear your name, and everybody will just *think* we did."

"Did what?"

"Did it," the dancer said.

It was brilliant, actually. A genius marketing strategy.

"That's a great idea, but it's not for me. I'm sorry."

She tilted her head at him. "Why did you even come to Trashlands?"

Tahiti had asked the same question. Coral too. How many times could he explain it?

"I'm traveling for work," Miami said.

"That's what they all say." She turned back to the door. Her black bra and panties, the only clothing she wore, were fringed, but not with cloth. This fringe rustled. Hard. He realized when she brushed past him what was sewn on her costume: the tines of black plastic forks. "You're taken, aren't you?" she said.

He felt he couldn't lie to her, even to get her out of his room. Somehow, she would know. She would call him out for it, like she saw the shabby room for what it was.

"I'm not, actually. I'm single." That old-fashioned word.

"But your tattoo?"

"It's old. Over."

"But you want somebody? You're taken by her?"

"I don't..." Miami said.

"I know someone in love when I see it," Foxglove said. She touched his cheek. He thought for a moment she might try to kiss him. He backed up until his shoulder hit the door.

She was right. The dancer was right. She had seen through him, like his sister might have.

He did want someone. He had wanted her from the moment he saw her, peeking up out of the junk.

Coral.

In the ruined ski lodge, Miami sat up. He could make out three shapes in the dark: the sleeping figures of Trillium, Summer, and the girl. Where was Coral? He slid off the jacket he had used for a blanket, and stepped around the junk on the floor. Faint light pulsed from an open doorway. There was a basement in the building, Summer had said.

He went down the steps. Dirt clustered in the corners. There had been another flood here recently and the muddy water had receded, or maybe snow from the mountaintop had gotten into the stairwell. There had once been snow enough to ski here, after all.

In the basement, he could see more debris, broken skis and boots. He thought that they should probably look through everything in the morning, try to find items that fit or could be sold. That was what Coral did, after all. And then he saw her, standing in the hallway.

It was near dawn already. Gray light leaked through the little half windows near the top of the basement. She faced the walls, the dimness casting everything, including her, into a veil of smoke. He walked down to her.

"You can't sleep, either?" she said.

"It's the open roof. I feel—"

"Exposed? You get used to it." She turned back to the walls. There was something hanging on them. "I feel a little sick. That's why I can't sleep."

"From the pills?"

"A side effect. I read it on the package."

Miami came close enough to see what she was looking at. Pictures hung on the walls, old-fashioned photographs in frames. Silently he stood beside her and studied them. *Ski Team*, one of the pictures read, below a group of people in puffy coats. *Junior Patrol*, read a photograph of children.

Squares darkened the paint on the walls where some of the pictures had fallen or been removed.

"How old do you think these pictures are?" Miami asked.

"From before the big floods at least. You think all these people are dead?"

"Probably," Miami admitted.

"Maybe some of them survived awhile, died of old age in their beds. Maybe they died peacefully."

"Maybe. If they were rich enough to ski, maybe they were rich enough to buy gas and islands."

Coral glanced over at him. "I hope they got away."

Miami tapped the cracked glass on one of the pictures. His finger made a clear dot in the grime. "Not this one. This old sport with the scarf? He deserved it."

Coral laughed. He saw her look at the picture of the children. "Do you have a partner back in the city?"

He felt his finger. "Not anymore. She left."

"I'm sorry."

"You know how it is. Everything is temporary."

"It shouldn't be," Coral said. "Some things shouldn't be. Like love."

"You and Trillium—you're together, right?" He thought of the gruff man. How many tattoos he must have given the dancer, Foxglove. How much older he looked to be than Coral.

"Yes," Coral said. One word, facing the wall.

You could never know a person, really know them, Miami had learned. Never guess what they truly might be capable of, or how they might change, change in a way that didn't include you, that left no space for you.

But no one could know a place either, he was beginning

to understand. No one could know Scrappalachia, not fully, not in a way that summed it up neatly. It was not neat. It was complicated, paradoxical. There were people living in the trunks of cars. Children living on their own. Summer crafted her own shoes. Coral made art out of trash.

"Are you happy?" Miami asked her.

She turned her head. Her eyes unfocused and her smile froze. He thought of the ground cherries, growing in the woods, where hardly anyone could see them, where he might have passed by them and never known.

"Sometimes," Coral said.

"Be careful with her," Foxglove had said in his room last night. "The person you love. Whoever she is. Don't hurt her. That's all I ask."

She lowered her hand from his face and left. She walked down the outside corridor, striped with pink light, down the rusted, unsteady stairs. He heard her call out musically to someone. A man answered, unseen in the night: *Let me walk you home, baby.*

Miami closed the door. His head pounded. This was such a strange place. The wine they brewed in tubs, out of rot, was strong and sweet, and there were hardly any bugs in it. He could see Foxglove's costume sold in the fanciest of city stores. What was the ink of her tattoos made from? Motor oil? *Pens?*

He would never be able to write about this place. He would never be able to get people in the cities to understand, to see. The columns of smashed cars, the community of scrap. If he opened his door again and stood on the balcony, he could gaze over the acres of rust and cooking fires, the music thudding under his feet. And the sign—where had they found neon? How had they made that, made any of this?—the pink light of Trashlands, lording over them all.

His basin of water stood on a clear plastic nightstand, next to a candle in a water bottle. He knelt, lowering himself to the floor. A mistake. He could smell the stale smoke. But still, he touched the short orange piles of carpet with his hands, running his fingers over the fibers. More plastic, rubbery, milled fine. He would never be able to get people to believe this.

And to love it, love it like he already did.

17

Rattlesnake Master

Eryngium yuccifolium

He could make it until the afternoon before he touched himself. Sometimes: the evening, if he was busy counting plastic or running numbers in his head. Even then he heard things. The clacking of heels, laughter. Through the low bass, he heard girls leading men to the back rooms, heard squeals and protests and the thudding of heads or bodies against walls. And crying. The crying was too much.

He locked the door of his office. He had made sure he had a lock that worked, that was solid. Unusual in this place. He was pretty sure none of the dancers had one. He even oiled the damn thing. He secured the lock, then sat back down behind his desk, in the chair that Summer had made, and closed his eyes.

It was difficult to be around so much beauty and so much power. That was the struggle: resisting the power. He could easily take anyone back here. It was his right as their boss, as the one who gave them food and a roof, a chance at a life. Letting them go onstage, giving them an audience—that was him doing them a favor. It was his duty, in a way, to make sure the dancers were doing their job.

A few of them had a reputation now—Summer and Fox-glove especially—and he was proud of that. Men came from miles away just to see them.

But women talked. That was the worst thing about them. They talked to each other, gossiped and warned.

Women were also disposable. Women were born every day, a plastic bag a dozen. But those two! He couldn't lose them. Men asked for them at the door by name. Tahiti had to run off the lovesick ones, the ones who didn't want to leave but had run out of currency. Who knows where they went, what happened to them. Rattlesnake Master hoped, for the sake of the women and girls of the world, the men didn't meet anyone unaccompanied on their way home. He hoped their wives and children were strong. Few girls were, he thought with a pierce of desire, once you got them alone.

Summer was on thin ice, though. Summer, he thought, was pushing it. She was turning men down, turning away work. And why? Because she was a fool, in love with an old man.

Any stirring he had felt, thinking about the nameless girls in the woods, subsided, remembering that old man. When the school bus had first roared into the yard and parked in a corner by the old quarry, Rattlesnake Master hadn't thought too much of it. They would move on. Everyone did. Most folks didn't like to live in the shadow of a strip club.

Then Rattlesnake Master had thought this might be a

good thing, a very good thing indeed. A school bus attracted kids, even now, riveted by the size of it, the mystery. Kids grew up. And some of them were girls. And some of them were parentless, defenseless.

The old man from the bus watched the kids like a hawk. Still, though Mr. Fall tried, he couldn't hold on to all of them, especially as they grew and became, as all children do, petulant, rebellious, aimless. Rattlesnake Master liked the aimless ones best, the ones who had something to prove.

But the kids born at Trashlands or the ones who moved here with their mothers, Mr. Fall swooped right up and kept in that school of his all day, every day. At dark, he made the big ones walk the littles home. They traveled in packs, so Rattlesnake Master couldn't come across a girl alone in a bend and call to her sweetly, like a wolf in a story. He forgot what happened in that story.

Rattlesnake Master had learned that Mr. Fucking Fall taught all the children to read, even the girls. He taught them about the past through his big shitty books, which they all called *the* book for some stupid reason. He taught some of their mothers to read too, some of the dancers at Rattlesnake Master's place, in *his* employ, and that was something that Rattlesnake Master couldn't stand. The old man had no business doing that. That was not the job of a teacher— a job to which Mr. Fall had appointed himself, by the way. Teachers taught kids, not adults who were past help.

Reading didn't help anybody, not the dancers who couldn't understand, who didn't have enough brains left in their heads after all the smoking and drinking and fucking they did, not to mention all the knocking around they had taken from customers or lovers. Naturally, their learning to read didn't help Rattlesnake Master either. What would they object to? What would they ask for next?

It didn't help if they got their hands on newspapers from the city, which happened sometimes, either from that old man or from men at the club, and saw the advertisements for Trashlands—ads Rattlesnake Master was very proud of. They'd see Summer, the goddess, and Foxglove, an angel in ink, mentioned, but not them. Nothing about their flat asses and stringy hair. As if any girl here except Summer and Foxglove had anything special.

And Summer loved that old man. It was fucking apparent. Everyone knew it.

She cooked for him. She made treats for all his whiny students. He stayed in her truck, half the time, when he wasn't crashing on the ground under his own bus in the dirt, a station which suited him. He had given up his bus, given up his own home, which was a pussy move, to a girl. The little redhead.

Trashlands didn't have a natural redhead, and that was something men always asked for. Foxglove was a bottle red, which was fine; she had other attributes. But Coral was *real*. Coral was sweet. And yes, she was older, pushing thirty, Rattlesnake Master would have to say. But Summer was certainly older than that, maybe forty. And Coral's hair was not only the color of a season Rattlesnake Master could almost but not quite remember, a color that made him ache in his very center of being, but her hair was curly as well. Wild as a late night. She had an innocence about her that seemed tarnished in just the right way. She had been taken advantage of, but only a little. Enough to get used to it. Enough to want it again.

She was as good as Mr. Fall's own daughter, though, so Rattlesnake Master never had a chance.

Not when she was young. Not when they had first come to the junkyard, dragging Coral's brat. But now that she was older…desperation had a way of piling on. His want for her had not faded over the years. Instead, it had only sharpened with time, just out of reach. She was still a prize. She was experienced now. She had been with two men that Rattlesnake Master knew about, her brat's daddy and Trillium. That was enough, that was perfect.

He wondered if she was sad enough, tired enough, desperate enough to dance for him.

Thinking about Coral had riled him up again. His eyes flickered to the lock on his door. He relaxed in his chair. There was a knock and his hand froze. "What?"

Tahiti's muffled voice: "Summer's back."

No peace. No fucking peace. He got himself together and opened the door. Tahiti stood there. "Well?"

"She's got a girl with her, someone they picked up on the road."

"Well, well, she can follow instructions, after all." Rattlesnake Master craned around the mountain of a man, looking down the hall. "Where is she?"

"Outside. She won't come in. She's got Coral with her too."

Did Tahiti know about Rattlesnake Master's obsession with the redhead? The bodyguard must know. Desire was easy to spot, like colored plastic in the water.

The reds always stood out.

Rattlesnake Master smoothed his hair. It was more gray than brown these days, but at least he had a lot of it, in waves down his neck. It gave him a hero look, like another one of those stories he could barely remember. He set off down the hall. The music boomed, and through a crack in the curtain he could see a girl spin on a pole. He barely registered her. He pushed open the back door.

The light outside always hurt after spending so long in the club. Sunglasses were on his list, but nobody found those intact anymore. He shielded his face with his hand. He saw a half circle of people. Summer. Coral and her fucking lover. And a new girl and man. "Introduce me," Rattlesnake Master said.

"This is Joshua Tree," Summer said. "She's from the Strip. Looking for a job."

She had a rotten mouth, but most people did. Eyes with energy. Dirty hair that appeared to be blond, and apple cheeks.

"Do you have a family?" he asked her. "Folks or kids?"

"No, sir."

"Have you danced before?"

"No, sir, but I've done other—"

"That's fine," Rattlesnake Master said. He didn't need to know. "Why don't you go inside? Get cleaned up. Are you hungry? We'll find you somewhere to sleep. Maybe you can stay with Foxglove."

"Oh she'll love that," Tahiti muttered.

Rattlesnake Master turned to him. "Tahiti, show the girl around. Get her something fried to eat." As the girl passed him, Rattlesnake Master got a whiff of her. "Maybe a shower first would be best." He turned his attention to the man in the yard. "Who's this, then?"

The stranger looked at the others, then when no one

spoke up for him, introduced himself. Rattlesnake Master struggled to control his face. *A reporter. A real reporter.* Fucking here at Trashlands.

"I'm boarding above the club," the man said.

"Paying?" Rattlesnake Master asked. It was good to be sure.

"Of course."

"Well, then, feel free to avail yourself of the other amenities of this business."

"I'm just here to write my story."

"Then ask me any questions you have." Was an article better than an ad? He hoped so. He couldn't wait for that old man to read this.

But the reporter said, "It's not really a story about the club."

Rattlesnake Master felt his forehead furrow. That would give him wrinkles. "What else is here to write about?"

Nobody answered him.

Summer said, "So you're giving the girl a job, right?"

"Yes," Rattlesnake Master said, distracted. But this didn't excuse everything. Summer couldn't stop refusing men just because Mr. Fall was jealous or whatever messed-up arrangement they had going on. They weren't done, Rattlesnake Master and Summer. They were done with what he could say in public.

The group turned to go.

"Wait," Rattlesnake Master said. "Coral, how are you feeling?"

He had heard about her accident. He had hoped it might be the tipping point, the push to get her onstage, to get her undressed. But she had found the money for medicine some-where. How, if not from him?

"Better," Coral said. But she didn't look better. She looked tired, and something else. Panicky. Scared. Was she scared enough? "The medicine works fast."

"Was it awfully expensive?"

"It was."

"I'm sorry. I know you were saving, for your boy."

"Thanks." She spoke the last word so quietly he would not have noticed except for how focused he was on her lips, her face.

"You know, this is not the sort of thing I normally say. I normally don't hire pluckers like yourself, Coral, especially at your age—but if you need money, you know how you can make it. You always have an opportunity here."

She didn't respond. Too embarrassed to talk about it in front of the others? He should have talked to her privately. But he could never fucking catch her alone.

Rattlesnake Master thought fast. "It can be a onetime thing. A show. One night only. You're that special, Coral. You know I'd wait for you."

Now Trillium spoke. "That's enough."

Tahiti tapped Rattlesnake Master's shoulder. He was back without the new girl. Rattlesnake Master hoped she had found her way to some lye. "Boss?" Tahiti said. "There's somebody you should see."

Dancers disappeared all the time. It wasn't like they had a contract. It wasn't like they had to give notice. They showed up, worked, and Rattlesnake Master fed and found housing for them. It was, he felt, a gentleman's arrangement.

The woman who sat on the couch in his office looked vaguely familiar—but then, she looked like a dozen others. Greasy brown hair, thin face. When Rattlesnake Master and the bodyguard entered the office, she stood. A skinny boy stood beside her, much taller than the woman.

"I'm here to ask for my job back," the woman said.

"All right," Rattlesnake Master said. "Sure."

Her face began to leak with a stream of tears. She hadn't expected it to be this easy, apparently. Or maybe there was more.

"Where have you been?" he asked, innocently enough.

"I had to leave. I'm sorry, but I had to. I found out where he was, and I had to go."

"He?"

She shook the arm of the tall boy. "My son. I found the factory."

"The factory?"

Rattlesnake Master became aware of a commotion in the hall, as the people from outside crowded in. Word traveled fast in the junkyard. Coral sneaked around Tahiti—or probably, Rattlesnake Master thought with a twinge of irritation, the man had just let her through.

You couldn't look away from Coral, even exhausted, even on the verge of tears as she too appeared to be. Her face seemed to glow, her skin to hum. It made a vibration inside him. The difference between the two women was striking. "Is it true?" Coral asked.

The woman in his office nodded. Coral ran forward and the two embraced.

"What the fuck is happening?" Rattlesnake Master said.

Coral looked into the woman's face. "Was there a boy at the factory named Shanghai?"

Now the boy spoke. "Sure. Shanghai. He makes things."

"He makes things?"

"Takes scraps of plastic and makes toys or whatever. I dunno. He hides them. But I stood near him on the line so I saw."

"How old was he?" Coral asked. The trembling in her voice—even Rattlesnake Master dared not interrupt her.

"I dunno," the boy said. "My age maybe?"

That was it. That was the answer she wanted. She closed her eyes. The other woman shook Coral's shoulders, excited, joyful, or sad. It was hard to tell. She pulled Coral close to her. What the fuck were these women thinking? A tear slipped down Coral's cheek. It took all of Rattlesnake Master's willpower not to reach forward and swipe it.

The woman said to Rattlesnake Master, "I was hoping to ask for a new place to stay."

"Sure," he said. "Take your pick of the empty junkers. I'll take it out of your paycheck. What happened to your last place?"

She didn't answer. "I was hoping for a job for my son too? As a bouncer? Or maybe he could be a bodyguard?"

Rattlesnake Master looked the boy up and down. "No way. He's like a beanpole. What is he, ten?"

"Fourteen, I think," the boy said.

"Maybe when the DJ dies, he can take his place. But not until then."

"He's very strong," the woman protested. "He worked in the factories."

But Coral interrupted them, her arms still locked around

the woman. Did she even know her? Were they linked by anything other than their bad luck and miserable lives?

"What was the price?" Coral asked. "For your son to be released from the factory?"

The woman looked at her straight. It was like Rattlesnake Master, Tahiti, the beanpole—none of the men were there in the room, or out in the hallway. It was Coral and the mother only in the world.

"One working car," the woman said.

18

Miami

The neon of the sign hummed. Miami looked up to see the letters, so bright they hurt his eyes. Something dark clustered above the *A*; a bird had made a nest there. How could a bird survive that glow, that noise? How could any of them? He walked away from the club with Coral, Trillium, and Summer. They had left the new girl from the mall behind.

What had Miami witnessed? Could he write about this? Did he have a responsibility to—or would it be worse if he told this story? How Summer sold a girl to the club, or how the girl sold herself. How Coral had found the factory and the price for her son's return—and she could not pay it.

Should he feel worried that they had abandoned the strange girl? She had gone into the club willingly, eagerly even, and had a wiriness that suggested she knew her way around a fight. But the man Rattlesnake Master...he occupied a bad place in Miami's mind instantly, the place where the men who hurt Mangrove lived, the forest of strangers and unknowable, unforgivable pain.

They passed a man vomiting into the weeds, his face splashed with neon.

Trillium was seething. "I'm fucking sick of this camp."

"It's just a bad day," Summer said. "You know Rattlesnake Master. He's like this with every woman."

"No, he's not," Trillium said. "He's worse with Coral." He picked up speed, walking much faster than the rest of them.

Coral couldn't keep up. She slowed as Trillium disappeared around a bend. Summer helped her onto the bumper of a smashed car. The long car had once been white. Through the slit of a broken window, Miami could see what looked like a fancy dress, rotting on the seat.

Summer touched Coral's arm. "You all right?"

"No." Hair hid Coral's face, but Miami could hear the break in her voice.

"How are you feeling?"

"Fine. I feel fine."

Summer looked up at Miami. "Maybe you should go on back to your room?"

"No," Coral said. "I want him here."

Miami felt his heart in his chest, heat in his face. She wanted him here. He had to say something, had to help. "Can't we find a running car in the junkyard?" He looked around. There were cars everywhere, the seat Coral perched upon, the walls that lined the path. Cars stretched to the sky.

"Everything that can run ran out of here a long time ago," Summer said. She patted Coral's shoulder. "We should get you home."

"Trillium's mad."

"Not at you, baby." She turned to Miami. "Do you have dinner plans?"

He felt adrift. Not hungry, not anything but lost. His room back at Trashlands was dingy in the daytime, poorly lit. Grease made a thick layer on the walls. The room had a not-so-faint fruit piss smell along with the smoky carpet, and you could hear everything through the walls: the thumping of the music, the thumping of beds on both sides of the room.

Summer straightened without waiting for an answer. "I'll cook for you at my place if you want. Mr. Fall's coming over, anyway. How do you feel about...cheeto casserole?" She helped Coral to her feet.

"I'll walk her home," Miami offered.

"That's fine," Coral said. "He can take me."

Summer gave Miami a look, but she raised her hands. Her nails were red, long and tapered like the lightning rods on old buildings. They hadn't absorbed the lightning, they hadn't stopped the water. They hadn't done anything, as the seawalls hadn't, as the sandbags hadn't. "All right, if you insist. I'll see you in a bit for dinner, Miami." Summer turned to walk back to her truck. "Be smart."

"I will be," Coral said.

"I wasn't talking to you."

Once they were alone, Miami felt the weight of Coral's embarrassment. That she had wept. That he had suggested a car from the junkyard, naively. Should he not have spoken up, not have said anything?

He had heard that children sorted plastic. They had written stories about it at the paper. He had even heard that not all of the children were there willingly. Being unsubstantiated, he had never written a story about that last part. But he had also never known anyone personally who had lost a child that way.

Of course, most of his friends in the city didn't have children. It seemed too hard to bring a child into this world. Too sad. Almost all of his friends said that.

Coral rubbed her nose. "The rainbow bus is this way."

"I remember."

"You really don't have to walk me if you don't want to."

"I want to," Miami said. He kept a slow pace with her as they headed back, alert for any stumbles or hitch in her breath, tuned in to her like a radio only his body could hear. "Is there anything else that can be done about your son?"

"No."

"Do they ever come back on their own, the children?"

"You're doing it again."

"Doing what?"

"The reporter thing. Asking too many questions."

Miami apologized, but Coral wasn't looking at him anymore. "Koala. That boy in Rattlesnake Master's office. His name is Koala. He's the only child I've ever met who came back."

Miami followed Coral's gaze. He saw children spreading cattails out to dry on the swell of a tanker tipped on its side. He imagined the children were going to eat the plants. And even though it was the reporter thing again, he asked, "Why would you and that woman both have lost a child that way? Why are children taken?"

"It's how this place runs. How you get your plastic recycled. It's too much work for adults to do alone. Too dirty. Too hard. So they take kids, make them do it."

How this place runs. Did Coral mean Trashlands? Or the region? Or the world? There were newer plastic buildings back in the city, but not, he realized, in Trashlands. He had seen no real building at all except the club, and that was an ancient structure, just patched up. The children were doing work that didn't even help their home.

He wanted to press Coral close to him. He wanted to shield her from bad things, the guilt that didn't let go. He didn't want to tell her: that hurt never went away. "Can I hug you?" he asked.

Something strange crossed her eyes. Like a cloud, or a jet plane with a white tail. "Why are you asking?" she said.

Then they were holding each other. She smelled of sweat and sunlight. When they broke apart again, Coral started walking.

19

Trillium

Foxglove waited at the bus, jiggling with impatience. Trillium was glad to see her. There was only one reason she would come here, and it was something for him to do. Work. A distraction. Her skin shone, frost on a window.

"No man with you?" Trillium asked.

"Just his money."

He kicked open the doors with his boot, and indicated she should go inside. Foxglove hitched up the steps. He watched her shimmering ponytail move like a snake in the dark.

"It's getting colder," she said. "Night's falling sooner. You're really going to stay here another year? You're not going to find a better place?"

"I don't know," Trillium said.

"I wish I could find another camp. Somewhere with palm trees. Fuck yeah."

"There aren't any more palm trees."

"Cocktails by the swimming pool."

"How do you even know about palm trees?"

"Mr. Fall's book."

"Ah, the book."

From the book, Coral had learned about the basin of the Amazon, dinosaurs, the hole in the layer surrounding the Earth. Sometimes, Coral said she looked up at the sky to try and see it, that hole in the ozone, if it looked like something she might know—a break in the ice over the river, a tear in her clothes. She always pictured it as angular, sharp with many points, like a star. She always pictured one hole in the ozone, though Trillium knew there were many. Too many to think about mending.

"What'll it be this time?" Trillium said. He patted the table, but Foxglove didn't move.

She raised her index finger. "He wants a nipple. He has enough for a finger."

"I hope he has a short name." Trillium turned to his tools.

"Is Coral all right?" Foxglove asked. "Did she get the medicine?"

"She's fine. We got what she needed, and it seems to be working."

"Where is she?" Her question was innocent enough, but everything about Foxglove seemed both innocent and not at the same time. She held his gaze blankly but steadily.

Most of the time, the tattoo by her eye looked like an eyelash, or bit of grime. Tonight it seemed to have the shape of a tear. It was fading, though. Fading away. She was going to need to freshen it up soon, if she wanted to keep it. Trillium did not bring it up. He told her, "Coral's with Summer and that reporter."

"Miami?"

"Have you met him?" He patted the table again and this time she hopped on.

"I've met everybody." She crossed her ankles and set her hands primly, finger extended, on her knees. "He seems like a good man."

"I wouldn't know."

Her head was faced away from him, and now he couldn't see the *Baby* tattoo at all. "He turned me down," Foxglove said. "So he's probably good."

Coral came home. Mr. Fall was spending the evening at Summer's, and Foxglove had to get back to work, her finger pulsing with *Adelie* in looped script. Neither Trillium nor Foxglove—nor the man whose name it was, according to Foxglove—had been exactly sure how to spell it.

Trillium cooked a handful of curly dock with some wild onions. They ate in silence.

Finally Coral said, "I'm going to keep looking. With Miami. For his sister's bracelet."

Trillium set his spoon down. "That's a waste of time."

"Yes. But I think what he's really looking for is closure. Coming to terms with his sister dying. I think writing a story about this place is just an excuse for him to be here. See it for himself."

"It's still a waste of your time."

"But we need the money."

Trillium began to clear the plates. He couldn't remember the last time he had left food on his plate, that he had not gone to bed hungry and woken up hungry. "You know the best way for me to make money is to move on."

"For you to make money. You. Not me."

"Go somewhere that doesn't have a tattoo artist, that hasn't had the same one for years and years."

"New people come here all the time."

"Doing a few tattoos a day is never going to be enough," Trillium said.

"We can't leave. He won't be able to find us if we do."

"He's not coming back, Coral." The thunder of his own voice surprised him. "It doesn't matter where we are. It won't bring your son back."

Coral looked down at the kitchen table. It was plastic. It came out of the wall on a plastic hinge, supported by plastic legs. When they were done eating, they would wipe the table with a rag and fold it back against the wall. Soon the bed would be pushed over for the night. They couldn't have the kitchen table and the bed out at the same time, there wasn't room.

He stacked the plates on the counter, cluttered with ink jars and old needles. Trillium would dip the plates in the water basin by the doors, scrub them with a solution of ground plastic. Everything was dirty, the counter, the water. The plates after he rinsed them would still be unclean.

"How did we get stuck here?" Coral asked quietly.

It had seemed like a good place. Not too far from the water, a safe distance from the trees. The junkyard made a kind of fortress, protecting them. But Trillium hadn't remembered, he hadn't called back the history from Mr. Fall's book: all fortresses have kings.

This king wanted Trillium's lover. Maybe because of her beauty or history. Maybe Rattlesnake Master wanted Coral because he wanted all things. Trillium had known men like that, men who collected what they didn't need: food that would spoil before they could get around to eating it, screens that didn't even work. Did the men think they would use everything? Did they think their families would return and be hungry? Did they think they would find other women? That sex and love were still guaranteed to them, just by virtue of being men?

Did they think it was all coming back: phone service and internet and jet planes and marriage? Or did they just not want anyone else to have it?

Trashlands was still a good camp, in many respects. The water provided plastic. The woods provided food. Mr. Fall had children to teach, children whose mothers left food outside the bus in thanks. Summer helped out a lot. Foxglove was a good friend to both Trillium and Coral.

But Trashlands. The club. Trillium saw neon in his sleep, etched on the inside of his eyes. He would never know if his hearing was going—as Mr. Fall suspected his was—because he just heard bass all the time. The beat lodged in his ears, a low throb.

And the men. The fucking men.

The men kept coming to Trashlands. They might as well have been walking out of the river. They might as well have been stamped from the factories, though the bricks that came out of those factories looked more distinctive than the men at the club. Those men only varied on the spectrum of how drunk they were, how intense the fights they started or ended, how far Tahiti or one of Rattlesnake Master's other goons had to push them back into the woods, how deeply the hired muscle had to shove them into the dust.

Trillium wished he could build a junkyard around Coral, a

labyrinth that only she would know the way out of. She had gone from one man to another; she'd never been alone like him.

But that was not unusual for women.

"How did you get stuck here?" Trillium echoed. "Or how did you get stuck with me?"

"Are you mad at me about something?" Coral said.

"Are you mad at me?"

"I just wish we hadn't spent so much on the medicine. We could have bought a car."

"It wasn't enough for that. And we had to spend that plastic. We spent it to keep you alive."

"I'm just not sure what kind of life this is anymore." Coral rose from the table and pushed it in violently.

Trillium jumped at the bang of the table hitting the side of the bus. She shoved at the bed. She couldn't push the bed out by herself, couldn't lift it, but she was trying. Trillium reached over and helped her.

"I'm just tired," Coral said.

"You should rest, then."

"I just need to be alone."

He finished cleaning up. It was nearly dark, everyone at home in their hovels. They had to be, before curfew. Foxglove had been right: night fell earlier. Soon the rains would come, then the snows. Sometimes they came at the same time, curtains of sleet, hard as arrows. Often part of the river froze, and Coral could only gather the plastic that floated in the white skin of the water, or risk breaking the ice and feeling around in the freezing currents beneath.

Trillium couldn't think straight on those days, until she was home.

She had gone outside after dinner. He could see her in the glow of their solar lamps. The lamps were mushroom shaped, and Mr. Fall said at one time they had been decorative. Trillium knew Coral was examining plastic, lining up pieces she might like to use tomorrow. She would feel better after she had done something, made some work. Trillium still wanted to think, still wanted to believe, that they all had a purpose, a higher calling, like her art.

The lights made orbs bounce off the crown of Coral's hair. He hadn't given her the present he had bought for her at the Strip with the leftover plastic, as Summer had suggested. What she really needed was a light, he realized. A headlamp. The kind men used to wear in the mines when they crawled on the ground and dug out coal, in these very hills that surrounded the junkyard. Before the land had sheltered the strip club and the acres of scrap, the hills had held minerals.

Maybe they still did, deep under the trees, and that was their secret. Dark riches waiting underground. But Trillium didn't think so. He was pretty sure his ancestors had taken it all out, used it all up. And not built enough roads. Or med centers. Not maintained them. When the floods came, power was knocked out easily to the places where the lights had always flickered, where the internet had never fully reached.

It was a piece of leather, folded slim, he had bought Coral. He had forgotten it, left it at the bottom of his pack, and then they had fought. It didn't seem like the right time to give it to her. Now it seemed like there never would be a right time, and he felt foolish for having gotten it. It was not what she needed, not what she would have chosen for herself.

He watched Coral from the windows of the bus. She had the pieces she wanted.

20

Coral

It was different when Shanghai was small. It was worse. There were more people alive, Coral thought, and they fought more. They fought over the little they had, which was not very much at all. Being so hungry, so tired, so hot and weak all the time, anything could set a person off. It was not unusual to see someone just bleeding. To walk by as an argument started up or as it escalated into men jumping to their feet, throwing objects, throwing fists. Coral learned to walk quickly.

It was not uncommon to see a dead body. She learned to see without seeing, to take in just enough to know to move on. *Don't think about it, don't think.* It wasn't remarkable enough even to tell Mr. Fall about at night, when they often had dinner cold so as not to alert strangers they had food.

I saw a body today. She wouldn't even say it. He would only say, "Oh?" Then he would say, "Do the ferns taste all right?"

"I don't like fiddleheads much," she would answer.

Then he would say, "Well, we can't be picky, can we?"

No, we couldn't be picky.

There was not much dairy. There was no meat. People foraged for roots, for nuts and berries, for the ferns, which curled into green fingers and had to be cooked well or they were poisonous. Some of the dead people Coral saw in those days had probably died from eating mushrooms or spoiled food. Mr. Fall had taught her to avoid cans with bulging sides. A small dent was fine. It likely meant the cans had just banged about. But dented outward meant a possible poison called *botulism*.

Once she had seen a severed human arm. She thought it was plastic at first, and reached for it. Then, as the movement of the river brought it closer, she realized her mistake and sprung away.

What's the matter? one of the men joked. *Water snake bite you?*

Some of the pluckers had been with their group, following Mr. Fall, for a long time—since they first boarded the bus, New Orleans said. But other men who joined later on weren't as loyal, weren't as kind.

Bones rested in river bottoms, but those were old, from the floods. If her fingers touched a smooth, slender thing, she knew what it was. She let it go, the bone drifting back to its grave.

Sometimes cans were buried in the grit, like the eggs of a creature. Mr. Fall was teaching Shanghai to fish, and between the two of them they would occasionally catch something, though the adults had to examine the catch carefully before figuring out if they could eat it. How big was the fish?

Bigger was usually out of the question. More flesh meant more time in which to harbor mercury. Frogs were certainly out, though Coral didn't see many of those.

For the most part, Mr. Fall said, they should leave the few living creatures of the woods and water alone. Let them have their chance, as we had had ours.

Coral and Shanghai would never know what *fresh* tasted like, Mr. Fall said. Crackers that crunched, cookies that fell to soft pieces in your mouth.

Water bottles ruined the world, Shanghai had said once. He lined the bottles up on a log and knocked them all down.

Do you remember bowling? Mr. Fall asked.

They did not.

In the Star-Glow camp, where all that was left of the drive-in theater was a sign and a graveyard of poles, Mr. Fall, Coral, and Shanghai lived near the rest of the pluckers. Being with a group made them a harder target, though it also meant sharing or hiding food. It meant noise, especially on those evenings when the pluckers had brought in a lot of plastic.

Excitement roared through the camp on those nights. Coral swore it had a smell: sweat, sour beer, and fire. She didn't sleep well, when the men had had a good day. She didn't trust them not to burn the whole camp down.

For a time, Mr. Fall had led the crew. That was when he had found Coral as a baby. He had taught her everything she knew: how to swim, how to search, what to look for. What plastic was good and what was not worth her risking it. More often than not, Coral wanted to risk it. Mr. Fall had to temper her excitement, urge her to be smart, as he did the whole crew, reminding them their lives were worth more than plastic.

But people died, they moved on. Other people came to the Star-Glow, other men. And soon there were more of the new people than the old, and they wanted a different leader of the crew, a younger man. One maybe not so careful, so cautious.

It's fine, Mr. Fall said. *I can get back to doing what I really love.*

Coral thought he *did* love pulling plastic out of the ground and out of the river. Finding treasure—and once, finding a tiny person.

But he seemed to be good at the other thing, too. Teaching. And children seemed to like it. Shanghai actually listened to Mr. Fall sometimes when he saw the big book come out, its pages wavy and worn as the river shore. The book was really several books, different volumes that covered different topics. But because the books all looked the same—hardback leather covers, with fancy gold pages and chipped gold lettering on the spines—as a child, Coral had thought it was only one book: a single magical volume which contained new stories each time they opened it. Mr. Fall liked that.

Sit down a spell, Mr. Fall would say, and Shanghai often did.

Coral met Trillium there, at the Star-Glow.

He, like others, had come to sell. Peddlers and con artists, healers and midwives, sex workers and cooks came there. It gave the camp what Mr. Fall called a *carnival atmosphere.* Along with the noise, the camp felt bright all the time, from the fires and the blazing solar lamps, colored bulbs strung along the tents.

Trillium came one day with his sign and his tools. He made poke tattoos, pricking skin with an inked needle. It was what he could carry with him. When she asked why he had chosen their camp, why the Star-Glow—he said he didn't know. He couldn't remember making the decision, exactly. He just wanted to go somewhere.

Mr. Fall had risen to greet the new man when he approached them. Evening crept down from the hills, and the lights around the camp flickered on. Mr. Fall said they weren't either of them interested in tattoos—Shanghai was much too young and thankfully, already asleep, because he probably would have begged for one—but the stranger was welcome to share their fire.

It was how he greeted most who might wander over, starving or lonely, lured by the bus's big shape. Trillium was the first who had come this close in a long time. And Trillium was different. When it became clear that Coral and Trillium were going to do most of the talking, Mr. Fall reclined on the ground away from them. He had a bit of plastic in his mouth, a straw he gnawed on, as he stared into the fire.

"You came to the camp for business, not a chance for love?" Coral had teased.

"Well, I've been lonely," Trillium said. "Who isn't, when they're alone? But I don't think…you can't think you're going to meet someone. Then you never will."

Trillium had had a love. She was gone. Not dead, though maybe she was by now. She had decided to start new with someone else. There was nothing legally binding her and Trillium, after all. They had not even inked their hands. They had not had children. It did not seem right to have children. He had faltered, saying this to Coral. He regretted it, from the look on his face.

"No, it's all right," she reassured him. "No one in their right mind would have a child now."

"It sounds like you were just a child yourself."

"My mind wasn't grown yet."

"You didn't know," he insisted. He admitted he had heard the story about her and the whale, from the drunk men who wanted tattoos.

"Well, stories don't feed us," she said. "Stories don't ensure Mr. Fall a position."

"My position is fine!" Mr. Fall said from the ground beside the fire.

"You're barely paid. You do all that work—and the parents barely feed you."

"They pay what they can. It's not about that. It's about taking care of the future."

"It's about dinnertime when there isn't any food," Coral said.

"Don't you want future generations to know how to read, know their history? Don't you want Shanghai to know? How can children change the future, unless they know what happened before?" He spoke facing the fire, as if it was a speech he was practicing.

Coral turned back to Trillium. "I'm sorry," she whispered.

"It's all right."

"He gets like this. It's the same debate we have over and over. What's right versus what we need to survive. We've been thinking about trying a new winter camp. Trashlands? Have you heard of it?"

Trillium hadn't.

"They placed an ad in a newspaper, looking for a teacher. They said they can pay."

"What is he to you? Your father?"

"As good as. The only parent I have. Do you have anyone left?"

"No," Trillium said.

It wasn't that she felt sorry for Trillium. It was true, she
didn't like to think of him alone, sleeping with his bag of
tools rolled under his arm, on the cold ground. He said he
had already lost one pair of boots to thieves in the night. He
had awoken another time to a man stroking his face. He had
no idea why; the man had taken off when Trillium stirred.
Coral already didn't like to think of Trillium suffering—
but that was because she liked him. She was drawn to him.
When he left, that first night, to sleep alone wherever he
was making his solitary camp in the Star-Glow field, she
felt his absence. She wanted him back.

She turned to Mr. Fall. He had not moved much. Only
the embers of the fire glowed now. "Mr. Fall," Coral said.
"Do you think Shanghai wants a man in his life? Other than
you, I mean?"

"Not really," Mr. Fall said. "But you might."

It was different than Robert had been, when she had been
young, so young, in the icehouse. Trillium asked Coral before they did anything. To walk with her, to talk with her,
to touch her hand, to kiss her. Mr. Fall liked that Trillium
asked if he could go with her to the river that ran through
the valley behind the hills, if he could join their fire at night.

Mr. Fall liked Trillium in a way that felt easy to Coral.
The men seemed close in age. They remembered some,
though not all, of the same things: for instance, drinking
cow's milk. Trillium remembered glass bottles distributed
by volunteers. Mr. Fall remembered cartons, children's pic-

tures printed on them. He had heard stories about it, if he hadn't seen it himself. Trillium didn't remember that part.

"Why children?" he had asked.

"They were lost," Mr. Fall said.

Looking back, Coral felt she should have known. She should have guessed something was about to go wrong. She was happy for the first time in what felt like forever, hopeful—but that remark about the lost children stuck in her brain. Something bad was going to happen.

Trillium started waiting for her at the bus every morning. He would walk her to the river, if she said yes. Mr. Fall rose first to start the fire, so Coral got used to waking to the sound of the two men talking quietly outside.

She stirred, waking Shanghai beside her. The boy bounded out of the bus. No matter how quietly she moved, he would hear—he would not let her wake without him. Coral rose more slowly. The air always felt freezing, the blankets furry with ice. Even though this was their place of refuge during colder times, a warmer place to shelter, it was still so cold. Everything was intense and unpredictable: two unrelenting seasons that simply blurred into each other after heavy, transitional rain.

Plucking was the best and worst after these rains. Plastic filled the world when the water receded, bags hanging in trees, water bottles topping the fence posts still standing.

But after the rain was when you would see the bodies.

In trees or on rooftops, floating facedown in a puddle that didn't seem deep enough to drown. Often the water was so powerful, surging above the riverbanks, it pulled the clothes right off the bodies. Most of the naked men Coral had seen had been dead.

Snow still fell at the Star-Glow, a lot of it. Mr. Fall had to dig to find roots for them to eat. Coral had to crack the ice crust of the river, and her hands when she drew them up were aching and red. The squirrels in their traps grew thin.

Then Trillium started coming to the bus before Mr. Fall even woke. Trillium brought kindling and bread. He knelt in the predawn and coaxed the fire alone in the cold while Mr. Fall went to the window to look.

"That is a good man," Mr. Fall said to Coral.

Shanghai had never asked about his father.

Many children did not have one. A woman and a child—or two or four—was the most common family unit. Coral had Mr. Fall. But most people did not have their fathers with them, or a man willing to be one.

Sometimes children drifted on their own to a woman. It was tough on her, if she didn't want their reaching hands—their warm bodies, desperate from nightmares, curling against her in the night. But usually, women just gave in. It was easier to put up with children by your fire than to force them out. They could be destructive, especially the ones who had been on their own for too long. Coral had heard of children rolling over a car. She had herself witnessed children beat a man who had tried to take away one of their sisters. They drew blood, going for his eyes first.

She had had her own run-in with the motherless, when Shanghai was not yet walking. Mr. Fall was away on one of his last plucking trips. She wore the baby wrapped on her chest, and she guessed the children thought: well, she still has arms. Maybe the children thought her weak, so recently split in half by the birth of her baby and by his father leaving. Children started hanging around the bus, begging and grabbing at her legs or hair, when they smelled the cook fire—and it was that Coral used to threaten them. She couldn't take on more children, more crying, more hanging on her body. More of them, less of her; she had so little left.

She reached into the fire—Shanghai asleep on her chest—and pulled out a branch half in flames. She waved it. The children leapt out of the way. *You don't come here at night*, she hissed at them. *You can come during the day to learn. That's it. You don't live here. I am not your mother. I am not your mother.*

The children stayed away after that. New ones to the camp were warned by the others: the old man will watch out for you in the day, but that red bitch? You stay away.

Most of the mouths fed themselves. They had learned to, early.

Men didn't come around, like the children. Mr. Fall was the one who kept men at bay. He was friendly, but intimidating. It was strange that Trillium wasn't scared off by him. Mr. Fall was a tall man, slender but strong with the muscles of their life's work, stronger than his years—and anyway, any man who lived to be almost sixty (they thought) was tough indeed. Was really not to be messed with.

But Trillium was gentle. Trillium was quiet. Trillium, when Shanghai leapt from the bus, barreling at him, put up with the hug that nearly knocked him off his feet. Trillium tried to teach the boy how to coax a fire, gave him lessons about making and using ink. But Shanghai wandered away, bored, or got frustrated and angry, lashing out at Trillium, spilling the ink. More than once the boy had kicked and scratched him, making gashes that took time to heal. Coral had the same marks.

Trillium was patient with the boy even though he did not want children. Coral had asked him about it directly one morning when they walked to the river. "Is Shanghai why you're here, spending time with us?"

"No," Trillium said. He seemed surprised at the question. "I'm here for you."

"I mean, do you want more like him? More children?"

"I never did."

"But me having Shanghai already...?" She trailed off.

"It's just part of you. Part of your life. There are hard parts and easy parts, just like anyone's life."

"I don't want more children," Coral said, loud enough that a plucker walking ahead turned around to look at them.

"No," Trillium said. She wondered if he was thinking about the violence, the scratches beneath her sleeves. "I don't imagine you would."

21

Trillium

Trillium had learned tattooing from a man in the tent city, a man who was covered head to toe in ink, so much that at first Trillium thought there was something wrong with the man's skin, that he had been burned by the sun or a fire. The tattoos crowded together, one long speckled rash that made his skin look green. It was only when Trillium crept close that he was able to pick out the knife, the snake, the heart in flames.

Most of the tattoos were old and faded. The man had done them himself. Out of boredom, he told Trillium, to commemorate people or places or moments in his life. But also, he said, he had done them as advertising. *Tattooing is the only job you wear*, he told Trillium, a boy still full of childhood stories and his daddy's beatings and not much else.

They did not have enough to eat in the tent city. There

was also no privacy. Trillium could walk right up and watch the man poke a dark, careful image into another man's thigh.

What was the first tattoo you saw being made? Coral had once asked Trillium.

It was a rose.

Then he was hooked. He spent most days watching the man. There was nothing else to do. There was no school, and there was danger everywhere. Men who would grab you. Hunger and hurt. Trillium saw his first dead bodies in the tent city: children who had starved, old men who had been left where they lay. The bodies were naked because people would strip them. Even then, shoes went first.

Initially annoyed, and then grudgingly appreciative of Trillium's attention, the man began to show him tattooing. He laid out his tools, told Trillium how he conjured ink from the few materials available to him, those he could barter for, forage, or buy.

He made ink from clay, from motor oil dripping from abandoned cars, from pulverized rocks—jobs he soon made Trillium do, along with making tattoo needles, which involved sticking sewing or hypodermic needles in an eraser, wrapping the ends in string, then disinfecting the needles with fire. Most of the man's tattooing was done with these sticks. The hardest part was finding clean, unbroken needles.

One day the man hurt himself. Gathering materials in the muddy fields, he slipped. His wrist twisted and snapped. There were medics in the camp then, and they set the broken bone, wrapping it in a kind of gluey cloth that hardened. But the man couldn't work. It was his dominant hand. And without tattoos, he couldn't eat.

Trillium did his first tattoo: an arrow on a woman.

He was nervous. She wanted it on the top side of her hand, the bony ridge where her veins and tendons seemed especially close. She wanted the arrow pointing toward her middle finger. *To remind me to tell the world to fuck off,* she said. Trillium knew already that the places on the body with less flesh hurt more: the thinner spots, closer to bone. He was afraid to tell her this.

He needn't have worried.

Good, she said, when Trillium explained to her about the bony places, the man cursing at him and yelling directions from his cot where he lay within earshot of the transaction. Trillium tried to ignore him. *I* want *it to hurt,* the woman said.

That was when Trillium had first begun to learn the mysteries of love.

Anyone could want anything. However many people there were still left in the world, there were twice as many wants, desires—and he could provide those to people in a safe way, in a way that kept him fed and out of harm. This was it, he had thought, bending over the woman with a needle dripping ink. He had found his way to survive.

He began to practice. Not on himself. Strangely enough, Trillium had no tattoos. The art was not like that, he decided. It would not serve to be selfish. He practiced on trees, on bits of boards that would wash up in the stream, on the prickled flesh of old oranges distributed by volunteers in the tent city, when they still had volunteers. Oranges that he would later eat, though the man said this was a waste of ink and also, unhealthy. If Trillium was to put the ink into people's bodies, he might as well put it in his own, he thought. He might as well eat it.

When he had told this part of the story, Coral had said, well, she would eat the oranges too. They were still fruit, still food. She had not seen oranges in a long time. She was starting to forget their bright taste.

Trillium began to look for other images to tattoo. Many times people would want a flower or an animal they missed in the world, but couldn't quite recall. But often Trillium didn't know the image either. He had never seen an ocelot, an orchid, or a polar bear—and he had seen a jet plane only at a great distance: a streak in the sky, headed by a gray dot.

He began to search for art to imitate, to learn from. Decades, he estimated, before seeing Mr. Fall's book, he studied what he could, like the safety instruction manuals the volunteers had passed out when he first arrived at the tent city, which were soon being used as fans and sun hats. Manuals patched the holes of their tents. The holes widened, as the days stretched on, and people lived in a place that was not supposed to be permanent, that was only meant to be a waystation after disaster.

But there did not seem to be a next station.

The safety manuals looked old. They were made out of a slick material that seemed to be not exactly plastic and not exactly paper. They gave directions on hygiene and food preparation and how to evacuate homes, which people no longer had, should they have to leave again in a hurry, owing to a *large-scale climate calamity*. Also: how to evacuate a jet plane, which people no longer had access to at all.

That particular manual, the jet plane one, was one of the first folded into bowls and plates. It seemed particularly worthless. It featured pictures of people in colorful clothes that did not look like outfits Trillium recognized: jackets with boxy shoulders, bags that were square. The tattooed man said these pictures had been drawn by a computer. Still, Trillium found them useful in practicing faces. Sometimes people wanted him to tattoo images of loved ones they had lost. They tried to describe these people. They never had pictures.

Trillium made them all look like the people from the safety instruction manuals. The woman putting on her oxygen mask before her child's, the child swimming in the yellow vest, the man opening the window of the jet plane to throw it into the sky.

Trillium began to get a reputation. He was better than the tattooed man, calmer, more careful with his lines. None of his tattoos got infected. He never poked too deep. The man's wrist healed, but it made no difference. Trillium, barely more than a child, had his fans.

The man drove Trillium away from his tent and refused to help him, to teach him anymore, or to lend him needles or ink. It was around this time that Trillium became separated from his daddy. Weather came to the tent city—but it wasn't floods, as they had all expected, like before.

It was a tornado.

That was the thing about the world: you could no longer predict it. You could no longer assume you could take from it what you had always taken—water and energy and shelter and food—and expect it would not ask you for anything in return. That deal was off the table.

The Earth had taken its shitty trade arrangement back.

Trillium didn't like to talk about this time. He knew Coral was not even exactly sure what had happened to him in the tent city, only a storm. *He* was not exactly sure what had happened.

There was a green cloud, the color of illness. A roar like a machine. The wind blew away the tents, blew a truck down the road. The people Trillium had lived with, sleeping in tents, in cots side by side, ran for the ditches. They waited out the rain, the wind that tore any words from their mouths, any crying, any prayers.

After the wind and rain, the people walked for a long time along a road because it was there and mostly solid beneath their feet. Unspeaking, they walked as if in a trance.

And after a while, Trillium veered off. He left the people he had lived beside, the others he barely knew. His daddy was not among them, not anywhere. Trillium went into the woods for no reason. He just wanted to stop walking.

He was not sure if anyone from his past was alive, not his daddy, not his teacher, not the woman to whom he had given the arrow tattoo. But there were many ways of dying, of disappearing from the world, from who you thought you were. You didn't come back from any of them.

22

Coral

Sometimes she was too tired to notice how shitty everything was. In the dark, it was easy to just glide by the messy countertops, the doors patched with cardboard and the windows smeared with grease. She could even forget the smell at night.

But in the morning, there it was again.

Mr. Fall said the bus perpetually smelled of cat food, which was strange because they hadn't found any in years. The sun through the holes in their curtains was unforgiving, alighting upon the dirt-speckled silverware, the dust clumps on the floor.

The floor tilted, which you realized when you stood. Mr. Fall had parked the bus on an incline, years ago, though every now and then he started it up, to make sure the engine still ran and to clear the pipes, he said. And though he would back the bus up and do a lap or two around the outskirts of the junkyard to ensure the tires still held—he kept reparking in the same dimpled spot. They had worn a hole in the hillside.

In the morning, Coral could see the jumble of Trillium's inks. The rags left where they fell. Nobody dusted or swept anymore. Why bother? Lint clustered in the corners of the bus, little universes. When Coral swung her feet out of bed, she felt grit.

The floor was cold, which meant snows were coming. She brushed the plastic off the soles of her feet, and slipped them into boots too big for her; she and Trillium both used them. When Coral wore the boots, she stuffed the toes with plastic bags. They crunched against her toes in her threadbare socks as she stepped out into the air. A white film, somewhere between dew and frost, covered the grass.

She was up before Trillium. It was the interim hour at Trashlands. Dancers were sweeping up at the club, refilling the beer tubs. Tahiti was probably catching a few hours of sleep. Nobody tried anything at dawn.

Mr. Fall's spot under the bus was empty. Coral didn't understand why he didn't just move in with Summer full-time— but she didn't understand why Tahiti and Foxglove didn't just talk to each other about their feelings, either. She didn't understand much about love.

Really, she didn't understand anything about it, she thought as she went for the kindling box, stashed under a truck shell half-buried in the hillside. Trillium had traded a lifetime of tattoos for the truck shell. It was a good trade, it turned out, because the man who had wanted tattoos forever had died not long after making the deal.

Later, the man's wife came to Mr. Fall to learn how to read. If she harbored malice for her man making such a careless decision, trading away good plastic and metal for tattoos, she didn't show it.

Coral shouldn't think of tattoos as foolish. Trillium thought of them as art that came to life. And he would never criticize one of her pieces—and they were the most temporary things in the world, left in the woods or on the river shores, to be washed away or destroyed.

She thought of how much she liked to watch Trillium work, and how often she wasn't there when he did it. She didn't want to bother him, get in his way. But when he tattooed, his hands in his gloves looked stronger, younger somehow. There was something desirous, mysterious, in that line where rubber met flesh. Lines crossed Trillium's face, though not as many as on Mr. Fall. Soft skin hung from his arms and sides. His hair was turning silver. He had a scar in his eyebrow, thin lips he drew together.

It was fine, Coral tried to tell herself, as the kindling caught fire, that she didn't know exactly how Trillium felt about her at the moment. There were gaps that surrounded him like mist, like he was only half there, half with her even when he stood beside her.

But Trillium didn't know a lot about her, either.

How it had begun with Robert. How she had felt about her teacher's long glances: glowing and confused. How cold the icehouse had been. How she had felt when he left her, like the floor under her feet had buckled, soft with decay, giving out.

How she had known she was pregnant: a fever.

What she had wanted and been afraid to do.

Trillium had never asked too many details; most women had children in tow. Coral didn't even like to say Robert's name and Trillium just followed her example. They didn't talk about it. They both understood that behind silence there was pain.

She understood that he filled the pain with art. He hunted it everywhere, with a thirst. He collected bits of images torn from books or packaging. Those images he couldn't take with him, like road signs, he memorized. He dreamed tattoos, he said, and spent his days working to make them better. He wanted to make the ink last longer, be safer, more vivid. Black stained his fingertips, as if he had lost them to frost.

For Coral, art was not like that at all, she thought.

One morning before Trillium came into their lives, she found a big orange rubber ball that had deflated in a field. It looked too wasted to be useful, a hole in the center, gouged out like a pumpkin. She used plastic sticks to scrape away a bit of mud to see if the ball might look better cleaned up. It didn't. But once she was done poking at the muck, she just left the sticks in. She placed another stick.

No, that wasn't right. An impulse told her to do it differently.

She took the stick back, folded it. It was thin, bendy plastic. Probably a straw. She found them floating in the river like ferns. She folded it again. She looked at the thing. She had made a star.

She placed it in the center of the ball. It looked both like it belonged there and strange at the same time. Random but not wrong. Just surprising. Nothing grew in the field but weeds. Nothing drifted in the ditch before it. The ditch smelled like death, as they always did.

Then there was the ball with the star in it.

What would she have thought, if she had come across it? She would have been delighted, she decided. Someone had taken the time to make this—and then just left it. They never left supplies. Muddy plastic could be cleaned. Bent plastic reshaped. Take more than you need, that was the rule. More than you thought you could carry. You were stronger than you knew. You might not know the use of a thing, you might not be able to imagine its potential—but that was not your job. Your job was to gather and bring it all home.

That was what Mr. Fall had taught her. She was relatively young—her eyes were still good, unlike his. Soon, she knew, she would have to scavenge for them both. If they ate, it would be because of something *she* brought home, something she got to first.

In the time she had spent in the field, staring at the orange ball, other pluckers had ventured farther. She saw New Orleans knee-deep in mud, lifting something out of the weeds, a blue tube called a *pool noodle*. Others had drifted into the trees, hoping to strike treasure.

She looked again at the thing she had made.

What would she call it?

She didn't tell Mr. Fall. She kept it to herself. She did other structures.

Not every day. She made pieces when they struck her, when they all but declared themselves. A bit of clear packaging small and curved. A length of wire curled up tight. She created when she felt the plastic she found wouldn't be missed, couldn't be used for anything else. She did it when she was alone, when she saw an opportunity. And, she began to learn, she did it when she had a bad day.

When the sun beat down. When everything in the camp smelled like rot, especially the people, and mud stuck to their boots and legs until it dried and flaked, and then the mud became another problem, the problem of choking dust. When she had seen someone dying or dead. When the camp had lost someone, especially a child.

Making helped her feel better. She knew that.

She had done maybe a dozen secret pieces when Mr. Fall came home and announced he had found something.

Coral was in the bus, wasting water from the jug to wash her face. Her eyes felt stung from squinting in the light. She let the water drip over her cheeks, feeling the tiniest prickle of plastic.

Shanghai burst through the bus doors. "What's for dinner?"

"Well, what did you find?"

He was skinny, all angles, knees that were always bruised, feet that were always bruising. Hair so blond it looked white. And eyes like his father's. Coral hated to think it, but it was true. She might not have even remembered what Robert had looked like, she told herself, except every day Shanghai became more and more his ghost. Wide-set eyes, high cheekbones, not at all like her own round face. He hadn't inherited her hair, either.

Sometimes she wondered if there was anything at all of her in him. She didn't see it. Maybe it would reveal itself later, when he was grown. The midwife said children changed so much.

"Chicken mushrooms," Shanghai said.

"Chicken of the woods?"

"The orange ones."

"Those are great. They taste so filling. We'll fry them up."

Mr. Fall stepped onto the bus. "You'll never guess what we saw today."

"Chicken of the woods. Shanghai told me."

"No. Something else. At the edge of the trees, by the bathhouse. There was a shrine."

"What's a shrine?" Shanghai said.

Coral smoothed her son's hair and gently pushed away his hands. He was climbing all over her. He was too old for that; he was heavy and it hurt. "I don't know. You're the one who saw it." His elbow jabbed her leg. "Ow."

At the small sound of protest from her, something flipped on Shanghai's face. "You hate me!" He stood up and shoved her. "You hate me!"

"No, sweetie."

He shoved again, then kicked at her. He began to huff, his skin reddening. The whites of his eyes widened, roving until they alighted on the curtains and he yanked them from the rods. He was panting. *Hate me, hate me.*

"Stop," Coral said. "Please." She felt torn between protecting herself and putting her arms around him.

Shanghai kicked the side of the bus. Mr. Fall took off his hat and fell silent. When the child got upset, Mr. Fall said he didn't know what to do. He said children had good days and bad days. But more and more, every day seemed to be bad for Shanghai. There would come a moment like this where his mood tipped into destruction, into fury, and Coral was never sure why. What had she said, what had she done to make him so angry? How could she bring him back?

This time she tried deflecting. "What did you see exactly?" she asked Mr. Fall.

He said, "It was like a plastic house, what we used to call an A-frame, only very small. As if for dolls. Inside was a swing made of straws." He shouted this last bit to be heard over Shanghai, twisting the curtains so tightly his fingers turned bloodless.

"Shanghai!" Coral tried to think. "I bet you can't catch crickets?"

"You hate me! You hate me!"

"It's a contest," she tried.

His eyes didn't seem to recognize her.

"Look!" Coral pointed to the window, where three insects crawled across the pane, exposed by the ruined curtains. "Stink bugs. We can eat them too. They taste like apples."

That was it today, the sentence that worked. The anger passed, flushing out of his face. He relaxed his hands and dropped the fabric. "That's disgusting." he said, crinkling up his nose. And he was a child again, incapable of hurting her, though her shins where he had lashed out told a different story. He was getting stronger.

"Apples are good," Coral said. "Even when they're bugs." He grinned. Tears shone on his face. Mr. Fall just stood there and watched, his hat in his hands. "Go out and grind some flour, then. There are acorns in a basket."

Shanghai veered to the doors, flying so fast it made her dizzy. When he was almost out of the bus, she called, "I love you."

He jumped down the steps and didn't answer.

Mr. Fall pulled up the chair next to Coral. "We don't need flour."

"I just wanted him to go outside. I thought fresh air might help."

"It seems to, sometimes. Are you all right?"

"As all right as I ever am. Is he all right?"

"He's fine," Mr. Fall said. As much as he loved her, as much as he loved both of them, Coral knew he refused to have to face Shanghai's moods, the striking out, the quick shifts in temper, though Coral was still breathing hard, though her skin throbbed with a bruise. "He's just a child."

"I made that thing you saw in the woods," Coral said.

"The dollhouse?"

"That's not what it is."

"What is it, then?"

She couldn't explain herself. She didn't know what to say. "It was scrap. Plastic we weren't going to use."

"That's fine," Mr. Fall said. "Don't worry about the plastic. But why did you make that little house?"

"I don't know."

"Why did you leave it there? Do you want me to bring it back?"

"No."

"Back to the bus? Shanghai and I could carry it, real carefully."

"No," Coral repeated.

Mr. Fall looked at her. It hurt to see him not understand. But how could she explain it? She didn't understand herself. "If you leave it in the woods, it'll get destroyed," Mr. Fall said. "Someone will trample it, or take it apart and use the plastic. It looks like you spent a lot of time on it."

"I did," Coral said softly.

"You're just going to give it away?"

"I guess so."

Mr. Fall got up from the table. Coral knew he wasn't going to yell at her. He never yelled. She had wasted plastic, but old, cheap pieces that probably couldn't be used for much. She had wasted time, that was all. He rested his hands on the chair back.

They had made that chair, Coral and Mr. Fall, from shower curtain rods and a rubber lid. It was comfortable, if unsteady. "This is your thing," Mr. Fall said.

"What is?"

"You make art and you give it away."

"It wasn't..." Coral faltered. "It's not art. I don't know what art is. I mean, from your book—I know that. But those are paintings. Those are sculptures. They were famous."

"There are many kinds of art," Mr. Fall said. "Maybe you just discovered the art of the future. Maybe you're making it."

"It was just something to do. I don't know why I did it."

"That's perfect." He lifted his finger and she could picture him teaching; she could imagine him standing in front of students, coming up with an idea, or reacting with support and excitement to something some child said. "That is what makes it your thing. You don't know why you do it. You just have to. You just do."

"No," Coral said. She was not sure why she was resisting. Only that she felt that the work she had done in the woods was hers alone. It was private. She hadn't wanted anyone to know, let alone try to figure it out. "Plucking is my thing. Having a child is."

Mr. Fall waved that away. "Plucking is a job. We do it to

live. We do it because it's better than robbing. It's not a calling. Neither is motherhood."

"What's a calling?"

"It's what you did in the woods, Coral."

No, she didn't understand anything about art—or love,
she thought as she trudged to the river. Her leg still ached
below the stitches. She imagined she would have a scar. Trillium slept on in the bus behind her. And if Miami showed up
there, Trillium would send him away. She doubted Miami
would arrive before the sun was high. Men stayed up late at
Trashlands. Miami was no different.

He was not special, she told herself.

She was the first to the river. Nothing had washed up
on the shore. The tree branches, low to the water, held no
plastic bags, tattered as ghosts. It was time to wade in. She
checked her boots, hoped the patches would hold. Cold
water could kill you. Wet socks could kill you. Sometimes
Coral remembered little things from a past she was not even
sure was her own. If rabbits get wet, they can die. Had she
read that, in Mr. Fall's book?

Into the water. The current flowed swiftly. The water
looked brown but not frothy. It was cool, it didn't burn. It
had no smell today. Coral's gloves were sewn from other
gloves. She pulled them on. Everyone used to have masks,
but those had fallen to bits.

She lowered her hands into the water, unfolded her net,
sweeping it through the current. Water rushed through her
fingers. She felt the occasional tug or resistance which meant
plastic had snagged on the net. She walked forward against
the river flow, weaving her net through the water. It was

hard work that required constant bending. If he hadn't returned to teaching, Mr. Fall would have gotten too old for
it. The work aged you fast. Already, Coral felt a bright star
of pain in her back.

She straightened, lifting her net. It felt light, but that didn't
mean anything; good plastic could be light. She waded back,
but misjudged the depth, sliding into a hole in the river bottom. Before she could move, water had rushed over the top
of her boot. Back on the shore, she sat on a rock and took it
off, dumping out the water and stripping off her wet sock.

"Find anything?" New Orleans stood on the bank, peering down on her.

"Not yet." Coral smacked her sock against a tree.

"Someone's looking for you."

Now she looked up. "A man?"

"Yes."

"Tell him to wait. I'm working."

"You tell him," New Orleans said. The sun blazed, and
Coral could make out a silhouette, as if the person who stood
behind New Orleans had broken off from the sun. "He just
tagged along." Quickly, New Orleans splashed downstream.
He didn't want to be part of this talk.

Coral looked back at the sock in her hand.

"What happened?" Miami climbed down to her. "Did
you get hurt?"

"No," Coral said. "Just wet."

"Getting pretty cold for that."

"Occupational hazard."

"Where did you hear that phrase?" He answered himself.
"Mr. Fall's books, of course."

"Where did you learn the phrases and words you use?"

"Well, the schooling I had. My newspaper. And other papers."

"There's more than one paper?" She had only ever seen one over the years. But thinking about it, maybe they had been different, just with the same kind of name. *Herald. Courier. News. Times.*

A look came over Miami's face, surprise crossed with something else, maybe sadness. "There are lots of cities still standing," he said. "Not just the one I live in. Cities with newspapers. And more cities forming all the time. New buildings, schools."

"This is my city," Coral said, spreading her arms to indicate the bank, the river of plastic. "My city of Trashlands."

"You could live in a city if you wanted," Miami said.

"You don't even know if your apartment is going to be there when you get back."

"They're holding my job for me. Expecting me to return. And if something were to happen, there are other apartments. Other places to live, like I said. You deserve more than this."

Coral laid her sock across her knee. River weeds had tangled in her net. She could see their tendrils, dark and slimy. It was just weeds she had caught. "I don't think we get more. I think people like you and me..." She paused. "People like *me*, we don't get that many chances. This is my life. This is it."

"It feels like you're trying to convince yourself."

Coral felt something rise up inside her. She was not sure how to name the emotion filling her chest. It was anger, outrage, shame. He had no right to tell her about her life—he had barely glimpsed it. He hardly even knew her. And yet, she felt the nagging pull of a different emotion, too: small but powerful. Doubt. Like the hand of a child.

What if he was right?

"I'm fine," Coral said. "You're interrupting my work."

Downstream in the river, New Orleans whooped. He had found a shoe.

"I can't leave," she said.

"But what if you go get your son, right now?"

"It's not that easy."

"I can find the money. We can look for a car—"

"*He's* not that easy, all right? He was never easy. What if he doesn't want to come back? What if he doesn't want me?"

What did he know, this man on the bank? What could he ever guess of motherhood? The hurt of her son, losing him— but even before losing him, the hurt of never really having him, never knowing how to help him, how to help herself.

Shanghai ignored her then lashed out at her. He ran to her, then screamed to get away from her. He was difficult, angry, loving, confusing. He could switch as quickly as the weather, cycle through emotions, come to her for comfort, hurt her bad. She still had scars on her arms and legs from his nails, his teeth.

She had been afraid of him. She missed him every day.

"You have no idea what it's like," Coral said. "Having a child. It's not like you think it is."

It was not like it seemed to be for others: a child who didn't run from her, who didn't yell, who didn't bite and scream and hurt people and himself. Those mothers, when their children were carried away by the collectors, they wept. Coral wept too, but partially, guiltily, on some level, from relief.

Another man was coming down the bank to the river. He moved cautiously, putting out his hands to navigate. It was Mr. Fall.

When had he started to move this way? As if just walking hurt him? How had she not noticed? The hair on his head had been gone for a long time—but what were those dark spots?

"Coral," he called. "Summer told me. You found where Shanghai is?"

"We think so," Coral said. Her chest trembled from raising her voice to Miami. Blood beat hot in her ears. If she stood up, she felt her body would not be able to hold her.

"And the price?"

"It doesn't matter. We can't pay it. We don't have it."

"But, Coral," her father said. "I do. I've had it here, all these years."

"A running car?" Miami asked.

Mr. Fall didn't even pause. "Coral," he said. "The bus."

23

Foxglove

The new girl sucked.

From the side of the stage, Foxglove watched her. She tilted her hips, not even a shimmy. She barely had any hips *to* shimmy. The silver shorts Summer had made her were sliding right off, and in a saggy way, not a sexy way. She couldn't even get through that basic move of a hip thrust with a straight face. Her expression collapsed into laughing panic. She covered her awful teeth with her hand.

From the front row, the men laughed.

Fuck them.

The song ended, and in the skip before it began again, the girl raced offstage, not even waving to the men, who didn't clap for her. She tripped over her shoes, and Foxglove took her by the elbow. She felt like she was pulling the girl up from the river.

"You're really bad at this." Foxglove yanked one, two

credit cards from the girl's shorts. That was it. Her only tips for the set.

"Hey," Joshua Tree said. "Those are mine."

"They're my fee for housing you. And nothing is yours. Don't you know that yet? Not even this." She pressed her hand on the girl's stomach. "Your body isn't yours. Your home isn't yours. And this plastic—" she waved it at the girl "—definitely isn't yours."

Joshua Tree took a step back. "You don't have to be so mean."

"I'm not even supposed to be working right now." Foxglove slipped the credit cards into her own halter top. They didn't look like much, but they could be used to jimmy open doors. They could be used as knives. The edges were sharp enough; someone could make them sharper. "I'm here as a favor."

"For me?"

"For Summer. Who asked me. And who for some reason believes in you."

"Summer's nice."

"Well, don't get any ideas that she can mother you because she's busy as hell. *I've* got to fucking mother you." She hiked up the girl's shorts and adjusted her bra. It was made from two tiny plastic cups. The cups had square bottoms and ridged sides. Mr. Fall said they had been used for coffee.

Foxglove tried to imagine using one of those tiny cups each morning, then throwing it away. Every day throwing it away. The trash disappearing into the ground. The cups never ending.

Now the cups barely covered the girl called Joshua Tree— a forgettable name. She was going to have to change it. Foxglove studied the girl's hair. Mousy, thin. "Look," Foxglove said. "What are you selling here?"

The girl thought.

"It's not a hard question."

"Fantasy? Myself?"

"That's right. And what's the appeal of you? What makes you different, more special than anyone else? Why should someone spend his hard-earned plastic on you?" This was a difficult question, but Foxglove was impressed. Joshua Tree got it.

"I'm new," the girl said.

"That's right. And that'll work for a time, depending on how many regulars we get. But then you've got to come up with something else. Some other reason men should want you."

"What do *you* have?" the girl asked. "What makes you special?"

Once Foxglove was new and once she was young. That made her special for a time. But not long. Other dancers had to tell her everything: what the blood was, why it started, why it stopped.

Her belly grew before her breasts did. She didn't understand; Rattlesnake Master had to tell her. He was not as patient a teacher as Mr. Fall would be. Summer explained it more to Foxglove. People hadn't believed who Summer was at first, which didn't make sense to Foxglove; Summer was just a woman, that was just who she always was. She taught Foxglove how to take care of herself and what grew inside her. She brought the girl more to eat, rationing from her own supply or bartering. She reminded Foxglove to drink water, to stay away from the fruit piss and the pills that seemed to be everywhere.

Summer was there to hold her hand when the pain came. One of the bodyguards went for Ramalina, the first woman Foxglove had met at Trashlands who didn't dance onstage. Foxglove hadn't even known Ramalina existed, that there was a healer in the camp. It was not an option she had understood: that a girl or woman could be something other than a body, moving for the pleasure of men.

Rattlesnake Master said he paid Ramalina and the guards extra not to tell anyone about the baby. Summer didn't have to be bribed—she refused. But the baby, when he came, was not a baby, not in the way the women had patiently explained to her.

Foxglove thought she had felt him moving before, inside her. She had thought she heard him whispering to her, telling her secrets at night while she slept, fitfully, on the couch in the back office. But when she woke she couldn't remember what he was trying to say.

Now she would never know.

Her baby was born silent and still, and Ramalina was going to take him away. She insisted Foxglove look at him first. Foxglove had shaken her head no, she didn't want to see. This wasn't him, this wasn't right.

But Summer said gently, "If you don't do it now, you'll regret it. He doesn't look bad. He looks sweet, like you."

And he did. Summer was right. He wasn't torn or broken. Something must have happened to break him, but you couldn't tell at all. He just slept. He slept forever. His eyelids were closed. She touched them and they were soft. She would never know the color of his eyes; they would never open. Was that the secret he had been trying to tell her in her dreams on the couch? Or was he trying to warn her?

He could not stay.

They let her hold him for a long time. Summer and a bodyguard kept Rattlesnake Master and the other men away. The music of Trashlands pounded behind the door. Beyond the curtain, drinks and drugs were sold, deals made. Girls danced onstage. They would dance forever, the music a fist at Foxglove's back. She had stained the office couch with her blood. And that would be there forever too, a stain like a blooming flower: a foxglove. And Foxglove would never sleep there—or with Rattlesnake Master—again. After that night, she would have her own trailer. Summer and Ramalina demanded it.

Finally Ramalina had come for the baby. This time Foxglove didn't want to let him go. Her arms locked around the bundle. "No."

"It's time," Ramalina said.

"It's not time. It never was time."

Summer knelt beside the couch. She put her hand on the back of Foxglove's neck, and pressed her forehead softly against the girl. Summer smelled of flowers—what kind of flowers? Foxglove had no idea. And cooking oil. And grief, which Foxglove knew had a salty smell; she remembered it from her mamma.

When Foxglove at last loosened her grip on the baby, everything gave in her body. Tears, her muscles. She felt blood slip. She would bleed until there was nothing left of her. That was fine.

"Where are you taking him?" Foxglove said.

"Somewhere safe to rest. No one can hurt him anymore.

He'll be with you forever," Ramalina said—and then she and the baby went away. She shut the door.

"How can he be? How can he be?"

"There are ways," Summer said.

Probably Summer meant the thought of him. Probably she meant he would stay in Foxglove's heart, or in her memory—but Foxglove wanted a physical presence. She wanted a mark. And she wanted it to hurt. *He* must have hurt. The pain must have been too much for him, to leave like that. Dying must have been less painful than living in this world with her.

She needed it to hurt bad too.

And so, years before Trillium came with his tools and his gentle ways, there was a man who bought a dance from her, a man whose arms were so green and black with ink it looked like he was wearing long sleeves. She leaned down to him from the stage. He had a bald head with a tattoo on it, a funny little leaf.

Do one to me, she whispered. *Tattoo me. And you can touch me for free.*

While the music thumped on, a woman named Maple danced, shaking a lot more enthusiastically than Joshua Tree had. On the side of the stage, Foxglove combed the girl's hair with her fingers. "We've got to do something about your name."

"What's wrong with my name?" the girl said.

"It's too common. I've met several Joshua Trees over the years. In fact, I think I have one of them tattooed on my ass..."

"All right. What's a good name for me, then?"

Foxglove thought for a moment. "JT."

"JT?"

"Simple. Sweet."

"It's not sweet. It sounds like—"

"Adventure. Ease. Men like that. A cowboy," Foxglove said. "It sounds like a cowboy."

"What's a cowboy?" JT said.

"Ask Mr. Fall."

"Who's Mr. Fall?"

"You'll find out. Here." Foxglove pointed the credit cards at the girl, not giving them back just yet. She made a sound of protest, but Foxglove said, "Hide this plastic. Find a place somewhere in the building. There are cracks and holes everywhere. Hide some of your earnings for the night—every night—until you're through with work. Don't let Rattlesnake Master see everything you earn."

"Why not?"

"Because if he doesn't see it, he can't take it."

Maple had finished dancing to more hearty applause. The DJ mumbled something from his high and distant booth. Foxglove had never seen his face, only a smear of movement, his features in bleary shadows. She wondered if he was handsome. She wondered if Rattlesnake Master would ever let him out.

"That's you," Foxglove said. "You're on again. Remember you're special. You're JT. You have something different to offer the world. And here." She pulled a pinch of leaves from her pocket. "Open your mouth."

The girl did so, obediently. Foxglove ignored her breath. She poked the leaves down the girl's throat and waited until she swallowed.

"Ugh," JT said. "What is that?"

"Smartweed. Take it, or Jack-in-the-Pulpit root. Rama-lina has both. You need to visit her and take them regu-larly. She grows them in secret for us. Promise me that you will. Now go."

Still chewing, JT stumbled onstage.

24

Shanghai

He woke in the bunkhouse with the others. He dressed, which was really only a matter of pulling on another layer of rags.

Sometimes children left the factory, and Shanghai was not sure if they had grown too big for the work, or if they ran away, or died. When the absence of someone was noticed— a blank space in the line, an empty bowl at mealtime— everyone seemed to figure it out at once. They all ran back to the bunkhouse, to fight over the child's things. Nobody had much. But a scarf, a shoe, even a sock, was worth a lot.

Shanghai liked to search the pockets. In the rush to take something, anything, clothes would be upended, pockets or blankets dumped out. Shanghai would drop to his knees, below the frenzy, and scan the ground, listening for the *plink* of something lost. Usually it was plastic. Once, though, he had found a knife, a small shiv; he forgot who had taught him that word.

The blade was the size of his index finger, solid plastic sharp enough to shave. That was a good find, a useful find. Why would the child who had left not take their knife with them?

And why would they not take pills, the thing Shanghai found most of all, raining on the floor, plinking like the coins he remembered finding in the river?

Sometimes the pills were homemade, herbs pressed into lumpy shapes. They smelled and were prone to dissolving. He had to be careful with those. But sometimes the pills looked machine-made: uniform blue or white with stamped numbers or letters.

Shanghai would dodge feet and hands, the shuffle of children fighting over rags, and stretch his fingers into the many cracks of the floorboards. He would dig out the pills and palm them. Later, on their water break, or at night in the few minutes they had to find their bunks before the lights went out, Shanghai would show his pills to Outer Banks, the redheaded boy.

His friend.

"I'm telling you," Shanghai said. "No one would leave this on purpose."

"That is valuable shit," Outer Banks said, peering into his hand. "I wish we knew what it was."

"Pills."

"Yeah, but some pills are medicine, for specific things. If you get really sick, they could help you. Not all pills fuck you up."

"All pills fuck you up," Shanghai said.

They heard the shuffle of footsteps, and Shanghai closed his fist.

"Maybe they're making new medicine," Outer Banks said when it was quiet again. "Like they used to. In a factory."

"A factory like this one?"

"No. Not like this. A factory in a city. Making medicine for rich men."

"Wouldn't we know about that?" Shanghai said.

"No, we wouldn't. Just like we don't know where kids go when they leave here."

"Yes, we do. They go to their graves."

"Just like we don't know where a jet plane is flying to."

That had happened exactly once but they all remembered it. They talked about it all the time. Shanghai remembered it with a clarity that sent a jolt of excitement through his body.

The sound had rattled the factory walls. Walls of clay, patched with the first generation of plastic blocks made years ago by children who were grown or dead—the walls quaked and shook. Another flood, Outer Banks said he had thought. An earthquake, thought Shanghai, who had been taught about such things. And the sound: a roar that was both high and low and near at the same time.

They abandoned their posts on the line. None of the collectors, the men in charge, who paced, hands on the guns at their hips, stopped them. The collectors ran too, they opened the doors. Everyone raced out of the factory to the open air, in time to see something streak through it.

It was a monster, winged. Behind it puffed a white tail.

Where was it going? Like the others, Shanghai craned his neck. His hand shaded his eyes.

"It's a goddamn aeroplane!" one of the guards said.

They followed its path. Why did it not burst through the clouds? Tear and burn into them, light them on fire? How did it not fall from the sky, into the trees, into the factory? Why did it not break the factory open and save them, save them all?

Come for me, Shanghai whispered to the jet plane. *Come back for me. Please.*

He thought no one had heard him. He thought, like most things he had said since coming to the factory, he had spoken to himself, in his head. But when he tore his glance away from the sky, from the jet plane becoming a smaller and smaller speck, Outer Banks stared at him.

The collectors were starting to nudge the children back into the building, poking them with the butts of their guns. "Show's over," one of the guards said. "Move."

Shanghai tried never to remember their names. They didn't deserve names. Their faces blurred into each other like clouds. But he must have been lingering too long, looking at the sky. A guard spotted him. He felt a jab, involuntarily arching his shoulders as the guard pushed the barrel of his gun into Shanghai's back. He fell to his knees. He was derailed by pain, disoriented by it.

"I said move," the guard said.

When the twinge of pain passed, Shanghai got up. Other children streamed past, not looking at the scene, not wanting to be drawn into it. Shanghai reached out and grabbed the barrel of the guard's gun.

No one had ever seen the guns fire, not since Shanghai had been taken. They were old, rusted. The collectors used them for hitting only.

He felt the metal dig into his palms. Shanghai wrestled

with the gun. Anger surged through him, hot as plastic. He
wanted to break the gun in half. He wanted to plunge the
pieces deep into the man's side. He wanted to break the man
whose eyes were wide at this small act of rebellion. Nobody
ever fought back. Nobody did anything but rise when they
were knocked down, but swallow the blood when the collectors burst it from their mouths. How dare the guard un-
derestimate him, embarrass him, force him to the ground?

Shanghai's hands were wet, starting to slip. Swiftly, the
guard yanked the gun back. The man raised the gun, preparing to swing it.

The redheaded boy put his hand on Shanghai's back. He
held his other hand out to the guard. "He's going in. We
both are." His voice was calm and slow, with a drawl Shanghai couldn't identify.

The guard lowered his weapon.

"Come on," Outer Banks said.

It was the first time Shanghai had been touched in years.

In the dark, at night, he counted his treasures to reassure
himself that they were there. The pills, the shiv, the odd
bits of plastic. With the knife, he had worn a groove into
the side of his old wooden bed frame, a hiding place for his
finds. The thin trench was covered by his mattress. He had
the top bunk, a safer, more desirable spot. Easier to sleep,
since you missed the turning and squeaking of a bunk above
you. Out of reach of rats or bugs or human hands. If anyone
tried to climb his bunk, Shanghai would hear it.

One row over, Outer Banks had a top bunk too. Shanghai
didn't know the name of the boy on his own lower bunk.
It was a spot that rotated. Kids on the bottom bunk didn't

last long. Either they found a top bunk as soon as possible, or something else happened to them.

Shanghai had decided it was best not to get attached.

It was true he could trade his treasures, and he did sometimes, bartering for clothing or bread when he was especially cold or hungry. But mostly he kept things, collected them. He felt safest when he had a big stash. Touching the pills made him feel secure. He had thirty-four. Well, thirty-two.

One night he had taken two of the small pink pills when his head throbbed with an ache that would not abate, even after he had swallowed handful after handful of the gritty water the collectors provided. When his shift finally ended, he had returned to the bunk to lie down.

Outer Banks had helped him. "These might be aspirin," he said about the pink pills.

"What is aspirin?"

The boy tried to explain, but Shanghai didn't understand. The pills ended up helping him, that was all he cared about. He filed it away in his memory: pink helps with pain.

Outer Banks had had a different other life. He had lived with his father alone in the woods. There had been a mother, but she had died, too early for Outer Banks to be angry at her. When the collectors came, as they always did, in this case setting fire to the trees, Outer Banks had gone with them, willingly.

"My old man couldn't afford to feed me much longer," Outer Banks said. "We were eating bark. We had dug up or stripped off most of the edible things in the woods. He had me later in life. He was older, and I don't know how much farther he could move, how many more times he could start over, make a camp for us somewhere else. It was good, really, when the collectors came. They promised to feed me—and they've kept their promise."

"Barely," Shanghai said.

They ate two meals a day at the factory. Mostly hard bread, and soup or gruel that were indistinguishable from each other, both watery and gravelly with plastic. Everything was gray: their food, their water, the rags they wore. Shanghai wondered if his hair had turned gray. He hadn't seen a mirror in years, just his own grim reflection peering up at him from the clouded water.

Shanghai didn't ask if Outer Banks thought his father was still alive. Was that a blessing, to worry about the person who had lost you, who was left behind? Or a burden? Whatever it was, Shanghai didn't carry it. He tried not to think of his mother. Never to think of anyone who had allegedly loved him.

Rolling onto his side on the mattress, the bunk squealing below him—too bad for the stranger on the lower bunk, trying to sleep—Shanghai took a round white pill from his stash in the trench. He peered at it in the moonlight spilling from the holes in the roof. He felt grateful it was a clear night. Rain and snow would leak from the roof onto his bed too: the one drawback of the upper berth. He turned the pill over in his fingers. So smooth. Factory-made. City-made. From The Els.

Shanghai wondered if he would ever see beyond the factory, ever live past its walls again.

There were numbers stamped on the white pill, but he couldn't really understand them. He had been taken by the collectors before he made it that far in his schooling, to high numbers. There was a letter on the other side of the pill though, and that he knew. *V.*

Sometimes Shanghai missed books. He remembered having seen one. He thought he missed it more than anything, missed the silence of leafing through the pages. He missed the discovery of learning stories from the past, like about the Apple computer and basketball. He missed places that he had never been to, like Disney World and England.

Sometimes he thought he smelled the book's smell: soft rot and dust. He would sense it in a stranger's hair as they passed, smell it in the very air. He thought it was a ghost he sensed.

In the bunkhouse of the factory, Shanghai was never alone. He heard coughs, snoring, and breathing. Someone was always awake, no matter the hour, crying or hungry or just there in the dark. Shanghai felt he was often that one awake, the one who couldn't shut it all off, who couldn't forget, roll over and let the blank oblivion of sleep come.

Other things came with sleep.

Men. Nightmares of men with guns and fire and cars with open doors, open arms to sweep you into them, grabbing arms to take you away. Shanghai was almost as tall as a few of the collectors now—he had heard rumors that some of his fellow captives *became* collectors, once they grew old enough, simply swapping their uniforms and getting a rusted gun—but he was still afraid of them. When he slept, they still came. They came to take him from his mother, from his warm bed and blankets. They came almost every night.

He considered the pill. If he held it up between his thumb and index finger, he could block out one of the holes in the roof. Moonlight seeped around the *V*, giving the pill a kind of corona.

Shanghai rolled onto his back, then swallowed the *V*. It stuck a bit in his throat, dry. He swallowed hard. Who knew what it was, what it did. He had learned that some pills were fun. Some pills made you floaty. They made the world lose its sharp edges. They made you not care.

Shanghai would like the world to lose its edges. He would like to not care.

The pill slid down his throat and in the dark, he waited for it to work.

25

Rattlesnake Master

The problem was that men were bored. Even tits got old, if they were the same tits.

Rattlesnake Master watched the dancer onstage, the new one. What's-her-face. He couldn't remember her name, if he had ever learned it. She looked young and scared and danced like her life didn't depend on it, which it did.

Her hair didn't appear to have ever been washed, and the teeth still left in her mouth looked gray. Still, she flung off her K-Cup bra with abandon. She had that way about her. The kind of person who would let herself go to hell and come back for more. The kind of girl you could really hurt.

What's-her-face was still new. A few men fumbled in their pockets for plastic to give to her. Not a lot, it looked like. She would be a novelty for a little while longer. Then what?

Rattlesnake Master turned from the stage. He was counting out paper money at the bar. It was confusing and he had lost track.

Paper money wasn't worth what was printed on it. Those numbers were meaningless—most people couldn't even read them. What determined money's value was the quality of the paper. Was it crisp? Rattlesnake Master had never felt a crisp bill in his own hands, but he had heard rumors. Those were worth a shit-ton. Was it whole? Not very many of those. Half bills were worth less, scraps even less than that.

He sorted the bills by size on the bar. Then he sorted again by condition. No one would dare touch the money. If a man was drunk enough to try, Warthog, who tended bar, would take care of them.

Rattlesnake Master studied the piles, muttering, "It's not enough."

Warthog, drying a cup with a rag, said, "It sure looks like a lot to me." He replaced the cup on the shelf. It was ancient purple plastic, printed with the words: *Spring Fling, A Night to Remember. March 13, 2020.*

Would anyone remember Trashlands when Rattlesnake Master was gone?

Not at the rate it was going.

"This is less than last month," Rattlesnake Master said. "What happened to drive down business?"

"It's getting colder? People don't like to travel when they're cold?"

"*People don't like to travel when they're cold,*" Rattlesnake Master mimicked the bartender's high whine.

Warthog seemed not to mind. He took another cup out of the tub with its inch of grimy water and dried it off. He was almost as tall as Tahiti, his cropped hair the same color as the water. His lips looked puffy, as if someone had punched him in the face.

(Rattlesnake Master frowned. Had *he* been the one to punch the bartender in the face?)

"People die in the cold. Freeze to death. Give up. Happens every year," Warthog said. "The big die-off."

"We can't lose customers because they're dead. We have to do something."

"Heat this place," Warthog suggested.

"That would take a whole fucking forest."

"Men'll come for the heat."

"Men don't need heat." Rattlesnake Master turned back to the stage. "Not that kind."

What's-her-name had finished her set. She ran off to Foxglove waiting on the side of the stage. Even from this distance, that girl looked extraordinary, slim and tender as some kind of flower, maybe a lily—was that a flower? She glowed, as if she stood center stage and not in a dim corner of the wings, as though she was lit by the majestic chandelier at its full power and not the glitchy spotlight they had rigged up from an oil drum. Rattlesnake Master could see flashes from beneath the robe she wore as she bent to talk to the new, shorter girl, her red hair sliding over her mouth.

He had always known Foxglove was special. She had that kind of energy about her. You couldn't tear your eyes away. She was the light in the dark room, a star on fire. She was the last bit of electricity in an almost-lightless world.

Rattlesnake Master thought he could have loved her.

But he was not in the habit of loving anyone. And that would taint her, make her less special. Love ruined women. Made them too soft or too hard, depending on how the love went. Made them want to run. Even when their bodies were here in the club, their minds weren't. They felt upset or thrilled, hopeful or worried. They were always feeling. You could see it in their eyes: a kind of darting, a drifting away.

That was one of the powers of Foxglove, Rattlesnake Master thought.

She wasn't in love.

The names on her skin worked like a token, like the red leaf he had found pressed in a wad of old paper money once, which had crumbled when he tried to touch it. Foxglove was the same way. But if you tried to hold her, *you* would crumble.

It was best not to fall in love. Best to touch, but not feel. Those names meant nothing to her, as the men had meant nothing. It was only skin, which she still had more of— thankfully, he thought, watching her fuss with the new girl's outfit. Love closed you up. Love narrowed your options.

Like Summer, striding over to him across the club floor, fully dressed as though she wasn't supposed to start work at any moment, her lips set in a grim, unflattering line. "She's good, right?" Summer said, nodding at the stage where the new girl had left and no one missed her.

"She's...fine," Rattlesnake Master said.

"Seems sweet to me," Warthog said.

"No one asked you."

"We're good, then?" Summer said.

Rattlesnake Master looked at Summer. Love had made her cheeks fuller, her eyes glossy but absent. Fuck love, he thought. "What do you mean? We talked about this already. The girl settles your debt."

"Then I'm out."

"You're *out?*"

"I quit."

Warthog's eyes widened and he wiped more furiously at a cup. Summer was rolling her shoulders back. But her feet, in the high heels she had made, tapped songs of anxiety on the floor. She bit her lip. She was going to draw blood. She was bluffing, and he knew it.

"This isn't the kind of place you quit," Rattlesnake Master said.

"I don't owe you anything," Summer said. Then quieter, "Anymore."

"This isn't a job. It's a life. Where are you going to go?"

"I'm not going anywhere. But I could."

"I loaned you your truck."

"I paid it off."

This was probably true, but Rattlesnake Master would have to check. He would definitely check. "That truck doesn't even run."

"It might. It might not. But it's none of your business anymore."

He couldn't believe he was having this argument with her, in the club, in front of the damn bartender and a handful of customers. "That cup is fucking clean already!" he said to Warthog.

Warthog moved to the back of the bar.

At least the men still watched the stage. The DJ pumped the music up. It was harder to be heard, but Rattlesnake Master lowered his voice. Let Summer strain to hear him. Let her struggle. "You are going to starve," he said.

She had the nerve to laugh a little. "Don't you know how

I cook? Don't you know how I make things? I can live on
that. We can both live on it, easily."

"You can't live on shoes. You're going to fucking die."

"We'll see," Summer said. She turned her back on him
and walked away.

"That bitch won't last the winter," Rattlesnake Master
said to Warthog. But Warthog had moved away, pretending to be out of earshot, doing some job that didn't need to
be done in a far corner of the bar.

Rattlesnake Master watched Maple finish her set. The
music didn't change, she just ran out of breath, got tired—
or got some sign from the men that they were sick of her.

The music came from a scratched silver disc, flimsy plastic
found on the floor years ago, when Trashlands was an abandoned theater. The disc had caught his eye, shining in the
dirt like he wanted this place to, a gem in a sea of trash. It
was, he felt, a metaphor. The disc still worked. Rattlesnake
Master had heard one of the dancers say that the disc could
get scratched to hell, but whatever happened you could *not*
get a fingerprint on it. A single thumb would break it.

Rattlesnake Master made the DJ wear gloves.

He had found the DJ, some skinny kid, hired him away
from his mother. Rattlesnake Master had told him if he made
a pass at the dancers, he would cut off his balls. The boy
seemed more interested in the bartender, anyway. He did
his job. He sat in the alcove overlooking the dance floor, a
balcony shored up with the finest Ikea—but privately, Rattlesnake Master still believed the balcony might fall down
any day, necessitating the need for a new DJ—and pressed
the button on a player held together with tape.

It was the number three the DJ had to press. Again

and again. Possibly the disc had other songs, but only one
worked. Maybe there had once been words, or more instruments you could make out. A guitar, a piano. Rattlesnake
Master could almost remember those.

But now there was bass, only and forever. The deep tones
rumbled in Rattlesnake Master's chest. He thought of the
beat of Trashlands as his own heart. He had given his life
to the club. He would probably die here, in the back office,
hopefully with a dancer's head between his legs.

He hoped he died before the music did.

The new girl was on again. She looked back at Foxglove,
uncertain or unwilling, and Foxglove made a shooing motion. When she still didn't dance, Foxglove swatted her.

"That's what we need," Rattlesnake Master said to himself, as Foxglove faded back into the curtain. "Two of them.
That'll bring the crowds back to Trashlands. That'll sell out."

"What, Foxglove and Joshua Tree?" Warthog had decided
it was safe to come back.

"Who's Joshua Tree?"

"The new dancer. Onstage right now."

"No, not her. She's terrible. We need Foxglove and somebody else, somebody the men haven't seen before, somebody
they might not see again."

"For what?"

The girl began her dance, a shaky hip thrust, off beat. Behind her, Rattlesnake Master could just make out the shape
of Foxglove, taller, curvier, a twin or mother.

"For a show," Rattlesnake Master said.

26

Foxglove

The only sound was the rustling her fingers made, going through plastic on the table before her. And in the distance, the sound of a stick hitting something. A tree. JT was striking it.

Foxglove had left the door of her trailer open to keep an eye on the girl, flitting about in the yard. Whatever. Foxglove returned to the table. Swiftly, she divided the durable plastic from the cheap shit, the virgin plastic from the already recycled. Blue rubber gloves stood out in the mess, the bright green bottle of a sugar drink.

Tahiti stood in the doorway. "You're taking a cut from JT?"

"It's my right," Foxglove said. "She eats a ton. And she talks in her sleep, disturbing me."

"I didn't hear anything."

"Well, you sleep outside." She felt something as she said

it, a kind of deep unsettling, as though she had upset her
stomach or taken a strange pill. Even now in the evening,
she could feel the cold in the air. Tahiti slept outside in that,
the kind of chill that would creep under your collar and inside your clothes. A chill like a man's fingers. It would only
get worse. The weather would turn into something insistent, something mean. "I should be paid for caring for her,"
Foxglove said.

Tahiti smiled. "You're good at it."

"I don't think so."

"I've seen you with her."

"Let's not make it a fucking habit."

"It's almost like having a daughter," Tahiti said.

"More like a pet." Foxglove pushed at the pile and it scattered, plastic pinging on the floor.

Tahiti bent to pick it up.

She thought of his arms, his back to the woods, his eyes
turning away as she showered. She thought of his deep scars
and the one razor-thin one. "Leave it," she said. "You don't
have to do that. Just keep an eye on JT. Please."

He looked up at her, holding her glance for a moment.
She looked away first.

Why had she talked to him like that? she thought as she
watched him return to the yard. Ordered him around? What
was wrong with her? She looked at the plastic on the floor.
Trash. It was all trash.

Outside, she heard JT talking. The tone of the girl's voice
changed, sweetening. She was no longer talking to Tahiti;
someone new had come into their space. Foxglove didn't
hear Tahiti send him off.

She reached over to the counter and dragged out her

shiny tray. It had been a present from Tahiti—everything in Trashlands was a present or a price. She rubbed it with her sleeve, peering at her reflection. Her cheeks blurred in the distorted surface. Foxglove often wondered how the tray had become warped, what was the story? Every time she looked at her face in the mirror, she couldn't help thinking of ruined cakes, children crying.

She looked good, though, she thought. She looked fine. She was not in the mood. She was tired, but she could do this. She could always do this. Find a spot for his name. She turned the tray over to its dull side, so the man wouldn't think she was vain, looking at herself. She covered the plastic she had been counting, so the man wouldn't try to steal anything, or think she could be undersold. She straightened her shoulders, and turned to the door. Rattlesnake Master stood there. "Oh, it's you," Foxglove said.

A hand blocked his way: Tahiti.

"I pay you to protect her," Rattlesnake Master said.

"I am protecting her," Tahiti said.

Foxglove slouched in the chair. "It's fine. Let him in."

Tahiti dropped his arm. Rattlesnake Master glared at the man, then stepped into the trailer, closing the door behind him. Foxglove tried not to feel panic at that *click*.

"What's up?" she said flatly.

"Where did you hear that old phrase?"

"Miami."

"The reporter? Well…" Rattlesnake Master pulled out a second chair to sit down without being asked. "He's everywhere, isn't he?"

"Did you want something? I've got to take Junior for her walk."

Rattlesnake Master stretched his hand across the table, finding Foxglove's hand. His fingers felt heavy and cold. She tried not to shudder.

She had taught herself to feel nothing at touch. It would wash over her like water. It would bead off her like oil. Nothing could get in. Even tattoos only permeated the top few layers of skin, Trillium had explained. Or maybe, she thought, he had lied to her about that, told her what she wanted—needed—to hear.

"I have an idea about you," Rattlesnake Master said.

Foxglove sat very still and waited for his touch to go.

"Seeing you with the new girl, how good you were with her—it got me thinking." He took his hand back, and Foxglove could breathe. He hadn't even noticed her discomfort. They never did. "Two of you together onstage, two beauties."

Foxglove stared at him. "You want me onstage with JT?"

"Who's JT?"

"Really? The new girl? Outside right now, probably eavesdropping."

"I'm not eavesdropping!" she squealed from behind the door.

"No, I don't want you and that bean sprout," Rattlesnake Master said.

"What's a bean sprout?" Foxglove heard JT say.

"I want you and someone lovely. You and someone else lovely. A show of two beauties who complement each other. Match. Like two flames. That's what we'll call it. Twin flames."

"How am I a flame?"

He reached across the table again and this time she

flinched. It happened too fast. She didn't have time to prepare, to mold her face, take her body away where she could only see and not feel what was happening to her.

But he didn't touch her hand this time. He pulled on her hair, giving it a firm tug. "Your hair, dummy. We'll do a show of two redheads. Do you know, redheads feel more pain than other people? You're more sensitive." He rubbed Foxglove's hair between his fingers. "We'll have to test that theory sometime."

She had curled her hair only this morning, twisting it up with rags she tied around her head. She felt foolish now, having done such things. Her hair would only get torn out, pulled. She would only be dragged around by it. It would only be used to find her, betray her if she ever tried to get away. The blinding beacon of her hair would never, ever let her get far, unless she escaped in a red past, in the red place of trees Mr. Fall used to talk about.

She would have to dye her hair again, darker, to get away from here. Summer was collecting walnut husks; Foxglove had asked her to. She was experimenting with clay and pigments, to cover the tattoos. They were both of them, both women, saving and waiting.

Foxglove could have reminded Rattlesnake Master that her hair color came from chemicals, but she was stuck on something he had said. "Where in Trashlands are you going to find another redhead?"

He released her hair and smirked at her, waiting for her to figure it out.

"Coral?" Foxglove said. "You want me to do a show with Coral?"

"A natural redhead. A girl never before seen onstage. The child who walked into a whale…"

"You are never going to convince her to dance at Trashlands. Not after what happened to her."

"No," Rattlesnake Master said. "You are."

"She won't do it. She knows the price to get her son back. That's all she needs."

"I heard. A running car. They don't have it."

"They do." News traveled faster than a slap. "The rainbow bus. Mr. Fall is giving it to her. It still runs."

This didn't seem to derail Rattlesnake Master. "Not without fuel it doesn't."

"They have fuel," Foxglove said, though uncertainly. Summer hadn't told her this part.

"The only person who has enough diesel for that old bus to run," Rattlesnake Master said, leaning forward, so close to her face she felt cold, "is me."

She stood in the doorway and watched until Rattlesnake Master went out of sight. JT was watching him too, bouncing on the balls of her feet. There was an energy Foxglove hadn't seen on the girl, a hopefulness in her lifted chin. Her eyes followed him down the path. Only her hands gave her away, pulsing into fists at her sides. Foxglove saw the skin on her fingers was red, torn or bitten. "JT?"

The girl glared at Foxglove. "What?"

"Are you taking the herbs I gave you?"

JT made a face. "I guess."

"You better know. You better be sure."

"They taste like shit."

"Well, giving birth hurts like hell, so." Foxglove felt, rather than saw, Tahiti's look. His eyes made heat on her neck like a coil of rope. Who knew what he had been told about her.

She wondered what JT had been told about how babies were born. Not much, she guessed. She suspected the girl had been shown, rather than told, what her body could do. Foxglove shifted. Her feet ached. Her back ached. She didn't know how she would stretch dinner, which was crickets and weeds. She couldn't keep feeding three people.

The chill across the yard tugged at her dress. Soon enough they would have to dig for roots under the snow. She wondered if JT would still be in her trailer then, sleeping on the floor. Would Foxglove have to find boots for the girl? Mend her warm clothes?

She asked JT, "Have you found your gimmick yet?"

"My what?"

"Your thing that makes you special, makes men want to come here for you? You won't be new forever—we talked about this."

Her face brightened. "Yes, we did. And I found my thing. I decided."

"You did?" Foxglove was skeptical. "What is it?"

Her cheeks bulged in a smile. "Tattoos."

Foxglove dropped her hand from the doorway. She felt Tahiti beside her, trying not to laugh. "That's not your thing. That's my thing."

"Well, it's so popular, I thought maybe—"

"No."

"It would be good to have two—"

"No, it would not. Two tattooed girls in a club is too many. Nobody would pay for that."

"Why do I need to be special, anyway?"

"Because being special keeps you safe," Foxglove snapped. There was a cupboard in her trailer called an oven. She kept clothes folded in it. Foxglove reached back to pull out a shawl. "I have to go out for a bit."

"It's almost curfew," Tahiti said.

"I know, but Rattlesnake Master asked me to do this. Keep an eye on JT."

He was ready to follow her. "I need to keep an eye on you."

"I don't need you," Foxglove said, then regretted it.

She pulled the shawl tightly around her head. It was more to hide her hair than to keep her warm. Most of the clothing she owned felt thin, starting to tear. That served fine for the stage, but off it, she shivered. She had only a few warm clothes—and now she would need more for JT—and they were holey, eaten by moths and the mice which had already started to burrow inside her trailer. She couldn't blame the insects or rodents. Everything living was just doing its best.

Leaving the trailer, she noticed two of the tires had cracked. She would have to replace those. She made a note to ask Coral to search for tires for her. Her clothes had holes, her tires had holes, even her shoe had a hole; she could feel the ground as she walked. Everything wore out at the same time. That was the law of poverty, Mr. Fall said.

She wanted to ask, *What was poverty?*

But she felt like the time for asking questions was over. She was too old for that.

She fussed with the shawl. Even with her hair hidden, she was still a woman. That alone made it dangerous to walk alone through the yard, especially this late. Men would be watching for a woman.

For a moment, Foxglove considered running. Just run-

ning now, in her thin dress and shawl with no suitcase, no
money. Out of the junkyard, into the woods. How would
she get through them? What was on the other side?

She couldn't remember. The world beyond Trashlands
was a mystery to her. Memories of before felt fuzzy at the
edges and came back to her at strange times: a word, a taste
of something sweet. She remembered her mamma as a tall
person with shaking hands. She yelled at Foxglove for taking too much time tying the rags on her feet, for complaining about the bugs in her oatmeal.

Pick them out, Foxglove recalled her saying. *You're not fancy.*

But now she *was* fancy, Foxglove thought. Fancy enough
that somebody else—often Tahiti—picked the bugs from
her food. Fancy enough that she wore real shoes, not rags:
shoes with heels. Fancy enough she could spend her money
on pills or weed.

She could say *no* whenever she wanted.

Almost.

Foxglove could not remember her mamma's name or face.
Or maybe she chose not to. She remembered her back, how
her hair looked streaming over her shoulders, limp as weeds.
She remembered the feel of Rattlesnake Master's arm, slith-
ering around her for the first time, lest she try to run. She
did not try.

Now she hurried down the path, wondering what she was
going to say. *Let's just get this over with. Let's both get what we
want and get out of here.* Her shoe stuck in some mud and she
yanked it free. She came down the hill to see Coral outside
in her little dirt yard, fiddling with something. "Find any
good plastic?" Foxglove said.

Coral looked up. "Not really."

"Me either. Not in my take today or the brat's."

"Are you looking after her now?"

"I guess. Trying to help her out."

"That's nice of you."

"I don't have much of a choice," Foxglove said. She watched Coral's hands, dividing the plastic like she was braiding hair. "You're feeling better?"

"All better."

"Drugs are wonderful, aren't they?"

"I wish they weren't so expensive."

"About that." Foxglove just had to say it, then she'd figure out what to do next. That was the way of it. That was her life: act, then react. Survive, then later—much later, if ever—figure out how she felt about it. "Rattlesnake Master came to visit me. He has this idea. I think it might help you."

Wrong thing to say. Coral went back to her plastic. "I don't need help."

"Yes, you do," Foxglove said. "For your son."

"I don't need Rattlesnake Master's help."

"You don't want his help, you don't want Miami's help…"

Something strange happened to Coral's face. She went both flushed and pale at the same time. She pushed away the plastic she was holding. It looked like a medicine bottle.

"Anyway, it's not help from Rattlesnake Master. Not a handout. It's a job."

Coral wasn't looking at Foxglove anymore. "He's already offered me a job. A standing offer. A long time ago, when we first came here. And then he re-upped it, in front of everyone. Trillium wasn't too happy about that."

"This is different," Foxglove insisted. "I'd be there."

"What do you mean?"

"This is a show. A show with you and me."

Coral looked at Foxglove through her hair. Foxglove knew her friend was older, but in some moments she seemed young as a child. Foxglove could picture her being led into child-birth by a much older man, a teacher whose lies she believed. Foxglove could imagine Coral trusting, not knowing what to do, what was right or what she was allowed to say, if she could tell. Not knowing anything. Foxglove remembered what that was like.

Say it. Just say it, she thought. If you're not clear, people can get ideas, wrong ones. People can take more than you're offering. She cleared her throat. "The show would be us on-stage, clothes off, pretending to touch."

"Pretending?"

"Completely. It would all be fake."

Everything is fake, Foxglove thought.

Coral busied herself with the plastic again, but she said, "How much is he offering, Rattlesnake Master?"

"Everything."

"What do you mean, *everything*?"

"Everything you need. The diesel he has buried."

Coral was thinking. Her movements no longer seemed purposeful, poking at the plastic as if she didn't really want to touch it. She asked, "What do I have to do?"

"Nothing, really."

"I don't know how to dance."

"You don't have to dance. It's not dancing."

"What is it, then?"

Foxglove tried to shrug but it came out more like a shiver. "Give the men what they think they want. Let them forget for a moment that everything is shit and hard, forget their lives. Give them a glimpse of something special."

"Am I special?" Coral asked.

There was the child inside her. The little girl who had been led into the icehouse by the hand of someone she trusted.

Foxglove, the child who had been left on the back porch, smiled. "You're very special, Coral."

Foxglove wasn't that child anymore, but they had a lot in common, her and Coral. Both had their ways to forget. Foxglove liked pills, how they didn't taste like anything. There was one pill she liked especially called *V*. It didn't take all the pain away—the pain on her skin from being tattooed, the pain deep inside her—it didn't do shit for pain. But it made her not care.

That was a great feeling, being alive and not caring.

Coral had her own thing: keeping her hands occupied. She was making something now, as Foxglove turned to go. She didn't know how to explain what Coral did with plastic. Maybe Foxglove had missed that day in Mr. Fall's school. Maybe she had been torn from the tent by then by Rattlesnake Master, who said the girl already knew everything she needed to know.

Coral was putting an arch together with water bottle pieces and cup lids. What would she do with that? Where would she put it? How would she get it to stand up and stay? Foxglove would never know. She didn't feel like she could ask any questions. She took one last look at it before she left.

It was pretty, in a way.

27

Coral

Trillium would be angry. He would try to talk her out of
it. He would say they could get the fuel another way. But
there was no other way, no other supply. The thought occurred to her that he might leave her. And though this made
the bottom drop out from her stomach just thinking about
the awfulness of being without him, it would be easy in its
own way. She would not have to make a choice then. The
choice would have been made for her, by him.

No, she told herself. She didn't want that.

She didn't want to hurt Trillium, who had been with her
for so long. And she didn't want to lose him. His steadiness,
his quiet love, the scarred spot in his eyebrow where hair
wouldn't grow, his deep blue eyes below. She had no real
choice—and that was fine, that was good, that was easy.
This was her life. She was happy. She was *happy*.

If she told herself that enough times, she might believe it.

She was going to do the show with Foxglove. One show, one night, and then they could go away, she and Trillium. They could go get Shanghai and start fresh, someplace better. Somewhere warmer, she thought, as she felt the wind curl up like a ghost from the quarry. And cooler in the hot times. Where would that be?

There was another part of her decision, as Mr. Fall had explained to her on the riverbank: if Coral left with the bus, he couldn't come.

Mr. Fall was needed in the junkyard. He couldn't leave the children. He couldn't leave Summer. And Coral and her son might want to start over someplace that didn't have a club spitting out drunk men nightly. Someplace that didn't have a Rattlesnake Master.

But maybe there were always Rattlesnake Masters.

Coral couldn't picture a life without Mr. Fall. She couldn't bear to think of it, and so she chose not to. It seemed far away, a time when she might drive off.

It was strange how the past and the future both felt bridged by impossible distances. You couldn't reach either of them, couldn't begin to imagine what you might find, like the time New Orleans had stumbled into an old, sealed basement. The house it belonged to had been destroyed, flattened by the floods. But somehow, the underground room had remained frozen, protected by felled trees and debris.

New Orleans described finding shelves of long boxes. Inside the boxes were games with instructions he couldn't make sense of, cardboard that folded open into his hands, tiny playing pieces like cars and pink plastic children. Everything was untouched. He couldn't think of what to do with them, how to make the games work or repurpose them—

the cars were so tiny; there was one game with a miniature hat, a dog the size of his thumbnail—and it seemed wrong, somehow, to disturb them. The room had been preserved for so long, surviving weather and riots and change, such change. And in all that time, no one had played them. No one had won or lost.

He put the flat lids back on the boxes, put the boxes back on the shelves. He just left them all there in the basement, sealing the room again with tree limbs and brush. Coral wondered where it was. She would never look for it.

She sensed Trillium at her back, in the bus behind her. He was waiting for her to come in. She had worked later than she meant to, past dark, past curfew. The piece was done. It looked done, anyway. A glittering arch of bits. She would prop it in a tree.

In the early days of her making sculptures, she had believed she was creating pieces for a specific person. Maybe Robert, who had said he loved her and left a part of her floating in the icehouse. Maybe he might see her work in the woods, and know somehow it was hers.

Then, after memories of him faded a bit like pain did, she thought maybe she was making pieces for girls like her, pregnant and scared. Some beauty for them to wonder about, to take their minds off their lives. Something the river had not spit up, ugly and wasted. Not twisted by floods and earthquakes and fire, forces that molded so much of their lives, but shaped by hands. A girl's hands.

Once Shanghai was taken, the pieces were for him. All for him. Ways for him to find her, to find his way home, ways for him to know she was still looking, still hurting, still sorry. Lately, though, she felt her pieces were for no one.

She made them out of habit. She made them because what else would she do?

Are you happy? Miami had asked her.

"You still hungry?"

She turned to see Trillium on the bus steps. "Not really."

"We have more crickets," he said.

"Crickets?"

"I could fry them up."

"Do you remember Mr. Fall saying crickets were good luck? It used to be lucky to have one in your home. Alive, I guess. I don't know if it's lucky to eat them."

But they ate everything and nothing at all. What did the children in the factories eat? That was something she tried not to think about.

"Well, it's what we have left," Trillium said. He was mostly shadow, backlit by the bus.

Coral thought about how sometimes when he touched her, if it had been a long time, his mouth fell open in pure amazement of the fact of her: her body, the feel of her skin. She didn't think he knew he did this. She didn't think he knew how pure he looked then, both young and old at the same time, shooting past her like a comet that would not pass by again. Because of their age difference, they would never grow old together.

"I'm not hungry," Coral said.

"Well, come inside. It's dark."

"It is?" Of course it was. Her fingers moved through shadows. The thing she had made looked like a tree root beside the big bus tire. When she stood, her legs felt weak, her knees stiff.

"Are you all right?" Trillium asked.

She had to get it out. "Foxglove came to visit me. I don't know if you saw her."

"Does she want another tattoo?"

"No. She asked me to perform with her. A show at Trashlands. A onetime thing. It would be just the two of us, her and me. I wouldn't be alone. Rattlesnake Master…" She faltered saying his name, the name of the man she had tried very hard to avoid. She had spent years avoiding him, maybe because she had failed to avoid Robert. Would she have been so afraid of Rattlesnake Master if she had never gone into the icehouse? What else might have been different about her life? "Rattlesnake Master has promised the fuel."

Trillium turned away from her. "I wouldn't trust anything that man says."

"And then we can go." Coral trailed after him. "We can take the fuel and the bus and get out of here. Get Shanghai back and go for good."

This was the deal. This was what she would give up: her home in the scrap, the river, her father, her friends. She was prepared to leave them. For him.

Trillium was not looking at her. "What does he want you to do?"

28

Miami

In his room he listened to the thump below the floor. It thudded through the carpet, making the stains shake. He couldn't imagine the music was easy to dance to, and yet, that's what the women did all night and much of the day, below him in that unfathomable dark. It might as well have been the ocean. He floated above it, hoping the ancient structure of the building would hold, dreaming of her.

Tahiti had not come back to Miami's room again, and Foxglove had not returned either. The other dancers left him alone. Maybe Foxglove had said something to them. Maybe they just knew.

In his narrow bed, he thought of Coral. He dreamed of her beneath her clothes, the many ragged layers. He dreamed of her sparking with light, those rags splitting open. He dreamed of warmth and safety and home. When he woke, he realized he had never really been asleep. Not fully. He couldn't rest with that music. *The song of the club.* That's what he would write, how he would say it. The siren song of Trashlands.

It had been difficult for him to write since coming here. Even though he was often alone, in a way he never was. Never without the neon, casting everything in pink. Never without the song.

He was used to traveling with ghosts. He had lived near his sister for a long time, and then, lived with the memory of her. She knew when to call—when they had phone lines that worked—knew to try to find him or come over to his apartment when he really needed her, when he was sick or heartsick, or down to his last ration. When his wife had left.

That day, he had mistaken the knock on his door for his wife, come home. When he had slid back the dead bolt and taken off the three chains, his hands were shaking. He had thrown open the door and saw Mangrove.

She fell into his arms. "Something bad happened. What was it?"

"My wife left." He was numb. It felt impossible to say her name.

"Oh," Mangrove said against his shoulder. "I was afraid."

"What were you afraid of?"

"I guess I was afraid of that. That something was going wrong between you two."

"Well, it did. It has been going wrong. And I didn't even notice. Or I didn't care. I didn't do anything about it."

"There's a lot going on," Mangrove said.

And she was in the thick of it, fighting, though Miami didn't believe there was much left to fight for. Mangrove fought against corporations, trying to get more of them to stop polluting. She fought against brick factories and the exploitation of workers. She fought against what was left of the government, how it had taken over air travel and transit, hoarding food and water and gas. She fought by running in the streets with others. She used her body as a battering ram, pressing into barricades, smashing windows, burning things. Often she smelled of paint and smoke.

The day Miami's wife left was no different. When Mangrove pulled out of the hug, a campfire scent hovered in the air. Her bracelet slid against her wrist, a pink plastic thing she had worn since they were kids. She always wore it, glittery and cheap, a bright, happy contrast to the rest of her: dark clothes, dark curly hair, a frequently glowering or intense expression. He wondered if the bracelet reminded her of being happy, of being a family: what she was fighting for.

"You've been to an action," Miami said.

"Well, I have to keep going."

"What was it this time?"

She wouldn't tell him. She never did. She kept him safe that way. "I'm going to be traveling soon."

"Where are you going?"

All she would say was that word. *Soon.* "There's a lot to be angry about, you know? There's everything, maybe especially in the places we don't like to think about."

"What are those places? Mangrove?"

She trailed down the hallway past him. "Do you have any food?"

Miami barricaded the front door behind her. By the time he had fixed all the locks again, she was in his kitchen, eating the core of his last apple.

"How long has it been since you've had a real meal?" he asked her.

"What's your definition of *real*?"

He thought about his marriage. His wife. How she had been slipping away from him this whole time, like Mangrove said their rights were eroding, like the city services had been cut off one by one.

At first, you didn't notice. The lights would flicker or the internet go out. Phone service was spotty. Then one day the phones just stopped. The power went out for a day, then another. Water trickled brown from the faucets, then sputtered out to nothing. Garbage bags piled up on the street corners. Nobody came to take them away.

Love was like that, he thought. Loving the same person for a long time, you started not to see them. Their edges blurred, and they became indistinct to you. His wife, Aletsch, had brought up points of disagreements, daggers of things that made her angry. Like how they didn't read at night in bed anymore (*there was not enough light*, he had thought). How she always had to instigate sex (*he was tired; it was exhausting, trying to survive*). How he never looked at her.

That last one was just untrue. Sitting in the kitchen, with his sister trying to drink his cooking oil, he thought he could draw Aletsch by heart: her thick hair, her heavy breasts. He could see her with his eyes closed, if he ever slept again.

"How is she going to survive without me?" he said, more to himself.

But Mangrove answered. "She'll survive. Or she won't. But probably she will. Probably she's got somewhere to go, some people to be with."

"What people?" Miami said. Most of their families were dead.

"I don't know. You might not know. You might never know what happens to her."

"I can't believe she's really gone. I don't understand."

"You might never understand it," his sister said.

In a way she was preparing him for her own absence, for the mystery of her disappearance from the world. Aletsch left, then Mangrove left.

His wife took some food, her sunhat, sweaters, a coat, and a plastic knapsack. She undid all the locks, left her ring on the kitchen counter—they could afford only one ring between the two of them, cheap metal they had talked about selling; they probably would have sold it; he could never sell it now—and walked out into the street, becoming a stranger.

Not two weeks after eating in his kitchen, Mangrove left on a mission farther than she had ever gone before. She tore into the country, into Scrappalachia on a task Miami was not privy to. Something about a factory, undercover. A fact-finding mission, that was all he could get her to say, that afternoon in his kitchen. But something went wrong. Someone was betrayed, and that someone was Mangrove. The action had been compromised, the message that came to Miami read. She had been killed.

She burst into a ball of her own flame, became indistinguishable from the lost and likely broken car, the bones of her fallen comrades. Mangrove, not unusually, was the only woman on the trip.

They could not bring back a body to the city, the message read. They could not definitively identify her—but they knew that she had been out there, and he should know that too. They could not risk such a passage for the dead.

So Miami risked it. He made the passage. He came to her.

★ ★ ★

She was not here.

Not in the bass, which did not beat her name. Not in the neon, which hurt his eyes and took away his appetite, falling over everything like a skin of pink plastic. Not in the anonymous bodies filing into and out of the club. And not in the junkyard.

He was embarrassed not to have realized how *big* Scrappalachia was, that Trashlands was only one junkyard out of many. That the junkyards were ringed with trees, struggling but alive, and mountains higher than his apartment building. He wondered if there were cities in some of those hills, and who lived there, what they did. He wondered if there was a newspaper.

He should have moved on when he had found no sign of his sister in Trashlands, not a single person who knew the story: the activists sabotaged, dragged from their car and killed. Maybe she had died here. Maybe it was not here at all.

He had thought he might have been able to find the spot somehow. In the city, accidents were often marked, noted with flowers, candles, cards. Though those memorials sprung up less and less, now that he thought about it. More people stole the candles. There weren't very many flowers. Too many people were killed to make a memorial of it.

He naively thought the people of Scrappalachia would have news about Mangrove, would have heard the crash or seen the flames. He should have moved on that first day when nobody had known anything about his sister.

But on that first day he had met Coral.

Something had drawn him here, to this yard with the club looming over it like an electric god. Maybe his sister

was not here—but a story was. Many stories. He told himself that as he got out of bed, the mattress groaning. From
his bag, he took out his notebook and a pencil, sharpened
to a nub. He had to conserve pencils and paper, think carefully about what he would say.

He started to write.

When the knock came at his door, he felt grateful, as always, for the distraction. *For a writer you sure hate to write*,
Mangrove had said to him once.

He hid the notebook and pencil. "Yes?" he said at the door.

A female voice he didn't recognize called out, "Knock.
Knock."

This again. He fumbled with the thin lock. "Listen, no
offense, but I'm not interested in—"

"News!" The girl swung into the room. She must have
been pressing her body against the door, just waiting for an
opening, like a cat.

It was the girl who had come back from the shopping
mall with them, the one called Joshua Tree. Being at the
club had not softened her edges, though her hair had been
washed and she wore fancier rags.

"What are you doing here, Joshua Tree?"

"I'm called JT now. And I have news." She held up a
flimsy plastic sheet. She waved it and the plastic made a singing sound, like a saw. Miami reached for it, but she slapped
it back. "No. I only have the one. I'm supposed to go to all
the boarders and tell them about it."

"Tell me about what?"

This she did not seem to know. His must have been the
first room she had come to. Words in black had been painted

on the flyer. She looked down at them, and the glimmer faded from her face.

She could not read, he realized.

"Can I see it?" Miami asked, softer.

She handed him the flyer, and he squinted at the letters. Whoever had painted them had not been able to read or write very well themselves. He said, "I'll read it out loud so you know what it says, all right? So you can tell other people."

She nodded.

He read: "Trashlands presents. For one night only. Twin flames." His voice caught on the word *twin*, and he faltered, thinking of his sister.

JT was looking at him. He continued reading.

But the next words were worse. "Foxglove, the angel in ink, and...and...*Coral*, the child who...the child who walked into a whale. Together. Onstage." He took off his glasses. He handed the flyer back to the girl and rubbed his eyes.

"What's the matter?" she said. "I'm not going to remember all that. Can you say it again?"

"No," Miami said. "I can't."

"Well then how am I supposed to do my job?"

"What do you know about this? Whose idea was it, to do this show?"

"Nothing. I don't know nothing."

"Who gave you this flyer? Who told you to advertise this shit?"

"Rattlesnake Master. But I don't know what *advertise* means—"

"And Coral agreed to it?" He couldn't believe it. "To dancing at Trashlands? Why is she doing this, after all this time?"

She stared at him. "Why do you think?"

There was a pause. Miami felt blood spreading through his body, as if he had chugged some of Tahiti's alcohol and it had gone straight to his head. It was anger he felt, and the hot grip of panic. He felt he was losing her. But he had never had her. "How many boarders have you told about this?"

The girl shook her head. "You're the first."

"Give it to me, please." He snatched the flyer.

"I'm supposed to... I'll get in trouble! You're going to get me in trouble!"

"Tell Rattlesnake Master you did what you were supposed to do. You told all the men. It's fine," Miami said. "I'm going to make it all right."

He found Coral in the river. She had waded up to her waist, despite the cold air. What did she do when the river froze? Miami wondered for the first time. How did everyone eat then, keep warm in their trailers that had no fireplaces, behind their windows that had no glass? She turned when he approached, saw it was him, and did not look again. Miami stood on the bank with the flyer. "What is this?" he asked.

"I'm busy," Coral said. "I can't look right now."

"You know what it is."

"I don't, actually."

"It's a Trashlands advertisement."

He saw her jaw clench. "Don't shout."

"What, I'll scare away the plastic?"

"What is it an advertisement for?" she asked.

"What do you think?" He couldn't look at the flyer again, see that handwriting. "You and Foxglove. One night only.

At Trashlands. You and Foxglove." He lowered his voice. Maybe he had been shouting. "Twin flames."

"Twin flames," she repeated. "Why does it say that?"

"I suppose because you both have red hair." He crumpled the flyer.

But it was plastic. It wouldn't crumple. It sprang back whole in his hand. It would last for a hundred years. They would have to live with it forever. His children would have to deal with it. He flung it into the river.

"Don't do that," Coral said. They watched the flyer drift past her, swallowed by the current, only to bob up again. "Someone's only going to pluck that out."

"Fine," Miami said. He stepped forward, into the river, and pulled it out himself. He shook water off the flyer. His pants leg was damp and his shoe squeaked with water. "I thought you never wanted to go onstage. I thought you hated that place. That man."

"It's complicated. I do. But Foxglove said she'll be there with me the whole time." Coral pulled some plastic out of the river, an awkward thing, blue as the tropical waters that he and his sister had been named for.

He wondered if the river had ever been that color. Coral brought the plastic to the bank and set it down. He should have helped her, but he could not bring himself to.

"He's paying me in diesel," she said. Water streamed from her hair and clothes. She must have been freezing. "Rattlesnake Master. He has drums of it buried in the ground, regular deliveries from some supplier. Where else will we find fuel that hasn't gone bad? I told Trillium we can take it and go. We'll leave that same night, go get my son, and get out of here."

"Where?" Miami asked. "Where would you go?"

"It doesn't matter. Just out. Trillium just wants to go somewhere else. He's wanted to for years."

"What do *you* want?"

A pause, during which the breeze slashed her hair. Anything could happen in a moment, Miami knew. His sister could have died in the flash of a decision: telling the wrong person who she was, just crossing the path of someone who would hurt her. His wife could have decided to leave in an instant. Shanghai was taken, as Coral had told him, in just such an instant.

Coral looked at the plastic she had pulled from the river, and Miami recognized it from his youth. Part of a slide. Would she know what that was? At Trashlands, he had seen no playgrounds.

He waited for Coral to say something, to answer his question. He waited for a long time.

Tahiti squinted at him when Miami appeared at the back door of the club, but it took only a moment for the bodyguard to smile. "Do you have trouble seeing?" Miami asked as Tahiti held the door open, ushering him into the dark and pounding hall.

"Yes," Tahiti admitted.

"Always? When did that start?"

"A while ago. Headaches and blurriness."

"I understand," Miami said. He tapped the frames of his own glasses. The lenses cost half a year's work and he knew the prescription wasn't quite right. He still had headaches too, and trouble discerning who was on the opposite side of the street.

But it was all right enough. It made the shapes of the world mostly make sense. And many people had headaches—from hunger, from just breathing the air. Despite the cost, he saw eyeglasses on people in the city, noticed often-squeaking hearing aids and wheelchairs. He had seen none of those things in Trashlands, he realized.

"Boss doesn't know about the eyes," Tahiti said. "I'd appreciate if you'd keep it between us. Something like that could get me fired." He tugged at his collar, where he had a jagged scar, like a bit of barbed wire.

"Of course."

"Summer fixed up a pair for me but then something happened."

"What?"

"Someone needed them more."

Miami was not sure what he expected, but in the back office of Trashlands, Rattlesnake Master sat behind a real desk, heavy and metal. It must have been ancient, pulled from the river whole. Or maybe Rattlesnake Master had built his office around it. Miami remembered what Coral had told him about the club: the building had already been here, a theater that survived the floods. Rattlesnake Master had just fixed it up, changed its purpose, added junk, added women.

The man leaned back in a chair Miami recognized as probably made by Summer, PVC pipes and a woven plastic seat. Another chair sat before the desk. A couch slumped in the corner. Candles shoved in sports bottles lit the windowless room. The light flickered over the walls, peeling red wallpaper plastered with flyers. They were old advertisements for shows at Trashlands, all of them as misspelled as JT's flyer. Plastic spread over the desk, beside a tarnished metal scale—and a plate of steaming meat. Miami was surprised to recognize it. Chicken.

Where had he gotten a chicken? Miami had seen no livestock around the junkyard, no farming even. Coral had told him the vegetable garden Summer had planted had been razed. Rattlesnake Master had taken some of her crops and burned the others.

To grow anything here, Summer told Miami when he asked her about it, *you need to do it in secret. You didn't hear that from me.*

The smell of the meat was disorienting, as was the fact that Rattlesnake Master ignored the plate. He was letting it get cold. He must have eaten meat often enough that he didn't need to devour it, as Miami would have.

"Come in, sit down," Rattlesnake Master said, gesturing at the other chair. "How's your story coming along?"

"Fine," Miami said. He didn't sit. "I'm here to cut a deal."

Rattlesnake Master leaned on his chin. "I like the sound of that. Go on."

"This show you're having, with Coral?"

"And Foxglove, our tattooed darling. I'm glad word got to you. I was beginning to worry our new employee wasn't worth it."

"She did her job," Miami said. "She did what you asked her to do, don't worry."

"But it's Coral you want to know about, isn't that right? I knew she would be a draw. Been watching that one for a long time."

Miami fought to control the heat that flooded to his hands. He wanted to squeeze the man's neck, to stop his smirking. "You want me to write a story about you, right?"

"Aren't you?"

"I wasn't planning to. The story was supposed to be about Scrappalachia in general."

"But Scrappalachia's huge! Scrappalachia is many things,

and many places, most of them not as sophisticated as Trash-lands. Why on God's plastic Earth would you want to write about anyplace other than right here?" He pounded the desk with one finger.

"It's not what I want," Miami said. "It's what my editor assigned. But here's the thing." He leaned in. "I think you're right. I think the real story is here at the club."

"The only story."

"The only story, right. I'd like to interview you seriously. An in-depth interview. And I'd like to interview some of the dancers."

"Foxglove is really the only one who can speak in complete sentences—"

"I'm thinking this is a cover story."

"The cover?" Rattlesnake Master said. "Really?"

"Readers love a self-made man. A man who made himself out of scrap."

"And made a kingdom too. I'm really more of a mayor, you know. Do you know what that is? Do they still have mayors in the cities?"

"They do," Miami said.

They were all just as corrupt and self-serving as this man.

"*The Mayor of Trashlands.* That would be a good headline, don't you think?"

"I do. And I think I can make it happen. I think I can convince my editor. But he's a stubborn man. To do that—" Miami leaned even closer, resting his palms on the desk, feeling the bits of plastic stab into his skin "—we need to come to an arrangement."

29

Foxglove

Foxglove fixed Coral's hair. She went slowly because the plastic bristles, on the brush Summer had made, hurt, and that girl's hair was a nest. "Have you ever," she asked seriously, working out a tangle, "brushed your hair before?"

She was trying to make Coral laugh, or at least smile, and it worked a little.

"I could make you a brush," Summer said. She was bent over Coral's hand, painting her nails a crimson color with another tiny brush. Foxglove thought the bristles of this one had come from human hair. The paint smelled noxious, like tattoos.

"I don't think anyone's going to see my fingernails," Coral protested.

But Summer said, "It's how you feel that counts."

How was Coral feeling? How did Foxglove herself feel? she wondered as a knot came free in the other girl's hair.

Memories flooded Foxglove, and she was not sure why: her first time onstage when Rattlesnake Master had pushed her on, then waited in the wings with his arms crossed. She had turned to the crowd and saw only the white orb of the oil drum spotlight, a distant planet that would not save her. She couldn't dance. She couldn't move. She sat down on the stage and waited until the song was over.

She hadn't known then that the song of Trashlands never ended. You danced until they decided you were done.

"You could make lots of things yourself, with your skills," Summer was saying. "You're such a craftsperson."

"The pieces I make aren't really useful," Coral said.

"Well, I don't know why you couldn't adapt. That's what life is about, right? Adapting?"

Foxglove couldn't see Coral morphing into someone who made objects people understood, let alone paid good money for. Besides, Coral was always leaving her shit in trees. Foxglove would come back from peeing in the woods and get tangled in a mess of straws hanging from a branch, or stumble over a pyramid of water bottles. Hearing her cry out, Tahiti would come running. He always got to where she was fast.

Those were the times she let him hold her, stopping her from tripping over Coral's art—or over her own shoes, coming offstage. It was always so damned dark. The music pounded in her ears, and she let the only man she trusted lead her off into the wings.

He stayed close as she made deals behind the curtain. For her whole life, she would link the musty, rank smell of old velvet with haggling, getting men to take less for more. Less of her body, more of their plastic.

"Aren't you afraid you're going to run out of room?" Tahiti had said to her after the last tattoo, when she had bargained her finger.

"I've got some parts I'm saving."

"And then what? What will you do then?"

"I'll figure something out." Foxglove didn't look at him. "Maybe we'll have saved up enough money to go somewhere else."

"You won't be saving nothing if you keep spending on pills."

"That's none of your business," Foxglove said.

Maybe he hadn't heard what she had said, the *we*. She disappeared behind the curtain, its folds settling around her like arms.

It wasn't that Foxglove hated Coral's art. Foxglove just wished she understood the pieces more. They made her feel inferior. She didn't like remembering that she knew nothing. That she had come from trash back to trash—she had only changed yards. Rattlesnake Master had said that to her.

She fluffed Coral's hair. "You look real pretty."

"You are real pretty." Summer blew on the nails. "Now to get you dressed."

Foxglove knew this was a source of anxiety for Coral, but Summer had brought options, a pile of shiny scraps she held up for Coral one by one as Coral made a face.

Coral made a lot of faces.

Foxglove put away the brushes and the bottles of potions, tallow and an oil of calendula flower. Both were used for softening skin. Coral had needed a lot of softening. Foxglove felt very tired, and they weren't even close to showtime. She would definitely need a pick-me-up. She had spent so much time with Coral, she had neglected herself. She left the two talking about clothes, and went to the back.

What she loved most about her trailer was that the bedroom had a door that locked. True, the door was flimsy. A man could bust in, easy. The door had been broken at least once. She could tell by the splinters at the top, the scratches around the hinges. But the lock still worked. The sound of its small bar sliding into place was the sweetest sound she knew. It made her shiver with pleasure. No, with relief.

She closed the door, locked it, even though it was only Summer and Coral in the next room. She considered her closet. She had told Coral it didn't matter what they wore. Which was true. Nobody would be looking at their clothes. Still, Foxglove pondered her own outfit. She wanted something that would catch the lights, something that wouldn't clash with their hair. She rejected a bra made from clingy plastic wrap. Too showy. She wanted Coral to feel safe, she reminded herself.

As usual, she knew Tahiti was right outside. If she listened, she could hear him, moving around. But she felt something different now, knowing he was there, so close behind the thin metal and plastic shell of her trailer. If she touched the wall, could he feel her?

Or had she changed things? Ruined them?

Today had been a clean day. She had stood below the shower, thrown her robe over the woodpile. Tahiti had held the curtain around her. The water always seemed cold, even in the hottest times. It was never relaxing to wash, only an obligation. And now, as the air shifted from unbearably hot to unbearably frigid, it was painful. The water felt sharp.

She washed below her arms, wet her hair with the hard soap, rubbed at herself until she couldn't stand it anymore.

Then she turned back for her robe. Tahiti stepped forward to put the cork into the shower bag, saving the water that could be saved. He got wet, he always did, but he never complained. He never slipped up and looked at her, either.

She stuck her arm into her robe. She tied the sash. "You never look at me."

"I'm supposed to protect you, not look at you," he said.

"What if someone came out of the woods when I was showering and grabbed me?"

"Then I would look at you, to grab you back."

"I don't like to be touched," Foxglove said.

"I know. I would touch you, though, to help you," Tahiti said.

"Because it's your job?"

"Because it's the right thing to do."

"How do you know?" Foxglove demanded. "How do you know I don't like to be touched?"

"I've been with you a long time. I know you'd rather get tattooed by a needle than be touched by a man. I understand."

Foxglove wondered if he did understand.

"Look at me now," she said. She was clothed in her robe, though the thin, wet fabric clung to her skin.

Tahiti did. When his eyes met her own she felt something inside her rend, break like the lock on her door—opening because *she* had unlocked it, not because it had been kicked in. That shuddering click that *she* chose.

"What if I only touch you?" she said.

★ ★ ★

Foxglove chose her clothes and she chose her drug: *V*, the happy numb. By the time she unlocked the door and went back into the main living space, Coral had dressed in a silver bra and shorts. Foxglove wouldn't have chosen that. It looked almost like what JT had worn her first awful night onstage.

But it was fine, it would do. Coral and Foxglove didn't clash. She had chosen a one-piece herself, green with its own silver stripe. It was stretchy and soft and had a yawning hole in the middle for her stomach, barely covering her back. It would be easy to take off, just a strap pushed from her shoulder and a shove down. She could step out of it, kick it aside. Men loved that shit.

Summer and Coral turned to look at Foxglove in the doorway.

Coral's eyes were wet. "I can't wear these shoes."

"Yes, you can," Foxglove said.

"I'll fall before I'm even onstage."

Summer had painted Coral's face with berries and clay to dull her redness. Foxglove thought she looked like an illustration, a picture in Mr. Fall's book come to life. A girl from a far-off place. Someone who had lived a long time ago.

Foxglove stretched out her hand. A pill lay there. "Take this," she said to Coral. "You won't feel a thing if you fall, then. You won't care."

"I can't take a pill." Coral looked at Summer, panicked.

Summer said, "Whatever gets you through, baby. I won't judge. And I won't tell Trillium or Mr. Fall."

Foxglove stepped forward in the tall box shoes that were a little hard, a little painful. Coral was right—but every day, every breath, was pain. The *V* would make it not matter.

The only pain she could feel for sure was the stitch of a new tattoo, which reminded her she was still alive, she was still fighting—she leaned down from the height of a million stars and folded the pill into Coral's small mouth. "We are none of us," she said, "going to tell a man anything."

30

Foxglove

Before they knew that Foxglove would not run, they chained her by the ankle. The chain was attached to Rattlesnake Master's desk. Or to the pole of the club. Or, if they thought she needed a little air or sunshine, outside to a tree.

Those first weeks were a blur. She took a lot of pills, because they didn't want her to run. They also didn't want her to remember. They wanted her weak and agreeable—and she didn't care. She didn't fucking care. She opened her mouth for anything, pill or water or the hope of food.

There wasn't much food, but she was used to that.

It was outside, staked to the one, nearly dead tree by the back porch, that she first saw Tahiti. She saw him as shade.

It was a hot day. Dirt blew into her mouth, and she was beginning to learn that some of the men at the club came for relief from the weather as much as for the dancing girls. In the yard she had no escape from the heat pressing down.

The chillers ran, monsters at her back, cooling the inside of the club only. Then the shade came. She turned and could make out the shape of a man. A man big enough to block out the sun.

Rattlesnake Master approached from the club behind her. When she heard the sound of his boots, Foxglove felt her heart jump.

Before she came to Trashlands, she and her mama had had a dog. They fed him scraps and he hung around, but Foxglove felt that they were not feeding him enough. Bones poked through his black-and-white fur. Her mama said they couldn't keep feeding three mouths, they were going to have to do something. Foxglove thought she meant sell the dog. The girl snuck him bits of her own meager dinner when her mama wasn't looking, trying to help.

Then one evening they returned after foraging to find the dog, waiting by their fire, his mouth pooling with blood. He had found a rattler, her mama said, bit the snake before Foxglove and her mama had to face it. The snake lay dead at the dog's feet. Her mama chopped and fried up the pieces. But the rattlesnake had bitten the dog too, and he would not last the night.

That's what I call a problem working itself out, her mama had said.

When she learned Rattlesnake Master's name, Foxglove knew what kind of creature he was. It didn't matter that his name referred to a plant and not a snake at all. He was the kind of creature that would kill her dog. The kind that had given her mama the idea of how to fix the problem of Foxglove too, the other mouth she couldn't keep.

The stranger who introduced himself as Tahiti was young

but huge. He had always been big, she would learn later. Even as a child, he was mistaken for older, more mature. His size had only caused him pain.

"Whoa, whoa," Rattlesnake Master said to the stranger. "The entrance to the club is that way, big guy." He pointed around to the front. "We don't want any trouble back here."

"I'm not here to make trouble," the man said. "I'm just looking for work."

Rattlesnake Master studied him more closely. "What kind of work?"

But the man pointed to Foxglove. "Why is she chained up? She steal something?"

"No, no. She's just precious, that's all."

"That's no way to treat someone precious."

"Do you have a better idea?"

"I'll guard her," he said.

"How do I know you won't just run off with her?" Rattlesnake Master asked.

"Chain me," Tahiti said. "Chain me instead of her."

As she stepped onto the stage with Coral, Foxglove thought of the chain. The spotlight blinded her as it always did. The kid in the booth played the stupid song. She had developed moves to use over the years: striding back and forth across the stage, floor work where she lay on her back and stared at her shoes kicking at the ceiling. She tried not to think of the grime below her. She had learned not to smile. Men didn't like that.

She thought of Tahiti.

Rattlesnake Master had allowed him to take the chain collar off a long time ago, after it became apparent that he too would not leave. They would none of them run. They were too broken or lost or lonely. They had nowhere on Earth to run to.

But before that, he had worn the chain, and that time had left its mark, the crude metal, welded from junk, digging into his skin. The wounds had scabbed over, then broken and bled again until they made a scar on his neck. Like another collar.

Standing beside the shower, shivering, Foxglove had touched Tahiti's scars with her fingers, then with her tongue. She had kissed them. She had kissed the side of his face, where he had other scars, then his forehead, then his mouth.

It was different when she was in charge, she thought as the spotlight hit her full in the face. She decided this was as good a time as any. She wound the strap around her hand and pulled the one-piece outfit down. The light struck her like a punch, but she didn't feel it.

She concentrated on Coral, whose eyes were as wide as stars. Foxglove took her friend's hand. "Look only at me," she whispered. She helped Coral get her top off. Foxglove flung it onto the floor dramatically, even though the drug had hit and she felt like she was swimming through something soft and warm.

Tahiti had waited to kiss her back. He hadn't touched her until she said to, and then, only where she said to and how she said, waiting for instructions, wanting to be led by her.

Foxglove cupped her hand around Coral's face and kissed her. Their bodies looked so different. That might be good or bad to the crowd, to Rattlesnake Master. She was sure he was out there, watching.

Tahiti's hand had hesitated on Foxglove's stomach, even though she said it was all right. He traced the extra skin there, the roundness that never went away, even after the baby did. At first it had bothered her. She had tried pills, starving herself, bitter herbs to make her belly shrink.

But after a time, she became used to it, even began to like it a little. It was the only thing she had of her son, besides the tattoo near her eye. Her stomach was the thing he had made.

Coral was making a sound, maybe whispering to herself, but Foxglove didn't hear it. She was miles away, feeling again Tahiti's fluttering hand on her belly, hearing him ask, *Is it all right to touch you here?*

Yes, she had said, and then she decided to tell him. *I had a baby but he died.*

I know, Tahiti said. *I was the one who buried him.*

He had always been there, the man in the shadows, shielding her from the worst of Rattlesnake Master, standing watch as other men came and went through her door. He never came in. Not until he was invited.

Foxglove didn't notice—the drug was so strong, the spotlight so bright—that in the audience at Trashlands, there was only one man.

31

Coral

In the icehouse, she remembered being afraid to speak. Then, being too cold. If she spoke, would she end everything? Ruin it? Would he not love her then? Would they spring apart instantly like rats when stones were thrown at them, like the river when she waded in and the waves parted around her body?

It wasn't that she wanted what Robert did to her.

But she wanted something.

She wanted to feel special. She wanted to belong. Boys her age had already found good trash, valuable plastic washing up right next to the camp, and she hadn't yet. She couldn't seem to get to anything in time. She didn't feel that she was very good at this life, that she was supposed to do it, even though she had been born into it.

Even though, what else was there to do?

They lived then at what was called the Settlement. Be-

fore the floods, the camp had been a kind of history park—
Mr. Fall had tried to explain it—where people had looked
at old houses for amusement, wandering around, observing
performers paid to make candles and grind knives. It didn't
make sense to either Coral or Mr. Fall. But the park had
survived, at least some of its buildings, with moss on their
roofs and plastic sheets patching the windows.

Men hunted in the Settlement, and some women too. But
Coral wasn't much interested in that work. The animals they
brought back looked scrawnier and scrawnier every day. It
seemed less like a necessity and more a mercy to kill those
animals. No, she thought. She was not a hunter.

Nor was she a nurturer, like Mr. Fall. Children gathered around him, drawn to the bus. They loved its huge-
ness, like a strange bug, one that would have been killed off
by weather or pollution. Soon Coral realized another force
drew the children to Mr. Fall: He was safe.

He would not hurt them. He would feed them if he and
Coral could spare anything, which they never ever could,
but still he produced acorns from his pockets, mushrooms
from his hat, or found berries somewhere, somehow. He
would keep the children warm by the fire. He would tell
them a story about the past, about the world that was gone,
something their mothers would be moved that he remembered when the children related it later. A song for something called *McDonald's*, the phrase *Yes we can*.

The camp was full of men who took food from children.
They took children for wives. They took them for reasons
Mr. Fall refused to tell her about, only that she had to be
back at the bus before nightfall. And she had to trust her
gut. But what did that mean?

Her gut was hungry. It rumbled with the ache that was absence or eating the wrong thing—a bitter root, a plant out of season. Plants were always out of season; there were no seasons.

She knew her gut would not alert her to danger because danger was everywhere and difficult to quantify. Was the coldness of the river worse than its smell? Was the plastic in the deep parts worth the pitfalls: sunken barbed wire that could cut her, a tree limb that could snag and hold her down, the bodies she might find? Was anything worth it?

Danger was in degrees, and she had become numb to it.

Children had been drawn to her old teacher, Robert, too. All girls, though Coral didn't make this connection until later.

Mr. Fall was quiet and kind. But Robert was magnetic, passionate, charming. She felt pulled to him, like a fire. She felt warm when she spent time around him, special when his gaze fell upon her. Singled out. When he was lecturing, his voice sounded rich as milk, a fullness she pretended she remembered. He assigned Coral extra work, because she was so eager and smart. He wanted to meet with her after lessons. First, in the dirt circle, ringed by trees, that the camp used as a school meeting place.

Then, alone in the icehouse.

The icehouse was one of the buildings that had survived. Coral was not sure how. It was squat and windowless, too small to hold classes in. It had a peaked roof and a door that latched. Inside were low shelves and a cracked, clay floor that tilted to a drain, clogged with weeds. The icehouse sat in the shade, beneath a stand of trees. It felt cool enough even on hot days to preserve the rare bits of game, or cheese from the goats staked around the camp. Otherwise, the icehouse was used for storage, holding tools that would be ruined by rain. Nobody wanted to live there because of the dark and damp. Because there was only one way out. One latching door.

Mr. Fall said the building was originally used to keep blocks of ice cool. But ice never lasted long, even in the icehouse.

Funny, all these years later, Coral couldn't remember anything Robert had taught her. What did he lecture about, all those afternoons in the dirt, sitting on the bumper or the burned-out couch? He had a book—but it was not Mr. Fall's book. It was a yellow book. Yellow as dust, yellow as the eye of a hurt dog.

She thought now, onstage with Foxglove, as the blaring spot of Trashlands hit her skin so hot, so bright, she heard a sound, a buzzing—she thought that Robert had read the children names from the yellow book, old names that were no longer popular, like his name. She thought he had talked to them about work they could no longer do and words she had never understood, not then and not now, like *upholstery* and *plumbing*.

It was strange what stuck in her mind, Coral thought, as Foxglove pulled off Coral's silver top and the light slapped her. *Upholstery, plumbing.*

Ditch Witch, that was another one.

In the icehouse she had floated above her body.

On the stage at Trashlands, she floated to memory.

She remembered the bits of straw sticking to her. That had hurt. Other things had hurt too. But nothing compared to

the hurt of after, when Robert was gone. The next morning, he was just gone.

She didn't know how long he had been the teacher for
the camp. Not long, he had told her. He had said something
about people not being friendly in the last camp, not being a
place that had appreciated someone like him. But she hadn't
understood that at the time.

Sitting alone on the burned-out couch the morning after
he had touched her, she thought maybe she understood.

She had been the first to arrive at the school that morning
and had claimed the best spot, the one directly in his view.
She didn't mind the springs that poked up from the busted
cushions of the couch, its hard back, its faint but ever-present
scent of ash. Other children showed up, took the bumper or
rested their backs against a tree.

After a few moments of waiting, someone said, "Are we
early?"

"The sun is in the right place in the sky."

"I've already had my breakfast."

"Shit, I wish I had breakfast."

Coral said nothing. She was privy to the secret knowledge of her body, how it had held Robert briefly, like a cage.
She knew things other children did not know. She was not
a child anymore. She felt like she had shot past the others.
They didn't understand.

"Fuck this," one of the children said. "I'm out of here."

It was the signal the others needed. They all scrambled
up, leaving her alone.

Coral waited a long time on the couch that smelled like
fire. The couch was still functional, was one of the many

thoughts that ran through her head. It was still comfortable, despite its lumps. She could wait forever.

In the end, Mr. Fall came to get her.

"I don't think he's coming today," Mr. Fall said cheerfully. He didn't know. His ignorance grated on her. She wanted to tell him. It wanted to explode out of her, the secret, what she and Robert had done. How she was special, different. "All the other kids are out playing. Don't you want to play, Coral?"

"No," Coral said. "I'm too old for playing."

"What would you like to do, then?" he asked.

She thought. She wanted to sleep. She wanted to wash. She wanted to float in the river on her back. She wanted maybe not to have the knowledge she now possessed about her teacher, the knife scar on his stomach, the way he had cried.

"I want to work," Coral said.

She liked to think, onstage with Foxglove, that she never would have returned to the school, even if Robert had come back. That it was lost to her forever. She had moved past it—and that was the morning she knew.

Mr. Fall had always talked to her and shown her what he did as a plucker, how they lived, preparing her for the kind of life she would have to lead. But after that morning, she went out with Mr. Fall and his crew almost every day.

She liked when the work was tough—the plastic snagged in roots or buried in mud, currents slamming her body so she had to brace herself just to stay upright—because then she didn't have to think. She had to concentrate on staying alive and on her feet. She didn't even have to figure out what the plastic was. Mr. Fall had taught her not to worry about that.

The numbers on the bottom of plastic were meaningless. A system meant to make people feel better about using so much. It wasn't a system at all. Still, you never knew what something could be, what they could make with it. Just get it, Mr. Fall had said.

She liked not thinking. She liked not being in her head. If Shanghai hadn't come along, she might have stayed outside her head forever.

But then she started feeling exhausted. Strange pains began deep inside her. Sharp, stabbing cramps. Even before she knew what he was, he was angry.

It was the midwife who noticed first.

The midwife at the Settlement was named Bee. She was younger than Ramalina, the midwife and healer Coral would meet years later. Bee wore her hair knotted in whorls she covered with bright cloth.

The midwife stopped Coral one afternoon when she was returning home with the other pluckers. "Are you feeling all right?" Bee asked her in a low tone.

Coral knew and did not want to know. She pretended she didn't. "What do you mean?"

Bee's hands were small and muscular. She placed her hand on Coral's arm, and pulled her out of the line of pluckers, off to the side of the path. "Talk with me a moment."

"I'm good," Coral said. "I have to get back to the bus and look at these."

"The plastic can wait."

"What'll I tell Mr. Fall?"

Bee reached out her other hand and snagged the shoulder

of a passing man. New Orleans. "Tell Mr. Fall that Coral and I are having tea. She'll be home soon."

New Orleans nodded and jogged back to the others. They had worn a track into the grass with their boots.

Coral had good boots. Mr. Fall had found them. The boots were getting too tight for her, but she didn't want to tell him. He would try to find new ones, and that got riskier and riskier. There were no more stores near the Settlement, no rubble that hadn't been picked through.

"Come with me," Bee said.

Bee lived in a shack attached to a hollow tree. Its roots meant her home was more permanent than a bus, which Coral found both exhilarating and frightening. Such confidence, to believe you would not have to run. To believe something would not come for you, roost you out in the night. Or to believe, if danger came, you could leave it all behind, everything you had made.

The shack was barely large enough for two people. The tree had been hit by lightning, making a chasm in the middle, and the midwife had widened the hole more with a torch, attached plastic siding and a steel roof. Corrugated steel made a door, secured with a padlocked chain. The midwife wore the key around her neck on a string. "I keep medicines here," she explained. "I can't have people just wandering in."

Coral watched as Bee unlocked the chain. The padlock clicked open with an audible *thunk*. Bee wound the chain and stashed the padlock.

It was dark inside. Moss grew on the roof, hanging down from cracks and seeping through the crude walls. Plants hung from the ceiling too, tied into drying bundles. Coral recognized a few. Lavender, yellow goldenrod.

"Have you eaten?" Bee asked, riffling through some plastic tubs.

"When?"

"Today? At all today?"

"This morning," Coral said. "Before we went out."

"What did you have?"

"Some corn chips."

"Not enough," Bee said. "Not enough at all. Do you know what protein is?"

Coral remembered a shape in Mr. Fall's book. Maybe a pyramid? Since Robert left, Mr. Fall had taken to reading to Coral in the evenings. But she was often too tired to pay much attention.

"You're going to have to start eating more bugs," Bee said. "Mushrooms. Meat, if you can find it. If it's clean. Squirrels are good."

"I'm no good at hunting."

"We should hunt for you, if we knew what was good for us. If we cared about each other." Coral didn't understand. Bee saw it on her face. "Do you know what's happening to you?" Bee asked.

Coral didn't know how to answer.

"Did someone hurt you? The man who lives with you, Mr. Fall?"

"No!" Coral said. "He's like my father."

"Then who…?" Bee pointed to Coral's stomach, the hard little hill that had appeared overnight, that Coral could see when she washed, which she did not do often. She knew she had stopped bleeding—but she had not bled regularly to begin with, and it was difficult to keep track. She knew she was tired and sick sometimes too, dizzy and nauseous. She felt strange pangs, like she was being stabbed from the inside. She thought it was Robert's ghost. She thought no one could see her stomach, the sudden insistent swell.

But Bee could see it. "I'd say about four full months ago."

"Five."

"You know who it was, then?"

Coral nodded but did not tell. She did not tell.

"Was it done in pain?"

She didn't know how to answer that.

"Are you in pain now?" Bee asked.

"Sometimes."

Bee got to work with things she pulled from the plastic tubs: jars and canisters and water bottles filled with seeds and dried, packed herbs. She measured and sifted. Coral felt very tired. She sat down on the ground. Bee had no chairs, but she had a lumpy gray shape on the floor that might have been a mattress. It filled one half of the room.

"I don't want this to happen," Coral said.

"Well, it's happening, whether you want it to or not."

"It isn't fair." She had never said these words to anyone, but they spilled out of her, like the herbs Bee poured into a bowl. "I didn't want this! He didn't say anything about this. He's not even here!"

Bee looked at her. "Men rarely are. They take what they want and they go. They don't stick around for what's next."

"What's next?" Coral asked.

Bee handed her a mug of something steaming. It smelled like mud.

"A lot of pain," Bee said.

★ ★ ★

On the stage, Coral was naked. On the stage, the music was inside her, and Foxglove was dancing around her, not looking at her, not looking at anything. The beat was the thud of Coral's heart. It felt like *his* heart. She remembered the kick inside.

What kind of world did her child spiral into? Coral had to spit plastic from her water. She had fed him a diet of bugs and weeds, and whatever floated down the river—the contents of dented cans, something stale called *snacks*. She fed him what she fed herself: nonperishables that should have perished years ago. After that day in the tree, Bee had started sneaking meat to her, finding it somewhere, trading for who knew what.

Bee had gone with her to the rainbow bus, to tell Mr. Fall. It was the beginning of a series of terrible things. It was the first awful thing after the icehouse: Mr. Fall's tears, his guilt, and his anger. Robert getting her pregnant had nothing to do with Mr. Fall, but he thought it did. He thought he had failed Coral. He blamed himself, thought he should have known.

"There was no way to know," Coral said.

"Hmm, there were ways," Bee said.

"You couldn't have stopped me. I thought it was going to be all right. I trusted him."

"I thought you were too young to be bothered by men," Mr. Fall said. "Too smart. I thought I had protected you."

"They're never too young. You should know that," said Bee, who wasn't being especially helpful.

Coral thought that would be the worst thing, telling Mr. Fall about the baby.

But they were all the worst things.

After she told him, he started working late, past when she had gone to sleep. She would half hear him rustling around. It sounded like someone looking for something in her dreams—but it was only Mr. Fall examining plastic, work they normally did before the sun fell. He started spending hours in the water. They needed more money, he said. More food. She would hear him muttering about it to himself. They were going to need a lot more.

She was tired all the time. Her stomach felt like a heavy bag, like she was padded with mud. She wanted to leave the river and go back to the bus on those long days, but Mr. Fall wouldn't quit searching and he wouldn't let her go home by herself. She had to sit on the shore and wait for him.

"It's not safe for you to walk alone," Mr. Fall said.

"One of the men can go with me. Like New Orleans."

"It's not safe for you to be alone with a man."

"Even a man we know?" Coral thought of New Orleans. He was shy and skinny like the telephone poles she had seen buried in mud. Once he had shared an apple with her. It had tasted sour and hard. Mealy and delicious. She had chewed the peel for a long time. It reminded her of plastic.

Finally, she won her freedom by convincing Mr. Fall that it had already happened, the bad thing. She was already pregnant by a man who was gone. She could not get more pregnant. She could walk herself back to the bus just fine.

Mr. Fall started hoarding food. Never before had the cupboards in the bus been so full. He filled plastic tubs with dirt. When Coral dug her fingers through one of them, she pulled up carrots. *They store better in there*, he said, and slammed the lid down.

She noticed he was eating less and less himself. She thought at first—stupidly, selfishly—that he had lost some of his appetite, being so worried about her all the time. But when he refused meat, savory lumps of meat from Bee, which she had melted into a stew, Coral knew something was wrong.

He grew thinner, his arms hollowing out. He lost the last of his silver hair.

She grew rounder in her breasts and belly.

People started to talk, to whisper about her weight. It was an awful thing, the whispering. Then it was another kind of awful when they finally directed their jeers at Coral's face. *Save some food for the rest of us, bitch.*

"People have been having babies for thousands of years," Bee said tartly when Coral told her about the whispers and the talk. She set a pot without a handle on the fire to boil. "You're not the first. You won't be the last. Hopefully."

"But to be my age—"

"It happens all the time."

"To be alone—"

"You're not alone," Bee said. "You have me and Mr. Fall. Stop feeling sorry for yourself. You don't have time for that. Don't waste your energy on it. Drink up."

Bee seemed to think Coral's job was to drink the smelly, leafy concoctions she made, to eat extra and productively, skipping the snacks or questionable canned goods in favor of food grown in the ground.

Plastic filled the ground, and who knew what metals, what poisons, had bled into it. But Bee said it was the only earth they had.

Bee seemed to think that Coral should be happy about

all this, that she should be excited, darning clothes, patching baby bottles. She seemed to think that of course Coral would want to take care of herself, to give up the tub beer New Orleans might try to sneak her every now or then. She must never think of pills, Bee said. She must never smoke anything. If someone was smoking—any cigarette at all, no matter how fragrant—she needed to get herself away as soon as possible. Same with car fumes, though fewer and fewer cars drove into or out of the Settlement.

Mr. Fall had his book. Bee had her knowledge of the earth, seeping the hardy goldenrod into honey. Honey was delicious, and Coral wanted to try some. But Bee said the golden syrup, flecked with stringent blossoms and leaves, was medicine only, for cough.

Coral once asked Bee what she would do when all the plants in the world were gone. But the midwife said she didn't use too much, that she always left some plants in the ground.

"But what about when the plants go extinct?" Coral asked.

"I won't let them," Bee said.

"People make everything go extinct."

"Then I'll find other plants. We'll adapt. We'll find a way."

Coral wished she had come to Bee sooner. She wished she had known what to ask. She didn't know that there were plants you could take, bitter teas you could swallow, to stop growing the cells inside your body.

Bee did that too. She helped people in every stage, she said. It was all part of the same work. But now, she said, it was too late. Coral had waited too long. The baby was coming—he could not be stopped—and all they could do was assist his passage, make it as easy as possible.

It wasn't easy at all.

Onstage at Trashlands, Coral had the idea she could try to read Foxglove's tattoos, that learning the many names would keep her mind off what they were doing. Foxglove seemed to be in her own world, not looking at anyone, even at Coral. Coral felt almost as if she had interrupted her friend in the act of dancing alone in her trailer. Maybe that was the drug. The pill made Coral feel unsteady, unmoored from her body like a shed sliding off a hill.

The tattoos, she reminded herself. Look at the names.

But Foxglove's long hair flicked over the names, and Coral saw them only for a second: *Dodo, Ibex, North Atlantic*. Coral told herself to remember those words, to ask Mr. Fall about them later.

She had wondered what would happen if she didn't listen to Bee. What would happen if she refused the meat, if she spit the weedy drinks back up, as she wanted to? If she drank the river water: putrid, sometimes green and sometimes red. If she took pills or beer. If she jumped from the top of the bus. Would that stop the baby, hurtling through time to her?

She thought later that maybe the bad thoughts she had had about him, how she had not wanted him, made him worse. The thoughts passed through her as violent and sudden as food poisoning. But maybe somehow he knew. Maybe that was why he was born furious.

He stayed angry as he grew. He grew restless, insatiable.

He never slept long and always fitfully, lashing out in his dreams. He never could bear to be without her—but when he was with her, he twisted out of her arms. He screamed at her. He bit her as soon as his teeth grew in. But then he kept on biting. She couldn't bear for Trillium, years later, to put his mouth on her breasts, even lightly, tenderly. Any touch there reminded her of those months—years—when her body was not her own.

Women wept for this. Women died for this, would kill for this, to have a child. But Coral thought, *What have I done?*

The anger, sadness, and hopelessness she felt about being pregnant—it must have permeated her blood. The baby must have sucked it all up like plants absorbed minerals or poison in soil. It was Robert's final and best betrayal to leave her with a difficult child, a baby who chewed her from the inside out, a child who would take everything she had and more.

He was more aware than most children, the other mothers in the camp said. He was smarter. Maybe that was why he didn't need sleep?

He was maybe allergic to some foods, Bee said, and suggested Coral cut out wheat and stick to acorn loaves. Maybe the grain in the field at the Settlement had gotten wet? Could she drink vinegar? Could she barter for milk from the camp's one surviving goat?

He was a challenge, Mr. Fall said, who knew nothing of babies or small children, he admitted, only children old enough to sit behind desks.

What are desks? Coral had thought at the time.

On the stage she thought, *Dodo, Ibex, North Atlantic. Upholstery, plumbing.*

Ditch Witch.
Desks.

Maybe if Shanghai hadn't come along she would have continued to learn. Adapt, Bee had said. Just before the baby was born, Mr. Fall decided the children of the Settlement had gone without an education long enough, and if he had to teach them himself, by gum he would. (*What was gum?*) It wasn't right for them to be denied, especially the girls who had been in danger from their old teacher, and Mr. Fall hadn't even known.

Now he would protect them all. Part of his lessons were about saying *no* and speaking up and trusting yourself, lessons that made Coral feel both relieved and angry.

No one had said those things to her before in a way that she understood. She didn't know what Mr. Fall had meant by your *gut*, other than a body part that felt hungry. No one had told her that her stomach too had a brain, and she needed to follow it, to keep herself safe.

What was safe?

Hollow, she guessed. Without child.

The baby was made of star stuff, Bee said, and history. Her ancestors. The cosmos.

The cosmos were fickle, Coral thought, as the baby grew into a child who kicked, who dumped the larders into the bus aisle, who pinched her arms and scratched her face. Once he could talk, he told her he hated her. He told her he wished they were dead.

Star stuff was fury, Coral thought. And fire.

He pushed his fist into her eye. He split her lip like a rose. He screamed and screamed.

It had been difficult being pregnant. But Coral would go back to it any day. Inside her body, she could keep him from hurting himself or others.

Outside of her she could do nothing.

Only love him with a desperation as intense as it felt hopeless.

She would have given anything at the time, she thought as Foxglove—not knowing her history, not knowing the rules Coral's lover obeyed, lowered her lips to Coral's breast and mimed kissing her there—anything to be only pregnant again. Only stared at. Only made fun of. Only always tired and fearful of what was coming next. Only assumed to not be able to do her work. She remembered what that was like.

The men talked, calling her the names of animals they had mostly only seen in pictures. They called her *brood sow*.

Fucking pig.

Cow.

One night, exhausted and pregnant, she had heard the laughter and her name, the speculations about her weight, as she walked past men drinking around a fire. And she had decided. She was going to prove herself.

There had been a rumor of an animal dead on the coast. A big one. She was going to convince Mr. Fall to go for it. She was going to go for it, pregnant, brood sow or not. She was going to go for the whale.

32

Trillium

He would work. Work was the thing. Work was the way he would survive this. But no customers came up the path to the bus. Night fell. He waited. And still there was no one.

Coral had left in the afternoon, shuffled away by Foxglove and Summer to get ready. He didn't want to see what she would look like, painted and preened for men. He would have thought them traitors, those women taking Coral away from him, helping Rattlesnake Master. But he knew they just needed to eat, same as he did.

He should have started packing, beginning the process of readying the bus to move, when it hadn't budged for so long. He had been planning—hoping—for a move. He had a checklist in his mind, which he had added to over the years, and would run through at night when he couldn't sleep, or in moments like this, when he was alone. He needed to inspect the tires. He needed to check the stock of spare parts.

Nobody showed up for a tattoo. Still, he laid out his needles. He shook the bottles of ink and opened the lids to smell if any had gone rancid. He was not a neat person, but now he swept the aisle of the bus. He made the bed. He pulled a strand of long red hair from the sheets.

He hadn't stopped her. It wasn't his choice. It wasn't his body. But he had to ask Coral, when she had told him—she was dancing onstage at Trashlands, in front of the monster they had avoided for years; she was taking off her clothes— and they had had a fight about it: Did she really want to go after Shanghai?

"He'll be changed," Trillium had said. "It's been a long time. He's not a kid anymore."

"I know that," Coral said.

"The experience will have changed him."

"I fucking know that."

"Trauma changes you," Trillium said. That was a word he had read.

Trauma. It had stuck with him for a reason, because he knew it intimately. Trauma lodged in his own body. Trauma kept him from returning to the woods. He would do anything not to go back there. Dim, unknowable, the sounds coming from everywhere and nowhere at once. Trauma kept Trillium wanting to run, to follow the road, *any* road, to keep moving. He had been denying that urge, the calling from trauma, for years. To keep Coral happy.

But she didn't know what she would find when she went to claim her son, how trauma could have altered him, as it had Trillium. He would never know what he himself could have been, what path he was on before he veered from it, left the road full of survivors and walked alone into the trees.

Trillium said, "He's a man now."

"He's not a man."

"As good as. He may not want to go with us. He might have his own ideas about what he wants to do with his life."

"Fine," Coral said.

This argument was not about Shanghai and she knew it. It was about her.

"I think you're doing this out of guilt," Trillium said.

"I think you're full of shit."

It was the most she had ever cursed at him, since the night Shanghai was taken, when she swore at the sky. That sky would give her nothing. It had brought them only pain. Hard rain, hard snow, and pain.

"You don't have to feel that guilt anymore. You've been holding on to it."

"I don't feel guilty," Coral said.

"It wasn't your fault."

"I know that," she snapped. "I was there. They snatched him from *me*—right in front of *my* eyes, remember?"

"I mean, it wasn't your fault how he was when he was with us. How angry he was. He hurt you. He hurt other people."

"How he *is*." Coral insisted on the word.

As long as her child was living, she would accept anything, Trillium thought. Even the boy's violence, even his rage directed at her. Trillium saw what she put up with because she thought she deserved it.

So her life would be a bit unsatisfying, not what she had hoped. So she made the bed most mornings and they both fell into it most nights too exhausted even to touch. And so she closed her eyes when they did touch. So he was not quite what she wanted, or, he feared, no longer what she wanted.

He didn't understand some of what she talked about. Some of her art—most of her art—was a mystery to him, and when he tried to ask her about it, to explain it, she got defensive. She got mad more and more. She fell silent. She went off on her own, into those woods where he would not go after her.

And so she had made this pact with Foxglove. She had had only two lovers in her lifetime that he knew about: Robert, if he could be called that, and Trillium. But now the world would be her lover. Scrappalachia and the drunk, ungrateful audience at the club, their heads stuffed with that song like rags, their bodies straining to get close to her. Rattlesnake Master would watch her undress.

Why put up with all that? Why did she not want more? Kick Trillium out, try to sell her art, tell him the way she wanted to be touched (did she know how she wanted to be touched?). Was there a way to please her?

Coral didn't think she deserved more. In a way, it kept them together.

"It's only one night," Coral said.

"No it's not," Trillium said. "It's forever."

Finally, he heard the shuffle of footsteps on the path. He opened the accordion doors to see Tahiti standing there. The man shook a bottle at Trillium, one of those big sports drink bottles. It sloshed and smelled, even from where Trillium was standing.

"You want a tattoo?" Trillium asked.

"No."

He opened the doors wider. "Well, come on in."

★ ★ ★

When Tahiti unscrewed the cap of the bottle, a medicinal smell filled the bus, strong as the turpentine Trillium used sometimes.

"Where did you get that alcohol?" Trillium asked as he found cups.

Tahiti poured two generous glugs. "Made it."

"Not wine?"

"Definitely not."

"And not beer?"

"Not that, either." He scooted one cup, a mug with a big chip like a bite out of its rim, across the table to Trillium. "My daddy used to make this, and his daddy before him. It's called *moonshine*."

"Moonshine?"

All this time in Scrappalachia, Trillium and Tahiti had never talked much. He thought they didn't want to anger Rattlesnake Master, and both of them always seemed to be working. Trillium had long wondered about this man, who, like him, had once wandered out of the trees, but who knew enough about his family he remembered their recipes.

"I've been brewing it in the woods, in a still I made out of a bucket and a pot I patched up." He looked down into his cup—proud, Trillium thought, but also nervous.

"Rattlesnake Master doesn't know?"

"He does not, no. He'd take the recipe from me, brew it badly, water it down, and sell it for five times as much as I'd ever charge. He'd do it faster than you could drink a single glass."

Tahiti knew his boss well.

"Coral came across me once." Tahiti raised his eyes.

"Coral?"

"She found my still in the woods. Probably would have thought it was another artist like her, making these wild pieces and just leaving them, like she does. I bet my still looked like that to her. Like I had just made it up. I guess I did." He shook his head. "I wish my mind was as creative as hers. But I was there, messing with the still, trying to get it to work, when she found me, so I told her the truth. Told her it was just booze. And I asked her not to tell Rattlesnake Master."

"She never told me either," Trillium said.

"Coral keeps her word."

She had made deals with Rattlesnake Master and that reporter. She had kept a secret for Tahiti. His lover was more of a mystery to him than he ever realized. He felt love for her, new, powerful love spreading through him, felt it suddenly and violently, like a punch to the chest. What else might he discover about her?

"She'll be fine tonight. Coral," Tahiti said.

Even hearing her name, Trillium felt something deep inside him. Her name spoken by another man. Her body was being viewed by other men. He would never know how many or if they were trying to touch her. He felt certain she would not tell him, even or especially if they tried to hurt her.

He felt a different emotion, gripping the sides of his heart—he could swing so fast from one feeling to the next—he was scared. "Why aren't you there?" he asked Tahiti. "Why aren't you watching Coral and Foxglove? Isn't that your job?"

Tahiti sighed, as if he didn't want to tell this part. "Only one man at the show tonight. One man bought out the whole club. Not much of a threat to either girl, an audience of one, and especially this audience. No rowdy crowd. So, boss sent me home. Foxglove and Coral both said it was okay. I checked with them first."

"One man," Trillium echoed.

Tahiti lowered his eyes.

Trillium was confused. This was good news. Wasn't it? Coral would be safe. "We should toast," he said.

"What should we toast to?"

Coral, Trillium wanted to say. He did not want to picture her alone on that stage while the music thumped, locking eyes with the single stranger who had paid for their way out of here.

Though Foxglove was there with her, young and wise Foxglove. Inking her over the years, Trillium had seen almost every square inch of her body, part by part. It was Coral's turn to see it now.

"Let's toast to your new life," Tahiti said. "You both starting over. With your son."

Her son. "Starting over." Trillium raised his mug.

"It's best to get it down in one gulp."

Trillium tipped his head back and fire rained down his throat. He had a memory, involuntary, of the first time he had touched Coral. The shot felt like that, like all the heat in the world. He swallowed. His head pounded behind his eyes, which watered and stung. The bridge of his nose felt tight. He sensed a headache coming on.

"Another round?" Tahiti said.

"No, no." Trillium choked back a cough. "You could

sell that for a lot of money. It's very strong. Is that the plan, to sell it?"

"Maybe. Someday. I haven't been much for plans."

The opposite of Trillium. He felt he had been making a plan to leave Trashlands as soon as they had arrived, studying the ancient maps Mr. Fall kept in the school tent, thin and patched, the borders all wrong. Trillium had been plotting where they should go. Maybe to a community north of here, though he had heard gangs had overrun the camp known as The Oval. Or maybe south to the Pig Bridge? He had been told stories of places from men when he inked them. Everyone had an opinion about which camp was best, safest, had the best wine, the best women.

Maybe the opinions of those men were not to be trusted.

Tahiti asked him, "Will you come back to Trashlands with the boy?"

"I don't know," Trillium said. He was starting to want another of the burning shots. "I don't think so. I don't imagine Coral would want to come back. And I've been thinking for a long time we could make more money if I was tattooing a new crowd."

"It's nothing to be ashamed of, you know, doing a show at Trashlands. Foxglove does them all the time."

And Foxglove was in another world half the time, Trillium thought, floating in a haze of drugs. Pills were the only bright colors left in the world, he thought sometimes, blue and orange and green. Pills and the pink sign of Trashlands.

Coral was not like Foxglove. She was present, too present, unable to get out of her head, to turn off her brain when Trillium touched her, let go of the worry and stress and just *feel*. Not like Foxglove, who seemed to simply switch it off.

"I guess you do the work you have," Trillium said.

"Well, Foxglove had nothing. Her momma left her with nothing. Except her body. And she didn't really leave her with that."

"Are you ever going to tell her that you love her?"

The answer surprised him. "I've told her. The thing is—" Tahiti poured another generous shot of moonshine for them both "—it was going to be women's time, you know? Before the floods, it was almost their time. Men had led the country, the world, for fucking ever."

Trillium knew. He had seen the presidents in Mr. Fall's book: one old white man after another.

"It was supposed to be their time. They worked for it. They waited for it. They suffered for it, and they planned for it. They were ready. It was supposed to be their time. And then it wasn't. The floods came. Fires came. Their time didn't come. And now it never will. It's too late. We're too fucked up. We can't get it together. We don't even have agriculture, man. Unless everything and every man burns down, and the world starts over—"

"Well," Trillium said, "it might."

"It's never going to be a woman's time. Not on this world. So what we have to do," the big man said, "is make our own world." He took the shot.

He wasn't waiting for Trillium anymore. They weren't toasting.

Tahiti wiped his mouth with the back of his hand. "No, not make our own world. No, no, let her make it, I mean. Listen to her tell you what she needs to make it. Sit down, sit back, and let her take the stage. It's her time, you know. You make it her time. 'Cause it's not fucking fair, man. It's not fair. And she would do—Foxglove, Coral, Summer—they would *all* do a real fine job of running a world. You know it. I know it. And men know it. That's why they hold them back. They should have been allowed to try."

Tahiti downed the rest of his shot, though Trillium didn't think there was much left in the glass. He drank from his own mug more slowly, feeling the moonshine burn.

He should let Coral decide where they went next. Forget his lists, all the maps, and let her choose. He wouldn't ask her the name of the man in the audience. She probably wouldn't even know.

33

Summer

Aestas

There was love in every stitch, her grandmamma used to say, drawing string through the plastic bags as she joined them together. Maybe her grandmamma, a tiny woman who had raised five children, three of them not born to her, would not have taught Summer to sew if she had known who Summer was: a beautiful girl with long hair. But maybe she had known all along.

There weren't going to be any children for Summer, and that was fine. She had had Foxglove and Coral to watch, and now this new girl, JT. They were all trouble, just different kinds. You couldn't keep pills out of Foxglove's mouth. She was like a baby, the way she downed anything she found. And Coral. What to do with Coral?

Summer remembered the moment she had met the girl. Summer had gone to the river, to wash clothes and maybe pick up some plastic bags; she was weaving a pair of sandals from them. At the river shore, plastic poked out of the dirt like tree roots, but it was broken and cheap. You had to get in to get the good stuff.

She was used to dodging pluckers. They came and went, like men, but this morning, a new one stood in the river. A girl, redheaded and small compared to the others. The girl stood apart from them. She seemed to be avoiding them.

"Hello," Summer called to her. "Where did you come from?"

The girl looked up. She was older than Summer had first taken her for, but young about the eyes. She looked lost there. "The rainbow bus," she said.

"I passed that this morning." Summer had thought what an interesting addition it could be to the junkyard, colorful and new. She hoped it would stay, tucked in by the quarry, a little jewel in the hill. She had smelled food cooking as she passed it on the path. A tall, bald man coming out of the bus had tipped his hat to her. She kept thinking about his eyes. "And before?"

"A camp called Star-Glow."

"Sounds nice." Summer hadn't heard of it.

"My father is going to be the teacher here," the girl said. "But we're only staying for the winter. We go to another camp when it's warm. I guess the children won't have a teacher then."

A teacher? Summer wondered if Rattlesnake Master was aware of this, had approved it. She doubted it. She wondered if this sweet girl knew about Rattlesnake Master yet.

But something about the last thing the girl had said seemed to frighten her. Her eyes darted away. The current brought a red container, maybe a jug for motor oil, near the girl.

Another man spotted it and splashed toward it, kicking up a spray. Rather than reaching out to grab the plastic, as was her right, the girl flinched and jumped back.

"Hey," Summer said. "She saw it first."

The man backed off. "Sorry, Summer."

But the girl wouldn't move. "It's fine," she said. "You take it."

"If you're sure?" Without waiting for much of an answer, the man ducked forward and snatched the container. Durable plastic, but light enough to float. Not cheap, then. Why had the girl just let it go?

Summer waved at the man. "Thanks, Venice." She watched the girl move warily away from him. She wore an old sundress—sopping wet, it clung to her skin—and high boots. The hem of her dress floated alongside her like foam. "Did you come alone, honey?" Summer asked. "With your father?" She thought pluckers normally traveled together, big crews of them. "Do you know anyone here at Trashlands?"

"I know a few people. New Orleans."

"Well, don't mind the other men in the river. They're fine. Harmless."

"No man is harmless," Coral said.

What had happened to her? Something had. When Summer went over to the bus later to welcome the newcomers, bringing a ramp pie, she saw it in the way the girl's father shielded her, coming out to greet Summer alone. And her lover protected her. He looked older than the girl. Silver in his hair, lines scored his face. He had spent too much time in the harsh sun, more years than her. He stepped forward to put his hand on the girl's shoulder, drawing her close, keeping her back from the stranger.

Most people would be curious about the strip club, but not Coral. She found labyrinthine detours around the junk-yard to avoid it. She fished for plastic alone, and if a group of men showed up, she would give up a prime spot to make space for them, to be away from them. If a man came to the bus for a tattoo from her lover, Coral would leave.

Even before she knew Coral's story, Summer knew it. It was the story of most women, including Summer herself, nights in junked cars when she was too young and the men were too old, times she felt she had no voice or could not find her voice; her voice lay puddled on the floor with her clothes. Times she didn't like to think about.

Soon Summer was protecting Coral too.

Once Coral had decided to take the bus, to trade it for her son, Summer had pulled the canister of diesel out from under her bed where she had hidden it. She knew the fuel she had saved was not enough. She thought maybe it was a start, though. Maybe it could get the girl partway.

But when she unscrewed the top of the canister, she reeled back, nearly sprawled across the floor by the smell. Turpen-tine, woodsy and dark, wet rot.

The diesel had gone bad. The fuel was useless.

She hadn't told Mr. Fall.

It was fine if Coral went onstage one time, Summer told herself, helping the girl with the clothes they had chosen for her. Summer had sewn the costume herself from the scraps of an emergency blanket; it had said that right there on the package Mr. Fall pulled out of the mud. *Emergency.* With her lips red and her hair brushed soft, Coral resembled a baby doll. Smaller than Foxglove, her round belly and muscular limbs. Summer had always wanted a doll. But that was not a treat given to children. Not to her.

"What if I freeze out there?" Coral asked as they waited by the red curtain.

"You won't," Summer said.

"I don't know how to dance."

"That—" She pointed to the ceiling. Somewhere out there, beyond the curtain, the DJ pressed Play again and again. He was cursed to do so. "That ain't really music."

Summer remembered singing, her grandmamma's strong voice as she stitched, singing of horses, a man called John Redcorn, a drink called champagne. Sometimes songs still came from the junkyard, children or dancers too new to know that Rattlesnake Master could find you that way.

"You just get into it," Foxglove said. She was on something again, probably the same pill she had given Coral. Her voice sounded flat. She checked the bottoms of her shoes for mud.

Summer squared Coral's shoulders. "Foxglove will be right there with you, every step of the way. She'll take care of you. They just want to see you. So long as you show them—" she adjusted a strap on Coral's costume "—you'll be fine. Foxglove will lead you. It'll go by fast."

Summer didn't want to tell her—Foxglove better not tell her—it could be addictive.

The attention, the lights, the lust from the men. At first, Summer had fallen into that attention like a drowning child. It swarmed over her, the men's affection, their desire, their fingers clutching plastic, wanting to lose it on her. Refusing was the enthralling part, ending her shift, calling it a night.

When you've never been able to say *no,* Summer thought, it could feel like power. But that was a lie.

"It's just one night," Coral said.

"One night," Summer said softly.

"And one man." Tahiti lumbered down the backstage. He stopped beside Foxglove, and they smiled at each other in a strange way. The air between them seemed to vibrate.

That was different, Summer thought.

The smile looked so odd on the girl's delicate face. Summer realized she hadn't seen her smile much at all over the years. Her smile was crooked, higher on one side. That perfect girl had a crooked smile.

"I thought the show was sold out?" Coral's voice started to rise. "It was supposed to be just this one show. Rattlesnake Master said—"

Summer squeezed her arm. "Hold on a moment. What do you mean, Tahiti?"

"It is sold out, but boss said there's only one man in the crowd. He bought out the whole place, for a private show. He wouldn't let anybody else come. And he paid highly for it."

"I bet he did. He'd have to."

"Boss told me to leave, but I can stay if you want."

"That's all right," Foxglove said. "Go on home. We're fine. Get some rest."

Get some rest?

"I don't understand what's happening," Coral said.

"Don't worry, honey." Summer touched her face briefly, then turned to the other two. "Stay with her while I figure out what the hell is going on out there." She found the opening and pushed through the heavy red curtain.

Rattlesnake Master liked to joke that finding the way through the curtain was like making love to a woman. Summer could have answered he had a lot of trouble with both.

She edged onto the stage. The center was lit with the spotlight, trembling a little as it waited. The pole glowed like a weapon—which it could be. She put her hand over her eyes to peer into the crowd. "The fuck," she said.

Tahiti was right. Only one man sat in the house.

The light bounced off his glasses.

Summer hopped off the stage. "What the fuck are you doing here?"

In the chair—which Summer had made—Miami scooted back. All the other chairs sat around him, pushed back and empty. Some were still propped upside down on the tables as if one of the dancers was going to halfheartedly sweep. Clubs operated differently in other places, Summer had heard from men. Dancers were called *entertainers*. They did not have to sweep or wipe the tables down with rags.

"Are you trying to mess things up for Coral? Make things hard for her?" Summer pointed at Miami. "You know she needs this money for her son. This money you basically took from her already, since she got hurt working for you."

Miami raised his hands. "I know. I offered to give her the money, come up with it somehow, but she wouldn't take it. I thought if I did this, she would consider it working—"

"It is working. Harder than you work."

"I thought she could get the fuel and move on. Like she wants to."

"Oh, she's going to move on. She's gonna move on and leave you behind." Summer needed to say that, she realized. To have him hear it.

We could go too, Summer had told Mr. Fall. They lay on the bed in her truck. On the ceiling the fabric stars glowed. *Maybe this is the sign that it's time to move on.*

What about the school? he had said. *What about the children?*

They're not your children.

They are, he had said.

Summer backed off a bit. "You aren't just doing this to see her naked?" she asked Miami.

"No. I didn't even want to be here at all. I wanted to buy out the show and go. But Rattlesnake Master barred the door."

"That man!"

"He thinks I'm writing about the show for my story."

"A situation like this…" Summer looked around the room, taking in the windows patched with black plastic bags to keep the light out, the chairs, the sticky floor. Rattlesnake Master had said Trashlands had been a theater when he found it, long ago. He had fixed it up, restored it to its former glory. He alone had seen the potential, he said. He swore there was a giant chandelier, dripping with crystals, he had hidden somewhere backstage and was saving, fixing it up bulb by bulb until it was ready to glow.

Summer looked at the bar. There was a glass case in front. Once, it had been used for selling food, wares displayed inside, but the glass was broken. The stage tilted lower on one end. Nothing about this place was restored. Nothing was glorious. Or magic, if you looked too closely. She bet the chandelier wasn't even real. "Coral's gonna be embarrassed when she sees you," Summer said. "Nervous. She's not gonna look you in the eye."

"What if I move the chair farther back?"

"That's a start."

"What if I take off my glasses?" He folded them up.

He looked more handsome without them, Summer realized.

"I can't see at all now."

"That's fine," she said. "I appreciate that. But keep a close watch on them, your glasses."

She tried to imagine a world of glass, how beautiful that must have been, how fragile. Glass drinking glasses. A tinkling chandelier. A brittle world. It had been broken, broken to bits.

The music was getting louder. It was close to curtain time, or that boy in the booth had seen Summer and was trying to chase her off on Rattlesnake Master's orders. Behind the bar, Warthog polished the plastic cups. He looked up at the DJ booth and winked, sharing a smile that Summer knew she was not supposed to see. He wouldn't have much to do tonight; she doubted Miami was a big drinker.

They should all just go home. It was a show for no one, she realized, except Rattlesnake Master. His pride.

"You can't touch her," Summer said.

"I won't come close."

"And..." She trailed off, trying to picture the scene. How would Coral react when she found out it was Miami—and only him? Should Summer warn her? Summer had seen the way the two looked at each other, how they helped each other. They were likely about the same age. If Coral had met Miami before Trillium, in another life, at another time...

"Just be respectful," Summer said.

"Always." Miami reached to tuck his glasses inside his shirt pocket, and Summer saw the pink of an eraser.

"And keep your pencil and paper away. This is not your story."

★ ★ ★

Outside her truck, Mr. Fall waited on the cinderblock step. Twilight fell around him like a shawl. Summer pulled her own shawl tighter around her shoulders. Cooler days were on the way, which was a relief. But that meant harder nights were coming too. They need to patch the tires on the truck, scare the mice out of the engine, find usable fuel.

"You didn't have to wait for me outside," Summer said. "You could have gone in. Aren't you chilly?"

"I like waiting for you," Mr. Fall said. "I like watching you come up the path." He could grin. It lit up the darkness like one of those prized LED lights: a glow, brighter than the moon.

All these years and he still waited for her.

She sat down on the step. He scooted over, but not much, to make room. "How's Coral?" he asked.

"She's going to be all right. Only one man's in the audience."

"One man?"

"It's fine, trust me. Don't worry. She's not in any danger."

"I feel like I failed her."

"You gave her everything you have. But diesel? Enough diesel to run a bus? That only comes from sex work, alcohol, and drugs. And writing, apparently."

Mr. Fall caught on. "*Miami* was there?"

He was quick. That was one of the things Summer loved about him. He had always loved her, not the idea of her. She was not a dancer at the club to him; it was just her job—one of her many jobs—not who she was. To men at Trashlands, she was lovely and unknowable. Some idea that they had. The worst men liked to think of themselves as fucked up.

And as tough when they got close enough to touch the girls, which was not allowed, at least not in the front of the club. They liked that it was not allowed and still they did it. They liked having a story for their friends. How far they went. What limits they pushed. Who they thought they broke.

It wasn't that way with Mr. Fall. "It's going to be fine," Summer told him. "Her friends are there. Just don't ask her to talk about it."

"I wouldn't do that."

"Don't nag her. And don't bring it up unless she does."

Mr. Fall grew silent. Summer thought she had been too strident with him, but then he said, "I don't imagine I'll have too many conversations left with Coral. I want to save the time we have on the good stuff. Good words only."

"I know you're going to miss her," Summer said. "But she wants to do this. This was her decision to make—dancing, leaving Trashlands, all of it."

"I know."

"It was good of you to let her have the bus."

Mr. Fall nodded. Summer wondered if he was thinking about the bus, parked beyond the next two rises. In the darkness the junk looked like monsters. Sometimes Summer thought the piles were moving. They seemed to grow arms and sharp teeth in the shadows.

Summer could run fast, even in the heels she made. She made them as comfortable as she could on purpose, in case anyone wearing them needed to flee.

There was love in the shoes. Love in the clothes. Love in the meals she threw together out of nothing. *Nothing* was the main spice. Whatever they had—roots or greens from the woods, puffs of corn or air or whatever was in those snacks—she could make something out of it.

She liked especially holiday meals, what passed for holidays in the junkyard. When they chose to celebrate their birthdays, she made cakes out of honey and corn. She would always find a present for someone, even if it meant unraveling her own things to sew together socks or the red scarf Mr. Fall was wearing.

But making something out of her food truck? Making it run out of here, run far away—she was not sure she could do that.

"You sure you want to give the bus up?" she asked Mr. Fall.

"It's served its purpose. It's time for a change, and Coral deserves it. She can do something good with it, and it's all I've got to give her. Her inheritance. As long as you don't mind me moving in here with you?"

"Of course not. But losing the bus...that thing runs, at least. We know it does, no matter how ugly it is and how much diesel it guzzles. I'm not sure about my truck."

"We can get it running again."

"But what if we don't?"

"We're pretty handy, you and me."

"But what if we *don't*?"

Mr. Fall let the words hang in the air for a minute. Then he shrugged, a movement so languid it didn't even disturb her shawl. "Then we spend our retirement here, the old dancer and the old teacher."

"Speak for yourself. I'm not old."

"We should stay for a little while, anyway. Until all the children can read."

Summer had spent years touching that face, in the darkness and in the day. They had not hidden their love, the way Foxglove and Tahiti seemed to be doing. They had not moved in together a long time ago only out of respect for Coral and their family unit. But now that was changing, breaking apart like hunks of plastic in the water, cracking and splitting into something new. They only had to see its next shape, what it could be.

The air felt colder. Summer threw one side of her shawl around him. "Did you ever think you might have your own kids?" she asked.

"Oh, we have plenty of kids."

"I mean, biologically."

"Well, it's too late now," Mr. Fall said. "But maybe. Maybe once I did."

"What would you have named them?"

Mr. Fall looked in the direction of the river. "Britannica."

34

Shanghai

He had thirty-one pills now, and Outer Banks said that was a lot. Enough to do something with. Something big.

"Do what?" Shanghai asked.

The redheaded boy whispered the word Shanghai had not thought of for years. He had not even dared to dream it, not since a child had run away and been caught and beaten in front of the whole factory, not since Shanghai realized the ones who left wouldn't leave such treasures as pills behind, wouldn't go without them willingly.

Outer Banks said, *Escape.*

They had noticed one of the guards seemed to be in his own world some of the time. They had decided this was not a world of daydreams, but the fuzzy world of pills. The man moved slowly, his reactions delayed, as if he walked through syrup or deep water. His eyelids had a habit of drifting down. His hand on his machine gun relaxed, almost casual.

A frayed strap held the gun to his shoulder. The gun was ancient—all guns were—rusted and gummed with mud. But even if the gun had no bullets, which it probably did not, or could no longer fire, it was heavy and metal. It was still a weapon. Shanghai had learned that.

It could still kill.

Outer Banks befriended the man. It was a slow process, consisting of eye rolls exchanged with the man when someone on the line did something stupid, like got their finger jammed in the belt, or wept before they knew they would be punished. Outer Banks laughed at the jokes the guard made, gruff comments about the way people looked, how skinny they were, how useless. Outer Banks made his own jokes to the man, under his breath, things Shanghai didn't hear. Or chose not to.

It was a cruel friendship, Shanghai thought.

"I'm just trying to get close to him," Outer Banks said. "He'll let his defenses down and trust me. It's part of the plan."

What a strange plan, Shanghai thought, trading sexual jokes with a man who most certainly would not be having sex any time soon, not with a willing partner.

Shanghai did not understand the language of men. Their easy ways, how violence tinged almost everything they did like a sheen of ice. Anger infused their bodies, gave their movements energy and purpose, a way to be in the world.

Outer Banks and his guard friend didn't hug, of course. That was too far. They would never do that. They would never even shake hands, at least not within sight of Shanghai. But they did touch in a strange, bruising way. Outer Banks bumped into the guard's shoulder. The man would punch him in the arm as he passed. They joked about how ugly the other was. They called each other names like *woman*.

Shanghai felt lost, and he felt he was losing his only friend—and for what?

Where would they go, anyway, if they got out, him and Outer Banks? What would they do? They had not thought that far. Only *escape*, they had thought. *Escape*. They had a skill: brickmaking. Surely they could lay the bricks too, build them into schools or med centers? Or fortresses? What were people making now?

They had shaped so many bricks, all day every day, the plastic sliding through their hands—surely the world was simply full of bricks by now. Surely Shanghai and Outer Banks and the other children had shaped the new world in their image. They were responsible for it continuing.

It would be glorious, Shanghai thought, outside the factory.

They just had to get there.

He saved the pills, re-counting them at night. He resisted the urge to take one. They couldn't spare a single pill, especially not the nice, machine-made kind. They didn't know how many they would need.

He saved food too, though this was difficult. The bread would mold, attract mice. Still, Shanghai kept several hunks stuffed in his greasy pillowcase. He remembered, or thought he did, greens of the field that would be all right to eat, safe mushrooms in the woods. Rats could be caught and cooked, though they had no way to make a fire. No matches or flint.

How would they keep warm? Or cool—it was difficult to know the temperature from inside the factory walls. Shanghai shivered at night so he guessed it was cold now. Maybe the greens and the mushrooms would be dead. Night fell early through the holes in the roof, and in the morning, the sky looked solid gray. How long would they walk until they reached the first marvelous city, made from the work of their hands? Would that be how they earned their first wage, on the strength of their past?

Maybe a rich man would hire them to build for him, Shanghai thought. He hoped there might be some adventure, some difference in the work, somehow.

He was tired of making squares.

Finally, it was time. Shanghai had slept fitfully for weeks, he thought—he had run out of room for hatch marks on his bunk post long ago. But on the one night he had finally drifted off deeply, he was shaken awake.

Outer Banks stood on tiptoe to reach the top bunk. When Shanghai saw his friend, he startled. But he felt alert and ready instantly. He had salvaged a plastic bag for the pills. He slid up and carefully slipped the case off his pillow. He knotted the bread inside. The knife he had found was in his pocket. He had nothing else to bring.

They had no water, no way to bring it. Shanghai imagined they would find a water bottle soon, fill it up at some stream. They had no shoes, only the rags they wrapped their feet in.

Shanghai hoped the snows had not yet come.

In the aisle, Outer Banks waited for Shanghai. All around them, the others slept, depleted. That was the only reason any of them could close their eyes: sheer physical exhaustion. They were certainly not dreaming. Shanghai snuck one leg over the side of his bunk. The bed squealed. He paused, waiting for the sound to settle, then pushed himself across the bed and hopped to the floor. The rags on his feet muted the sound.

But his bunkmate was already awake.

Shanghai saw the boy's eyes shining in the darkness. The boy had pulled the blanket up, as if it could protect him. Shanghai didn't know his name. He had never learned it. None of the lower bunkers stuck around for long.

"It's your lucky day," Shanghai whispered to the boy. "You're moving up. The top bunk's yours now. Take it. I've left you the blanket."

"We gotta go, man," Outer Banks hissed. His eyes darted around the bunkhouse.

But Shanghai said to the stranger, barely more than a child, he realized now he was finally looking at him, not much older than Shanghai himself when he had been taken. "Wait till we're out of the room, then get up on the bunk. Take it before somebody else does."

The boy nodded, a motion so slight it was almost impossible to see.

"Shanghai," Outer Banks said.

Shanghai moved to go, then turned and crouched down to the stranger. From the plastic bag, he pulled out a blue pill. "This one helps with sleep. Save it. Take it when you really need it."

A skinny arm came out from beneath the blanket. The boy took the pill.

"Let's go," Outer Banks said.

Down the aisle of the bunkhouse, through the unlocked

door. The door was always locked, but not tonight. That was the plan. And another part of the plan: the collector outside the door, the one who had opened it, was their guard friend.

But when he saw Shanghai, the man said: "Who the fuck is this?"

He had been smoking something. A leafy scent drifted in the air. Shanghai thought he smelled pines in the smoke, a spiciness that felt familiar.

"My buddy," Outer Banks said. "I told you about him."

"I don't remember no buddy."

It was much colder outside than Shanghai had expected. Their breath lingered in white puffs, and he could feel damp through the rags on his feet. He and Outer Banks would have to find shoes quickly. To find or make coats. They could stuff their shirts with leaves, he remembered. They could make a shelter of branches—his mother had taught him that. If the rivers and streams had frozen, they could crack the crust on top to reach water.

But first there was this man, barring the way.

Shanghai held out his hand. That was how you greeted people, right? Outside the factory, before the factory, an old man had taught him...

But the guard used the butt of his gun to push Shanghai's hand away.

"He's the one with the pills," Outer Banks said.

"In that case." The guard balled his hand into a fist and fake-punched Shanghai's side. Except it wasn't fake. Shanghai's stomach muscles cramped. He bent over, his body pulsing with the jab. "Just kidding, man. Where are the pills?"

It took Shanghai a few moments to recover. He fumbled for the bag. Outer Banks took it from him and spilled a dozen pills out into his own hand, bright and strange, many-colored, the teeth of little monsters.

"Nice," the collector said. "What are they?"

"Different kinds. Homemade and mass-produced."

"Mass-produced!" the man whistled. "Nothing's mass-produced anymore. Those pills are old, man."

"They keep for years, you know that. Besides, manufacturers in The Els—"

"What the hell do you know about manufacturers in The Els?"

But the man was reaching for the pills, anyway. Outer Banks let him pick up a couple, hold them between his thumb and forefinger in what light there was from the moon, from the solar-powered security light above the doorway of the bunkhouse, cracked but still emitting a weak pink glow.

The pink stirred something in Shanghai's memory.

"These pills are good," the man said.

"Hell yeah, they're good," Outer Banks said.

"Where did you get these?"

"My man has his ways."

My man, Shanghai thought. *That's me.* He thought he had never been anyone's man before. His stomach ached where he had been punched.

"All right," the collector said.

"A dozen, like we said?"

"Hold on. A dozen for *you* to get out. You never said anything about a friend. Two of you, it's twice as many."

"Twenty-four pills?" Outer Banks was incredulous. "You've got to leave us with more than that. What'll we trade for food? We don't even have shoes."

"Not my problem," the collector said. "I'm taking a big

risk, letting you go. What will they say, in the morning when they find you gone, huh? Two of you? What will they do to me?"

"You could go too? Come with us?"

The thought of traveling with this man, a collector, with his rusted gun, his easy fists, made Shanghai's stomach lurch again. He felt the sick spread of a bruise.

But the collector said, "I am going, in my own time. I've got plans. I'm getting out of here. You know where I'm going?"

Hell, Shanghai thought.

"There's this place, not too far away. Let me tell you. It's a club—and they've got girls, man. Girls for miles. Dancing all night with no clothes on." He spread out his hands, setting the scene for them there in the damp, cold darkness. "There's this one girl, a redhead? Prettiest thing you've ever seen. Red hair like a river."

Rivers weren't supposed to be red, even Shanghai knew that.

"This girl—for some plastic, right?—she'll tattoo your name on her body. Like forever. You're on her body for life."

Shanghai was remembering something, but he didn't know what. It was the pink glow of the security light, the woodsy scent of the man's smoke. It was the tattoos. He had known a man who tattooed. He recalled the action more than the person. The ink, the sticks with needles on the ends, the bottles lined up...

"Thirty pills," the man said, upping his price even more. "Thirty if you both want out. Thirty and I can stay at the club for days, sleep in that bitch's fucking lap, tattoo her face."

It was everything they had.

Outer Banks flashed Shanghai a look. It was a look Shanghai had not seen on his friend's face before, not when a boy had been punished for stealing and his blood had dripped on the factory floor right in front of them, a smear that was not cleaned for days. Not when it was so cold, his friend's toe had turned pink, then white, then he said he could no longer feel it. It was a blank look, a beaten one. Outer Banks did not know what to do.

"Twenty pills," Shanghai said. "But we'll give you all the good ones." He leaned forward and thumbed through them. "The good ones are factory-made. Smooth and strong. Pills for sleep, pills for pain. Pills for forgetting. Girls like the pills for forgetting." He thought he remembered that. Or maybe he was making it up.

Either way, the collector stuck his big finger into the pills. They made the faintest clacking sound, like stones on a riverbank. Finally, the man said, "Deal."

Moving quickly now, they counted out the pills. Shanghai was grateful he could count that high. He felt cold in his joints, could see dawn crimping at the edge of the sky. They had to hurry. Shanghai did not know if the collectors would look for them once they realized the boys were missing, or what they would do if they found them. He did not know if this guard could really be trusted.

Just in case, Shanghai selected another blue pill. "You should take this one," he said to the man. "Right now. It's sweet and smooth. One of my favorites." One he had used before, a pill that caused an almost instant, heavy sleep that prickled on the edge of his brain, fizzed his thoughts and slowed his movement into nothingness. "We'll throw it in extra. For free. A bonus, just for you."

Bonus. That was a word he had learned in his old life. It meant something people liked.

The man sure liked it. He grinned at Shanghai. He had several black caves where teeth should have been. He popped the blue pill in his mouth and swallowed. Opened his mouth to show he had taken it. His tongue was a big hank of meat.

"It should work fast," Shanghai said. "You'll feel real good."

"All right, man," the collector said. He held out his hand, his hand that had punched Shanghai hard enough to hurt. An old greeting, but one Shanghai knew.

Shanghai shook it.

Outer Banks and the man hugged, a strange gruff hug, the gun in the middle like a baby. "Don't be a stranger," Outer Banks said. A thing you said to someone you hoped never to see again.

Seven years and Shanghai was free. He expected someone to leap out of the trees, to materialize from the road before them—which wasn't much of a road at all, more like a path being swallowed by leaves—and take them back.

No one did.

Behind them, the collector called out, "Trashlands! That's the name of the club. Trashlands!"

They turned to the trees and ran. They kept the buildings over their shoulder, but Shanghai could feel them back there, a kind of presence which hummed with pain. Years ago, the buildings of the factory and bunkhouse had been a huge warehouse. It had made cars then, not even whole ones, but parts, the collector had told Outer Banks. What kind of world was that, with enough cars that a factory could make a single piece?

A few more minutes of running and Shanghai started to believe that maybe no one was coming. Maybe the woods were not guarded, the road not rigged. The road, such as it was, sloped down, then around a bend. No fires loomed out of the darkness. Or torches or men.

Soon the buzz of the factory faded. Whether it was the generator or a pressing on his head, it was gone. Shanghai was starting to feel, now that he could sense more than simply fear, other sensations: the cold through the rags on his feet, the pain in his stomach from the punch. The wind. The dawn.

Outer Banks slowed. "Nice move with the sleeping pill. That's what it was, right?"

"I guess," Shanghai said. He was still not sure they should talk or stop running. Every sound in the air made him flinch. A crack of branches or the scurrying of an animal seemed magnified. He was so used to walls blocking everything. "Where are we going?"

"Trashlands? I mean, why not? If it's as big as he said, I bet they'll have construction work. Or guard work. Guards for the girls."

"I don't think we should stay on this road."

The woods had encroached, narrowing and breaking the road. It split in the middle. Living things struggled through the cracks, weeds that didn't need much sun or water. Bitter things you couldn't eat.

"I don't think the collectors are coming. I don't think we're worth it, not in the dark," Outer Banks said.

But it wouldn't be dark for long. Maybe they should bed down in the woods, get some sleep under the cover of trees. Shanghai remembered the woods as being bad, but he was not sure why. Something came from them. Worse than the collectors?

They decided to rest once light had broken through the upper branches. They found a place within sight of the road but not, Shanghai thought, able to be seen by anyone. Their drab and patched clothes blended in. Flooded and burned, pillaged then ignored, the woods looked brown and gray. Half the trees were dead. He and Outer Banks settled on the needles that had fallen from one tree. They were prickly and soft at the same time, orange as poison.

Shanghai worried he would not be able to sleep, with the sounds of the woods closing in, the vastness of the sky, the cold, and the men coming. Always the men were coming.

Still, he fell asleep in the woods.

The sound of shoes—hard shoes, *real* shoes—stirred him. A man walked, but not on the road they had come from, the way that led back to the factory. Through the trees, on the other side of the thin woods, was another road. Shanghai could see movement.

His neck ached and tree needles clung to him like icicles. But what he felt most of all was stillness. Fear grabbed his throat, squeezing him, rooting his body. He couldn't warn Outer Banks, still sleeping beside him. He couldn't scream.

He froze in emergencies. It was why he had been taken to the factory. He was an easy mark. He knew this without even remembering it fully. He was a target, he let himself be lost. He knew he had done this, all those years ago.

Shanghai looked through the trees. The man walked alone. Shanghai didn't recognize him. He was not a collector, then. He walked slowly, glancing up, then down at something in his hand.

Shanghai felt breath return to his body. He was able to move a bit, to shake his friend's shoulder, hold his finger up to his lips when the boy's eyes snapped open, confused and alarmed.

Outer Banks knew what to do. He slid up slowly. "Do you have your knife?" he whispered.

Shanghai felt for it at his side.

They watched the man. He seemed oblivious to danger, to them. Outer Banks looked back at Shanghai, his eyes very white. The freckles on his face stood out. "Let's go," he mouthed.

"Let him move on. He doesn't see us."

But his friend had already turned, and was creeping through the trees to the other road. Shanghai followed, bending low, feeling every crunch of leaves. The man seemed not to hear them, or he didn't know what to listen for. He had stopped, his back to them.

Outer Banks crouched until he was almost on his stomach. He inched forward, easing into a ditch below the man. He lifted his hands.

"No, wait!" Shanghai said.

Outer Banks grabbed the man's ankles.

They were the things that came from the woods. They were the something bad, Outer Banks and Shanghai. They were the men Shanghai had been warned about as a child, all those years ago.

The man on the road fell. Onto his knees, then, shouting in pain and surprise, tumbling over the bank into the ditch. Shanghai straightened, the knife in his hand. How had it gotten there? He didn't remember grabbing it. It shook as he stuck it out.

The man fumbled to stand. He saw Shanghai and held up his hands.

There was so much Shanghai didn't know, he had never been told or he didn't remember about people, about men. If men ran the world, as they said in the factory, why didn't he know? Why did he not understand how to do things? How to hold the knife straight, what to say to the man?

He said nothing.

The man had a knapsack with him. It had fallen into the ditch. Outer Banks rummaged through it.

"What do you need?" the man said. "Take what you need."

"Everything," Shanghai found himself saying. "We need everything."

"You can't take everything. I'll die."

"We'll die, then. Would you rather *we* die?" The man didn't answer. Shanghai turned to Outer Banks. "What's he have?"

"Some food. Some clothes. What's this?" He held up a small piece of paper. Words were printed on it. Outer Banks turned the paper over and over.

He could not read.

Shanghai said, "Give it to me." He kept the knife pointed shakily at the man and reached out his other hand to take the paper. It took him a moment to figure out what he was looking at, to make sense of the letters he had not seen for years. "It's a bus ticket," he said. "Is that what this is?"

"There's a bus around here?" Outer Banks said.

Shanghai shoved the ticket deep in his pocket.

"You don't want to do that," the man said. "It's only the one. There are two of you."

"We could sell it. Exchange it for two."

"It doesn't work that way. It won't be enough money and you can't sneak on. They count the riders. There are guards."

"I know what buses are," Shanghai snapped, though he didn't, not really. He remembered a bus—but it was parked. A bus with his mother, he thought, its middle painted brightly with a stripe. He had never seen a rainbow in the sky, only on a bus.

"You have to have permission to get a ticket, apply for it in advance."

"Why do *you* have permission?"

"I work…" the man began. "My job…" He was having trouble.

Shanghai saw his hands shook, like the knife.

"We work." Outer Banks got right in the man's face. "We work doing things you can't even imagine. Our whole lives, right? We worked." He looked at Shanghai.

"Pretty much," Shanghai said.

"We worked and worked, and for what? For nothing. For you. I bet we made the bricks of your house. Your *work*. And we never saw any money from it."

"From the factory?" the man said. "You came from a factory?"

"Damn right we did."

"How did you get out?"

"Escape." Outer Banks sounded proud.

"We paid our way," Shanghai said. "But there's not much left. We don't have much food."

"I have food," the man said. "You can take it. All of it."

"All right."

"And shoes." Outer Banks pointed at the man's feet. "We want your shoes."

The man looked at his feet, dusty shoes with laces, then back at Shanghai. There was no way his shoes would fit either of them, but Shanghai didn't want to undermine his friend. Maybe they could sell the shoes.

The man asked, "What factory did you come from?"

"It doesn't have a name."

"Were you kidnapped? Taken in the night? From your mother?"

"What do you know—" Shanghai began.

But Outer Banks interrupted. "Yeah, we were taken. That's not fucking news. Everybody knows their bricks are made by children. They still use the bricks. They still buy them cheap."

"You've been there," the man said, "since you were a young child?"

"Yes," Shanghai said.

"How old are you now?"

"You ask a lot of fucking questions," Outer Banks said.

Shanghai and the man were locked eye to eye. The man's eyes were brown as glass. He lowered one of his hands slowly. He pointed at Shanghai's neck. "Where did you get that plastic?"

Shanghai didn't have to look. He knew. He had worn it out of the factory, beneath his ragged shirt: the last piece he had made from plastic that was just too colorful, too different, to waste on a brick. It was pink plastic. No, not quite the color pink.

Coral.

His mother's name. Coral-colored, it sparkled all over with stars. He had twisted and strung the plastic out in a thin rope, wound into a necklace. He would not trade it. He would not let the man touch it.

"I made it," Shanghai said.

"But where did you find it?"

"Get your fucking hand up," Outer Banks said.

"Where did the plastic come from?"

"Where it all comes from. The trash. The wrecks. The rivers. Everywhere. What does it matter to you?"

"I was looking for a bracelet," the man began.

"It doesn't matter what you were looking for," Outer Banks said.

Strangely, the man smiled. A sad smile. But smiles were supposed to be for when you were happy? Shanghai didn't understand.

"You're right," the man said. "It doesn't matter."

No, Shanghai did not understand men. The stranger had not raised his hand again as Outer Banks had demanded. He had not removed his shoes. He licked his lips. They were cracked, bleeding from his fall.

Maybe he was not as rich as Shanghai had believed, when he first saw him on the road. Maybe his life was not as easy. The hems of his pants looked ripped. He squinted as though his eyes or head hurt him. He looked like a child in some ways, especially in his eyes.

Shanghai saw then what he would not understand for a long time, what lovers would say to him in the future— women who tried too hard with him for too long, men who loved and left him; he would be with both in his long life— that you could be a boy inside a man. That you might never leave the night when you were taken, or when something was taken from you. Your body might leave that place, grow up, grow strong—but your mind would still be back there, forever in the fear and sadness.

Shanghai and the man were alike that way.

"I think I know who you are," the man said. "I think I know your mother."

"What do you know about my mother?"

"I know she misses you. I know she's sorry. I know she feels guilty, even though it's not her fault. Your disappearance ruined her life."

"You're saying I ruined her life?" Heat rushed through Shanghai. He felt a ringing in his ears, like the machines from the factory.

"He doesn't know your mother," Outer Banks was saying.

But the stranger said, "Coral? In the rainbow bus? With Trillium and Mr. Fall?"

How did this stranger know so much about him? Shanghai remembered the bus, how crowded and dirty it was all the time, how it smelled like poison from the fucking ink. The strangers who would wander in and out to be tattooed. And his mother was never there. She was off in the woods, doing something without him. He went into the woods, in the night, and she never found him.

"Coral told me how hard things were between you. She told me—"

"Nothing!" Shanghai said. "She told you nothing." He took one step forward and plunged the knife into the man.

It went in easy. The man's shirt was thin. He had lost his coat in the tumble from the road, and he wore no layers, as

Shanghai's mother had taught him to do, as he and Outer Banks would have to do if they wanted to live.

The knife went in, and it drew Shanghai close to the man, their shoulders and bellies joined by the blade. The man's brown eyes went very wide and his mouth fell open. Then liquid filled the space between the two of them, spilling from the man's stomach onto Shanghai's hand. Blood found the cracks in his fingers and sleeve like plastic filling a mold.

Shanghai let go and the man fell onto his side in the ditch. The knife stuck out of him. The man grasped his hands around it, but he could not pull it out. Shanghai looked down at his own hands. They were splashed with red.

"Fuck," Outer Banks said. Then he said, "Check his pockets."

Shanghai did not want to go back to the man. Outer Banks came close and leaned over. Shanghai did not want to look in the stranger's face, to see if his eyes were open or closed, his deep, dark eyes like an ancient river. Why did Shanghai feel like he had betrayed that river, betrayed his own home? He fell to his knees in the ditch and crawled, fumbling at the man's pockets.

In the first pocket, he found a knife.

"I fucking knew it," Outer Banks said.

But the knife was closed, the blade folded. In the man's second pocket, Shanghai found a piece of plastic, printed with words. He could read it. Outer Banks could not. *One night only*, it read. *Twin Flames.*

35

Mr. Fall

She left in the morning. That was best. She left after breakfast. She left with water and plastic and the food they could
spare.

And the diesel.

The canisters filled the back of the bus and cluttered the
aisle. Seeing them, Mr. Fall couldn't help but remember the
last time the bus had been so full, the last time it had traveled so far. Earth flecked the canisters. Mr. Fall wondered if
the lights of Trashlands would finally dim now, the power
for its generator gone.

He could not remember how much fuel the bus took, but
it was a lot. He was not sure where else to get it anymore,
or how long even this much diesel would last. Would they
have to leave the bus somewhere if the fuel ran out? Bar the
doors in the middle of some lonely road, and go ahead on

foot? Was it a gift he was giving Coral, the bus she had been raised in, or a burden, a target on her back?

A full tank—that was a phrase he had not heard spoken for some time. He would have to write it down. That and *Fill 'er up.*

Summer had been encouraging him to start writing, to make his own book. She said Britannica did not contain everything, which had shocked him at first. But of course she was right. She usually was. The world had changed since the book had been published. Changed dramatically.

He would begin writing his book in the margins of Britannica. He would write down sayings, what they did for food, how they gathered plastic, how they lived. He supposed he had been a little inspired by that reporter.

It's not an outsider's place to tell our story, Summer had said. *It's* our *story.*

Mr. Fall had thought Miami could have become an insider, could have become one of them, given enough time.

But he kept that thought to himself.

He thought Trillium told the story of Trashlands in a way, with some of the tattoos he made. They were a record of animals, of place names. He thought Coral told it too, with her art. People would come across her pieces and maybe go home and tell others what they had seen. In that way, his daughter would live forever.

But who would remember how the people of Trashlands used willow bark for headaches, scraping it off the trees and grinding it into paste? How they whittled plastic into knives? How the children caught rats and sometimes yard cats for pocket money?

Pocket money. That was another phrase he would have to

write down. He was almost certain Summer didn't know it. He would ask her about it later. Later. After Coral left.

He couldn't bring himself to say that part, to think it.

They had made plans in the way people did, optimistically. They had lied. She would bring Shanghai back to the junkyard, she promised—he would want to see Mr. Fall. She was sure the boy would remember him.

But once you left a place, it was hard to come back. Mr. Fall knew that. You forgot the way. Or the way was blocked by debris, floods that washed away the path, fire that cut a new path. You ran out of money, plastic, food. You were needed in a new place. You needed other places, other people, more.

Such had been the way in his own family: his male relatives, picked off one by one by the promise of work. Work was always in another place.

After his family had left their flood-splintered home, carrying what they could on their backs, they lived for a time in a Walmart parking lot. His father had been a cobbler (another word for his book?), and they bartered for food and clothing in exchange for repairing shoes, patching soles, and waterproofing boots. His father tried to teach him the work, but Mr. Fall felt his mind wandering. To the flood, to his mother and girl cousins. They were gone. They would never be seen again.

His brother, uncle, and the male cousins who were left fetched water for others in the Walmart lot. They hunted the little field mice, groundhogs, and frogs in the ditches, selling the meat. There *were* frogs—Mr. Fall remembered them singing. At night, their song was a hopeful thing that soon became mournful.

His family dwindled until it was only his father and

brother with him. Then his brother decided to head south alone. There was a rumor that a mine had opened up. They needed workers. His brother sent postcards for a while. His father read them aloud in the battery light of their tent, then passed the postcards around the camp to grateful strangers.

With no televisions in the camp, and the internet flickering on and off on their phones, people were desperate for new things to read, to occupy their minds, even everyday details of someone else's family. Though only a child himself, Mr. Fall remembered helping some of the people of the camp with the words. They were grateful and sent over watercress they had collected from a stream. Another time, a dead rabbit appeared at the foot of their tent, dressed and raw (and still too much looking like a rabbit, Mr. Fall thought, but it was meat), sent by another family in thanks.

Soon the postcards stopped coming. Mr. Fall worried that something had happened to his brother, but his father said it was probably only the mail having trouble. Roads had been washed away. There were gas shortages, price gouges. Letters piled up, were lost or stolen. Strikes happened. Mr. Fall thought it was selfish for those who still had jobs to strike from them, but his father explained that workers weren't being paid. Hospitals closed just when the stream of patients, their lungs filled with water or smoke, became untenable. Groceries couldn't keep bottled water, rice, or meat on the shelves. It became more common to see plastic bottles than crops in a field. The ground was too saturated to plant.

No one knew to collect the plastic yet. No one knew it was all they would have.

Once their screens stopped working, his father got news from a thin newspaper. The people of the lot passed around each paper that arrived, dated days earlier, with reverence, like a holy artifact, their only way to try to understand. *What was going on?* People would still turn on their screens every few days, to see if there was reception, to look at pictures of missing loved ones, but soon, those batteries died.

The parking lot lapsed into a kind of permanence. Tents had overtaken the parking spots. Someone set up a kitchen with an oil drum grill sizzling at all hours. Portable toilets appeared, dropped off from a truck or stolen, Mr. Fall could not remember.

And when a school started in the largest tent, he enrolled.

The Walmart lot became a community, a camp, the first one where Mr. Fall would live. When the weather turned cold, some people began to build permanent structures out of wood they had found. It was flood wood. Swollen and warped, it would not hold, but the people did not know that.

This was before we knew about building with plastic, Mr. Fall would say when he told this story to children.

He was a teenager when his father died. From what, he would never know. Something that had no name, no diagnosis, and probably a simple enough cure: antibiotics, or oxygen, or even just rest. It was a fever illness, and it came on fast. His father was buried in the fields beyond the Auto-Zone. Then Mr. Fall had no one. He packed everything he or his father owned worth packing and strapped the bag to his back. He took the first ride out he could get, just people going elsewhere. Anywhere would do.

It was an easy decision to go. Moving, not thinking. He would never come back.

It would be hard to write that down, to help the people of the future—if there was some future where strangers would find this book, where they would want to read it—understand. Letting go—that was how you lived. Holding on too hard, too long, could end you, sure as an animal stuck in mud.

Later, he heard that people in the camp had overrun the Walmart. They had broken through the glass doors with homemade battering rams, taken cough syrup and canned food, what vegetables still arrived at the store: wilted, pale, and sandy. They took flats of bottled water held aloft on their heads. They were starving. Salvation seemed just below the glowing sign. Mr. Fall did not know if police came next with clubs and canisters of gas. If any of those men still had jobs, still served orders.

But he knew what had directed him to Trashlands, all these years ago: neon. The last sign of his father. The last light of family. Flickering, calling to him through the trees.

He steered the bus to it, the brightest light he had ever seen.

And yes, this neon, pink not white like the Walmart sign, had flickered on top of a building that ended up being a strip club. And yes, the light lit a junkyard with rats and bugs and a thousand dead cars. It was still a good place to stop.

Plastic stopped there, lapping at the banks of the river. They had been needed there, the work they all did: Mr. Fall's teaching and Trillium's tattoos. Coral had been important to the place—her friendship with the dancers, her kindness, her art. And Summer. Summer needed him. He needed her.

The light had been right. It had led him to love.

Summer wrapped cornmeal cakes in a plastic bag. She had been busy all morning, her movement in the kitchen waking Mr. Fall. The smell woke him too. The flour in oil, the sweetness of corn and the spiciness of insects. It had been dark when he stirred from the bed and moved to the counter to kiss her. Her outline looked purple and shadowy, and the hot plate, hooked up to a small solar panel, glowed.

"How long have you been up?"

"Awhile." She lifted the meal cakes out of the oil with a spider strainer made from strips of woven water bottles. She had to work fast or the plastic would melt. Mr. Fall knew she worked to put her feelings somewhere, to put her sadness to use, getting things done. "He's leaving today too." She nodded at the screen door.

She had started a fire in the barrel outside, and a man sat before it.

Miami stared into the flames. He wasn't wearing his glasses, and without them, Mr. Fall could see the bags beneath his eyes, the weary skin that aged him or indicated he too had suffered. Sleepless nights, nightmares, despite his apartment in the city, despite his job.

"He wants to get an early start," Summer said.

"Does Coral know he's leaving?"

She looked at Mr. Fall. The heat from cooking had stuck her bangs to her skin. He wanted to sweep the hair away and kiss her forehead. He wanted to go back to bed. He wanted to keep them all home and safe.

She said, "You're going to have to tell her."

There were no right times. There was only this time: Trillium was inspecting the tires around the back of the bus with Tahiti. The bodyguard had picked up eyeglasses from somewhere and was marveling at the details, finally able to see them. Foxglove, who had gotten up too early and kept complaining about it, nursed a mug of Kentucky coffeetree pods. Coral took the cakes Summer gave her and put them in her backpack. She looked up and saw Mr. Fall.

"The reporter's gone," Mr. Fall said. He needed to tell her before he said anything else, all the speeches he had prepared to say. "Miami. He left this morning, early. He wanted me to tell you—"

"He doesn't need to," Coral said. "I know."

Mr. Fall looked at her, this person he had raised. He had taught her to read, to fish for plastic in the river, to light and bank a fire, to watch her back. But somehow she had learned other things too. How to love, even when there wasn't much hope. How to see art in the plastic the dead had pitched into the river. How to see a thing as another thing: its potential, its new beginning as well as its end.

He remembered finding her in a Dairy Queen. So much of what he remembered was gone. So much seemed like it was never meant to be. Beautiful dreams that were never really beautiful, he would tell the children.

He never told Coral that she couldn't have been in the building while it burned. She couldn't have survived without a mark on her. Her baby hair, sparse as it was, didn't even smell of smoke. No. She had been left there after the fire had cooled. Maybe her parents had started the fire or flocked to it, knowing the smoke would draw someone wanting to help—or more likely, someone hoping to find some salvage. Instead they found Coral, her hair the brightest thing for miles, so red it was almost electric.

Maybe it was all just too much. Maybe her mother had

seen a decent enough spot and just let her baby go, swaddled in a fleece blanket with a card that bore her name sign.

In a way, he thought as he looked around the junkyard, Summer refilling Foxglove's mug, Golden Toad clamoring on the big bus tires—he would have to shoo the child out of there—they were all abandoned. By their families, by their homes, by the way they had lived before.

Coral was looking at him. The sun rose higher in the sky, and with it he felt she was aging, gaining lines on her forehead, white through her hair. Maybe it was the harsh light, or leaving that made her seem wise. Not a child anymore.

"Do with your life what you wish now," he told her. Part of the speech he had practiced. It had sounded different, in his head.

"I can't do that."

"As much as you can then, do it. Beyond surviving, what does it matter, Coral? Marriage, a job—you're not bound by those things. They've never pushed down on you the way just living has. Be what you want," he told her.

She tightened the straps of her pack. She had something clutched in one of her hands, a bit of paper. He couldn't quite see what was written on it, but he thought…was it a bus ticket? How had she gotten that? He wanted to ask her about it.

He wanted to say, *Go after Miami, if you want to.*

He wanted to say, *Go on your own.*

There was no time. She tucked the paper away. "Thanks for teaching me, Dad."

Summer said, "She's gotta go, love."

The others had already said their goodbyes. Trillium moved to get on the bus. Mr. Fall shook his hand, then embraced him. Both men felt thin to the other.

Golden Toad climbed onto Tahiti's shoulders. Mr. Fall stooped to hug Coral one last time. She would never grow taller, she was too old. Whether this had been the height of her genes, her biological parents, or the result of malnutrition, exhaustion—his fault, he felt—he would never know.

Coral broke from the hug first. "Look out for my work."

"I always will," Mr. Fall said.

"Teach JT to read."

"Good fucking luck with that," Foxglove said.

And that was it. Coral boarded the bus. Trillium closed the doors. The rubber pads made their familiar, soft sigh. Summer took Mr. Fall's arm and they stepped back. Foxglove was waving, her hand in a fingerless, knitted plastic glove. Through the big front window, Mr. Fall could see Coral standing behind Trillium in the driver's seat.

She should sit down. She should use the seat belt still attached, the buckle half-rusted to the one bench. He had taught Trillium to drive years ago and the man was careful, but the road would be bumpy. They would have to dodge fallen trees and cars and who knew what else—people probably. It was not Mr. Fall's place to tell her these things. But still, he wanted to shout at the windshield. *Drive safe!*

Coral waved.

The bus backed up. One of its taillights still worked. The bus still made the *beep beep* sound. It would wake the others in the junkyard, alerting them, if they did not know already: Trillium and Coral were leaving.

Mr. Fall's daughter, the artist, the girl who walked inside a whale, was going away.

Trillium honked the horn once, a stiff sound, creaky with disuse. Then the bus rattled down the hill, the last rainbow.

36

TRASHLANDS

Scrappalachia (OH)—Few outsiders have seen the hills of Scrappalachia. Those who live here were born here. They will likely die here, among the mountains, the bones of shacks, and the trees still standing. Most of the people in Scrappalachia work as scavengers. They have a name for the work they do, those who call this wild and winding place home, the work that has become their life, their children's life, and their survival: *plucking*, so called because they "pluck plastic from the water," according to Coral, a thirty-something woman who lives and works in a junkyard in what used to be southeastern Ohio.

Pluckers follow the "plastic tide," as Coral called it in an interview. It is a transient life, with most working in crews or family units who travel together to two camps in the course of a year: a camp for warm weather and a camp for colder temperatures. They move to more hospitable ground as the weather changes, but also, they must go where the plastic is.

Tides move plastic, though floods can bring more or less to an area unexpectedly. Wildfires and earthquakes can destroy or scatter the contents of factories, trains, even small cities on the outskirts of the region.

Since the United Nations World Plastic Act, no new plastic has been made (legally), and all plastic objects must come from recycled sources. Pluckers provide this material, doing the difficult, often dangerous work of reclaiming plastic from the wild. There is plenty.

"I imagine we'll be here forever," Coral said one morning as she pulled plastic from the river historically called the Hocking, near her home.

Pluckers like Coral wade up to their waists in water that is often foul, discolored with toxic chemicals or run-off, or diseased. It is undrinkable. It is not unusual for pluckers to see dead animals or human corpses.

There are no showers or sanitation facilities at the camp where Coral lives. There is no grocery or medical facility. There is a school in a tent, an unlicensed midwife who does much of the doctoring for the residents, and a club.

A strip club called Trashlands.

Once plastic is retrieved, pluckers weigh it, and sell or barter it at open-air markets. There is no question: they are not getting a good deal. Plastic is still very much a buyer's market, and those who salvage it can barely afford to live off what they make in trade.

Most of the pluckers at the Trashlands camp can read and write, thanks in no small part to a man called Mr. Fall, a former plucker and Coral's father, who conducts lessons for the children of the camp. His only textbooks? An incomplete and badly damaged set of Encyclopedia

Britannica, a reference book last in print in 2010, decades before the floods.

In many ways, Scrappalachia is repeating its past, when this region was called simply *Appalachia*. Back then, residents often worked manual labor jobs, in retail, in maintenance, and in the mines, which have mostly dried up.

Like the pluckers of today, miners worked long hours for meager wages, and, due to the remoteness of the region, were forced to spend much of their paycheck right back with their employers, purchasing food, clothing, and household goods at what was known as the company store.

The equivalent of the company store in the junkyard where Coral, Mr. Fall, and other pluckers live is Trashlands. It sells food, booze, and sex. An unlicensed, unregulated, and lawless place, formerly a theater, the club looms over the junkyard.

Most of the residents live in old cars. Music pumps from Trashlands constantly; the club never closes. The owner has managed to rig up old industrial air conditioners to solar panels and a generator, blasting cool air during the hottest times, which can get near tropical in the swampy, humid region.

Also connected to a generator is a giant pink sign on the roof of Trashlands, visible for miles, advertising the club—the first working neon this reporter has ever seen.

The sign, the music, and the club's reputation seem to be working, bringing business into the area. The only strangers the junkyard ever sees are for the most part, men: here to lose a night or three at the club, to room in the lodgings upstairs, to spend plastic and possibly commission a tattoo of their name on the skin of one of the club's more popular dancers, a young woman named

Foxglove. *[Foxglove refused to be interviewed on record for this story.]*

If a strip club seems out of place for the region, you don't know Scrappalachia.

Here, great beauty coexists with great pain, seemingly for millennia. The hills, mountains, trees, and cliffs of the region look majestic, yet are scarred with environmental and industrial devastation. Burned and demolished structures dot the landscape, much more so than in The Els, where buildings are quickly rebuilt to make the best use (and reuse) of precious land. In Scrappalachia, land goes to rot. People can too.

Summer, a woman in her forties who recently retired from dancing, described the junkyard as "a vortex. It sucks you in." She said in an interview, "You get indebted, and it's hard to get out."

Dancers, like the miners before them, are expected to pay their employer for food, for costumes (if they don't make the clothes themselves or barter from Summer, an accomplished seamstress) and for rent. Dancers, like the pluckers, live in abandoned vehicles or makeshift shacks rented to them by the owner of Trashlands, a man named Rattlesnake Master.

Rattlesnake Master owns the club, but he also claims to own the junk—a claim that seems dubious but also, in a place like Scrappalachia, difficult to challenge. And rent is steep.

"You don't have anything left over at the end of your shift," Summer said. "If you want to survive, you have to do other things."

JT, the newest dancer at Trashlands, didn't seem to mind. "I like the opportunity," she said. "If I do more, I can make more. Back at the Strip, where I lived before, there wasn't much. I was willing, but there wasn't nobody to give me that chance to proof *[sic]* myself."

In her limited free time, Coral, a single mother whose son was trafficked into plastic sorting labor several years ago, [see in a previous edition: "The Cost of Cheap Bricks? Children's Lives"] makes art. She creates sculptures out of plastic too damaged or old to be recycled. One could imagine her pieces fetching a high price in The Els for those comfortable enough to collect art.

But in Scrappalachia, Coral gives her art away. She leaves it for strangers in the woods. She never goes back to see if her art has been appreciated, destroyed, or stolen. She'll never know.

Though Coral does not like to talk about the art, she finally admitted, "It's not about the money. It's about doing something not connected to money. It's not about surviving, I guess. It's about living."

It was startling for this reporter to find such inventiveness, artistry, and creativity in a place such as Scrappalachia. Though in The Els we have become accustomed to long lines for bread, in Scrappalachia, the people long ago learned to use insects for flour. Though El residents wait hours for our buses, which frequently break down, and we endure blackouts, brownouts, and long stretches without clean water, the residents of the junkyard have almost never known such luxuries. They've done more and they've done it with less.

We have dismissed—and this reporter includes himself—the people of this region as backward. We have assumed their ways to be strange and not our own. We have attributed one story to Scrappalachia: that of people left to sift through our trash, to make meager lives out of what we threw away.

But though there is one song at Trashlands, the same tuneless track played day and night at the club, there are many songs of the region.

The song of the child forced to grow up too soon.

The song of the teacher who alters his whole life to save a stranger. The song of the mother who sacrifices for her son. And the song of this stranger, this outsider, forever changed.

[Ed Note: This piece was mailed in anonymously. Our longtime reporter is missing, presumed dead.]

37

Miami

In the darkness of the club, he'd found Coral. He had to fight his way through the curtain, ratty and stinking of mildew, that separated the club from the backstage, and there she was. Shivering in the costume she had pulled back up.

"Someone should get you a robe," he said.

"Summer's gone to get one." Coral crossed her arms over her chest as if suddenly she realized he was there. "It was you, wasn't it? You're the man who bought out the show?"

"Yes."

The thing about not wearing his glasses was that although he couldn't see distances, he could see close-up even better, see to count her freckles, the heat that flashed across her cheeks. Her lips had been painted. Inky lines extended above and below her eyes, flicked on the tips. Up close, it looked garish. He could see she had a small scar on her temple.

They all had scars. This one was shaped like a ring.

"What did you see?" Coral asked.

"Nothing. I don't have my glasses. I can't see five feet away without them."

She reached up and touched his face. The explosion of that hand, as her fingers grazed his cheekbone. "You have long eyelashes. I didn't notice with your glasses on. What happened to them? Did you give them to Tahiti to borrow?"

"Tahiti?"

"Summer found a pair for him, but then we had to…"

"I know."

Her expression was falling—even Miami could see it.

"Without my glasses," he said quickly, "you and Foxglove looked like moving blobs. Very artistic. Abstract, is what they call it. That was all I could see onstage. But I could see the floor beside me pretty well. Let me tell you, it's disgusting. You don't want to look at it close."

She gave a real laugh, but it was tinged on the end with sadness. How long could they stand in the hall like this? Rattlesnake Master was close. Summer was coming with that robe. Soon Coral would collect her payment, the canisters of diesel, and go.

"I didn't want to come tonight," Miami said.

"Why did you, then?"

"Rattlesnake Master locked the door. I can't get out. I still can't get out."

"There's a door backstage. I'll take you there in a minute. Thank you for doing that. This. You must have paid a lot, to buy out the show, for him to turn away anyone else."

"The price was a cover story," Miami said.

"What's that mean?"

"It means it's time for me to go. I'm going to stay up late

tonight and finish writing the story and then I've got to go back and file it."

"Back to the city?"

"Yes."

In a minute. His brain stuck on the phrase. Coral said she would show him the door *in a minute.* What could he say in one minute? What difference would it make? He pulled out two pieces of paper. "I have something for you."

She took them. "What are these?"

The words printed on them were straight and uniform, really printed, from a machine. The letters looked official and final. "Bus tickets," he said.

"For a bus to the city?"

"Yes. My city."

She read. "Who is Mangrove?"

"My sister."

"And..." She tripped over the name on the ticket. "Aletsch?"

"She was my wife."

"Why do you have these?" Coral asked.

He had been carrying them all this time. The most sentimental things he could hold on to, really, even more than the knife, which he was never going to use, or the bracelet, which he was never going to find.

"I bought them a long time ago, just in case my family needed them. And then I held on to them when my wife left and Mangrove disappeared, because—I don't know. I thought my family might be coming back. They're not, though. Mangrove is dead and Aletsch isn't my wife anymore. I used to think I was a fool for keeping the tickets, carrying them around. But now I'm glad I kept them. You can get some good out of them."

Coral looked up. "I can't take these tickets."

"You don't need to show ID on the bus. Or money. You just need to show the tickets. Two people, two tickets. They don't expire."

"Two people?"

"You and your son." He said it quickly before she could stop him. "You don't have to come to me. You don't have to see me ever again. But there's no date on the tickets. You can use them anytime. If you decide you want to go somewhere. If you—you and Shanghai—want to go elsewhere, now you have a ticket."

Coral looked down at the tickets for a long time, so long he wondered if he should put his glasses back on to see if someone was coming down the hall, so long he wondered if he should just go, find the back door of Trashlands himself and leave.

Then Coral said, "Where do you live in the city?"

38

Coral

The world looked different behind the windshield of the bus. Higher. The ground, the bushes, the straggly trees. Mr. Fall, Foxglove, and almost everyone Coral had ever known passed by, smaller. And then they were behind her.

The bus rumbled, the engine sounding thick and low as though angry at having being ignored. Dead leaves fluttered from the windshield. The bus dipped and Coral lost her footing for a moment as Trillium avoided a rut.

"You should sit down," he said.

The steering wheel looked huge in his hands. Mr. Fall had wound the wheel with rags to make it softer. He said he had gotten callouses when they had driven from the casino camp to Trashlands.

Coral didn't remember much about that journey. The grief and disbelief of losing her son was still so raw. She couldn't enjoy the trip now either. They were leaving Mr. Fall. Leaving Summer. Miami had left already.

She gripped the back of Trillium's seat, her fingers slipping into a hole in the old fabric. The bus came to the end of the narrow pathway. On one side, the river ran below in the gully, colored with trash. Ahead of them was a gate, higher than the bus. Trillium braked and the bus huffed to a stop.

"I'll open the gate," Coral said. She went down the steps before he could protest. He opened the accordion doors for her, and she ran in front.

The gate had no lock. It was ancient, the metal bowed and rusted, patched by wooden planks. It rarely opened. This was the back path to Trashlands. No sign indicated what was just inside. Rattlesnake Master wanted men's first glimpse of the place to be the other end of the junkyard, the direct path to the club, cleared and wide, lighted by his lamps.

Coral pushed at the gate. Rust flaked off into her hands. She saw someone had graffitied on one of the wood planks: *Good luck. The world suckz.*

Well, maybe it did, but she would take that luck. She shoved hard. One side of the gate shot open and she pushed it out of the way. The bus passed through, Trillium giving her a wave. The red of the one working brake light reminded her of neon. She supposed it always would.

It was time to close the gate. She dragged it back across the path. Before the gate shut, she looked back. The path climbed to a hill, then down another one where the bus had parked all those years. Was there a depression in the hillside now? Would Summer and Mr. Fall park the food truck there, or would someone else move in? She heard the babble of the river below. She heard, but faintly now, the song of Trashlands. She closed the gate.

The woman who had returned from the factory with her son had drawn a map for Coral on a potato chip bag. She drew the road away from Trashlands, a turn at what she called a *keystone* bridge: an overpass that had once shuttled trains. She said the bridge was high enough the bus could pass under. And they would know the factory was close when they saw the crashed aeroplane.

She said two pieces remained of the broken aeroplane, as big as a whale. Like a whale, they were gray. Vines grew over the debris. The plane's tail was intact though, she promised, pointing north.

The bus rattled over the road. Coral couldn't sit down. She needed to figure out what she would say to him, how she would greet her son, to ask him what he had been through. Did she have a right to even know? Could they talk about it?

She wondered, if he had not been taken, if he eventually would have asked her: *Who was his father? Where was he?* Years ago, she would have said something had killed Robert, a not unrealistic lie. And maybe not even a lie. Gangs were already gathering back then, men going camp to camp with clubs and wire cutters. Shelters burned, food and girls taken. She remembered Mr. Fall saying they needed to find a camp with a gate.

And now she had driven right out of one.

But if her son asked her—today or tomorrow or whenever she found him, when she traded the rainbow bus for his life—who his father was, Coral would say the truth, as much as she knew it.

She had made a bad choice, but his father had made a worse one.

The bus rocketed over the road, pitted with holes. Coral was jostled almost off her feet as Trillium swerved to avoid debris. Branches twisted with plastic bags and blue rubber gloves, a broken pod coffee maker.

"We're not going back for it," Coral said.

She took a seat on the bench. The fabric was so ancient it crackled. She fiddled with the two halves of the thing Mr. Fall had called a seat belt, but she could not figure out how to get it to fasten. She'd never worn one before, not when they'd traveled earlier. The buckle was speckled with rust, rough in her hands.

Trillium slowed.

"I don't think we should stop for that plastic," Coral said. Then she leaned forward.

Trillium had paused in front of a place where the road split off into sections. You could turn left or right down other roads, or continue straight. Or even, Coral thought, move sideways, though that road had worn metal sides and weeds in the middle. She suspected it might be a railroad.

"This isn't on the map," Trillium said. He had pinned it on the visor where there was also—there always had been—an old bit of plastic with a stranger's broad, smiling face, a name they didn't know, and the letters *CDL*. Mr. Fall kept it up there for luck.

Coral peered at the chip bag map. "Well, maybe you don't turn at all until the bridge."

"I just didn't expect there to be so many choices." Trillium started driving again, slower this time, as if the turns had made him alert for more danger. He headed straight.

So many choices, Coral thought. It was not simply driving forward or driving back, as she had thought. You could turn, different ways. You could follow those railroad tracks. She had thought she had two choices: Trillium or Miami, but that wasn't it at all. She could go somewhere else with her son, with or without Trillium. She could go back. She didn't have to live in the city to be with Miami. Could he live back in Trashlands with her?

She had never even asked. She had the address of his newspaper; he had said to send any messages to him there. She had the bus tickets, two of them.

Coral had been fiddling with the pieces of the seat belt, the frayed cloth with its heavy metal ends. Absently, she pushed the two ends together and they fastened with a hard *clink*. "I figured the seat belt out."

Trillium slowed again. "There's a man."

Out of the trees, a stranger ran up to the bus, waving his arms. Coral could see through the big front windshield he wore clothes that were barely more than scraps. Rags were tied to his feet. His hair was long, down to his shoulders, jagged but golden. His eyes looked wild, scared. He raced right up to the bus, forcing Trillium to slow.

Coral unsnapped the seat belt she had worked so hard to close. "Stop."

"Seems like a trap," Trillium said.

The man was young, a boy. The front of his clothes, the palms of his hands, which he held up, were coated with red.

"Stop. Open the doors," Coral said.

"Coral, wait."

But she was already going. Down the bus steps, pushing through the accordion doors, onto the road. The boy had run through the woods, past the broken aeroplane, under the keystone bridge, but Coral didn't know this.

"There's someone hurt," the boy said. He was out of breath. He was taller than her. "I hurt him. We're putting pressure on the wound but he needs help, needs stitching. Is there a camp back there?"

"There is," Coral said.

"Can you take us?"

"Coral!" Trillium shouted through the open bus doors. "What about Shanghai?"

But Coral knew who the boy was. She had known him right away.

39

THE BOOK OF MR. FALL

I had been living in the city for a long time, which was maybe five years, maybe three. It was hard to remember. I had a clock that did not need batteries or power so it worked. I wound it every day so I would arrive at the school on time, though most of the children trickled in when they could, when they remembered or their mothers did. When the children woke in their beds of rags or the cold of their shelters became unbearable—then they would come to school.

It was a real school building with hallways of classrooms, an unused cafeteria—we had no food—and an empty nurse's office. All the medicine had been pilfered long ago. A row of school buses were parked behind the building, beyond the playground with its rusted swings.

The teachers mostly came to the school and worked because what else would we do? No one was being paid, except sometimes by parents; some children still had family.

Once you had secured a sleeping place in a tent or shed or a broken-down car, once you had found or stolen your food for the next couple of days, how could you pass the time? You wanted the familiar, on some level. To do what you had always done.

You could only plan a few days in advance. So teachers would also stop coming. A child would disappear one day or the next, and I would never know what had happened to them.

Then new ones would drift in, drawn by the promise of pretending everything was fine.

There was no television, no internet, no electricity. A few solar- or hand-powered radios still cranked out the news. Mostly it was just the old emergency broadcast played again and again, then static. I had books for my class to learn from, a row of them I had found in a classroom with the ceiling falling down.

An incomplete set of Encyclopedia Britannica.

This was what I taught from. I do not know what the others taught. Mostly from their memories, I thought. There were about seven of us, seven teachers and classes in a school that could have held dozens more, our rooms full to the limits, many more kids than adults. Teachers stood in the front of their classrooms with the broken and boarded-up windows and the light that came in from the cracks, and they said what they knew, what they remembered. Who could say what would be important for children to know?

Women did not have the right to vote for a long time.

Neither did people of color.

Voting was choosing someone to represent you.

Anyone could be president. It was said.

Cars were fueled by gasoline and diesel.

Dinosaurs roamed the earth, and no one knows for certain what happened. No, it wasn't plastic that killed them. There was no plastic then.

Yes, people knew that plastic was poison, but they didn't care. They wanted to make money.

Money was how you collected things and survived.

Collecting things was supposed to be very important.

I don't know why.

I don't know why.

It seemed important at the time.

The radio had gone to static, as it did for most of the day. I had been talking about the Triangle Shirtwaist Factory Fire to a full classroom of glassy-eyed, starving children. Most of their feet did not touch the floor. Several of them slept on their desks, relieved to have found a flat surface. I did not wake them. They needed the sleep, the safe place.

I kept the radio on low in the background, just in case. As long as the charge would last, it buzzed softly, a fly in the room.

And then one day the static changed. To an emergency broadcast, but a different one. One I had not heard in a long, long time, since I had been a child and the flood swallowed our home. But I remembered the word they said on the broadcast; I had taught it to the children.

Evacuate.

Evacuate.

Children, I said. *Like we've practiced.*

And they had. Some of the children looked around for something to throw, a trash can or debris from the junk pile in the back, in case it was a man with a gun. But it was not a man with a gun.

Another child began to climb on his desk thinking, as I had too, that the emergency was water, another flood. But it was not another flood.

A third child saw it first, the way the clouds changed color, yellowing like a bruise. Orange licked their undersides. The clouds filled up the cracks in the walls, the broken windows.

Fire! the child, New Orleans, said.

We ran into the hall. Other doors were busting open, other classes filling the halls, the children mostly too tired or too hungry or too used to upheaval to cry, but the teachers looked to me.

I had started this school, reopening it in the old city. I had, before triple-checking the classroom to make sure no child was left inside, loaded the books onto an AV cart that still had wheels—first kicking off the TV in a crash of glass and plastic—and strapped the books down with my belt.

The teachers asked me what to do.

The buses. Go to the buses!

The fire was coming. We could smell it now. When we pushed through the back doors of the building, we could hear it, a crackling in the distance, lapping up everything.

My class linked arms and stuck together. I pushed the rattling cart of books ahead, into the smoke. I heard the children coughing. I saw, through the clouds, teachers loading their groups onto buses. There were enough buses. We would make it. We would all make it.

I kicked open the nearest bus. It had been spray-painted black.

Get on!

The children listened. They remembered how to. They filed in behind me, scrambling onto the bus as I unbuckled the belt on the cart and began to throw books into the stairwell. We had to save the children, but I was going to try to save the books too. I emptied the cart and pushed it away. I looked down the aisle.

The children stared back at me, sitting two or more to a seat. Quiet, waiting.

I threw myself into the driver's seat, and felt around madly for keys, keys. But there they were, right there waiting. I started the engine. It sounded like a monster. It sounded like fire.

I looked around the schoolyard through the clouded windshield.

Some of the buses were not starting. Some of the buses did not have keys still in the ignition or stuck in their visors by the CDL, as the black bus had.

But the black bus was full. It was full. It was so full, children sat in the aisles. They sat on each other's laps, clutching each other as if they were family. They looked up at me.

The fire poured over the hills.

Put on your seat belts, I said to the children.

And I drove them out of the fire.

★ ★ ★ ★ ★

ACKNOWLEDGMENTS

Thank you to my wonderful agent, Eric Smith, my amazing editor, Margot Mallinson, and everyone at PS Literary, MIRA Books, and HarperCollins, especially Roxanne Jones, Lia Ferrone, and Quinn Banting. I'm thankful for the tireless work of Kim Yau and Taryn Fagerness. For their support of this book and of my work in general, I'm grateful to Mike Chen, Rene Denfeld, Heather Edwards, Jennifer Key, Bishop O'Connell, Liz Pahl, Curtis Sittenfeld, Jeff VanderMeer, Christina Veladota, and Andy Veladota. Thank you to the Philip K. Dick Award committee. Ellee Achten and Stacy Jane Grover are brilliant and were insightful first readers of this book. Elizabeth Stinaff, thank you for the last-minute assist. Thank you to my family, especially Andrew Villegas and Henry: I love you, and you keep me going every day. The West End Ciderhouse was my place to write when I didn't have one, and Athens County became